Jagged Hearts

You're Beautiful! Enjoy!

LIZZIE LEE

Lizzie Lee

Cover artist: Jada D'Lee

Cover Image by: iStockphoto/Pixabay©

Edited by: Sally Hopkinson

Pre-read by: Sherry Franklin, Paige Britton, and Lizzie Lee

Reviews for *The Blessing*:

"Lizzie Lee has written a very real and in-depth story, with flawed and imperfect characters that you will want to embrace and love. The entwined love story between Trevor, Veronica and Greyson will tug at your heart, yet have you rooting for them until the end. If you enjoy twists and turns, and a story that will heighten your emotions, this is the series for you. The Blessing will pull you in, grab you by the heartstrings, and won't let go until you're wanting more."

-Z.N. Willett, author of *The Red Carpet Series* and *Acquired Asset*

"… a spellbinding rollercoaster of a story that will have you both soul-searching and falling in love with every turn of the page."

-Ciara Shayee, author of *Pinky Promises*

"… Ms. Lee has created a cast of incredibly likable and engaging characters. I look forward to reading more of her stories in future."

-Elise de Sallier, author of *Hearts of Honour Series* and *Innocence.*

"An absolutely amazing, beautifully written, incredibly gripping tale. This is a story of love, loss, redemption and, above all, family. I laughed, I cried, I screamed, I rejoiced."

-Amy, *Goodreads* reviewer.

Thank You!

Sherry and Paige, thank you for your support on developing the foundation for this story. Without you two, I would have never had the courage to continue moving forward in my writing. You have no idea what your friendship and belief in me means.

Sally, I can't express how grateful I am to you. The work you did on this project was completely transformative. I feel so confident having you by my side. Your support means the world to me, and I'm so lucky to have you as a friend.

Ciara, your friendship alleviated so much of my stress. I don't know where I would be without you! Thanks for always being free when I need you. I couldn't ask for a better friend.

Jamie, you are fantastic. Thank you so much for all of your help! Navigating through all of this has been difficult at times, so it's a blessing to have a friend like you.

Nicole, thanks for reaching out to me and taking me under your wing. I feel so much more confident because of you. I can't wait for our friendship to continue! I'm blessed to have such a talented friend.

Jada, thanks for inspiring me with your beautiful cover designs. I'm so lucky to know such a talented person.

Caroline and Morgan, thank you so much for introducing me to the world of romance novels! Sharing Johanna Lindsey's paperbacks with you both will always be a wonderful memory.

Sara, thanks for taking me under your wing last minute. Your guidance means so much to me.

The ChickLits Book Club, thank you for reading my work and helping me to become more confident in my writing and sharing it with others.

My family, thank you for supporting me every step of the way! I couldn't do any of this without you.

Table of Contents:

Prologue

Death with Dignity

Sometimes, death was beautiful. It *was* the last chapter of someone's story, after all. When it came to my mother, my fingers still fumbled numbly on her very last page, afraid to turn it over because I knew once I did, I would never be able to flip to the beginning of her story again. Her story had been told, and mine, I felt, was just beginning.

Certain moments felt as if they would play in my mind forever, circling over and over again—teasing my mind's eye despite my effort to evade the thoughts completely. I didn't want to forget the images which swirled around in my mind; however, I didn't want the images of her—the images of that day—to haunt me forever. When my mind was quiet, I saw the white, seemingly endless hallways of that constricting hospital; I smelled the faint stink of antiseptics and urine; I pictured the way the fluorescent lights had reflected against the large windows of her hospital room, which had peered out at the dark, ominous sky. Time moved forward in my memory, and I was hit with the sounds of dozens of machines, screaming at my jaded mind that the end was imminent. That room colored my memories, and, no matter where I was, I could close my eyes and see it all clear as day. After all, this was the last room my mother had ever seen—the room where I had felt a part of myself slip wordlessly into the same void.

I had spent *hours* in that room, ignoring the walls which had felt as if they could have swallowed me whole as I sat at my mother's bedside. With my feet glued to the floor, I would squeeze my thighs together, trying desperately to hold everything in to avoid using the ladies room, fearing if I had, I would have come back to find my mother gone. With my thighs smashed painfully against each other, I had made sure I hadn't missed a single instance. As time had ticked on, my body had become almost as atrophied as hers. I had been waiting for something—*anything*—to happen.

Hours had passed, and I had begun to furiously blink my eyes in an effort not to nod off. My gaze had remained on her face for as long as I had been able to stomach it. While my eyes traced her features, I had noticed she looked very much like a shadow of the woman I had grown up with. Her ashen face had caused my eyes to veer off toward my father, who had no longer cared to hide the emotions he felt. The grief swimming in his eyes had done little to assuage the pain in my heart.

On that final day, the look of resignation on my father's face had nearly killed me. Being as young as I was, I had looked to my father for comfort and guidance as we tread through foreign waters. When I watched my father, I had felt even more lost—even more uneasy. *He knew.* Deep down, in the depths of his consciousness, he had known that day was the end. In his eyes, that knowledge had been clear as day. Perhaps, I had easily recognized it because I had known, too. So had my sister, Eden, who had spent most of the time with her eyes glued to the floor beneath her perfectly polished white sneakers.

Despite being older, Eden hadn't been able to stomach it. As I had watched her, the energy in the room became even more suffocating. The tension had been so thick, the walls of the already small hospital room in the bleakest ward felt as if they were closing in around me.

I have to escape ... I have to get out—if only for a moment. A moment of fresh air ... A moment for some clarity ... Peace. Finally, a few moments of peace. Just a few seconds ... Just a moment to breathe ... The air in here is far too thick ... The walls are so constricting. Mom ... I can't. Mom ... I—I can't think. I can't breathe. Mom ...

With my mind and body somewhat out of synch, I had risen from my chair and left the room. As I traveled down the corridor toward the ladies room, I had watched one foot move in front of the other, never wanting to acknowledge the images attached to the cacophony of sounds surrounding me. Instead, I had focused my mind on the matter at hand: moving down the hallway and to the right.

I had locked myself in a stall and placed my head in my hands until I had been able breathe again. My heart had raced in my chest, pumping against bone as if it were trying to break free. Surprisingly, no tears had ever come. *Not yet. You have to be strong, Veronica. Be strong for her. Be strong for the one person who has always been strong for you.*

Earlier this morning, I had promised myself I wouldn't shed a tear—at least, not in front of my mother. I had to be strong for her like she had been strong for Eden and me every day. In the bathroom, I had heaved on air for several minutes before my legs had found their strength again, and I managed to rise to my feet. Composed, I had left the small sanctuary I found in that bathroom stall, returning to my mother's room.

Slowly, I had drifted out of the bathroom and begun down the hallway. Like before, I had ignored the sounds around me; I had allowed them to mix into one massive blur made up of a variety of noises produced by the patients around me. The blur had been a comfort, which had quickly been shattered by one sound I had been dreading to hear.

A long, menacing beep filled the air, effectively erasing my mind of anything other than the room at the end of the hallway. *My mother's room.* My throat had tightened, and my chest had grown heavy as the persistent beep strained against my ears. The walls had moved in on me, and the corners of my vision had become fuzzy. One nurse had zoomed toward my mother's room, and then another. And another. Before, finally, the NP had flown down the opposite hallway with a doctor in tow. It was then when I had realized I hadn't been moving. In my horror, I had stopped to watch; I had observed the entire scene with a weak stomach and fractured heart.

Time suspended as I had peered down the narrowing hallway and attempted to will my legs to move. The world had been muddled around me, but I had managed to propel myself forward. I never had understood the idea of "out-of-body experiences" until I ran toward my mother's room. In those moments, I had found that my body had been weightless and moved of its own accord. When I had looked out at the scene surrounding me, it was as if I were in a theater watching a film— nothing had felt like it was happening to *me.*

It couldn't be. Nothing awful happens to me; awful things happen to everyone else.

I had been lost in my thoughts—my senses had run wild as my world fell apart. As I had heard my sister scream, I came back; my thoughts had returned to the present as I shot down the hall.

My legs had shaken, but determination had kept them moving until I had reached the room. The commotion had rung in my ears so loudly that my mind hadn't been able to block it out—as much as I had desperately tried. My sister's voice had turned my body to ice, shooting through me like poison in my veins. Her hysterics had driven my mind wild and shattered the image I had held of her for a moment.

All my life, she had been someone I had thought was impossibly perfect. So, when I had found her rocking back and forth in a chair near my mother, I saw her looking more human than ever. The only thing that had been more disturbing than her wails had been the chaotic sounds coming from the machines surrounding my mother's bed. My eyes had drifted away from my sister and widened in horror as they took in the sight of doctors and nurses clustering around my mother, trying to revive her; they had moved with little success. While I had watched them, my eyes increasingly widening with horror, I had felt myself drop to my knees. The sting from the fall had shot up my body, but nothing other than the sight before me had mattered.

She slipped away ... right through our fingers. This morning, she was fine, and by twilight, she closed her eyes ...

"I'm calling it," her doctor had murmured as he peered down at his watch. "Seven twenty-eight."

Then, they had dispersed, allowing me a clear view of her. She had appeared just as she always had. Although, now, she had been far thinner—the bones on her face were more prominent than ever, but she still had the same ethereal beauty.

As I had studied her, I found she looked as if she had fallen to sleep—slipping into a state of unconsciousness she would soon wake up from. However, even at fourteen, I had known her eyes would never flutter open again. I had known ... but still, I had allowed myself a moment to dream.

My eyes had pulled away from her, moving to my father, who had collapsed against his chair. With his face buried in his hands, he had quietly sobbed; his shoulders shook enough to rock the chair he sat on. Then my eyes had moved to my sister, finding her in a similar state. I had been the only one semi-composed. After a long pause, I had risen from the floor—my legs had still been unsteady as I had moved to my mother's bed. I had peered down at her for a moment before my hand reached out, and my fingers brushed along her hand, avoiding the IV jutting from her vein. I had held her hand for a long time as my tears came and went. I held on until her palm was cool against mine.

After that, my memory became fuzzy. I could remember my father composing himself just enough to reach for me, taking me in his arms. I remembered, despite my distress, I felt almost childlike as he had carried me out of the hospital room and to his car. Looking back, I suppose I had been childlike—I was fourteen, after all; however, in that moment, I had felt so much older than my years. I had seen more than any fourteen-year-old should.

Too much. Far too much. So much, I wanted to scream.

The most disturbing thing I had seen that day was the look in my father's eyes. The light in his eyes had extinguished; as I had peered up at my father, I had barely recognized the haunted man before me.

The memory of the beginning of such a tumultuous period of my life had my mind reeling. The images of the hospital faded as the image of my dim apartment replaced it. Looking ahead, I wondered what type of woman I would be if that event hadn't shaped me. After that day, I had learned to cherish everything in my life.

Every. Single. Thing.

I accepted the good with the bad, carrying the weight when I had to. And I *always* had to ... just like Trevor. My past allowed me to understand his pain so completely. He believed he was alone in this; in his beautiful, jaded mind, I was sure he believed he would carry this weight on his own. But I would carry it with him if he let me.

I would carry that weight with him because a man like him deserved the world. A man who reached for the light in the darkest of times was the sort of man I could give myself to.

My mind eased as I thought of him like I always did. *Trevor Warren. Trevor, my sinfully handsome neighbor with a baby to care for and a jagged heart. One day, we'll let go of our demons and find happiness—together.*

1

Don't Get Lost in Heaven

A cup of tea and maybe I'll feel human again ...

Sliding off my reading glasses and rubbing away the weariness, I sighed as I wondered how much longer I'd be able to stare at these words before I became too antsy. As my right foot bounced against the leg of my chair, I mentally chastised myself for procrastinating this long.

What on earth were you thinking, Veronica? Do you think?

My eyes skimmed over my messy living room, trying to remember the last time I had a chance to clean. Since graduating college four years ago, my life had become consumed with work. Every second of every day, I seemed to be pouring over some sort of project—never feeling good enough regardless of whatever it was I was doing. The never-ending cycle of projects spurred my adrenaline and focused my thoughts on something other than my past, which I was always grateful for. I didn't feel lonely—despite what my sister may think. I didn't have the time to feel lonely.

Besides, who needs people? Why surround yourself with people who will inevitably let you down? God ... You're so dreary, Veronica. Can't you lighten up for a bit?

Tossing my pen onto the counter, I closed my eyes and took a deep breath as I tried to refocus my thoughts on the matter at hand. My deadline was tomorrow, and I couldn't seem to concentrate to save my life. *God, I shouldn't have procrastinated this much.* What was on my horizon tonight had my stomach in knots. Despite my previous objections, my sister, Eden, finally managed to twist my arm, cajoling me into going out for the evening. The thought of dating had left a bad taste in my mouth for quite some time.

Since college, I had avoided romantic attachments. After having my heart fractured and my trust completely shattered, the idea of "opening up" made me feel violated. The thought alone caused the hair on the back of my neck to raise as my entire body grew frigid. Closing my eyes, I remembered the breathing exercises my therapist thought me. With my body vibrating with tension, I breathed in and out until I managed to shut the memory of *him* away into the little box I formed in my mind—locking the sounds, feelings, and images up so I didn't have to face them.

Run away from it. Run away like you always do.

A groan escaped me as my eyelids fluttered open, remembering myself. As I stared off into the space ahead, I considered whether tonight was a good idea or not. I hadn't tried to put myself out there—instead, I had built a wall. A wall I had quickly grown fond of. With my barriers, I was invincible … *wasn't I?*

My thoughts drifted back to that dark place I tried to avoid. I remembered the days when I was dead set on a "happy, fairy tale ending"—the type of ending every girl dreamt of. However, those endings didn't exist in my experience. In fairy tales, the ending highlighted an enamored couple during their honeymoon stage. *Were they happy after that?* The story never went on to tell their fate.

I had believed I'd found my prince charming in the form of my college sweetheart. My fairy tale love had twisted into something dark—something unforgettable. Something which had the power to keep me awake night after night years later.

That was the trouble with darkness—it was inevitable. To ever have light, you needed darkness. At least, that was what I had told myself since it happened. A bitter laugh escaped my throat as I considered the ridiculousness of my thoughts. *When was he* ever *a fairy tale? Are you joking, Veronica?*

Due to my past, I didn't understand my sister's insistence. She knew everything.

Every.

Single.

Ugly.

Detail.

She wanted me to be happy, but she didn't understand I was "happy" right now. I was surviving, at least. *Moving forward ... always moving forward. It's all I can do, isn't it? Keep moving—keep reaching. Even when it feels pointless. Even when I want to turn around.* Which was more than I could have said a few years ago. I worked so hard to wear a mask—to exhibit the woman I always wanted to be: intelligent, successful, and wildly confident. I wondered if she saw through the guise.

Of course, she does. She's known you your whole life.

The thought of her seeing right through me made my heart ache. Eden felt so much more than everyone else. She always had. Her empathy knew no bounds, and when it came to me, her little sister, she felt every one of my emotions as if they were her own. She felt my despair; she felt my fear of losing myself. Eden wanted me to be happy, and because of her good intentions, I agreed to a single date, making no promises for a follow-up.

My gaze moved to my cell as I tapped the screen, looking for a message from the elusive Hayden, a man Eden was *sure* I would fall for in an "instant." I rolled my eyes at the memory as I picked up the phone, tapping on my sister's contact. Scrolling through our last conversation, I read up on Hayden again, memorizing facts about him as if I were heading to an exam. The way she gushed about him in her text messages caused me to worry.

Why does she have to be so convincing if he's so great? With a sigh, I abandoned the phone on the table and leaned back in my chair. *I wish she could just let me find happiness on my own. I don't need to find happiness in a man. Besides, I'm pretty sure that's impossible. If I'm not happy with myself, how on earth can I be happy with anyone else?*

Eden had always been rather codependent—unable to fathom how anyone could get on in life without a constant companion. Truly, we couldn't be more dissimilar. Which was perfect, in a strange way. We complimented each other well and knew each other as if we had been fused together.

The vibration on my phone startled me, and I nearly laughed when I saw Eden's picture shine on my screen. I tapped the phone to unlock it before pulling up her message. My eyes scanned the words on the screen while my body attempted to stifle a laugh. All caps. I was sure, to anyone else, this message would have seemed to be sent by a crazed lunatic. Her bubbly and sometimes overbearing attitude oozed through her message. *This girl is lucky I love her so much. I don't think I could handle her insane extraversion otherwise.*

ARE YOU GETTING READY, YET?!? VEROINCA, GET ON IT! HAYDEN IS SUPER EXCITED TO MEET YOU. QUINT HAS BEEN RAVING ABOUT YOU ALL MORNING!

I read the message, snickering at the idea of Quinton, my brother-in-law, "raving" about me. He loved me like a sister, but a cerebral man like Quinton wasn't the type to "rave" about anything. His wife, on the other hand, couldn't seem to stifle her excitement. Eden and Quinton dealt with their emotions very differently. Eden's heart was on her sleeve while Quinton's was tucked underneath a few of his many layers. Eden and her husband had the perfect chemistry—opposites intertwining to form something beautiful. Although, I wasn't sure if I could stomach a relationship, part of me did envy my sister for hers. In my darkness, I had run from everyone and everything around me; in her darkness, she had run into Quinton's arms.

Perhaps Hayden isn't half bad.

Outside of being Quinton's friend, Hayden was *respectable* enough—accountant by day, taking care of his elderly grandmother by night. He was *safe.* Nothing about him sounded controversial or the least bit exciting. Maybe he was just what I needed. I needed nice. I needed *safe.* Maybe a night out with Hayden could turn my view of men on its head. Maybe, after tonight, my anxiety would be assuaged slightly, and I would be able to let my barrier down a smidge.

You need this more than you think.

My fingers reached out and brushed the ceramic mug in front of me, checking to see if my tea was still warm. As I felt the subtle warmth underneath my fingertips, I sighed, numbly reaching out to grab my drink. After a long sip, I reached for my phone and, with a stiff hand, I replied.

Eden, it's nine o'clock in the morning. My date isn't until seven. What on earth do you expect me to do so early?

I grinned at my phone, knowing she'd be annoyed with my response. Although I loved her confident, gregarious nature, it could be trying at times. Especially so early. *Doesn't she know the rest of the world sleeps?*

> Ronnie, when was the last time you shaved your legs? It's not a crime to take care of yourself, you know? Do you want me to come over there and help you get ready for tonight?

My eyes widened as I stared at the message. *Oh, please, Eden. Not again. Not today. I can't deal with your antics. I'm nervous enough as it is.* The pressure suddenly swallowed me whole, causing me to lean back in my chair and wonder why on earth something as simple as a date had to be so debilitating. I knew why. In my darkest corner, where I locked everything away, the past threatened to escape again. It threatened to escape and bounce around in my mind until I would eventually be reduced to tears. Tears ... or anger. I never knew which emotion would eat me up. Today, I felt it would be tears. *I have enough to deal with, Eden. Not today.*

> I'm twenty-five years old. I think I can get ready myself.

She responded within seconds. As I read her message, I wondered if I had any true chance of dissuading her.

> Do I have to remind you what you showed up in last time? Jesus, I want to burn that sweater, Ronnie! A sweater? On a date? Is that some sort of joke?

I rolled my eyes at her comment. Although, she's right—the sweater had been hideous, and I had used it more as a security blanket than anything else. As much as I had wanted to look and feel beautiful, I was worried if I tried too hard, I would give the wrong impression.

What really is the wrong impression? When I was in sweats and a T-shirt, I had apparently given the "wrong impression."

Perhaps I was being cynical. *But the past changes you.* Even if I had truly trapped it in the darkness, it would still have the power to shape who I was today. *It's been years ... Why am I still like this?* With a sigh, I texted back as my agitation grew.

I think I can manage, Eden.

If you wear a sweater and a frumpy pair of pants tonight … so help me God.

Why, oh why, did I give her the keys to my apartment?

A horrible feeling that she'd just show up bubbled in my stomach. If she did come, I would convince her to allow me to cancel the date and spend the evening with her. A girls' night out sounded far better than a night spent uncomfortably with a stranger.

Do you think maybe you and me could do something tonight instead? I don't know if I'm feeling up to another blind date. Not after last time.

Mere seconds ticked by before I received a reply.

Veronica, you're going. Do you need me to come over?

With a roll of my eyes, I quickly typed back to dissuade her. As my fingers moved across the keyboard, I bit down on my lip, wondering whether her presence would truly be a troublesome thing. With my anxiety, my sister could potentially ease my mind. She felt like home, after all. Just being around her transported me back to a happier time. *No. She's just going to make me more anxious!*

Eden, no! Don't worry about me.

My phone buzzed immediately, and an annoyed groan passed through my lips as I viewed her reply.

Let me get Harper ready. Then, we'll be on our way!

Another groan passed through my lips as I dropped my phone on the table. Of course, she was coming over. God forbid she allowed her baby sister to live her own life. She was fiercely protective of me and had been since our mom died. It's as if she filled that maternal role as soon as it had become vacant. Whenever I needed comfort, she would hold me like she would when we were both very little; whenever I felt down—which was often—she would tease me and chatter away until I had forgotten what I had been so upset about ... even if just for a moment.

After what had happened—after the darkness which had surrounded me for years finally became suffocating—she had never given up on me. Even when I had wanted to give up on myself, she never did. Time had dulled the wounds of my past, but I was sure time wasn't the only factor in my recovery. I was sure Eden had been a factor, too.

"God, Ronnie. Haven't you had time to take a shower before we stopped by?"

My eyes moved to the clock, huffing as I saw only an hour had passed since she had told me she was coming. *It's nice to see you, too, sister.* I backed away from the door and ushered her inside. My subtle annoyance dissipated as soon as I saw the blissful look on my niece's face. Harper was all smiles as she stumbled past the threshold of my apartment. She had been here many times, but I supposed everything seemed exciting when you're a toddler. After she finished her assessment of my place, Harper's eyes peered up at me, and her smile grew. Although she was young, I could already tell that she was just like her mother: bubbly, outgoing, and intelligent mixed in a very small package.

"Auntie!" she screamed as she rushed toward me. "I bring Polly!" She held out her stuffed unicorn for me to appraise.

Lowering myself to my knees, I wrapped my arm around her for a moment before turning my attention to her toy.

"Polly has to be the cutest unicorn I've ever seen. Did you just get her?"

"Yep," Harper proudly announced. "Mommy get yesterday."

"It's very cute."

"Veronica," my sister snapped, always referring to me by my full-name when she felt stern. "Go take your shower. Harper and I can watch cartoons. I can't help you if you insist on looking homeless all of the time."

Eden waved a hand at my sleepwear as her face morphed into a dissatisfied grimace. *Gosh, Eden. Like you don't own a pair of pajamas.* I nearly snorted at my own thought. Of course, her pajamas were most likely the fanciest thing a lingerie store had to offer.

"Sorry," I said unapologetically. "I didn't think you would come over so soon. It's barely past ten, and my date is *hours* away. Am I really such a lost cause?"

"Veronica," Eden started, her tone similar to the one she frequently used with her daughter when she attempted to reason with her. "You're *not* a 'lost cause.' Don't put words in my mouth. I just want you to look and feel your best tonight. Is that so wrong? Hayden's a solid guy, and I think you're really going to like him. I'm just here to make sure you actually give it a chance."

I remained silent for a moment, knowing that it would be wrong to snap at her for what she was doing. She was trying to make me happy; the only problem was her idea of happiness and my idea were dissimilar. I didn't need anyone. *Why feel alone with another person when I could feel lonely in my own blissful solitude?* Truly, I never felt alone when I was by myself. I only felt alone when I was surrounded by people who *made* me feel that way.

"I'll go take a shower," I conceded. "Don't have too much fun without me."

Eden smiled as I left, seemingly satisfied now that I bent to her will. The more I pondered it, the more hopeful I became about the evening ahead. *I suppose a date can't hurt too much.* The optimistic notions didn't last long. As I undressed and slipped under the scolding water of my shower, my thoughts found the darkness inside of me once more. I cringed as images invaded my mind; reaching to turn the shower handle, I adjusted the water to its hottest temperature to focus on the sting of the water, distracting my mind.

"Just relax, Veronica. Everything will be all right."

"Do you got her? Are you sure about this?"

"Fuck off with that shit now. It's fine."

Hands on my skin. Nails digging into my flesh. Pain. Pain. So much pain. I opened my mouth to scream but I couldn't make a sound. Maybe I was dreaming? Maybe this was all one, horrible nightmare? Mom! Mom! Dad! Somebody, please!

My eyes startled open. Tears mixed with the hot water pouring down on me as they ran down my cheeks. In this moment, I wanted to scream. I wanted to slam my fists against the shower walls until the pain inside of me finally released. Of course, I didn't do either of those things. Instead, I washed my body silently. I scrubbed and scrubbed until my skin turned pink. And then, I scrubbed some more—never feeling clean enough. A knock on the door was the only thing to pull me from the trance.

"Ronnie? Are you almost done in there?"

It's then that I realize I was sitting on the floor. Water poured down on me, and I sat immobile. Turning my head up toward the now lukewarm stream, I wondered how long I had been sitting like this. *How long have I been in the shower? I must be freaking everyone out.* As I tried to move, my limbs didn't seem to want to respond. My heart thumped wildly in my chest as I slowly began to rock back and forth, wishing my anxiousness would be expelled for a moment so I could feel normal again. Faintly, through the haze of my mind, I recognized the sound of Eden banging on my bathroom door. *Stand up, for God's sake! I can't let her see me like this! God, why do I have to be so freaking weak!*

"Veronica, is everything okay? The shower has been running for a while. I think it's time to get out now."

Her voice was calm, as if she were speaking to a child. Despite my lack of response, I listened to her. Instead of answering her, I reached out with my hand to feel the chilling water against the pads of my fingertips. My body felt so numb—barely registering the water beating down against it. My gaze dropped to my flesh, finding goosepimples everywhere. I shivered, leaning back against the tiled wall as I tried to will myself to stand once more. My muscles tingled as if they were trying to resist falling asleep. As pain shot through my limbs, I decided to stay put and ignore the sounds coming from my sister.

Just a few more minutes. This can't last much longer, can it?

The bathroom door flew open, revealing a concerned looking Eden and Harper standing in its entrance. Eden's face quickly morphed into shock as she took in my appearance on the floor of the tub.

God, sis, please don't look at me like that. I hate when people look at me like that. Pity. Who wants to see pity?

I closed my eyes, as if by doing so, they'd disappear. I listened as she told Harper to go play and relaxed as I heard little feet shoot down my hallway. I kept my eyes closed as Eden approached me and wordlessly turned off the water and stepped into the tub. Sinking down to my side, she wrapped her arm around my shoulder and pulled me against her, soaking her clothes in the process.

"Ronnie, what's wrong? Did you fall or something?"

From the way she posed the question, I could tell she wouldn't believe me if I said I fell. She knew what happened here; I was thankful that she didn't want to say it aloud. This was one of the things I loved so much about my sister: she never pushed or pried. After I didn't immediately answer her, she wrapped her other arm around me and rested her cheek atop my head. We stayed like this for a pregnant moment, waiting for my heart to return to a normal pace.

"You can tell my anything. You know that, right? I'm always here, little sister."

"I know." I paused, sitting up and brushing the wet hair out of my face. "I don't know what happened. One second, I was fine and the next ..." I shuddered, causing her to tighten her embrace. "Sometimes, I can't control it."

"Was it some sort of anxiety attack?" she asked slowly.

With my eyes cast down, I nodded. "They come and go."

"Do you know what triggered it?"

I stiffened in her arms. She knew everything, but that didn't make discussing it any less painful. Whenever the words escaped me—whenever I verbalized what happened—I felt weak. I felt like a victim all over again. I felt like what happened was my fault.

"Sometimes, I just think of it, you know?" I said as my body sank along the tiles. "Images bombard me, and I can't escape it. One moment, I'm in the present, and the next, I'm yanked back into the past. It's like a part of me will always be there—in the past—reliving it again and again."

"Veronica," she responded, her voice quivering slightly. "I—"

"You don't have to say anything, sis," I said, cutting her off. "I don't need you to say anything. Just ... well, thanks for being here. Your being here helps."

"I just wish ... " She stopped, shaking her head.

"What?"

"Nothing."

"Eden," I pressed. She had never been one to not say *exactly* what she was thinking.

"I just wish Mom were here. She knew how to deal with everything."

"I know. Me, too." Resting in her arms, I took a moment to enjoy the silence surrounding us before I added, "I'm just happy we have each other. I don't know where I'd be without that."

"You'll get through this. I mean, look how far you've come already! You don't have to compare yourself to other people; just compare yourself to where you were a year ago. You've come so far. And I know you always want to say it's because of me or because of work or because of your friends. But, it's not. It's because of you."

I smiled at this, hoping she was right. If I came this far all on my own, maybe I could find my old self again. That was what I wanted more than anything. I wanted to be the girl I was before.

"Why don't we just stay in tonight? I'll text Quinton and say we had a change of plans. If you don't want to go on a date, you don't have to. I thought I was helping ... " She trailed off, seemingly apologetic.

"You were helping, Eden," I muttered, wanting her to feel better.

"Not in the way you needed help." She paused, giving me one last look before standing up and reaching her hands out for me to take. "I should have been more considerate."

"Don't do that," I reprimanded.

With a gentle tug, she pulled me to my feet. My body swayed for a moment before I managed to straighten up and regain my balance. Eden jumped out of the tub and grabbed a towel, easing it around my body before giving me a hand to safely step out of the bathtub, knowing I couldn't trust my legs just yet. With my arm draped over her shoulder for support, Eden helped me to my room, ushering me to my bed. I took a seat, feeling unbelievably better already. Taking a deep, relieved breath, I watched Eden as she rifled through my closet to find a casual outfit that she still deemed "acceptable." It took her a moment, and when she came back to my bedside, she had a small pile of clothes in her hands—lingerie and all.

"This will do, I think. You get dressed and I'll go fix up some lunch and call Quinton. We'll just have a girls' night in, okay?"

While her voice was hopeful, her eyes were raw. My eyes shot to the floor in response, not wanting to see a look that was so similar to my own.

"That sounds good," I commented as I moved to get dressed.

Eden gave me one of her trademark blinding smiles before she turned on her heel and left. I was quick to get dressed, not wanting to feel exposed for any longer than I had to. I slipped on my underwear before sliding my legs into the nicest pair of leggings I owned—which were a gift from Eden, of course—and then slipped on my bra, fastening it before sliding on a pastel blue T-shirt.

After taking a deep breath, I slowly rose to my feet, making sure my muscles felt okay again before propelling myself forward, moving toward the bathroom. I washed my face and brushed my teeth before running a comb through my hair. Appraising my reflection in the mirror, I found a girl I barely recognized. Gaunt face, sunken eyes, and sharp features ... this didn't look like me. *Well, this will have to do for now.* Deciding to pay no mind to my reflection, I moved back into my bedroom, eyes searching for my phone to message Hayden with a quick apology.

"Hi!"

I jumped at the sound of the little, familiar voice. Forgetting the search for my phone, my eyes came to rest on Harper, who stared up at me with wide, curious eyes.

"Hey, sweetie. Did you have fun playing by yourself for a little bit?"

She shrugged, obviously not wanting to talk about herself—which seemed rare for a child her age. Only a few months ago, she had been completely egocentric, and now her focus and concern rested on me alone.

"You not feel well?" she asked as she watched me take a seat back down on the bed. She watched me for another moment before moving to climb onto my lap.

I helped her up, wrapping my arms around her before answering, "I'm fine, sweetie. How's Polly holding up?"

She smiled at the mention of her favorite unicorn. "She good. Boring now, though. You and me play?"

"Of course, you and I can play," I confirmed with a smile. Her smiles were infectious; now, I was smiling naturally. "In fact, I have a surprise for you."

Her eyes widened, and her little body shook as she began to giggle in excitement. While grocery shopping the other day, I had found the cutest little Fisher Price tea set on sale in the toy department. Not having children of my own or any pets after Salem, my black cat, passed, it was nice to spoil my niece. She deserved it, too. Although she was trying at times, she was a wonderful, caring little girl.

"What it?"

"You'll just have to wait until after dinner to see," I said as I slowly began to feel like my "normal" self again.

"That long time!" she complained with a pout.

"It's not that long, Harper," I reasoned. "Besides, good things are always worth the wait."

2

Linger

I needed to escape from my apartment. A few days had passed since my date fiasco, and I had spent every minute drowning myself in work. With a migraine and numb fingers, I became certain that if I read another sentence, I would surely pass out. *Maybe I could invite Eden over for a family dinner? I can't stomach another hour of work, and I don't think I could handle being alone tonight.* Usually, I preferred solitude but lately, I didn't trust myself when I was alone. My mind had been wandering too far for my liking—it touched parts of me I had managed to contain for years.

When was the last time you cooked for anyone other than yourself? I wondered, redirecting my train of thought to something bearable. Other than the few occasions I cooked macaroni and cheese for Harper, I couldn't recall the last time I made more than a dinner for one—which may be a good thing considering I never branched out and instead stuck to making the same few dishes I knew by heart. Perhaps today, instead of focusing on negative things, I would crack open one of the many cookbooks I purchased and never had a reason or inclination to use. Half of the books were far above my level of expertise, but if I relaxed for a few hours and pulled my mind away from my work, I was sure I could figure *something* out.

Dropping my pen on the table, I pushed away from my work and decided that, at three o'clock in the afternoon, it was time to abandon my papers and leave my apartment for a while. I cracked my fingers, which tingled from being overworked, and made my way to my bathroom, stripping out of my clothes before turning on my shower. *Today will be good. Today will be good.* I practiced the mantra in my head, believing that if I repeated positive affirmations to myself long enough, my outlook on life would change. *Dr. Leung would be proud.*

My shower was short—I had felt anxious about lingering in the shower for too long—and I spent a half hour getting ready while listening to an episode of one of my favorite podcasts, styling my hair and applying makeup before slipping into a casual outfit and a pair of Converse. As my podcast came to its end, I grabbed my keys and purse before heading out. I didn't know what it was, but grocery shopping had a way of easing my mind. Whenever I was stuck on an idea or I'm mentally exhausted from work, I hopped into my car and drove to the supermarket. *I guess there's something about buying fabric softener that was calming for the mind.*

After sliding into my Honda Civic, I shot my sister a text, inquiring about tonight. She was as prompt as ever to respond, letting me know that Harper was thrilled with the idea. The image of Harper bouncing around filled my mind as I read the message, causing me to smile as I replied.

Although I enjoyed being single, I had always wanted children. I used to think that I would be a young mother—hoping to have children in my early twenties. However, my past had ruined that for me—*he* had ruined that for me. *That bastard ...*

Knowing there was a point in my life where I envisioned having children with *him* always made me feel ill. Now, I didn't know if I would ever have children. I didn't know if I could put myself through *that* again. Once, I had wanted marriage, children, and a white house with a traditional picket fence. Now, I just wanted to get through the day without my past plaguing me. I became so engrossed in my work and following every dream I could; so, the past hasn't touched me like it once had. However, I was sure it would find a way to invade my life again. Soon enough, I would be wading the tumultuous water once more—praying for an escape.

I drove to Safeway while contemplating my latest "side project." Since I was little, I had always wanted to be a writer. Some of my fondest memories consisted of sitting on my mother's lap while she read to me. Stories such as *The Giving Tree* became favorites of mine because of her. Even now, I could hear her voice in my mind, reading to me; I could hear the intonation in her voice. The memory of this was stronger when I was writing. When I wrote my own little stories and worked on the illustrations, it was like she was sitting beside me, reading over my shoulder as I sketched.

"Oh, Ronnie. That's perfect. You can't imagine how proud I am of you."

My imagination brought a tear to my eye. Sometimes, when I was alone, I imagined what she would say. The words and phrases I made up still had meaning—although, she wasn't here to relay them to me. Shaking the thoughts from my head before my vulnerability set in, I reached for the radio, turning up the music until it was my focus, other than the road ahead.

"That's lovely, sweetie. Who knew my daughter was so talented?"

I parked close, turning off my car with a sigh. Closing my eyes for a moment, I considered why I was thinking of her so much *now*. I thought of her often, but those thoughts were fleeting. Usually, the thoughts brought a warm feeling, but now, the remembrance was more bittersweet. *Is something coming? A change, perhaps? What's wrong with me?* Opening my eyes, I opened the car door and slipped out, enjoying the heat of the spring sun. I couldn't understand what was wrong with me, but there was a feeling in my gut that was hard to ignore. A feeling that suggested something was coming—something *different*.

When did you get so superstitious, Veronica? I ignored the feeling as I moved down the parking lot and entered the store. As usual, I was sure I was just being ridiculous. I had never had foresight before, so, why would it spark now? Grabbing a cart, I decided not to give it anymore thought. My gut-instinct didn't have the best track record, after all.

After sanitizing the cart and pushing past the rows of check-outs, I pulled out my phone, researching recipe ideas as I dodged other patrons. *I could make parmesan chicken again, or maybe shrimp tortellini?* I shopped around for my normal groceries as I waited for an idea to come. Harper wasn't picky, but she wasn't exactly adventurous either. If the recipe wasn't too "out there," she was easy to satisfy. I decided on chicken parmesan, knowing she would love it, and gathered all the ingredients before heading to the frozen food aisle to get some microwavable meals for the rest of the week.

Microwavable meals for one ... maybe it's time you started getting more creative? Just swallow your pride and buy one of those fancy "meals for one" cookbooks you always made jokes about. They would be fitting, considering you're always on your own. Maybe you can grab a bottle of wine while you're at it and listen to Sad FM: listening for lonely twenty-somethings with—my inner ramblings came to a halt as soon as I saw him.

Something about the man before me was captivating; I couldn't look away if I tried. And I didn't want to try. Despite my usual reservations, I wanted to stare at him for as long as I possibly could. Maybe it was his tattoos, or maybe it was his angular face, which was almost too rough to be considered conventionally handsome. As I studied him, I found there was something about him—something I couldn't put my finger on—which made my knees weak. He was tall—well over six feet—with tattoos covering every bit of exposed flesh from his neck down. Gazing at his strong build and sharp jawline, I found it hard to breathe. I just wanted to gaze at him. *He's handsome.* Intimidating, but very handsome. *I've never seen a man like this ... at least, not in person.* He looked like something off a movie screen, despite his edgy appearance. *He looks like a dark, fallen angel.*

I continued to watch him as he stared at a display of boxed wine. There was something about the way he looked at the drink which unnerved me. It was almost as if he were challenging it—as if he were attempting to prove something to himself. I had never seen someone look at an object like that. But, that wasn't what disturbed me; what disturbed me was the familiarity the image of his face brought. I felt tied to him. Even though we hadn't exchanged so much as a word—or even a look—I felt as if I *knew* him, like he and I were the same. As I watched him, I made up a story for him in my mind—something which I frequently did when watching a new, mysterious person. In my head, I imagined he battled his own demons—just like me. I imagined an entire life story for him. I imagined that he overcame the battle but still carried all the scars. I imagined he and I were similar. Similar enough to be friends ... or something more.

Where is your mind, Veronica?

Knowing I couldn't just stand there and gaze at a stranger, I breezed past him, walking down the aisle until I reached the store's selection of rosé, eyes searching for Eden's favorite brand. As I reached for her preference, I felt his eyes on me, causing goosebumps to rise on my skin. The way he studied me made my heart race. I wanted to look back, turning my head slightly before I flushed and stopped myself, moving my cart forward instead. I tried desperately not to turn; it was so tempting after viewing him for such a long time. I couldn't control myself for long. Impulsively, I looked over my shoulder, wanting to see his eyes. *You'll probably never see him again. So, what will another glimpse hurt?*

His eyes were dark, almost black, and soulful. They looked like they had seen so much, and yet, they still held a spark. The lustful look in his dark eyes made me melt. Realizing we were both gazing at each other like idiots, I looked away, flushing everywhere. As I moved, I caught a glimpse of him; his mouth opened as if he wanted to say something. Part of me wanted to turn and greet him, but another, more prominent part, knew the conversation would lead to nothing. I would still be suffering from the same anxiousness that made every instance with a man hard. *Perhaps he could be different*, I considered as I walked away.

Moving aimlessly through the store, I couldn't erase his face from my mind. There was something about him ... something that made me desperate to reach out. I wished I could understand the strange pull I felt. I wished I could understand the familiarity. *Think about something else. He looks like danger, and you've had your fill of that.*

While I cooked, the handsome face from Safeway was all I could think of. Seeing his face in my mind's eye was so soothing. Strangely enough, thinking of him provided me with the same relaxation I got when I thought of my mother. With his eyes in my mind, my muscles relaxed, and my posture straightened. For a moment, it was as if I didn't have a care in the world. I smiled, thankful for the small glimpse I received from a handsome stranger. *Maybe I'll continue to think about him*, I thought, knowing it was probably weird considering he had, most likely, forgotten me completely. *Out of sight, out of mind.* I wasn't perturbed by this though. This was my imagination, after all; I could do as I pleased when I was inside my own head. If daydreaming about a rugged, handsome stranger was what I chose to do, then that should be the end of it.

I wish I knew his name ... What sort of name would a man like that have? Kurt? Blane? Jaxson? God, why didn't I have the courage to speak to him? I wished there was some way I could discover his name— just for the sake of my own fantasies. *I could always look him up on social media.* I snorted at the idea. What on earth would I have looked up anyway? "Hot, twenty-something with plenty of tattoos and sex hair"? The thought alone caused me to feel embarrassed. *Maybe I could make a name up for him? What are bad boy types in romance novels usually named? Jax? Brandon? Ace? Draven? He sort of looks like a Draven. I like that name, too.*

I understood that I would never know his true name; and "hot guy with sex hair and tattoos" just seemed to be too much. *H.G.S.H.T. You could call him that! H.G.S.H.T.: Hot. Guy. Sex. Hair. Tattoos.* I rolled my eyes at the thought and glanced down to check my recipe. While I felt silly thinking about a complete stranger, he occupied my thoughts in a way that was far better than my usual musings. *Even though we've never spoken, this stranger has helped me in ways he'll never know.*

"What are you daydreaming about?" Eden teased me as she gently kicked my foot beneath the dining room table.

I knew I had been quiet for the duration of our dinner. Which wasn't too unusual; however, I usually contributed *something* to the conversation every now and then. I was sure Eden was just worried about me again; pity would color her expression and she would grow quiet, too. I hated seeing her that way. It made me feel worse; it made me truly feel like a victim. *You were a victim, Veronica,* I reminded myself—just like I *always* had to.

"Nothing," I finally answered her, unable to meet her gaze. "I think I had some good ideas for a book today."

I looked up to find her eyes brightening at this.

"Really?" She smiled, leaning forward to get a better look at me. "You scrapped your other plan, then?"

"Yeah. I hit a major road block with that one. I just couldn't seem to get around it, despite my persistence. This one is different. I think it might be good."

"Well, out with it," Eden insisted with a smile. "Why don't you run it past us?"

"I don't think it's ready yet, Eden. I don't want to jinx it by talking about it too soon."

"Come on, Ronnie. Just—"

"Baby, leave the girl alone. This is part of her creative process," her husband, Quinton, interjected with a wink in my direction.

Eden laughed at her husband before she retreated and leaned back in her chair. Eden and her husband have the perfect chemistry. The way he looked at her ... It was as if she were the only woman in the entire universe. The love in his eyes was so abundant; it was obvious to anyone who witnessed them together. They were truly one soul in two bodies. They're everything I wished I had. *Maybe one day, if I let down my guard* ... Would it ever be possible for me to share something like that?

"Babe, I can't help it. My sister is brilliant," Eden bragged, pulling me from my thoughts.

I suppressed an eye roll in response to her compliment. I always hated when all of the attention was on me. Whenever any attention was directed my way, I just wanted to bleed into the walls and disappear. Thankfully, I had grown up with an extroverted, gregarious sister whose boldness had allowed me to fade away. Every now and then, I had wished I were more like her; I would wish I was outgoing with a wealth of friends. While I loved my alone time—*I was an introvert, after all*—there were times I wished I was more popular. *I shouldn't have isolated myself for so long.* After what happened, I had shut everyone out; I had wanted to be alone. Now, I missed the support system I had let slip through my fingers. *Maybe another therapist would be a good idea?* I had gone to therapy for two years after graduating college, and yet, I felt more lost in this moment than I had back then. *Who can I talk to? I feel ... lost.*

I sat in a trance for the remainder of dinner—listening but never contributing much of anything. I smiled when appropriate and laughed when I needed to, but my mind was somewhere else. Eden felt it, I was sure. She had always been so intuitive, especially when it came to her sibling.

After they left, I was faced with an empty apartment. Which had never truly felt *empty* until recently. Faced with it now, I wished I had someone—someone to open up and share my soul with without fears or reservations. The funny thing was I didn't believe I could *ever* have something like that, despite yearning for it so endlessly. If I ever wanted that, I knew I needed to change.

I didn't want to feel weak anymore. I didn't want to feel like a victim. I wanted to feel like *Veronica* again. And for that, I would have given anything.

3

Dreams

The summer air warmed my face and caused me to wonder why I insisted on spending so many of my days locked away in my apartment. June in Evergreen was lovely—nothing compared to a Colorado summer. With the crisp air and the beautiful scenery, the state felt like something out of a dream. Despite living here my entire life, I was still enamored with this place. It was just so *cozy*; just right for me. This was where my roots were; this was where I felt safe.

Closing my book and allowing it to fall to my lap, I shut my eyes, exposing my face to the hot sun. I soaked up the vitamin D and felt my entire body relax under the sun's rays. It was quiet around me; it was the time of day where everyone was at work and their children were in daycare. This was what I loved most about my job: how it afforded me flexibility and free time to enjoy a beautiful day. As the sun danced across my face, I thought of him—the mysterious stranger from Safeway. A long while had passed since I saw his face in person, yet, he was still in the forefront of my mind. I liked him there. It was as if he were my little secret. In my imagination, he was mine and mine alone.

When I daydreamed about him—or fantasized about him, too—I could control his every action. Everything he said or did was up to me. I needed that sort of control. That sort of control meant there was no way I could get hurt. Perhaps that was where my love for writing stemmed from; when I was writing, I played with a controlled world where everything was safe for me. Life was unpredictable, and unpredictability didn't fare well with me.

I opened my eyes and picked up my book. *No need to focus on the negative, Veronica.* Today was too beautiful for negative thoughts. The sun was shining, the breeze was just right, and my time was my own. I knew I shouldn't feel so sorry for myself, especially under such lovely conditions.

After a few more chapters, my eyes grew weary. Bookmarking my page, I slipped the book into my purse and stood, brushing off the grass from my outfit before I grabbed the beach towel I had brought to sit on. *I need espresso, and I need it now.* Last night, I couldn't sleep at all. After tossing and turning, I had given up on sleep and had spent the evening editing in my living room before I had passed out on the couch in the early hours of the morning. I had awoken restless, but it had seemed like I had grown used to the feeling.

Pushing my tiredness aside, I slid into my Civic and placed my bag on my passenger seat. I took a moment to adjust the music to one of my favorite indie rock playlists before abandoning the parking lot for a coffee shop down the road. It was packed around lunchtime, and thankfully, I had an abundance of patience and nowhere to be. I parked in the one spot available before heading inside, rifling through my purse as I made my way through the coffee shop's doors. *ChapStick, no ... Coin purse ... Where, oh where is my freaking wallet?* I smiled as my fingertips grazed the familiar leather and raised my gaze as I pulled my wallet from my bag.

The vision before me stopped me in my tracks. *It's him!* my mind screamed. *It's the handsome stranger from Safeway!* For a moment, I wondered if I was daydreaming again. The way he watched me ... it was something out of a fantasy. There was no way a simmering gaze like that could be real. It was so intense—so filled with longing. It made me want to go to him; my cheeks flushed, and I turned away instead.

I couldn't avoid his gaze for long though. It was impossible to not steal glimpses of him. I watched him out of the corner of my eye, curious about him despite having been too anxious to utter a word. I didn't regret watching him because I found he was watching me, too. I could feel his gaze dancing along the lines of my body. For a moment, I wondered if he daydreamed about me the way I did him. *Doubtful. Why would someone like him—who could probably have anyone and does probably have everyone—spend their time thinking of me?* Nevertheless, I was hopeful. I was hopeful because, despite his rugged, almost threatening exterior, there was something about him that made me feel ... *different.*

Unable to help myself, I finally met his dark gaze. Once our eyes locked, it was impossible to look away. It was as if we were the only two people in the room—the only two people in the world.

"Trevor!" the barista called out, causing the man to break eye contact with me.

My gaze remained locked on him as he stepped forward to grab his coffee and sandwich from the counter. As he turned away, he paused for a moment, looking at me with a contemplative expression. It was as if he were debating whether he should come talk to me. Despite the shyness I felt under his scrutiny, I wanted him to talk to me; I was desperate to hear what his voice sounded like. It would add a much-needed layer to my fantasies. I was sure the voices I had been making up wouldn't do his real voice justice. In my fantasies, his voice had been just as rough as the rest of him—a deep, musky baritone.

My eyes remained on him as he shifted back and forth on his feet, appearing lost in thought. After a few awkward seconds, it seemed as if he had made up his mind. He made a beeline to the front door with his eyes cast down the entire way. He seemed nervous, which was laughable to me. *How could someone like him be nervous?* His eyes only rose when his body came close to mine. His gaze was quick but sent a shiver down my spine. I smiled as my body flushed. I wanted to talk to him, but my anxiousness prevented me. *He's too attractive, and I'm not bold enough for this. Next time,* I promised myself as he dashed out of the coffee shop. Until then, I would hold on to the image of his strong body moving toward me as well as the passionate look in his dark, emerald eyes.

Over the next few weeks, the attractive stranger—*Trevor*—had drifted in and out of my head. When I had closed my eyes, he was there; when I had taken a moment to breathe, he was the first thing I saw. I was sure this sort of fixation was not normal, but I just couldn't help what my mind wanted to see. My overactive imagination ran wild with images of him. Even now, as I ran under the hot, July sun, I thought of him.

With a relaxing melody playing through my earphones, I ran down the Elk Meadow Loop. Running had always been so freeing— especially when the air was warm, and the sun was high. This afternoon, the trail was practically empty despite the decent weather. The clouds were a little gray, but it was nothing to detour me.

As I ran, I allowed my mind to wander. I thought of work before my thoughts drifted to ideas for my children's book. As my legs continued to propel forward at a steady pace, my thoughts moved to Trevor, and that was where they stayed. *That's where they* always *seemed to stay.* I blushed as his image conjured up in my mind. I couldn't believe that a man, whom I had never uttered a word to, spurred such reactions from me.

I'm sure he spurs this sort of reaction from lots of women. With looks like his, there's no way he's single. I'm sure he has a girl at home. Wherever his home is.

Suddenly, my thoughts were brought back to the present as I saw another runner coming toward me from a few yards down the trail. Every time I was alone and would see another person—even if it was just one—my heart would begin to accelerate. The reaction was embarrassing, and yet, it was one that I couldn't help.

Out of my control, I felt my anxiety slowly begin to take over. It would creep into my consciousness, toying at the edges, and then would slam into me all at once, leaving me completely immobilized. I slowed down my sprint and wondered if I should feign taking a break, so I didn't have to make eye contact with the man running toward me.

I decided it was a wise idea and stopped running, stepping to the side of the trail to peer down at my phone. I understood that, if he were dangerous, looking away would not be a wise choice; however, even in my anxiety-induced haze, I was able to tell that this man didn't have sinister intentions. I believed he was just out for a run, and I was just incapable of acting normal around men.

I attempted to control my breathing as I counted to ten in my head. I felt him growing closer and closer. When he was a yard away, I could barely breathe. As he moved one foot in front of the other, my heart began to race as my knees grew weak. I felt the air around me shift as he ran past me and continued down the path. My heart began to race so rapidly I feared I would pass out on the trail. Images conjured up in my mind as well as conversations I had once heard while drifting away in a haze.

"Just wait! Can't you be fucking patient?"

"You said once you were done—"

"Well, I'm not. Just go somewhere and chill. She isn't going anywhere."

My knees gave out as the thoughts filled my mind, and as I drifted through the haze, I felt myself slowly fall to the ground, landing on my bottom. The music was still playing in my ears, but I couldn't recognize the song; I barely registered the noise at all. I barely recognized my surroundings as I lowered my face into my hands in an attempt at willing away my anxiety. Of course, it didn't work—I sat alone as I rode it out.

A minute felt like an hour as I waited for my heart rate to slow to a normal pace. I closed my eyes, trying to focus my mind on something more pleasant. It didn't take long for my thoughts to morph into the image of the man who had been entertaining my every imagining. I didn't know why he was appearing in my head now, but I was grateful for it.

As I focused on his face instead of my haunting past, my anxiety started to calm. With the memory of his eyes in my mind, I forgot about what was ailing me moments before. In that moment, all I saw was him. *His dark eyes. His strong jaw. The ink covering his skin.* After a few minutes of this, I could finally breathe easy. My mind registered the sounds coming from my 90s rock playlist as I came back to reality, and finally, I was able to raise from the ground. *You did it. You got through it. You're stronger than you think.* All thanks to my strength and the images of a handsome stranger.

After my ... *incident*, I had kept to running around my small apartment complex. While I didn't talk to my neighbors, I knew them by name. I felt safe around my apartment complex. It was filled with mostly families and a few older couples. Although I hadn't seen everyone who lived here, I believed I could be one of the only singles.

Being early August, all the children were still on summer vacation and had congregated at the park in the middle of our complex. I ran past, receiving a few appreciative glances from some of the dads standing at the park's edge, which just made me cringe with disgust.

They're supposed to be watching their children—not me. Just feeling their eyes on me made me want to run back to my apartment so I could put on three more sports bras so my breasts wouldn't move an inch. While I ran past them, I paid them no mind, continuing toward my apartment. *I've run a few miles already. Maybe I can just call it a day.*

While my legs propelled me forward and my thighs began to sting, something caught my eye and nearly stopped me in my tracks.

It's him! It's Trevor... God, is it creepy that I know his name? Whatever. A girl is allowed a little fantasy, isn't she?

He was even more attractive than I remembered—even more captivating. I felt like a voyeur as I slowed down my run to sneak glances in his direction. He was with an older, equally attractive man.

I wonder if that's his father?

They were both around the same height and had equally strong features. As embarrassing as it was, I couldn't seem to take my eyes off of the pair of them as they walked toward the leasing office.

Is he moving in here?!

Suddenly, his gaze moved in my direction, and I nearly fell flat on my face as I quickly diverted my gaze. I prayed to God he hadn't caught me leering at him like that. My cheeks flushed as I ran toward my apartment; I felt his eyes on me the entire way.

As hard as I tried—*God, who was I kidding? I wasn't trying* that *hard*—I couldn't seem to focus on the novel in front of me. While I loved a good romance novel, it was hard to focus on its words when I had such an amazing image before me. In my apartment, I had a beautiful picture window. And in this moment, that picture window illuminated the most incredible view: Trevor, my brand-new neighbor, moving into his apartment. I felt almost guilty as I looked out my window, overlooking the parking lot. I just couldn't help myself though. Trevor and a man, whom I was now positive was his father, were moving furniture under the hot, summer sun.

I leaned forward in my seat to get a better look at the pair as Trevor lifted the bottom of his thin cotton T-shirt to wipe some of the sweat off his face. For the first time in a long time, I felt ... God, the feeling was so foreign to me I barely recognized it as my panties dampened. I felt turned on. *Really* turned on. I couldn't remember the last time I had felt so desirous.

Dropping my gaze, I peered back at my novel. *Novels are safe ... reading is comfortable ... staying inside won't hurt me.* Life hadn't been easy for me, and reading had always provided me with the most delicious escape from reality. While lost in a book, I managed to forget everything else. Through the author's words, I was able to live vicariously through the characters, enjoying their adventures as if they were my own. *Perhaps one day, I could have my own adventures*, I thought as I peered down at the handsome man below.

Biting down on my lip to stifle a moan, I watched my attractive neighbor as he and his father lifted furniture from the moving truck to bring inside. *I wonder where his apartment is? I wonder if he's close?* I had no idea which apartments were vacant as I watched Trevor, admiring his inked skin glistening with sweat under the hot sun.

It should be a sin to look so good.

My eyes were glued to him as he bent down and lifted a chair, blushing at the way his ass strained against the dark fabric of his skinny jeans. As he moved with the chair in tow, I nearly jumped in my seat. He was headed toward *my* apartment building. *Holy. Freaking. Shit. Veronica, this is going to be your year.*

My thoughts surprised me. Trevor was attractive—more than attractive—but I never truly entertained the thought of actually opening up and speaking with him. I considered my options while I kept my eyes peeled for his return. He came back down with an exhausted smile, returning to his truck to peer inside the back seat. *I wonder what he keeps looking at?* For the duration of the time Trevor and his father spent unloading the moving truck, Trevor has periodically checked the back seat of his truck. I peeled my eyes, trying to get a better glimpse of what he was so intrigued by, but had no luck.

My curiosity was satisfied moments later after Trevor reached into the back seat. I gasped at the sight before me: Trevor with an infant.

So, that's what he's been checking up on for the last hour. He has a child ... a baby that can't be older than a few months. Disappointment coursed through me at the sight. I felt deflated and foolish. *Of course, he has someone who loves him. And they have a child together, too.*

Although the disappointment stung like a shot to the heart, I still admired the way he and that baby looked together. Even from my perch far away, the love in his eyes was evident. He gazed at the baby as if it were his entire world. *I'm sure it is his entire world—his very meaning.* Seeing him with the child caused me to feel strangely maternal. *I wish that were my child he was carrying in those tattooed, muscular arms ... Christ, Veronica! What are you saying?* I reprimanded myself as I shifted my gaze, suddenly feeling far too voyeuristic.

Despite never "knowing" him, the loss I felt was profound. It was as if a piece of me was missing suddenly as a possibility faded to black. Leaning back in my seat, I allowed the feeling to wash over me. I closed my eyes and let the small heartache pass. I felt silly—what reason did I have to mourn the loss of a relationship I never had?—but I couldn't help myself. For a moment, I mourned the news as if a long-time lover and I had separated. *As if you really had a "long-time lover" to know the feeling.* He *wasn't much of "lover," was he?*

As my thoughts drifted, I considered what it would be like to be Trevor's friend. He looked as if he needed a friend; I needed one desperately. All the friendships I had formed in high school and college either fizzled out due to my anxiety, depression, and tendency to isolate myself, or my friends had moved around so much, I never saw them. Outside of Eden and Quinton, I could count the people I hung out with on one hand. I could use someone new in my life, even if that meant a platonic friendship with a man who made my heart sing.

It could be nice to surround yourself with someone of the opposite sex. It had been a long time since I had any male friends—or males in my life in general. Outside of my father and brother-in-law, I had avoided them. I never would have admitted to that out loud. The anxiousness they had unintentionally caused had been debilitating. One moment, I would be fine, and the next, I would be spiraling out of control—feeling myself slip away, morphing into a person I wouldn't recognize.

After so many years, I had become tired of fearing the unknown; I had become tired of my past deciding my future. *Why was I still letting him have such a hold over me? After all this time, I thought I would have forgotten him completely.* I snorted at the thought of ever forgetting Preston. The scars from the wounds he inflicted were so deep I was sure they would never fade away.

"Don't look at me like that, Veronica."

"I think I hate you."

"You think? Veronica, you can't decide on anything. You never know what you want. That's part of the problem."

"I hate you," I whispered. With the music blaring, I doubted he heard me.

Days passed, and I had kept to myself. Alone in my apartment, I had rehearsed different ways of approaching Trevor. I had practiced conversations in my mind, but none of them had felt right. I had considered baking him a "welcome to the apartment complex" batch of cookies but then believed the gesture would come across as too awkward and desperate. While most people could pull off a friendly act like that, I knew I would have stumbled over my words and scared him away. Besides, I didn't know how I would have reacted if I spoke to him. In my head, he had been thrilled to see me, stating he wished I had come sooner; in my head, he had embraced me and had been very, *very* single. Of course, fantasy and reality rarely mixed, and in this case, I doubted fantasy and reality would so much as flirt.

I pushed those thoughts aside and tried to focus my attention on something more *pleasant*—such as my attractive neighbor and his adorable baby. In his time here, I hadn't seen him with a woman once. I never saw a single woman enter his apartment. *Maybe he's alone after all.* While that would have been lucky for me, my heart broke for his little baby; it wasn't easy to grow up without a mother. *Someone so young and so innocent doesn't deserve that.* After my mother passed away, it had taken me a long time to accept it.

I couldn't imagine what it would be like to grow up without a mother at all. *To not even have a glimpse of her smiling face in his memories.* I cherished every single memory I had made with my mother—the good and the bad. Although her life had been cut far too short, it had been filled with love and happiness. She'd had the brightest of smiles and a feeling of warmth about her, which were impossible to forget. When I had been with her, I had been home. No matter where we had been or what our circumstances were, when she was around, it had been impossible to feel anything other than joy.

Perhaps the negative memories I have of her have become clouded, erased by the good. Once, someone had told me you may not remember what a person said, but you remember the way they made you feel. With my mother, I had felt invincible.

The thought of that little baby being motherless made my heart ache. I knew the baby wasn't mine—I knew its life was none of my business—however, I felt so drawn to the little one and its father. I felt like I belonged with them. *I could do some good. If Trevor is alone, he could need some help.*

I turned in bed and stared out the window as the sun began to shine through my blinds. I smiled as the heat hit my face and closed my eyes as I soaked up the vitamin D. *Maybe you're being weird, Veronica*, I considered as I laid in bed. *You keep referring to this man you've never spoken to by his first name as if you were friends. You're constantly thinking of him. Is that healthy?*

I rolled over onto my back and sighed. I understood I was probably being ridiculous. *Obsessing over a man you've never spoken to. Maybe today you could go introduce yourself? What could it possibly hurt?* I mulled over the idea as I rocked back and forth on my mattress. *I should bake something though. Maybe a pie or a batch of cookies? It would be too awkward to go empty handed.* I mulled over the idea more, wondering if I should finally pull the trigger. *He lives across the hall, for God's sake! What more of a chance do you need?*

When I had initially found out my handsome crush lived across the hall from me, I had wanted to faint. The thought of him so close, yet so far away, had nearly brought me to my knees. I had wanted him even more. The feelings he had conjured up from the depths of my consciousness had my mind spinning and my body warming with desire.

Suddenly, my fantasies had become more real. Every day, I had dreamt of his hands on my body—his lips covering mine. The thought alone caused me to blush.

My hands began to move over the curves of my body, and as I closed my eyes, I pretended my hands were his. Shutting out the darkness in my mind, I slowly began to touch myself—circling a nipple with my thumb while my other hand snuck down my body. I imagined his body on top of mine, his weight pressing me into the mattress as he reached between my legs and found the spot where I desired his touch the most.

Just as my fingertips reached my needy clit, a cry interrupted my musings. Howls sounded from across the hall and caused me to pull my hand away as if I had been caught in the act. The thought of Trevor wide awake with his baby while I was an apartment away touching myself caused my body to shudder with embarrassment. *Would it be a good idea for me to go help them? I wouldn't want to impose.* Before my mind registered what my body was doing, I was up and out of bed, sliding into my favorite robe and pair of slippers before I headed to the front door of my apartment.

Just see what you can do and don't overstay your welcome, I told myself as I exited my apartment. Now that I was in the hallway, the baby's cries sounded more hysterical. Hearing the wails caused me to worry. I thought back on my days babysitting my niece and remembered the many ailments she'd had when she had been younger. Like me, Harper seemed prone to bad luck.

Lost in thought and distracted by my concern for the baby inside my handsome neighbor's apartment, my usual anxiety didn't take over as I reached out to knock on the door. While I waited for an answer, my body was void of a single symptom. The pleasant change shocked me. My contemplations ended as the apartment door swung open, revealing the face that had haunted my thoughts.

He was even more devastatingly handsome up close. His hair was wild; his features were severe—so much so, he looked almost more intimidating than traditionally handsome. His eyes were something that would stick with me forever: dark, emerald green eyes swimming with so many emotions I couldn't name. My gaze dropped from his face, and I quickly became captivated by his body as well. His muscles were taut and impressive without being bulky, and every inch of his exposed flesh from the neck down was covered in beautiful ink. Despite his harsh exterior, I was completely at ease around him. I couldn't put my finger on the exact reasoning, but there was something about his aura that was very soothing. *Even now, with a frazzled look on his face and a crying baby in his arms, he has the power to relax me.*

With a worried expression and little patience, he gave me a quick once-over before he said, "I'm so sorry if we woke you. I'm pretty sure he's getting sick or something."

The look in his eyes distracted me momentarily before my gaze dropped to the little boy in his arms. *Poor little guy. Everything is going to be okay.* Despite being sick, this little boy was the cutest thing I had ever seen. With bright eyes, chubby cheeks, and a round face, he was a beautiful baby. I fell in love with him instantly.

"Poor baby," I muttered, wanting nothing more than to take the little guy in my arms in an attempt to lift his spirits. *I wonder what has this little guy so fussy.*

"He's been crying like this all morning. I have no idea what's the matter with him."

I could tell that Trevor was trying to stay calm, but there was a blatant edge to his voice. He was worried about his son. When I met his gaze again, his eyes were wild and frantic. In this moment, it was apparent that this man had never dealt with this sort of situation before. *Maybe this was the first time he's had an issue like this on his own?*

"Can I come in?" I inquired, hoping I would find a way to solve his problem. I may not have been a doctor, but I knew a thing or two about taking care of children.

With an eager smile, he stepped aside, inviting me into his apartment. The furniture and the décor were sparse, which made it apparent to me that two men decorated. While my eyes scanned the apartment, my heart began to soften. Images of Trevor "decorating" this himself filled my mind and made me smile. The baby's bawls quickly brought me back to the present though. My mind refocused on the matter at hand as Trevor led me to the couch in his living room and took a seat. I took a perch at his side, and my concentration poured onto his son.

"Do you think he could be teething?" I asked after a moment. It was the first idea my mind could conjure. I remembered how horrible it was for Harper when she had been teething. Eden nearly had a heart attack when the teething started, believing her daughter's symptoms indicated something far worse. She hadn't calmed until we had searched her symptoms online and were led to articles on different parenting sites.

I tore my eyes away from the baby for a moment to peer up at its father. Trevor looked completely aghast and I stifled a giggle. I didn't want to laugh at him. He was stressed out and worried about his son. I could only imagine what he was going through in this moment, watching his son in tears with no idea how to help. His brows were knitted together in concentration, and the muscles along his strong jawline were twitching from the stress. When his eyes finally rose to meet mine, I couldn't help but smile at him. He was just so *adorable*—a word which I was certain he had never been called—when he was deep in concentration.

As I found confusion being the only thing lighting Trevor's features, I asked, "Have his sleep patterns been different at all? Has he not been eating like he's supposed to?"

Trevor shrugged, clearly baffled by my question. I studied him for a moment, wondering why he seemed so skittish around his son. *The little guy must be at least six months old by now. So, Trevor can't be lacking for knowledge so completely.*

After he hadn't spoken up, I continued, "I have some Baby Orajel, if you want to give it a try?"

He looked at me for a moment as if he were trying to decipher what exactly Baby Orajel was before he finally gave me a tense smile.

"That'd be great! I'd be so lost if you hadn't dropped by."

"It's no problem," I said with a wave of my hand. "Let me just go across the hall and get it."

"You live across the hall?" he questioned, his deep voice going up an octave.

His cheeks became flushed. *Why does he look so embarrassed?*

With a befuddled look, I questioned, "Is that a problem?"

"No—no. I don't even know why I said that."

Weird. I had never seen a man so absurdly attractive stumble over his words like that. It was endearing. His soft heart and deep, tender voice were such a juxtaposition to his overall look. I was sure that despite appearing tame now, he had been primitive before. He didn't look like a man who was meant to be domesticated. *God, he's everything I don't need. Everything that I'm usually so afraid of.* That thought was what troubled me the most. *Out of all the men in the world to choose from, why was I so drawn to the ruggedly handsome, seemingly dangerous man before me?* Before I could give it any more thought, I returned my attention to the flustered man and child in front of me.

A tiny laugh passed through my lips as I said, "I'll be right back."

I caught the hopeful look in his eyes as I left his apartment and returned to my own. Once inside, I made a beeline for the bathroom, grabbing a half-used tube of Baby Orajel from the nights I had spent babysitting Harper. I smiled, thankful I hadn't thrown the ointment away once I hadn't had a use for it.

When I returned to Trevor's apartment, I found his son was still wailing in his lap. Despite not having a connection to the little guy, I felt utterly helpless as I looked at him. His bawls pulled at my heartstrings and, for a moment, I could barely breathe as my anxiety began to set in. *What if it's more than just teething? What if you don't know what you're doing?*

Putting a calm face on for my panicked neighbor, I took a seat back down on the couch and twisted the lid off the tube. *Calm, Veronica. Stay calm. You've got this.*

"Can you get him to open his mouth? I have to put this on his gums," I said, holding up the tube for Trevor to inspect.

Trevor gave me a tight smile in return before he reached down and gently squeezed his son's cheeks, causing the baby's mouth to pop open in a tiny "O." The baby's brows were knitted together in discomfort and his little body heaved in his father's arms as I squeezed a bit of ointment onto my fingertip.

"Aw, he must be so uncomfortable," I commented sympathetically as I applied the ointment to his gums.

By the time I was finished with the application, his loud cries had turned into soft whimpers.

Trevor emitted a sigh of relief before running a hand through his unruly mane.

"Thank you so much," he said gruffly, sounding exasperated. "I thought he'd never stop crying. I was getting worried."

I shrugged, knowing I didn't really do that much. Nothing more than Trevor could have done.

"What's the little guy's name?" I questioned as the baby stared up at me with guileless, jade eyes.

"Greyson," Trevor answered, pride ringing in his voice. "But I call him Grey."

Grey. That's perfect, somehow.

"That's a great name," I mused as I reached down and tickled the little guy's belly.

As strange as it was, I felt as if I had known this little boy his entire life. *It feels so right being here.* Sometimes, it felt like there were moments that were meant to be, as if the universe had done everything in its power to bring certain people together. *Right now, feels like one of those moments.* It felt like the world had come to a standstill; it felt like, for once in my life, I was right where I needed to be. *Goodness, Veronica. How ridiculous can you be? You've just met them, and you're harping about "fate"?*

"How do you know so much about kids?" Trevor asked, pulling me from my contemplations. "You were great with him just now."

"My older sister has a daughter. She's a toddler now, and I babysit her all the time."

He regarded me for a moment, a small smile tugging on the corners of his lips before he straightened up in his seat and said, "Since we're neighbors, I suppose I should introduce myself." An uncomfortable laugh escaped his mouth, which caused my heart to flutter in response. "I'm Trevor Warren. I moved in just a few days ago."

"I know," I couldn't stop myself from admitting. As soon as the truth left my mouth, I was unable to stop my blush. I didn't want him to think I had been watching him. *God, he was so captivating.* "I watched you move in."

His eyes widened for a moment, and I watched his expression with my heart in my throat. I felt nauseous as a pregnant silence filled the air. Finally, his face relaxed, and he smiled at me, ever so softly, in a way that made my heart skip a beat. I couldn't remember the last time a man affected me like this—if ever. Even my ex—who I had done anything for; who I had destroyed myself for—had never made me feel like this.

"And you are?" he prompted with a roguish grin.

"Sorry," I replied with a blush as I realized that, once again, I had been staring off into space. "I'm Ronnie Clark." I gave him my nickname, wanting to hear the name fall from his gorgeous lips.

There's nothing like a crush calling you by your name. It makes my heart flutter and my palms sweat.

"Ronnie? Is that short for something?"

"Veronica," I supplied with a shy grin.

My heart was beating so wildly I was afraid it would burst through the confines of my chest. *Just being near him is ... intoxicating.* He was an enigma, and I wanted to spend all my time figuring him out. So hard, yet, so soft; so rugged, yet, so wounded. Although I barely knew him, I felt like I could see past the hard exterior, which I was sure scared many people away. Past the scars, tattoos, piercings, and dark glances, I saw a man who was tender; I saw a man who had dealt with his fair share of hurt. In this moment, I wanted to reach forward and comfort him; I wanted to take away whatever pain life had caused him. I wanted to help carry the weight.

"Well, Ronnie, I'm glad you live close by," he said, his voice now light and cheery. The cheerfulness in his demeanor perked me right up, and before I knew it, I was smiling, too. "I'd never be able to figure this stuff out on my own." He gestured to his son, who was now laying in his arms with a curious look on his face.

Greyson's eyes were glued to me—curious and filled with wonder as they scanned my face. His eyes darted to mine before dropping to my nose, and then, to my mouth before, finally, they came back to meet my gaze again. He broke out into a smile as soon as he got a good look at me.

"He looks like you," I mused as I stared at the boy's bright, jade-colored eyes, which were a similar shape to his father's.

As soon as the comment left my mouth, I felt Trevor stiffen at my side.

"He looks a lot more like my brother, actually. Greyson's my nephew."

While his words hadn't given much away, the tone of his voice spoke volumes. Hesitantly, I peered up at him, afraid of what I might find lurking in the depths of his dark, soulful eyes. The way his voice had quivered, mixed with the way he had tried to mask the pain, gave me some understanding of the situation. Which was good because I doubted he was in the mood to expand on it. *Who would want to share all their dirty laundry with a stranger?* Something horrible happened. This, I understood. As much as I wanted to know exactly what that something was, I didn't dare ask. I could understand wanting to keep the past buried.

"So, it's just the two of you, then?"

I wondered if there was someone helping him. Truly, I couldn't help but wonder if there was a *woman* in his life helping him. Judging by his appearance, I knew there had to be *someone* in his life. *A man like him* ... I couldn't imagine a man like him would be single.

"It's just the two of us," he confirmed, causing my body to sag against the couch in relief.

I watched him for a moment as I wondered what it was about him that made him so special. Just being around him felt like a trip back in time. A vacation to a date when I had been younger and happy; a point when I had felt truly *alive*. As he met my gaze, the weight of the world seemed to lift from my shoulders, and I could finally exhale.

4

Honey and the Moon

Staring at my reflection in the mirror, I barely recognized myself. *Veronica ... you opened up ... you trusted someone.* I studied my reflection. My eyes were bright, my cheeks were tinged pink, and my skin had a glow for the first time in a long while. I felt exhilarated; I felt *free.* For a moment, I felt like the girl I once was: the girl who laughed; the girl who smiled without needing a reason; the girl who loved with her whole heart.

I smiled at my image, unable to help it. I felt so light—like I was floating on a cloud. Who knew a brief interaction with a handsome neighbor could help start to mend the wounds that were still raw and irritated? The wounds gnawed at me—scratching at my consciousness until I paid them the attention they craved. Even in a moment of contentment, they bit at the edges of my mind.

"Is she all right?"

"Of course. I look out for her, you know."

"She just looks so ... dazed. Was it too much?"

"No, I've done this before. So, will you fuck off with this shit? What do you want me to do? Take her to the doctor for a little checkup? Piss or get off the pot, Ace. You're starting to piss me off—"

He didn't say anything else.

My eyes dropped from the mirror as I took a step back. *Oh, Mom, what is happening to me?* As usual, I awaited her response, and, as usual, I received none. However, I still liked to believe that she was out there somewhere, guiding me. The sensible part of me knew the goosebumps, which appeared on my flesh when I thought of her, were merely a coincidence and not a supernatural phenomenon of sorts. *A girl can dream, though.*

The thought of going through life without her was a bitter pill to swallow. During college, the image of her was what had kept me going; it had kept me from succumbing to the darkness, which surrounded me. During those formative college years, I had laid awake in bed, with Preston's arms wrapped securely around me, picturing her. With tears in my eyes, I had wanted nothing more than to be enveloped in her embrace. I had wanted the strength and security it provided. Even now, I yearned for that comfort. *Regardless of age, a girl needs her mother.*

Images of her kind smile filled my head. In my mind's eye, I could picture the wrinkles that would appear near the corners of her eyes when she smiled with her whole face; I could picture the freckles dusting her pert nose and the slight tan she would have on the tops of her cheekbones from being outside; I pictured the way her green eyes would sparkle when she laughed at a story I told her. I remembered the way she would stare off into space at times—lost in her own thoughts. Sometimes, whatever she was thinking about would make her smile. When I was younger, I had been dying to know what was floating around in her thoughts. When I would ask, she would smile and explain she was thinking of my father.

"Daddy, again? You always see him. Why would you daydream about him?"

"I love your father, Ronnie. One day, you'll know the feeling. I'm sure you'll find a man you'll want to dream about, too."

I smiled at the memory before my thoughts began to drift again. *I wonder what my mom would think of Trevor.* I wished she were here so I could ask for advice. I felt utterly clueless when it came to men. I was sure I could guess what she would say. When I was younger, and she was healthy, we would often talk about boys from school. She would inquire after my "type," and would tease me when I grew bashful. "Looks aren't everything," she would say. "You'll grow older and looks will fade, but what's inside … Ronnie, that's the most beautiful part. Don't get too wrapped up in appearances, sweetheart. Look at their heart."

A smile tugged on my lips as I remembered her words—her voice—and the way she had looked at me when she had given advice: soft eyes and a kind smile that illustrated the unconditional love she had felt for Eden and me. Sometimes, when I remembered her this way, I felt like she was standing by my side, giving me the same warm smile from my memories. *I wonder what she would think of me now. Am I the daughter she dreamt of having?* "Nothing you could ever do would disappointment, Ronnie," I vividly remembered her saying, answering my silent question.

I kept her in my thoughts as the day moved forward. The image of her in my memory put my mind at ease, allowing me to focus on the present. My present consisted of the handsome man and the little baby across the hall. *I've been alone for too long. God, I'm so tired of being less happy than I could be ... less happy than I deserve to be.*

Do I deserve happiness? Was my past truly my own fault? I hated to think it, but part of me believed I victimized myself. I blamed myself for every scar—for every bit of darkness in my mind. *It's not your fault! Don't think that!* The sound of my mother's voice shouted in my mind. For a moment, I considered maybe the delusion I was having of her was right; I hadn't deserved what happened to me. I hadn't deserved the pain—past or present. And I definitely hadn't asked for it.

I focused my mind on something else as I got ready for the day; my thoughts found much more pleasant company with Trevor.

"Just go across the hall and talk to him. How scary could it be?" I questioned my reflection, feeling foolish for doing so. I closed my eyes for a moment, pretending I had some sort of guidance.

"Ronnie, you're still so young, sweetheart. The right man will come along. Don't rush it. Don't force yourself into a relationship with someone you don't love just because you feel like you have to."

She smiled at me for a moment before she broke into a fit of giggles. I smiled, too. I loved seeing her like this: relaxed as she lain in bed underneath the blanket I made for her with Eden's help. She had been tired and had spent most of her time in bed. Any more than twenty minutes off the mattress left her feeble and exhausted. I was scared for her, but Daddy had told me time and time again not to say a word—he didn't want Mom to see us suffering, too. So, instead, I told her about school and the boy I had my eye on since the beginning of last semester.

"Sweetheart, you're only eleven years old. This isn't something you should wo—"

"I'm almost twelve," I interrupted as if the few months made all the difference in the world.

"Yes, you're almost twelve," she conceded, her eyes softening as she peered over at me. "I can't believe how grown up you are. My daughter is almost a teenager!" I returned her smile, enjoying the pride in her voice. "Well, even twelve years old is too young to be worrying about things like this. The right man will come along—it doesn't have to be right now."

I frowned. She didn't understand. "Mom, but you don't even know what he looks like! He's the hottest guy in the whole grade!"

She giggled at this and reached out to touch my hand. "Appearances aren't always important. You may think you know what you want, but when you meet the right guy, appearances are the last thing you'll think about. You'll think about what's on the inside; you'll care about how they treat you—how they want you to grow. The right man might not be the obvious choice. The right man may not be perfect, but he'll be perfect for you."

I grinned, knowing she was probably right. She was always right about everything. "What was it like when you met Daddy?"

She leaned back against the pillows behind her and flushed. Even after all of these years, mentioning Daddy still caused her to glow.

"I ran into him in college ... Well, you know the story, sweetie. I ran into him, quite literally, and the books in my arms flew everywhere. He apologized profusely and helped me gather my things. And then, we got to talking. Since both of us had finished our classes for that day, we decided to grab a cup of coffee. The coffee turned into dinner, and the rest was history. He wasn't the usual type I'd go for. He was stern and focused, even back then. However, I felt myself falling for him. Every minute we were together, my feelings grew. And then, I forgot about everyone else. It was like he was the only man on Earth, and I was the only woman ... as silly as that probably sounds."

"So, you just knew?" I questioned, hopeful I'd meet a boy one day and experience the same love my mom had.

"I knew from the moment I saw him. Of course, I didn't know that the emotions I felt were love. But, I felt something. I was captivated *by him from the start. Something about him drew me to him like a magnet. I can't explain it. When you experience it for yourself, you'll know!"*

"I don't feel that way about Kent," I admitted with a laugh.

"I know." She smiled. "You'll find someone who makes you feel like your father makes me feel, someday. Just don't go looking for it. Don't force yourself into a relationship just to be in a relationship. You'll find that person someday, and it will be when you least expect it."

I smiled and stiffened as I heard heavy steps coming from behind me, indicating that my dad had entered the room. If he'd been listening, I would die from embarrassment. I felt my cheeks flush as I continued to look at my mother.

"So, you knew I was 'the one' right away?" I heard him question, his voice gruff and teasing.

"Don't let it go to your head," Mom responded with a grin.

Dad continued to her bed and sat down on its edge, giving me a smug grin. "So, boy trouble? Anything you wanted to discuss with your old man?"

"No, Dad." I rolled my eyes.

"Well, if I managed to win over the heart of your mother, I obviously know a thing or two," he replied, giving my mom a loving smile.

As much as I loved to watch them like this—so happy, carefree, and in love—I felt like I was intruding on a special moment between them. I stood up to leave just as my dad bent down to kiss my mom on the forehead before smoothing out her curls.

I watched them for a moment before I said, "I've got some homework to do today."

Dad gave my mom one last kiss on her temple before he turned his gaze to me. "Okay, sweetie. Dinner's at seven-thirty."

And, after that, he was back in his own little world with my mother.

I smiled at the memory of them together. My mother and father were absolutely perfect for each other in every possible way. The love and respect they had for one another seemed to transcend time. I knew, even after all of these years, my dad loved my mom with the same intensity. Whether she was with us or not didn't seem to matter to him. The love she had given him—the love she had given *us*—was palpable and limitless. Time apart would never dull it, and there would never come a day when I didn't think of her.

"Mom, what do I do now?" I wondered aloud as I studied my reflection.

You follow your heart and let go of the wheel, I imagined her saying. I smiled, although I knew my mind supplied her response. I smoothed out my hair and headed out of my apartment while my heart fluttered in my chest. For some silly reason, I was worried Trevor would hear the quick palpitations, which would embarrass the life out of me. I couldn't help my erratic heartbeat; I was excited to see him. His presence was so soothing, and on a day like this one, I needed that.

After taking a deep breath and gathering my thoughts, I knocked gently—almost timidly—on the door. I heard Greyson's cries and Trevor's footsteps as he approached the door; I felt my heart beating so loudly in my chest that I was afraid it may burst. The door swung open to reveal a frazzled looking Trevor with a fussy Greyson in his arms.

A few uncomfortable seconds passed before I started. "I just wanted to check on you and Greyson."

Grey gazed up at me with teary eyes and a curious expression. He was so adorable as he took in every inch of my fresh face. I wished I could go back in time to when I had experienced such doe-eyed innocence. *What I wouldn't give to start over and change a few of my actions. What I wouldn't give for a second chance.* Trevor stepped aside and with a shaky hand gestured for me to come in.

"He's doing much better. Thanks for your suggestion earlier. You're a lifesaver," he told me as he ushered me toward the living room.

Despite trying to keep my composure, I couldn't tear my eyes away from his butt as he walked in front of me. *Holy. Freaking. Hell.* My reaction to him was an overwhelming one, and I couldn't remember the last time I felt so fired up. *What is it about this guy?* While he wasn't watching me, I took a moment to study him. I was too bashful to do so in the past to the extent I wanted to, but now that I wasn't under his gaze, I scrutinized every inch of him. His legs were strong—muscular through the fabric of his jeans; his shirt was tight enough to reveal the cuts in his upper back; his skin was covered in beautiful, intricate ink.

I had never dated a man with tattoos before, and as I looked at Trevor, I wanted nothing more than to trace each beautiful design with my tongue. My tongue darted out and licked my bottom lip as I pictured it. While I licked my lip, Trevor turned to look at me. I quickly pulled my eyes away from his body, and with a flush, I focused on his face.

"It's no problem," I answered. "I babysat my niece, Harper, all of the time. You're my new neighbor, so helping you out is the least I can do."

I peered at him for a moment longer before my eyes dropped to the fussy, little man in his arms. Grey was no longer crying; instead, he was kicking his feet and smiling up at his uncle. I was thrilled to see he was okay. Seeing him in pain earlier gutted me.

"We were just watching cartoons if you wanted to join us?" Trevor asked as he took a seat on the couch and gestured for me to do the same.

I can't remember the last time I spent an afternoon not buried in my work.

I didn't respond to the question right away, so Trevor continued, "I took today off work to take care of Grey."

I tried not to giggle as he stammered through the sentence. I wondered if I made him as nervous as he made me. *It's a good nervousness, that's for sure.* Although, the thought of him being skittish around me was almost a laughable one. I was sure *plenty* of women hit on him each and every day. Especially now that he had an adorable baby in his arms. There was something about an attractive man with a baby that seemingly made every woman's ovaries explode. I knew because, in this moment, I felt like I couldn't get close enough to my hot, inked-up neighbor. I sat down at his side—closer than I normally would have—and tried to control the flush that was creeping toward my cheeks.

"Having weekdays off are the best," I said to him, praying I didn't look too flustered.

"What do you do?"

"I work from home as an editor. It's my dream job."

My dream job allowed me to be an introvert all day ... perfection. I giggled at the thought of having to work with other people again. It wasn't that I wasn't a team player—*I was*—I just preferred to be alone. I loved my own company, I supposed, which was part of the reason my sister constantly referred to me as a recluse.

Trevor gave me a curious look, probably wondering what on earth I was giggling about, and I was quick to continue. "I've never been too keen on working with tons of people. I used to work at an office, but with all the office drama and cliques, it was absolutely terrible. I'm just happy to be free of that."

I had never really fit in with anyone, anyway. I didn't know what it was, but I had always felt like an outsider. I supposed it was due to the fact that I felt many of the most gregarious and outgoing people around me were fake, and being genuine myself, I wanted to avoid those types at all costs. Women never really seemed too fond of me. Perhaps it was because, at the publishing house I had worked at before, I had been my coworkers' junior by at least fifteen years. There were maybe one or two women I had connected with, but they weren't friends outside of work and the occasional drink.

Being that young, had caused it to be hard to tell who to avoid in the industry, and being faced with the power of cliques daily, I had wanted nothing more than to leave it all behind and work from home. Of course, some of the men in the office had been nice to me. But, with my aversion to anything male, I had never wanted their company. After one man in particular had gotten a little too friendly with me, I had decided that sitting behind a desk was no longer for me.

"I know what you mean," Trevor answered, breaking my train of thought. "I usually keep to myself when I'm at work and just think about what I want to do when I get home."

So, he's a homebody, too.

"And, what is that?" I questioned.

"Play with Grey, of course," he responded as he reached down to poke his nephew's chubby, little belly.

I watched with a smile as the little guy threw his head back and laughed as his uncle's fingers tickled his belly. *What a beautiful sound*, I mused.

"I understand that." I smiled. "When I worked in an office, all I thought about was my cat."

Great. Now this man is going to think I'm a crazy cat lady. I blushed before I continued to say, "Wow, how sad is that? You probably think I'm some crazy, loner cat lady." *Which wouldn't have been too far off the mark back in the days when I had Salem.* When I had Salem to come home to, I had thought of her constantly while at work. She had even been the screensaver on my computer then. At work, everyone else had had pictures of their families, and I had multiple pictures of my cat littering my desk.

"Never," he scoffed as his eyes ran over my body appraisingly. I shuddered under his gaze and while a part of me felt slightly uncomfortable another, more prominent part of me felt exhilarated. "What kind of cat do you have?" he questioned as his eyes popped back up to meet mine.

"She was a black cat named Salem." I smiled, remembering how loving she had been. She was unlike any cat I had seen before. Part of me believed she thought she was a dog because she had been extremely affectionate and loved to play. She was so unlike Stitch, the cat I had as a young girl.

"Salem?" Trevor questioned with a smile. "You a big *Sabrina the Teenage Witch* fan?"

"Well, I was when I was twelve. That's when I named her," I explained.

My dad had gifted Salem to me a month after my mom passed away. He had wanted me to have a companion, and Salem had been the best companion I could have asked for. When she had looked at me with her big, green eyes, I felt like she could understand me. On the nights when I had cried in my bed, Salem had nestled up against my side and purred against my cheek. In a strange way, it had felt like my mom had still been there—still watching over me.

"I never had any cats or dogs growing up. I guess my parents didn't want them messing up the house. I had a hamster, though. He was pretty cool. My brother named him Finn."

"Finn? That's a cool name. Where'd he get that from?"

His face became ashen, and my heart dropped to my stomach as I watched his entire demeanor change. His shoulders slumped, his jaw clenched, and his jugular vein began to pulse. Grey must have realized the change in his uncle because his eyes shot up to study him, and his body became uneasy, as well. I wondered if I hit a sore spot with him. Of course, I understood that something happened—something horrible—but I didn't dream of bringing it up to him. I remained quiet, waiting for his demeanor to change. As I waited, different scenarios danced unpleasantly across my mind. I knew far too well what it was like to lose someone; I knew far too well what it was like to lose yourself.

"I'm not sure," he finally said, his voice quivering.

He was short with me, and I understood, not begrudging him for it. The wounds he had were fresh. So fresh that I almost felt them myself. As he brooded beside me, I could feel his energy—his pain—as if it seeped from his pores and became part of the atmosphere around us. I wanted to reach out to touch him, but I kept my hands to myself. I didn't know how he would react to me attempting to help him. Not all men wanted to admit to being emotional; it made some men feel weak. Perhaps Trevor was unaware of his own strength. I barely knew him, but I could feel his fortitude.

He was a strong person despite what he may have thought. I had gotten good at reading people, and while I felt like there was a part of Trevor that always would remain a mystery, I felt as if I could see something within him that others couldn't. Or, at least, *he* couldn't.

In the miniscule time that I had known him, I could feel he lacked confidence. It was in the way he held himself—in the way he spoke quietly, as if he were afraid of saying the wrong thing. My heart went out to him. Maybe that was why I felt so safe around him—why I felt like my old self—because he and I were the same in many ways. We both had our demons; we both had monsters we hid in our closet.

Wanting the afternoon to take a pleasant turn, I changed the subject to get to know more about the handsome, albeit wounded man. I could tell he was grateful as we fell into easy conversation about our jobs and our plans for the upcoming few weeks. I watched as Trevor's confidence grew as he spoke. With every word, he seemed to feel better. An hour flew by like a minute, and I knew that despite wanting to stay to talk to my new friend, I had to work. *Veronica, your deadline is in a few hours! Get your butt out of here!*

"Shit," I murmured, interrupting Trevor mid-sentence. "Sorry." I blushed at my lack of decorum. "It's just I have a deadline later in the afternoon, and I've got to get back. I'd forgotten all about it."

I quickly stood up before Trevor said anything else. I knew if he continued to talk, there would have been no way I would have left. There was something about his voice as he conversed with me. Its tone was so rich and relaxing. I supposed his deep voice made sense; it was strong and masculine, just like the rest of him.

"Well, I'm glad you stopped by," he said, standing too. "It's nice having another adult here to talk to," he continued as he ushered me to the front door. "I love Grey, but he's not much of a conversationalist."

I snorted at his comment and gazed at his face for a moment before my eyes dropped to the rest of him. He was so tall—so strong; he looked like one of the men I read about so frequently in my romance novels. *Heck, he could easily be on the cover of one of them with his muscular frame and strong, intimidating face.* Realizing that I was ogling him, I turned my attention to Grey, who was happy in his uncle's arms. He smiled up at me, capturing my heart. *What an adorable, handsome, well-mannered little boy.*

"Would you two want to come over for dinner?" I posed the question before really thinking about it. As soon as I gave it some thought, I flushed at my forwardness. I had never been so forward with a man, but Trevor wasn't just any man. He was different.

Before I could amend my statement, Trevor quickly jumped at the opportunity. "That'd be great! I can't remember the last time I had a home-cooked meal. It's been microwavable dinners ever since I moved into this apartment."

Well, that wouldn't be the case if you let me take care of you. My eyes widened at the thought. I managed not to flush as the image of me "taking care of him" flashed through my consciousness. I remained calm and collected under his gaze.

"Aw, that's too bad," I commented, trying to seem coy instead of nervous. "You never order takeout?"

"No, too expensive," he replied as he looked down at his baby. "His baby food is pretty costly, and I can't afford to be throwing money away on pizza and Chinese food all the time."

"I totally understand that. I go to the store with a giant stack of coupons because, otherwise, I wouldn't be able to afford half the stuff I want." The way he watched me so intently took my breath away. I leaned back against the door and emitted a shaky breath. *What is this stranger doing to me?* "Sorry, I'm rambling again." He smiled at me, his eyes bright and playful. "Is five o'clock too early for you to come over?"

He didn't spare a second; right away, he shook his head and smiled at me. His crooked grin made my heart begin to palpitate. I gave him a smile in return before I moved to leave. *Five o'clock couldn't come soon enough.*

I stared at the paper in front of me, but my mind didn't register a single word. I would have been frustrated if my thoughts weren't pleasantly consumed by *him*. His unruly hair, strong features, and the mirth which constantly played in his eyes captivated me even when I was alone. My thoughts were filled with him, and I felt amorous. For so long, I had felt like an intruder in my own body. When someone used you like that, you felt far removed from your own flesh.

Maybe it's because I never wanted to admit to those horrible, nightmare-inducing things that happened to me.

When I had woken up that next morning—wondering why my muscles were sore and my mood was so belligerent—I had felt as though a piece of me died. The piece which had trusted; the piece which had wanted to be consumed by another person, finding myself between thin sheets and their body. I had woken up, feeling pain unlike anything I could imagine and, in that moment all those years ago, I had found I was a different person entirely. I had gone from a girl who was beginning to enjoy sex, to a woman who had never wanted to think about it again. For years, I hadn't thought of a man's touch; when my mind had slipped and I had, my thoughts had always been negative, inspiring an episode that would leave me reliving some of the worst moments of my life.

I remembered the pain I had felt when I had first tried to masturbate a little over a year ago. I had believed time would heal my wounds; I had thought time would cause me to feel less *dirty* and used. I had imagined that after a few years, I would have found myself again and would have been able to ease back into a normal life. But, as I had touched that spot between my legs, I had realized nothing would ever feel normal to me again.

Touching myself had started off fine; with my eyes closed and my fingers determined, I had allowed my mind to drift from one fantasy to the next. The pleasant thoughts had only lasted for a few minutes before they had transformed into my devastating memories. I had nightmares that night, and since that day, I had been afraid of doing anything remotely sexual. The days of me being lascivious had past. *Until this moment, when all I wanted to do was find some release.*

Today, I yearned for some relief. *Maybe you can try it again, Veronica. It may make you feel better. Prove to yourself that you can do this. Prove to yourself that you can move on.* I sat still for a moment as I contemplated what trying could hurt. My behavior felt borderline unhealthy at this point, and I knew—*I knew*—I needed to set myself free from this cage I had somehow locked myself in.

Rising from my seat, I took one deep breath, preparing myself for what I was about to do. My muscles felt relaxed as my body felt awakened. The flames within me caused my breasts to feel heavy and sensitive and my core to gently pulse as it begged for release. I drifted to my bedroom and dimmed the lights before stripping out of my dress. I looked around as if I feared someone was watching me, which was ludicrous considering I lived alone.

After emitting a shaky breath caused by excitement and the fear of the unknown, I slipped out of my bra, almost smiling as my nipples puckered in the cold air. I stood still for a moment, allowing my amorous feelings to consume me as images of Trevor began to slip into my consciousness. I thought of his dark eyes and severe features as I slipped out of my underwear and took a step toward my bed.

My heart was beating rapidly in my chest as I feared my efforts could turn sour. I felt like I couldn't do this out of fear that it might break me. I hated myself for allowing the man I gave my heart to so many years ago to still affect me today. He had destroyed me in the past, and I would be damned if I allowed him to continue to do so. He wasn't in charge anymore—I was. I couldn't enjoy the present chapter in my life if I kept rereading the chapters in my past. With this in mind, I crawled onto the bed, laying on top of the covers before I closed my eyes.

I stilled for a moment before my right hand slowly drifted down my body until it reached my core. I paused for another moment, giving myself one last chance to wonder if doing this would be good for me. *What if it leaves you with nightmares like the last time?* I would never know until I pushed myself to find out. Slowly, I began to run my fingertips along my folds, preparing myself to go deeper.

As I circled my fingers around my pussy, I thought of him. Trevor's strong, masculine face filled my thoughts, and before I knew what my body was doing, I slid one finger into my warm depths before adding another. I moaned at the sensation, enjoying the pleasure I had been denying myself for so long as my left hand found a breast and began to play with a sensitive nipple. I thought of Trevor as I used my thumb to play with my throbbing clit. I imagined him staring down at me from beside the bed for a long while until he couldn't resist and decided to join me. In my fantasy, I smiled at him, eager to feel his body between my open thighs.

"Is this what you wanted? Are you going to be a good girl for me, Veronica?" my fantasy questioned as he slid off his belt.

I nodded as I gave him a coquettish smile. Although, that smile quickly faded into a look of apprehension as my eyes took in the impressive size of his cock. I began to close my thighs, worried that I might not be able to take him inside of me. With a confident smile, Trevor stopped me as he took off his clothes and joined me on the bed between my legs. He kissed me once on the mouth, giving me a moment to enjoy the taste of him before his lips trailed down my neck and torso. I gasped as my body bucked off the bed.

"What are you doing?" I questioned in shock as he lined his mouth up with my core.

He gave me a wolfish smile before he answered my question. "What does it look like I'm doing? This night is meant to be about you, Veronica. I want to watch you get off."

My eyes locked with his, captivated as I watched him lower his mouth to my pussy. The way his tongue moved up and down my folds caused my back to arch off the bed and my body to quiver. The way this man touched me had the power to make me feel sated before I even came. He kissed my clit and licked me everywhere before his fingers found my pussy again, taking me home.

As the fantasy played in my head, I rubbed my legs together to stimulate my clit. It felt divine. I focused on Trevor as I moved my fingers in and out, pretending those fingers were his. I was so close. So close I could almost taste it. My pussy began to tremble around my fingers, and as I pictured Trevor sliding his thick length into my pussy, I came apart completely. I shouted out, feeling an orgasm more intense than anything I had ever experienced. I rode out its waves, committing the overwhelming feeling to memory. *I feel so alive! So free!* I screamed in my head as my pussy pulsated around my fingers.

I lay in bed completely sated for a while; my fingers were still inside my pussy long after my orgasm consumed me. I stared up at the ceiling in disbelief. I couldn't believe I accomplished that. *I was sure it was an easy feat for some. But for me ...* I had an aversion to sex for so long—never desiring it. Now, I felt myself changing. I felt like a woman again—or at least, the woman I once was. The orgasm was as sweet as it was liberating. It proved that I was in control. I was in control of my body, my life, and my present and future. I took hold of the wheel again, and I wasn't going to let go.

From this moment forward, I refused to be a pawn in someone else's game. I knew I had to rewrite my life; this time, I was going to be the hero in my own story—not a girl who allowed the world to affect her. *Now, I would affect the world.* No longer would I feel like a nameless victim; instead, I would feel like *me*: Veronica Elizabeth Clark. I wanted that identity back. I wanted the life my mom so desperately wanted for me. I knew all I had to do was reach out and grab it. I had to take the plunge as I did mere minutes before.

I flipped onto my side and gazed out of the picture window in my bedroom. The sun was high in the sky, and the clouds were scarce. It was a beautiful day—a new day. As I stared out at the sky, my thoughts drifted toward Trevor again. *I can't believe I just got myself off while thinking of my neighbor! The man I'll have to see tonight.* I was sure I would have a permanent blush on my cheeks throughout the entire dinner. I was sure Trevor would wonder about type of girl he was allowing into his life. *The type of girl who would play with her pussy while thinking of him.* How would I face him? After an elongated moment, I decided I didn't care. I had nothing to be embarrassed about. If anything, I was proud of myself—content that I had taken another step forward. Another step closer to owning my life again.

5

Helium

With a relaxed smile on my face, I weaved around shoppers, moving from aisle to aisle at the local Safeway store. My thoughts were consumed with Trevor—the man who had provided me with such relief today. *Knowing me, he'll never know the change he has inspired.* What had happened this afternoon had been private to me. I had found more than a physical release; during my orgasm, I had found a mental release, too. After this afternoon, I felt energic—*light.* The weight of the world wasn't crushing my shoulders like it once had. *One small step in a long journey.*

A soft smile tugged on my lips as I meditated on the differences in my body. I had never realized how tense my muscles had been; I had never realized how little I smiled unless provoked by a loved one. Although today had been a small step, it had caused me to really see my truth—to see what I had really been like for the past few years.

No wonder Eden worried so much! I've been in denial about who I've become for so, so long.

Until today, I had believed I had been successful at hiding my pain—hiding my shame—but now, I was positive I had been absolutely transparent. In the past, I had always preferred to suffer in silence, but now I was sure my silence spoke a thousand words. Maybe it was outlandish to believe Trevor was my savior of sorts—I didn't know him very well—but he had begun to mend the wounds I hadn't realized were still open; wounds I believed I could cover up and forget about. The thought of seeing Trevor tonight gave me a glimmer of hope for my future. *I wonder if I'll have nightmares tonight. With Trevor as my friend, my dreams may be safe.* A friendship with Trevor could be a brand-new start.

A brand-new start was more than I had ever allowed myself to hope for. I doubted I was good enough for him. While my life was "put together," I felt damaged beyond repair. While I appreciated the solace my neighbor had provided me with, I knew if I wanted to be saved, I couldn't wait for someone to rescue me. I had to save myself. *I had to try to be the hero in my own story.* Suddenly, I felt determined. I couldn't live in the past forever, and if I wanted to make a change, I had to start straight away. I was tired of pushing everything off to a tomorrow that may never come.

With a new determination, I gathered the ingredients for the night ahead. *Tonight will run smoothly. Tonight will be the fresh start; a new and improved Veronica*, I told myself. After years of a horrid personal life, I wanted something to finally go my way.

I was jittery as I finished up dinner. The only man I had ever cooked for was my father, and I was positive he would have been inclined to tell me *anything* I had made was good. Although, I had been out of practice when it came to cooking for more than one—despite the few times I would make easy meals for Eden's family—I found I wasn't *completely* useless in the kitchen. I had grown used to making the same few meals, but tonight, I planned to switch it up by trying a new recipe.

My mother had loved to cook. She had grown up at my grandmother's side in the kitchen, pouring over recipe books and experimenting with different ingredients. Before she had met my father, my mother even considered being a chef; after she had given it a try, she had found the stressful work hadn't been for her. So instead, she had found her happiness in cooking for our family every night. I would spend my evenings perched at the kitchen table, watching her as she gracefully moved around the kitchen; watching her cook always had had a way of distracting me from doing my homework. As she had cooked, we would talk about my classes, boys, and the drama that seemed to surround my peers. I remembered the gentle sound of her laughter as if I had heard it just yesterday.

"He touched my hand today," I revealed with a giggle I couldn't suppress. *"He asked to use my pencil and this thumb brushed against mine as I gave it to him."*

I sat up in my chair, feeling proud of the small advancement.

"He did, did he?" Mom laughed as she put her knife down on the cutting board, abandoning her onion to look at me.

I flushed, wondering if I had said too much. I was not supposed to date. Dad said I couldn't go out with a boy until I was thirteen. And, even then, he had to be there. How embarrassing! *All my friends would totally laugh at me if they saw me on a date with my* dad *there!*

"Well, it didn't mean anything," I pacified.

"I don't believe that. I saw that look on your face, Ronnie. So, you think he meant to 'brush' his thumb against you?"

I flushed even more, letting my hair fall around my face to hide my smile. I couldn't help but smile. One of the most popular boys in school liked me: Veronica Elizabeth Clark.

"I think he did. I think he likes me, Mom."

"I'm sure he does. What's not to like?"

"You have to say that." I laughed. "You're my mom."

"I would say that even if I wasn't your mother," she insisted.

I felt a smile pull on my lips as she crossed the kitchen to come stand next to me. She wrapped her arms around my shoulders and kissed the top of my head.

"The man who wins your heart will be so very lucky, Veronica."

Tears pricked my eyes as I thought of her. *What I wouldn't give to have you here, Mom.* Staring off into the distance, for a moment, I pretended she was by my side. When it was quiet and no one else was around, I found that it was easy to play make-believe. For a small passing of time, I pretended she never died; I pretended those dark nights with my first "love" never happened; I pretended I was happy, carefree, and perfect—just the way I had once imagined I would be. I wished I could turn back the clock to a time when I was young and naïve. I wished I could transport to a moment when I had still been untouched by the harsh reality of life. *You're not the first person to lose someone, Veronica. You're not the first person, and you won't be the last.*

"The pain will pass in time, Veronica. I know it's hard, but you're not handling it. You're not even trying."

"Piss off."

"What did you say? You're not my little girl anymore. I've been giving you so much slack, but it's been over a year! You have a bright future ahead of you! Why squander it?"

I looked at my father as if I were seeing him for the very first time. "I'm handling it! Dad, we barely talk about her! You never say her name! Did you fall out of love with her at the end? Why can't you talk about her ever?"

"That's enough, Veronica." His voice was filled with venom. "We do talk about her. But how would you know? You're never around. You're always locked away in your room! I never shut you out. You shut us out."

"I don't have to listen to this."

"You're not the first one to lose someone, Veronica. We all lost her. We—" He stopped for a moment, taking a deep breath. His eyes filled with tears, causing me to quickly advert my gaze. "I'm sorry. I don't understand your hostility toward me. I know you want your mother—I know I'm probably a poor substitute for her—but I'm your parent, too. I remember when you were a little girl. I remember when you would cry when I wasn't holding you and now—now you can't stomach being in the same room as me. Just help me to understand how to fix whatever is broken between us."

"Dad ..." I looked at him, wishing there was a way for him to no longer feel like a stranger. He had moved on already.

He had barely mourned her loss. Already, he had found someone new, and he expected me to be all right with that fact?

"I'm sorry," I said before I moved to return to my room. He would figure out the root of the problem eventually.

"The pain will pass in time."

I supposed he should know, shouldn't he? It had been a little over a year, and that pain had apparently already passed and moved to acceptance. I wondered what my mother would think. I wondered if she would be happy or heartbroken. I was heartbroken for her. She wasn't here to feel the pain, but I felt it. I felt everything now that she was gone. Time healed all wounds ... Whenever someone said that, I wanted to laugh. I knew it hadn't been that long, but I highly doubted I would ever get over this. If I got over this, it would be as if I were forgetting about her. And if I forgot about her ... No. I knew I never would.

I wiped the wetness from my cheek and exhaled a breath I wasn't aware I was holding. I didn't understand why I felt so nostalgic tonight. I didn't know why so many memories were suddenly coursing through my thoughts. My eyes closed, and I took a deep breath, relaxing as the cool air filled my lungs. Perhaps the past taunting me suggested something important was on my horizon. My eyes opened with another realization. If I kept looking over my shoulder, I would miss what was ahead. It was a simple thought but an important one, nonetheless. *But the future could be so frightening! The future is out of my control.* I shook these thoughts from my head as I gazed up at the time displayed on the digital clock above my oven. *Jesus, he'll be here any minute!*

Knowing it was unlikely for the wistfulness in my heart to subside, I went to turn on the television in my living room, flipping to a random channel before I returned to the kitchen. The noise from the TV always distracted my mind and made me feel as if I weren't all alone in my apartment. Thankfully, I was quick to become lost in my work, and before I knew it, it was five o'clock.

Although dinner wasn't finished, I rushed to the bathroom to check my appearance. Grabbing a tissue, I quickly fixed the smeared mascara around my lash line before tousling my hair in an attempt to give my curls more volume. Of course, wanting my heavy curls to be voluminous was a lost cause. Despite my annoyingly uncooperative mane, I was pleased with my appearance. *This is as good as it's going to get, Veronica.* I threw my hair in a high ponytail and smiled at the fact that my cleavage was now on full display. Unable to help myself, I adjusted my breasts so my cleavage was more prominent in my dress. *I love it when his eyes are hungry as he takes in my appearance. It's one of the best feelings in the world.*

After I was finished, I returned to the kitchen and tried to pull dinner together as quickly as I could. Five minutes went by without a single knock on my front door. Then, ten minutes passed without a disturbance. Suddenly, I wondered if he was coming. Maybe he'd been polite earlier; maybe he had no intention of coming to my place.

I could go knock on his door. Maybe he forgot? Maybe something happened to Greyson?

The thought of him forgetting was disheartening. I'd been thinking of our dinner all day; even *considering* his potential indifference made me want to die of embarrassment.

Of course, the first man I have feelings for in years, doesn't like me. How typical.

I looked at the clock—twenty after five and he still wasn't here.

Great, Ronnie. This is just great. You're going to have to avoid him from now on. How will you be able to look him in the eyes after this?

If this had been his way of standing me up, I planned to avoid him at all costs. I would be far too embarrassed to ever talk to him again. *And here I thought things had gone so well.* Earlier today, I had honestly believed we had a connection. Strangely enough, it had felt as if I had known him for years. Now, it all seemed ridiculous to me.

Earlier, it felt like he knew me. It felt like he saw through the walls I erected. Now ... now I'm so confused. Did he truly feel nothing?

I wanted to believe there was still hope, but as I stood watching the clock, I convinced myself that hopefulness was truly wishful thinking. Trevor wasn't coming; I had spent my entire afternoon embarrassing myself. My face flushed, and I cringed as I felt the blush creep down to my neck and chest, which caused me to look like a spotty, red mess. *The first man I feel safe around—the first man who inspires romantic feelings in me in years—doesn't care for me.*

Knock! Knock! Knock!

At the sound, my heart leapt to my throat. My breathing came to a halt as my eyes shot to the door. *He's here! He's at the door! Play it cool, Veronica. Don't look too distressed. He'll sense your discomfort from a mile away. Deep breaths, Veronica. Deep breaths.* My shaky hand came up to smooth back my hair before I rushed toward the mirror hanging in my entryway, giving my appearance one final once-over. I barely recognized the girl who stared back at me. Her face was flushed, her eyes were bright, and her skin was luminous. Surely, this woman couldn't be me. My smile widened before I finally moved to answer the door.

As I swung the door open, my jaw nearly dropped. He was so devastatingly handsome, unlike any man I had been with before. His dark eyes took in my appearance, following my every curve before they shot back up to my face. His soft lips—well, they had *looked* soft; I had never felt them—formed into a crooked grin just as Grey began to squeal in his arms. I smiled at the little baby who had managed to quickly capture my heart. His carefree grin caused my soul to warm. All the tension in my body was eliminated, and finally, I felt like I could speak.

"And I was starting to worry about you two not coming."

I gave him a teasing grin, hoping he didn't realize how worried I truly had been. Stepping aside, I ushered them into my apartment.

"Sorry we're late." Trevor gave me a sheepish smile before he looked down at his nephew. Greyson giggled as he gazed up at his uncle, who rewarded him with a loving look before he returned his attention to me. Handing me a box of chocolates, he continued. "We went to the store to buy you these, and then Grey had a bit of an accident."

As soon as the words left his mouth, he grimaced. I tried very hard to suppress a laugh.

"That was really thoughtful of you, Trev."

His eyes lit up at my response. I held my breath as I looked at him, feeling every cell in my body awaken as though parts of me had been numbed until now.

"You guys can make yourselves at home. I'm just finishing up dinner."

Now that they were finally here, and my mind was at ease, I could actually finish the meal they came for. Although, knowing Trevor was only a room away made it difficult for me to concentrate. *God, I can feel him. Even when he's in the other room, it's like he's standing right next to me.*

While I attempted to focus on setting the table, my thoughts remained with him in the other room. *Heavens, I bet I could feel him from a mile away!* The attraction in the air around us was nearly palpable—at least, it was for me. I could feel it like electricity surrounding me, causing every hair on my body to raise in attention. If he could inspire these sorts of reactions just by being in such close proximity, I wondered what feelings he could conjure with his mouth. *And his hot breath against my cheek* ... I paused, nearly dropping a handful of silverware on the kitchen floor.

I had gone years without desiring any sort of sexual attention—denying myself so many basic pleasures—and now, I wanted *everything*. It was an odd thing to reconcile. The feelings Trevor inspired were so foreign to me; part of me felt they must have been inherently wrong. Part of my mind screamed I shouldn't have these feelings while my body amorously screamed for attention. I had been unhappy, untouched, and repressed for longer than any person should.

I finished setting the table and placed the salad, garlic bread, and manicotti down before I stood back and gave my handiwork one last glance. Satisfied, I quietly rushed back into the living room to retrieve my guests. What I found stopped me in my tracks. He was looking at the photographs displayed on my bookshelf. I watched as his eyes scanned photos of Eden and me before settling on a photograph of my mother and me. This was one of my favorite pictures with her.

She looked so young in the photo—so full of life. Her smile captivated any room and had the power to make time feel meaningless. In the photograph, she had her natural hair. I remembered how it felt: so soft; so similar to mine. I would run my fingers through it and inhale the scent of her luxurious shampoo as she would hold me in her arms and read to me under the tree in our backyard. She had been so attached to her hair. She had believed it made her beautiful. Little had she known she had been stunning regardless.

Her beauty had come from within—a place inside of her where the cancer couldn't touch. That beauty had shone through—making her externally beautiful even on her most difficult of days. After starting chemo, she had let Eden and me, along with a hairdresser, cut her hair before shaving her head. She had felt so unattractive afterward, which had broken my heart. When I had looked at her, I saw the most gorgeous woman I had ever known.

Without saying a word, I closed my eyes and took a moment to ease my mind. Thinking about her made me feel so emotional—so ripped open.

"You're so beautiful, Mom."

"Even like this?"

"No matter what."

"Not as beautiful as my little girl."

"Really? I think I look like you."

"You do, sweetie. We have the same eyes and the same smile." She grinned at me and reached out to tuck a strand of hair behind my ear, allowing her a chance to see my face more clearly. "And the same heart," she finished, touching her chest where her heart beats.

Touching my hand to my heart, I opened my eyes. While I still felt vulnerable—knowing Trevor was seeing a part of me I was never comfortable sharing—the thought of my mom helped me to feel stronger. Tonight was about new beginnings—fresh starts. I viewed this as a small bump in the road. I wasn't going to withdraw into myself like I would normally do in a painful situation. I knew if I wanted someone in my life—someone like Trevor—I needed to open up; I had to let someone in. *I've had these walls erected for far too long.*

"Are you ready for dinner?" I asked, my voice sounding cold and uncomfortable.

Trevor must have felt the awkward note in my tone because as he tore his eyes from the picture to glance at me; he looked remorseful. Suddenly, I felt remorseful, too. He shouldn't have felt bad. I was the one who told him to "make himself at home" after all. I couldn't begrudge him for doing what I asked.

I felt even more uncomfortable as he began to apologize.

"Did I—"

"The manicotti is ready. And I made garlic bread, too," I interrupted him in the cheeriest tone I could manage.

As I led them to my incredibly humble kitchen, I tried to gain control of myself. *Come on, Veronica. You've been excited for this all day. No man has ever made you feel this way. Chase that feeling! Stop dwelling on the past. You won't find him there.* I wouldn't find him in the past—and I was thankful for that. The past had consisted of memories I longed to forget. *My future* ... While I didn't know Trevor well, I liked to imagine—if only for a fleeting moment—that my future somehow laid with him. *With him and with Greyson.* The attachment I felt for them was absurd. It amazed me that two people could capture my attention so quickly and completely. I was constantly reeling from it.

I heard Trevor take in a breath as soon as we reached my kitchen table. I felt myself smile, happy to impress him. Turning to gaze at him, I nearly blushed at what I saw. His eyes scanned the table before meeting mine. I felt a pull to him again; the one I felt whenever our eyes met.

"Jesus, Ronnie. You didn't have to do all this."

"Well, it's my way of saying, 'welcome to the neighborhood,' " I explained as I felt my face heat up.

I couldn't stop smiling at him. *Heavens, I couldn't stop* looking *at him.* I felt like a young girl developing her first crush. However, Trevor Warren was a million times better than Orlando Bloom or even the cutest member of the many boy bands I grew up being absolutely obsessed with.

I ushered him to take a seat, and he quickly did so, situating his baby safely on his lap. I took my seat across from them, keeping an eye on the pair, almost as a way of reminding myself I truly wasn't alone.

"So, have you lived in Evergreen long?" I asked as I began to plate his food.

His eyes lit up as I handed him the plate from across the table; I felt proud of myself. It had been just *me* for so long, and now that I had two new people to cook for—well, *one* until Grey became a little bit older—I felt right at home. *God, what was I saying?*

"Born and raised. I spent the last five years traveling all over the U.S. and spent the last two years in Cali before I decided to come back."

As Trevor talked, Greyson distracted himself by reaching for his uncle's food. His chubby, little hands were eager to grab at whatever he could reach. I didn't blame him; I knew baby food and formula weren't tasty, thanks to a moment of curiosity I had experienced when Harper had been a baby. After Trevor finished speaking, he noticed his nephew's reach and quickly shooed his hand away. In an instant, Greyson became fussy, and I sensed a potential tantrum.

Greyson's bottom lip began to quiver, and his cheeks puffed out, but before he could cry out, I quickly suggested, "I have some yogurt if you think he'd like it."

Trevor broke into a relieved smile. Popping out of my seat, I went to the refrigerator and grabbed a vanilla yogurt after a quick check of the expiration date. After grabbing one of Harper's abandoned plastic baby spoons from my utensil drawer, I returned to the kitchen table with the small container and spoon in hand.

"I hope this helps," I said as I handed it off.

"I gave him his bottle before we came over," Trevor explained as he opened the yogurt and scooped up a small amount before spooning it into his nephew's mouth. Grey took a small bite before he smiled in approval.

As I watched the pair, I couldn't get over how adorable the baby was. With chubby cheeks, big jade eyes, and a smile that was absolutely infectious, he had to be the cutest baby I had ever seen. He gave my niece a run for her money. His presence was so warm—so soothing. He had such a wonderful energy radiating through his little body. I couldn't imagine the kind of man he would grow up to be. I was sure he would be just as kind as his uncle. *God, I'm acting as if I know them well.*

I didn't know if I was a good judge of character—my past decisions had really caused me to question everything when it came to reading people—but something about the man across from me suggested he had a kind heart. Past the rugged appearance, past the copious amount of ink, and past a jagged scar, which ran across his neck and another crooked one, which cut through his left eyebrow, I could tell he was *good*; I could tell he was patient and selfless. Suddenly, I realized I had been staring at them both for a long while and felt my seemingly permanent blush deepen a shade.

"Yeah," I finally went on to say. "But, he's watching you with your hot plate of food and probably is wishing he had something more substantial than formula."

"You're right about that. I'm never sure what to feed him half the time. Everything just seems so risky."

Trevor grimaced, and a small grin tugged on my lips in response. *Perhaps I could buy him a baby book?* I was constantly at Where the Books Go, after all. I was sure I could pick something up for him. He looked so lost, and I was positive he could use a bit of guidance.

"I understand that," I replied, wanting to make him feel more confident about his situation. He was doing wonderfully. "I used to be terrified when I would watch Harper. Children seem so small and fragile; it definitely takes a while to realize they're not as breakable as we think."

"I just can't believe how *little* babies are," he mused.

I watched Trevor as he feed his little guy. The love between them would be obvious to whomever observed them. While he claimed he didn't know what he was doing, he was obviously doing *something* right. All the little things didn't matter; no one ever remembered the little things, anyway. All one remembered was how a person made them feel. And I could tell just by looking at the pair before me that Trevor made this little baby feel very loved.

Greyson gazed up at his uncle with such reverence. He looked at Trevor as if he were his entire universe—his Earth, moon, and stars. Which I was sure, in many ways, he was. Greyson's world was so small now—it was easy for Trevor to consume it. However, even when Greyson's world became bigger, I was positive Trevor would still remain a prominent part.

"You're really good with him."

He smiled, obviously content with the small compliment. "I don't know about that," he replied. "He's just a chill baby to take care of. He makes my job pretty easy."

So, I supposed he wasn't one for receiving compliments. I guessed that was something we had in common. I disliked attention, too.

"You don't give yourself enough credit."

Doesn't he realize the wonderful job he's doing? Even I could see how deep their bound was.

"Well, thanks for saying that, Ronnie. I don't know if I believe it, but I appreciate the compliment all the same."

I smiled at him, and he smiled in return. For a fleeting moment, I could feel the connection between us. There was a synergy between us as our eyes met. In this moment, everything else faded away, and there was only *us*. In this moment, there was no future and no past—nothing outside of the three of us in this room. *What I wouldn't give to remain in this moment forever.* But, like all things, the moment faded into the air as soon as we returned to our food. Thankfully, I could still feel the aftereffects of his heated stare. Goosebumps covered my skin, and a blush burned my chest as I tried to concentrate on the meal before me.

After a few minutes of silence, we fell into an effortless conversation; it was as if we had known each other for years. We talked about nothing. We talked about everything. After a while, Greyson nodded off in Trevor's arms, and our dinner came to its end. I couldn't remember the last time I felt so carefree—so my own age.

"I better get going," Trevor said regretfully as he gazed down at the sleepy baby in his arms. He grinned at him for a moment before he returned his attention to me. "It's past Grey's bedtime, and he's going to get cranky if he's not in his crib soon."

"I totally understand," I responded with a smile despite being hesitant to watch them go. "It was really nice having you over, Trev. I could definitely use a few more friends around here. Outside of my sister, I'm practically a hermit."

I hated that I had to refer to him as my "friend." I wanted to be more than that already. However, I was far too shy to put myself out there and pose the idea to him. With a baby to worry about, a romantic relationship was probably the last thing the man needed. I watched a frown tug on Trevor's lips before he quickly regained his composure. I wondered if he felt the same way. *Did he want to be more than "friends," too?*

"I definitely hear you. Grey's pretty much the only person I hang out with these days."

Before I registered what exactly I was saying, I blurted out, "Well, maybe we can all hang out together, then?"

When was I ever this bold? While I used to have a "quiet confidence"—*according to my mother*—it hadn't been seen for a long time. There was a change brewing in me, though; I could feel it.

"My door is always open," Trev said, giving me one last look before he pivoted on his heel.

"I won't be a stranger, then," I responded as I watched him walk to his apartment.

I didn't know where the feelings came from—feelings so old they had been long forgotten—but I was going to chase them. I leaned against the doorframe and smiled, enjoying how relaxed my body felt; enjoying how relaxed my *mind* felt. I felt like the Veronica I once was. The girl who had yet to be broken.

You're not broken, Veronica. You never have been. You're better than that. Now, it's finally time to summon the courage and expel your demons, allowing yourself a chance to finally move on.

Easier said than done.

Although, I wanted a life; I wanted a future; I wanted to find the control I once had over myself. Regardless of the possibility of a future with Trevor, I wanted to ride the waves of the change that had sparked in my life. Even if this thing with Trevor led to nothing more than friendship, I would forever be grateful for his part in this. He inspired me to peel off the layers of damage on my wounded spirit like dead skin and find the courage to search for myself again.

6

Strawberries

"*Why are you looking at me like that?*"

"*Like what?*"

Nudging my legs open with his knee, he joined me on the bed, lifting my right leg to place a soft kiss to my ankle before his lips ascended to the one place where I desired them most. He licked the skin of my thigh, nipping it with his teeth before he pressed a soft kiss against my flushed skin; his stubble tickled me, causing my core to become even more lubricated. I heard him chuckle, obviously satisfied by my reaction as he shifted closer to my pussy.

I felt his hot breath against my wet folds and shuddered at the tantalizing affect caused by his warmth against my opening. The knowledge of his lips being so close to my core made me want to weep—made me want to beg for him. Desire coursed through my veins as my back arched off the bed while my body beseeched for his special attentions. I gazed down at him, wanting to see his handsome face situated between my thighs. He was perched between my open legs, his mouth nearing my pussy as his blazing eyes were focused on my face. I captured his gaze and felt my body flush—felt my nipples grow erect as he looked at me with an intensity that nearly caused me to reach my release.

"*Tell me where you want me to kiss you,*" *he insisted with a wolfish grin.*

Had it not been obvious? I opened my legs wider and watched his eyes as they dropped to my core, which glistened under the dim lights of my bedroom. He smiled at the sight before he raised his gaze to capture mine.

"*You have to tell me, Veronica,*" *he persisted. "Tell me what you want.*"

"*Here,*" *I told him as I ran my fingertips across my wet folds.*

"There?"

    Now, he was being smart. I rolled my eyes, feeling freer than I had in a very long time. "Kiss my pussy," I requested, feeling bold. He was quick to respond. My back arched off the bed as a response to his ministrations. I couldn't think; all I could do was feel. His tongue worked me over until I writhed beneath him. His hands kept me in place, forcing my butt to stay on the mattress as he devoured me.

    "Trev ... that feels ... that feels—" I gasped as I felt my pussy pulse against his fingers and lips, sending me spiraling while leaving me speechless. While my pussy fluttered rapidly, he continued to pay special attention to my clit, sucking and licking while I rode out my orgasm. My back arched off the bed despite his strong arms pinning me in place. I cried out a string of words, which I was too far gone to recognize. I fucked his face with an urgency that was unlike anything I had ever experienced. As I came down, it was as though I was falling from a cloud—drifting slowly back to Earth.

    "Thank you," I whispered, feeling as if my strength was depleted.

    Trevor smiled at me with the cocky, inspired smile I had quickly grown to love.

    "Are you ready for me?" he questioned as he climbed up my body, positing his throbbing cock at my entrance.

    I felt the tip of his erection brushing against my core as he awaited my answer. Goosebumps covered my flesh, and my nipples puckered as I stared into his eyes, searching for something in his dark, passionate gaze.

    "Honey, do you want this?"

    "Yes," I urged as I reached out to take his muscular ass in my hands, directing his hips forward.

    His muscles flexed against my palms as he thrusted inside of me in one fluid motion. Every time he made love to me, I wondered if I would ever grow used to it. Could a woman ever become used to such a sensation? *It seemed impossible to me; regardless of the copious number of times I had been with him, I found that I yearned for him like I did when he first touched me—when he first fucked me. Every time felt like the first time with him and, deep down, I knew I would yearn for him forever.*

"You feel so incredible." He groaned against the skin of my neck before he placed a wet kiss against my collarbone. "You're so tight—so perfect."

I gasped at his words as I found another orgasm quickly approaching.

He must have felt it, too. He lifted his head to kiss my lips once before lifting his body off of mine to turn me over. I giggled as he flipped me and gasped as he took ahold of my hips and pulled me up into a kneeling position. I loved when he took me like this. I loved the way he always rested his forehead against my back as he bucked wildly into me.

"Oh, Veronica ... I can never get enough of you."

I moaned, bucking my hips against him as he thrusted inside of me so deeply, I felt like I could have fallen to pieces at any moment. He bent over my body, kissing my back as he continued to plow into me. I gasped for air and arched my back as I allowed him to take me. I was close ... so close ... For a moment, the rest of the world faded away and there was only us.

Forever us and only us in this moment.

"Veronica ... baby!" he cried out as his hips bucked wildly against mine.

As I awoke in my bed, my body came to life. My eyelids fluttered open as shock coursed through me while my pussy pulsated uncontrollably. Alone in my bed, I fell to pieces. I rode out my orgasm as my mind reeled in disbelief. *Did my dream really cause me to come?* After my body settled down, I stared up at the ceiling and contemplated what had just taken place. That dream had been so vivid ... so *real*. My body still ached as if Trevor had touched me—had fucked me just like I had imagined. My nipples were still erect from his imaginary touch; my core was still wet from where I imagined his throbbing cock to be. I ran my hands leisurely up and down my torso as I enjoyed the aftereffects of my release. *Heavens, I feel like I'm coming alive!* I was alive—all because of Trevor.

As the sun rose to welcome the day, I felt reborn. My current state of convalescence gave me a fresh perspective. The awakening Trevor inspired had me reeling. Our paths had only crossed on a few occasions, and yet, I found my outlook on life had begun to change. I felt like *me* again. Now that I was "awakened," I wondered who I had been for the past few years; I wondered how others had viewed me as I had trudged through life like a functional zombie. Had they seen through the fake smiles and fictitious stories? I knew my sister had seen through my act.

Eden ... How dreadful a sister have I been to her?

Of course, she'd never complained about my behavior. She had tried relentlessly to set me on the right course, but I had always deviated. I'd wanted to go my own way despite my respect for her. When everything in my life had fallen apart, she had taken care of me; she had cared for me when I hadn't been capable of caring for myself. She had embraced my ugliness—carried the weight of my pain. After my incident—after the few nights that had altered my life entirely—I had quickly become withdrawn. I wanted to live in my own head—living in my own fantasy—knowing that would have been the only way I could feel powerful. In the real world, I had felt powerless. In my early twenties, I had walked through life feeling as if my identity had been ripped away from me. Thankfully, my sister had found me in that haze and brought me back to reality.

Even now, I remembered the way she held my hand; I remembered the way she would remain silent while giving me a shoulder to cry on until I was willing and able to share. She had rested her head on my shoulder as she hummed the familiar melody of a song our mom would sing to us growing up.

"I don't know what to tell you ..." I buried my face in the crook of her neck and suppressed a sob. I couldn't cry in front of her—it would break me.

"You don't have to tell me anything." She ran her fingers through my hair before she pulled me close. "We can just sit here for as long as you want."

I nodded and kept my mouth closed. If I said something ... if I told her ... God, I knew she would look at me differently. Would she be able to still see the girl she had grown up with after I uttered the words? *Tears welled in my eyes, and I blinked them furiously away. I couldn't help but blame myself, even though the rational part of me screamed that what had happened wasn't my fault.*

"I'm happy you're back," she said. "I missed you while you were away. God, Ronnie, so much has happened. I could have used having my baby sister around." She kissed my forehead, and I melted against her, appreciating her comfort and remembering the way she used to hold me like this when we were little.

"I'm happy, too."

"It's you and me, little sister. You and me, forever."

"Forever," I agreed.

She was silent for a moment before she asked, "You'll tell me one day, right?"

"One day."

She pulled me back to appraise me for a moment before she let me go and spit into her right hand. With a warm grin, she held her hand out for me to shake. Despite my mood, I smiled at her antics. As children, we had done this many times. It had been our version of a pinky promise. If we shook on it like this, it became an agreement set in stone. It was part of the "sisterly oath" we had created as children. I wiped the moisture off my cheeks before I spit into my right hand and reached out to give her a firm shake.

"I promise," I said before we broke the shake.

"One day."

"One day soon."

She had always had a knack for making me feel weightless when the entire world was crushing my shoulders. Ever since Mom had passed away, she had looked out for me. She had quickly become my world—the one person I looked up to. As I graduated high school and began college, I remembered all I wanted to do was make her proud. That sentiment was what had made telling her my horrible truth so very hard. For a strange reason, I had believed once she heard what happened, she would feel disappointed in me. *Maybe that was because I was disappointed in myself.*

I had been disappointed in myself because I felt, deep down, that I could have done something to stop it. A prominent part of me had believed I could have done something to save myself, which had been both illogical and impossible. In that horrific moment, my world had been an out of control blur. My body had been so lethargic I couldn't have moved a single finger, let alone defend myself. The only thing I had been able to do was piss myself—and that hadn't so much as slowed them down. They hadn't stopped; all they had done was laugh. That night hadn't been the only night I felt paralyzed; I had felt paralyzed for many nights to come. *Until I returned to Eden.*

I knew I had to pay her back. I had to do something to show my gratitude. Slipping out of bed, I grabbed my phone and quickly pulled up Quinton's number in my contacts. *Maybe he could help me shop for Eden? Now that I don't live with her, I have no idea what she has. She's a shopaholic, after all.* While being in a crowded mall caused me to feel claustrophobic and anxious, I decided that today I would put on a brave face for her. She had always put on a brave face for me, after all.

After shooting Quinton a quick text message, I hopped out of bed and began to get ready for the day ahead. I went through my morning routine and started a pot of Earl Grey while I began to read a chapter of my latest book selection. A few cups of tea later and a few chapters in, I received a response from my brother-in-law.

`I hate the mall. But I'll help you, sis.`

Quinton had been exhausted by the time we left Colorado Mills. Both of us had grown accustomed to the small shopping centers around Evergreen, which caused a mall like this to be a complete shock to our senses. As sad as it was to admit, I had spent most of my time shopping at Safeway and King Soopers. I didn't usually make thirty-minute trips to

Colorado Mills to spend my money frivolously. However, I would do anything for Eden.

I peered down at the bags in my hands and smiled at my purchases. While I wasn't exactly "fashion forward" myself, I believed I did all right shopping for her. Of course, her husband, who was well attuned to her shopping habits had proved to be a giant help.

"Ronnie, do you want to stop somewhere and grab a bite? You should at least feed me after what you made me endure all afternoon."

He smirked at me as he unlocked his Toyota Yaris and popped open the trunk for our bags. While he complained, I knew he only teased. The love he had for my sister was unreal. I basked in the warmth of his presence because of it. He was truly a brother to me—looking out for me in a way that many of my blood relations didn't bother doing. A moment spent doing something for Eden was a moment spent well in his mind. They had been in each other's lives for so long, and while they hadn't always been romantically connected, I had known from the start they had been destined to be together. Even when they were young, awkward teens who couldn't climb over the friendship barrier to reach one another, I had known.

"We could go to Yard House," I suggested, knowing he loved a good sports bar.

His smirk widened into a grin of approval. "That's perfect, little sis."

I loved when he called me little sis. I had always wanted an older brother who looked out for me. So, I knew I was lucky to have Quinton in my life.

Seated in a booth surrounded by flat screens and a rowdy crowd, I finally felt relaxed. As much as I usually hated crowds, whenever I felt small— unsure about myself—they had their perks; being surrounded by sound made me feel invisible. In a crowd, I felt like I could be myself. I could slip through the cracks of people's notice and exist however I wanted.

"Do you know what you're getting, sis?" Quinton asked as his eyes glossed over the menu.

I gazed at it for a moment before deciding on the cheapest thing I saw. "I'm getting the Vampire Tacos. How 'bout you?"

He stared for a moment longer before he closed the menu, and his eyes met mine. "Carnivore Pizza and a Nitro White Ale." He paused for a moment, as if he were debating what to say next. "Ronnie, not that I don't enjoy your company, but what brought this on? You don't exactly reach out to me very much, and God knows you hate shopping."

I flushed, feeling remorseful for how I had abandoned my family while I had been lost in my own little world. I had believed I had tried; I had truly thought I carried the weight well. However, he was right; I hadn't reached out to him. I had barely reached out to anyone. The only time I had seen my family or friends was when one of them had initiated it. I had never meant to be so tight-lipped, but then again, I had never meant for many things to happen.

"I wanted to do something nice for my sister," I said after a long, awkward moment. "She's always doing everything for me, and I felt like I never adequately returned the favor."

"She doesn't expect you to," he replied. "She does everything because she loves you."

"You sound just like her." I laughed, recalling the countless times she had told me the exact same thing.

"Well, I *am* married to her," he replied with a chuckle. He leaned back in his seat and appraised me for a moment before his gregarious smile faded into a more serious expression. "Ronnie, she understands that you're going through a lot. She loves you. She doesn't expect you to pay her back for merely being a sister."

"But I want to," I quickly quipped. "Or, I at least want to *try*. God, Quinton … I've been lost for such a long time. I haven't been a good sister to her. She deserves—"

"Stop," Quinton silenced me. "You've done what you could. You both have. Stop berating yourself all the time."

"I'm sorry," I whispered as I dropped my gaze. "It's just for the first time in a very long time, I feel like *me* again. I recognize myself when I look in the mirror. You can't imagine what that feels like after feeling like an alien in your own body."

He nodded at this, studying me for a moment before his expression lightened and he continued. "You've been growing better each day. We've all noticed. When you graduated, we barely recognized you."

He stopped speaking as his eyes began to water. His eyes darted across my facial features while morphing with discomfort all while my mind recalled unpleasant memories. The memories irritated raw wounds.

"You've been getting so much better," he continued. "But it's been a slow process. And now, all of a sudden, it's like you've morphed into your old self overnight."

I wish my transformation was as easy as he made it sound. This wasn't a fairy tale. A prince didn't come and kiss me, waking me up from a seemingly endless nightmare. I'm still living in that nightmare, and I fear I'm the only one to save myself.

"Eden's been so thrilled for you. I know she hasn't expressed it, but seeing you like this makes her happier than I've seen her in a very long time."

"Has she been very upset?"

How have I not known this?

"Just worried. She *is* your older sister, after all." He winked at me before he leaned forward in his seat. "If you don't mind me asking, what brought this on? It's like a switch inside of you was flipped or something."

"I don't know," I answered honestly. "I don't feel like I'm fully rehabilitated or anything like that. But for the first time in a long time, I have hope. I *want* to fight. I've spent the last few years believing I've been fighting these feelings inside of me, but truly, I was just sweeping them under the rug and ignoring them. Now, I finally feel like I have the drive and determination to make a difference."

The air was heavy between us, and it took Quinton a few moments to reply.

"Eden and I ... we did all we could. You can't imagine what it's been like on our end—wanting to help but finding it impossible. I'm just so happy you've found what you need. Whatever sparked this change in you, I'm grateful for it."

Trevor ... I smiled as I thought of him.

"I'm grateful, too."

My laughter sounded almost foreign to me as it fell from my lips. I could laugh freely again; I could breathe easy. As old wounds began to mend, I felt like the old Veronica my family knew. Quinton was far easier going, too. In the past, he must have taken direction from me and my emotional state. If I had been happy, he had been happy; if I had been upset, he had been upset, as well. His other half, my sister, seemed to be the very same way.

"God, it's been nice seeing you like this. Eden's going to be absolutely ecstatic." He smiled as he mentioned his wife's name, which caused me to smile, too. *They're so in love. I want that.* "She's talking about you constantly. Always worrying like some mother hen. Now, she can finally rest easy for a while."

I nodded before I looked toward my building, wondering what Trevor might be up to now. I didn't know his schedule—otherwise, I would have dropped in to see if he needed my help with Grey. *Come on. That's definitely* not *the only reason you wanted to drop by.* I smiled at myself, knowing my gorgeous neighbor gave me more than enough reasons to drop in unexpectedly.

"Ronnie? What do you look so happy about?"

My eyes snapped away from the apartment building as I felt a flush stain my cheeks. When I met Quinton's gaze, I knew he was suspicious. *More than suspicious considering the way he's looking at me.* His eyes were bright as he took in my blush, and as he studied me, his smirk transformed into a brotherly grin. He ran a hand through his cropped blond hair before he leaned back on his heels.

"Ronnie, who has you blushing like that?"

"No one," I quickly stated. *Too* quickly. So quickly Quinton could only smirk in response.

"Do you know you're a bad liar?" Quinton asked with a smirk.

"No?"

His blond hair swayed around his face as he threw his head back and laughed. My flush deepened. I wasn't ready to tell him about my love life … or, lack thereof. I didn't want to jinx things with Trevor. We barely knew each other, and I felt that if I spoke of what we had aloud, my chances with him would somehow disappear.

"It's nothing," I continued, cringing as Quinton cocked his brow while his eyes livened with a challenging stare. "He's no one, Quinton!" I stressed. "Truly."

"*He's* no one, is he? 'No one' makes you blush like that?"

"Like what?"

"Sis, I can't remember the last time I've seen you look this way."

"What way?" I inquired, growing self-conscious about my apparent transparency.

"Ronnie, you're flushing like a kid developing their first crush. Are you sure he's truly 'no one'?"

I didn't want to think of Trevor as "no one." He had quickly become so much. He had quickly become *everything. Being with him … So far … it's been life changing. Oddly life changing. I wish I could understand it.* In the short while I had known him, he caused me to wonder if I had ever experienced true love before—or *any* romantic love, for that matter. Once, I had believed I knew myself—knew my emotions—but now, I wondered if I had been disillusioned. Perhaps, life had misled me, muddling my mind until I hadn't known which way was up. What I had once believed to know about love may have been nothing more than a convoluted idea developed over years of watching silly romantic comedies and cartoons displaying beautiful princesses and dashing heroes. While Trevor was a far cry from how I had imagined my prince charming to be, I found he was far more appealing than any of my silly fantasies ever were.

"He's not 'no one,' " I finally murmured.

"Who is he?"

"My neighbor, Trevor."

"Trevor?" Quinton smiled with approval. "Is he nice to you?"

I grinned. *What a brotherly thing for him to say.* I had always appreciated how protective Quinton was of me. He only ever wanted me to be happy.

"He's more than nice. He's wonderful."

"Well, I hope he deserves you then."

"I don't know about that. We're not 'together' or anything. We're just talking."

"Talking is good. Do you think it could ever become more than that?"

I considered it for a moment. While I hoped it would become more—which astonished me considering how I had shied away from so many chances at different relationships over the past few years—I didn't know everything that went on in Trevor's life. He obviously had an abundance on his plate: a new apartment, a new job, a new baby, a new life … I was barely able to wrap my mind around the stress he must be under. We couldn't be just friends forever. I already knew I would never be satisfied with that. *For now, maybe … But I can't do forever. There has to be* more. *I can't be satisfied by a friendship for the rest of my life. Not with him …*

"I don't know. He has a lot going on," I explained, shifting on my feet. "I'm not sure if the timing is right."

"Well, maybe one day." He smiled at me for a moment longer as he leaned against his Jeep. "I should probably get going. I know Eden's going to have dinner ready soon and will start calling me if I don't head back. It was nice seeing you, sis."

He pulled me into a hug and gave my back a few pats before he pulled away. A boyish smile lit up his face as he turned his head and looked toward my apartment building. Turning his gaze back to capture mine, he jokingly waggled his eyebrows as a cheesy grin pulled at his mouth. I snorted at the priceless look on his face. If anyone wanted me to be happy, it was Quinton. I believed that, in a strange way, he felt responsible for what happened to me.

As illogical as it was, he felt as though he failed at protecting me. I knew he wanted to hunt down my ex-boyfriend and his pack of disgusting friends to make them pay for their sins; however, I had convinced him to remain with Eden and me. Looking back now, I didn't understand why I had done that—why I had protected them. I wouldn't have minded seeing those pricks suffer. I supposed I had been far more forgiving then—or far more afraid. I wasn't afraid anymore.

"I'll see you tomorrow."

Watching him as he walked away, I leaned back against my Jeep and considered my next move relating to my sinfully handsome next-door neighbor. Was I ready to pursue something, or was I lying to myself?

A quick squeal pulled me away from my contemplations, and my eyes quickly followed the direction of the sound. *I wonder ...* No, if Trevor were out here, I was sure he would say hello to me. *Wouldn't he?* Just as I turned toward my apartment, I heard a loud squeal and stopped in my tracks. Although I didn't know the little guy well, I recognized the adorably loud sound. With a smile tugging on my lips, I turned and walked toward Trevor's truck. As I approached, I watched him duck down out of my line of sight.

Was he trying to avoid me?

I hoped not. Now that I was recognizing my feelings for him, I would be gutted if he didn't return my sentiments at all. *Not that I expect him to like me ... but I can't deny feeling* something *between us when we're together.* He had to feel it, too.

"Trev?" I questioned as I approached his truck.

He appeared in front of me with a happy baby snug in his left arm and a large pizza in his right hand. His bumptious act was more than transparent as I saw the uneasy look in his eyes. His usual crooked grin seemed weary today. I wondered what inspired this change. *Could it be because—no, there's no way he could believe there was anything between Quinton and me.* As I gazed at him, I wondered how long he had been standing near his truck. *Was he watching me?* While part of me was worried about his view of what he had just witnessed, another part of me was downright delighted he felt so invested in me.

"How's it going, Trev? I didn't even see you over here," I said casually as I tried to calculate what was going on in that handsome head of his.

His expression was apprehensive despite his obvious effort to camouflage it. His eyes darted pensively over my body before they snapped back to meet mine. *God, it's times like these when I wished I were a mind reader.*

"It's all good now that I'm off work."

He paused for a moment and shifted uncomfortably on his heels. It was strange to watch a man who appeared so rough and powerful act so incredibly nervous. With his sharp jaw and intense features, I was sure he inspired a sense of unease in many people. So, it was odd to find him skittish. He gave me a once-over, and his brows knitted together, appearing calculating before he gave me an uneasy smile.

"You want to come up to my place and have dinner with us? We were just going to veg out on the couch, watch some movies, and eat pizza."

Nothing sounded better.

"That sounds good. I was planning on ordering take-out and watching reality TV," I said nonchalantly, not wanting him to know how excited I was by his offer.

I couldn't take my eyes off of Trevor as he locked up his truck and moved toward the apartment; his steps were strong and purposeful, his eyes were bright, and his expression satisfied. I walked beside him as he carried the animated baby in the crook of his left arm while balancing the pizza on his right palm. As I kept my eye on them, Grey's gaze shot up to meet mine. His jade eyes peered up at me with such understanding it took me off guard for a second. *Is it strange for a baby, who isn't biologically mine, to capture my heart so quickly?* He looked at me as if he knew me—*really* knew me. *Maybe this guy feels the same pull as I do?*

Wanting to hold the little boy in my arms, and knowing Trevor needed help, I suggested, "I can take Grey, if you want? I don't want you to drop the pizza," I teased him and winked.

His eyes sparked, and a smile tugged on his full lips, causing my breath to catch in my throat.

He handed me Grey, who squealed as soon as he was placed in my waiting arms. He nuzzled my chest and smiled up at me. His chubby, little cheeks flushed, and his jade eyes sparkled as he looked up at my face as if he were memorizing me; after a moment, he reached out and began to play with my hair. His little fingers ran through my curls, tangling them slightly before he looked up at me again and giggled. Looking at him, my heart melted. I may have not known the full story, but I discerned his biological parents were no longer in his life. The only person he seemed to have was Trevor; while I knew Trevor was a wonderful father to him already, it still broke my heart knowing he didn't have a mother to care for him.

I understood what it was like to suffer the loss; I wouldn't wish it on anyone. *What I wouldn't give to take away the pain. What I wouldn't give to give this little boy the world.* As he peered up at me with his beautiful eyes, I silently promised him: *I'll do everything I can possibly do for you, Grey.* I would do anything to make him happy.

Grey rested his head on my breasts as he continued to play with my hair, blissfully unaware of the rest of the world. *I hope I can always see you this happy, Grey. You and your uncle.*

"He's a giant flirt," Trevor commented with a laugh.

For a fleeting second, I swore Trevor looked a little jealous of his own nephew.

"I'm sure you'll have plenty of girlfriends, Greyson," I told the little guy as he nuzzled my breasts and continued to play with my hair in his chubby hand.

While we made our way to Trevor's apartment, I couldn't ignore the feel of his eyes as they traced over my curves. I knew he tried to hide his glances, but I wasn't obtuse, and I always noticed them. With a sidelong glance, I watched him as he peered down my sweater. Normally, I would have commented on the behavior, but when Trevor gave me this sort of attention, I never minded. When Trevor looked at me, every fiber of my being ignited, and there was nothing within me that wanted to extinguish the flame. *I'm sure his touch would do that, too. I'm sure his strong arms and soft mouth would cause me to burn even brighter.* I grinned at the thought as Trevor's eyes continued to roam my frame.

Upon reaching the apartment, I felt Trevor's agitation. He practically kicked his front door open before leading us to the living room. A tense hand ran through his untamed hair as he glanced around the entryway. He threw me a stiff, uncomfortable smile over his shoulder as we reached his living room. He set the pizza box down on the coffee table by the couch before he turned fully to look at me.

A light from the ceiling fixture shined down on him—its shadows highlighting the curves of his muscles and every sinfully attractive piece of ink. My nostrils flared as my breath caught in my throat; I couldn't look away from him. His body was strong but not overly muscular. His features were severe. Nothing about him was soft; nothing about him seemed *safe.* He probably should have made me apprehensive, but as I took in his handsome appearance, unease was the last thing I felt. Instead, all I felt was want and a neediness that was impossible to ignore. It had been so long since I had wanted anyone—it had been so long since I had felt something other than fear and foreboding when faced with the opposite sex—which made my longing for Trevor even more painful and difficult to stifle.

"Do you mind watching him while I take a quick shower?" Trevor asked, seeming stiff.

Staring down at the small boy in my arms, I grinned and confirmed I would be all right. As soon as Trevor disappeared into what I assumed was his bedroom, I took a seat and turned on the television while holding Grey comfortably against my chest. His wild hair tickled my skin as he bobbed his head around. He was studying my hair again—running his chubby fingers through my curls before he giggled and attempted to stuff it into his mouth.

"Come on, little guy. None of that," I told him as I gently pulled the hair away from his wide-open mouth.

He peered up at me, giving me a quizzical look before he broke into an infectious smile. Every time he smiled, I felt a smile tugging on my own lips, too. His smiles were so pure and filled with so much love. Reaching out, I traced the lines of his face with my fingertips. Ever so gently, I memorized the feel of his soft cheeks, the thin skin of his eyelids, the delicacy of his long lashes and, finally, his tiny lips.

Perfect. This little boy was so perfect.

A long time ago, I wanted a child of my own. I had imagined having a huge family one day along with a man I had loved. Every time I had closed my eyes, I could see the picturesque white picket fence of my dreams; I could see the large back yard and perfect house, which would be filled with children who resembled my husband and myself. When I was young, I'd had so many ideas for my future. But as time had ticked forward and the cruelty of life had become apparent, those dreams had faded away. Only recently had these dreams simmered back into my consciousness.

"You're a charmer. Do you know that, Grey?"

His response was a giggle. As he reached out for me, I gave him a finger to hold on to, smiling as I watched his tiny fingers wrap around my slim thumb. Our eyes met, and my heart swelled in my chest. In this moment, the entire world seemed to stop, and the only thing that mattered was us. In this moment, our bond was fortified. *I love him*, I thought. I never believed it would be possible to love a baby so completely who wasn't biologically mine; yet, in this moment, I found I could. Maybe I felt so drawn to him because I understood the pain of not having a mother. *Or, maybe it's because he's such a little charmer.*

"I bet you could get anyone to love you, couldn't you, Grey?"

He laughed at me.

"You know I'm here for you, right? Always," I promised.

He stopped laughing for a moment and gazed up at me. My eyes welled with tears as I looked at his open expression. *God, I want to give him the world. I hope I never have to give him up.* Rocking him back and forth in my arms, I considered what my life would look like with him permanently in it. Perhaps I was getting ahead of myself, but my mind always conjured up images of the future I could have with Grey and his uncle. As a constant reader and an amateur writer, my mind wandered, and my imagination frequently ran wild. Closing my eyes, I opened my mind, allowing images of the future I dreamed of to flood my brain.

"You can do it, Grey! You're doing so well!" I encouraged as he stepped toward me. I smiled as he grew confident with every movement.

He squealed as he reached me. Throwing my arms around him, I congratulated him. I never felt so proud.

The wheels of my mind turned. Grey reappeared in my head, older this time. Trevor was there, too.

"Daddy, I don't want to go. You come with?"

"Buddy," Trevor said, kneeling to look his son in the eye. "This is something you have to do on your own. You're a big boy, now. And big boys go to school." Grey's bottom lip trembled, causing Trevor to throw his arm around him, pulling him close. "You'll have fun, little man. You'll meet friends. You'll—"

"I'm not little," Grey interrupted his father, frowning.

Trevor smiled at this, enjoying the small, yet significant moment with his son. "No, you're not little anymore. You're in pre-school now. You're growing up."

"I grow up a lot."

Trevor chuckled at this, and I felt my eyes well with tears. He has grown up—so much faster than I wished he would. It was all too fast. I wanted to turn back time and pause it. I wanted to remember him this little forever.

"You grew up a lot," Trevor agreed, looking emotional himself. "And I'm so proud of you."

"Love you, Daddy," Grey responded, hugging his father.

Time moved forward in my daydream. Now, Grey was a preteen. In my imagination, he was handsome; as I pictured him, I wondered what his father and mother had looked like. I wondered who he resembled more.

"I don't know if she likes me, Dad," Grey whispered, making me feel guilty for eavesdropping.

"Well, you two are friends, right? Have you thought 'bout asking her out?"

Grey was quiet for a moment, and although I didn't have a clear view of his face, I could imagine his calculating expression—the one he would usually have while deep in thought.

"I don't know if Mom would like that. She said I'm not old enough."

Now, it was Trevor who was quiet. "Well, she and I can talk about it. We'll see. If you like this girl, I'm sure we can make something work."

"Thanks, Dad! Maybe we could see a movie or—"

"Let me talk to your mom before you run wild with ideas." Trevor chuckled.

My thoughts shifted, and Grey was older now. He was graduating high school, and Trevor and I were in the crowd, watching him with tears in our eyes and cameras in our hands. In my daydream, Trevor looked older and more distinguished. His dark hair had bits of gray, and his muscular frame was just as perfect then as it was now. *Trevor is going to be a very, very sexy older man.* I smiled at the thought, and my mind shifted to something different. This time, Grey was young again, playing with a few other children in my fantasy backyard.

"No, Dean, you do it like this, see?"

"I no like it this way," the toddler, Dean, responded with a pout.

"Well, that's the right way," Grey insisted as he took the toy out of the toddler's hands.

Dean began to cry, causing the little girl next to him to tense up.

"No, Grey! No. You be mean!" the little girl screamed, becoming fussy in her seat on the floor.

Grey's eyes widened, and he sat back on his heels. "I'm sorry. I just try to help."

Trevor came in the room, frowning. "Guys, what happened this time?"

"Daddy, I just try to show them," Grey explained, becoming anxious.

"He took my toy!" Dean screamed as he clenched the action figure close.

"Dean, your brother was just trying to help you. You don't have to cry."

"I just help," Grey agreed.

Dean sniffled, looking at his father for a moment before he turned his gaze to Grey. "Sorry," Dean muttered, setting the toy on the floor before he turned to face his brother. "Sorry, Grey."

"It's 'kay," Grey said with a shrug.

Dean nodded before reaching out and wrapping an arm around his brother. Grey hugged him back, playing the perfect role of an older brother.

"You're so good with him."

A rich voice pulled me from my contemplations. My eyes left Grey just in time to find Trevor taking a seat at our side. Grey came to life in my arms as soon as he saw his uncle. The way he looked at Trevor warmed my heart. He looked at Trevor as if he were Superman; he peered up at him as if he were his entire universe. Wanting to hear his adorable laugh, I reached down and tickled his little belly. He squealed, throwing his head back, causing his hair to fly everywhere.

"Thanks," I answered as I continued to tickle the baby. "He's so easy-going. If you ever need a babysitter, you know I work from home."

Trevor gave me a quick once-over. His gaze hovered around my breasts for a moment before he responded. "Well, I might have to take you up on that." He glanced down at my chest again and bit down on his bottom lip before he tore his gaze away and glanced at our pizza. "You want anything to drink before we dig in? I've got soda, water, and orange juice."

"Soda," I answered as I popped open the pizza box.

As soon as he was gone, I reached for a slice of cheese. I couldn't remember the last time I had pizza, and this particular one smelled divine. Grey's eyes were wide with wonder as he watched me reach forward and grab a steaming slice of pizza. His mouth cutely dropped open in awe as he watched me bring said pizza to my mouth for a small bite. A laugh escaped my lips as he reached for the pizza, gazing at it as if it were the holy grail.

"Baby, I don't think you're ready for pizza just yet."

Grey pouted at me as if he understood me perfectly.

"Is it good?"

My face flushed as I turned to face Trevor, who had an attractive smirk on his face as he handed me a bottle of Coke. I stared at him dumbly for a moment, captivated by the intensity of his eyes before I took my drink. Feeling his stare, goosebumps appeared on my flesh, and I shuddered, desire rippling through me. Licking off the pizza sauce from my bottom lip, I took a moment to compose myself.

"It's amazing. Thanks for this, Trev. I was starving."

"Same. I haven't eaten all day."

Trevor sat down next to me with plates, utensils, sodas, and Grey's bottle in hand. He set everything on the table before glancing at the pizza; after a moment of him mulling something over in his head, he looked at the bottle of formula. Of course, he wanted to feed his nephew first. I heard his stomach as it grumbled in protest as he reached for the formula. The way he always put his nephew first—even in the smallest of ways—was lovely.

While I watched him, I wondered what his life was like before Grey. Judging by the scar cutting through his left eyebrow and an additional scar on the side of his neck, which was partially covered by his black and gray lotus flower tattoo, I knew his life had been rough. *Was he a brawler? Was he a violent person?* No, I could feel he was not. His energy was far too soothing. Everything about his aura suggested he was a giving and loving man. While he may have been violent in the past, he certainly wasn't violent now. The way he was around the baby told me everything I needed to know about him. He treated Grey like he was the most important thing. Everything he did illustrated how wonderful he was as a guardian.

"I can feed him if you want," I suggested as I noticed how tired Trevor looked. He looked exhausted, physically and emotionally. "I used to do this for Harper all of the time."

He gave me a grateful smile before he handed me the formula. I felt his eyes on us as I fed Grey. I didn't look up at him, but, as usual, I could feel the heat of his stare. My eyes were on Grey—he was so precious as he drank. His eyes were closed, and his eyelashes fluttered against his flushed cheeks. His little hand clenched and unclenched as he took each sip while his body stretched from side to side in my arms. His head rested against my breasts and, in that position, he seemed oblivious to the outside world. When I finally had the courage to meet Trevor's gaze, I was no longer hungry for food. My breasts felt heavy, and my core began to throb between my thick thighs. His dark eyes left me feeling dizzy.

I closed my eyes for a moment and imagined Trevor's hands on my body. *His strong arms around my waist ... his soft lips on mine ... his hands touching my breasts ... pulling down a cup of my bra before wrapping his sweet lips around my nipple. Sucking, sucking, and sucking, as his fingers slipped into my panties and played with my pussy. His thumb rubbing my clit until I came so hard, I was gasping for air and calling his name. His hands leaving my core and taking his cock out of his pants... wiping the pre-come off the tip before rubbing it against my folds. Him impaling me ... fucking me until I don't know my own name ...*

Grey's giggle brought me back to reality, and I pulled his bottle back, realizing he was finished while cursing myself for fantasizing about my neighbor while his nephew was in my arms. *How awkward ... Stop being so ridiculous, Ronnie! Stop letting your mind run wild!*

"You okay with watching a Disney movie?"

Wow, he's been looking for a movie to watch this whole time, and I was too busy thinking about his cock to notice? I felt a blush stain my cheeks and prayed Trevor didn't catch it. *How embarrassing would that be?*

"Of course!" I replied over earnestly. *Jesus, Veronica! Pull yourself together, please. Don't let his cock distract you! He's just a man. Only a man ... Besides, you love Disney movies.* "I love this movie." *God, I sound lame.*

Trevor gave me an appraising glance before he smiled and pressed play. Despite my age, I knew I would never grow tired of watching these animated classics. I remembered watching *The Lion King* with Eden. We had watched it constantly and even sang incompetently along with the songs, butchering each and every lyric. The memory brought a smile to my face as I leaned back against the couch cushions and pulled Grey comfortably against me. It was simple moments like this that were always impactful.

As the movie progressed, I noticed how quiet Trevor was. He was as stiff as a board at my side, and I turned to look at him; I found tears swimming in his eyes. I doubted these tears were due to the movie despite Mufasa's death being so tragic. While the nosey part of me wanted to know everything, I knew it was best to respect his boundaries. If he wanted to tell me, he would. I didn't feel as though I knew him well enough to ask what was going on in his head.

"Trev? You okay?" I gently pried.

He loosened up at my side before he turned to give me a bashful smile. "Yeah, I'm fine. Just some dust in my eye."

Just seeing him this vulnerable tore at my heart. "It's okay, Trevor. Mufasa's death made a lot of people cry," I teased him.

And then, he was laughing. *I made him laugh!* Knowing I was able to take his pain away—if even for just a moment—made me feel wonderful. His smile was just as infectious as his nephew's. I breathed him in and felt his happiness flood my senses. As his loving aura embraced mine, I knew Trevor Warren was what I wanted. I knew we had issues, but I wanted him in my life. If I could bring myself to open up, I could be good for him; I could be good for Grey, too.

I just had to try.

For them—and for myself—I have to try.

7

Wildflowers

The end of summer brought renascence. Everything felt so fresh—so disenthralling. The past few weeks had given me such hope. I had felt myself flourishing. I never realized how repressed and withdrawn I had been. For so long, I believed I had been getting better; for so long, I felt like I had been healing, but truly, I had been avoiding everything that had made me *feel*.

In the few shorts weeks which I had known Trevor, I had felt *everything*. My old, everyday schedule had been thrown out the window and replaced with a new and improved one I loved far more. Every morning, I rolled out of bed with a profound sense of optimism and would spend a good while washing my body and masturbating in my tub before I would sit down with my breakfast, a hot cup of Earl Grey, and a book. I had come so far so quickly. I had made more progress in the past few months than I had in years. *All thanks to my sinfully attractive neighbor.*

I leaned back against the hard cast-polymer of my cramped tub and relaxed as I practiced my favorite part of my new morning routine. Closing my eyes, I listened to the *crackle* that came from the lavender candle I had placed on the countertop of my sink. I dipped my head into the water, enjoying the sounds of my bones softly *creaking* as my body relaxed in the warmth of the tub. When I resurfaced, I inhaled the rose petal scent of my bath bomb as my hands slowly drifted up and down the curves of my body. My fingertips ran over my sensitive nipples, causing them to pucker and harden between the pads of my fingertips. While listening to the soft sound of my bath bubbles *pop*, my right hand drifted down my body to the apex of my thighs, touching the spot that yearned for some attention. My fingertips were gentle at first, teasing my clit as well as my folds before they delved a little deeper; I slid a finger inside my throbbing core. With my eyes closed and silence surrounding me, I thought of *him*: my handsome friend who starred in each and every one of my fantasies.

It didn't take long for me to reach my brink. I worked my clit until I had felt my orgasm approaching, and then I began to move my fingers even faster to push myself over the precipice. My legs trembled, and my eyelids fluttered as I felt my pussy begin to pulsate. I cried out softly and found my release while I pictured Trevor in my mind; in my fantasy, we came together, and his body trembled over mine as he filled my core with his come.

Coming down from my high, I settled into the water, which was now lukewarm, and contemplated a time when I wouldn't have been able to achieve this. Now, those days seemed so foreign. My past felt as though it happened to a different person entirely. In this moment, the old me was forgotten; now, I swam in blissful, uninhibited waters.

With a relaxed body and mind, I finished washing up before I pulled the plug and watched the bathwater drain. I sat in the tub for a moment longer before I finally stood and got out, knowing I had to ready myself for the day. Trevor would be here within the hour with Greyson. By then, the sun would be up, and I would have a lot on my plate. Taking care of a baby while I worked from home was no easy feat. However, for Greyson, I would sacrifice anything. Even if he wasn't truly *mine*. Besides, he was such an easy-going little boy, which made watching over him no trouble. In fact, it had become the highlight of my day. Over the course of the past week and a half, I had babysat Grey several times while his uncle had been away for work. Usually, I babysat when Trevor's mother had been too busy. *She could be busy as often as she liked. I loved watching her grandson.* With Greyson around, I felt like a little girl again. To him, everything was new and awe-inspiring—such a wonderful thing to see. It made me feel like I was seeing the world for the first time, too.

"Thanks so much for this, Ronnie. My mom had some lunch with her friends—"

"You don't have to explain." I waved him off. "I love watching him."

Holding my hands out, I reached for the very eager baby in Trevor's strong, tattooed arms. Grey squealed as soon as he left his uncle's embrace. I wrapped him in my arms and pressed my lips to the soft skin of his flushed, little cheek.

"I'm glad you do. God knows my dad needs a break."

Trevor laughed before his eyes leisurely followed the curves of my body. My nipples hardened beneath his gaze; his eyes were fixated on them for a moment before he smirked, obviously satisfied with how my body responded to his attention.

"I'll call you when I'm on my way back," he finished.

"Of course."

I felt almost awkward—holding a baby while openly lusting after its caregiver. *Any woman in my place would do the same, wouldn't she?* Especially when Trevor looked like this: his hair untamed and damp from his shower, his white shirt molded against the muscles of his torso, his ink on display for the world to see, his dark—almost black—eyes crackling with intensity, the jagged scar slicing down his eyebrow crinkling as he smiled at me, and the long, muscular legs perfectly exhibited in his work jeans. I licked my lips as I looked at him and flushed, realizing what I was doing and how long I had been doing it. Thankfully, Trevor was too distracted with everything going on in his own head to note my attentions. I wondered if he could see through the shades of his self-deprecation to even notice me. *Hell, it wasn't until recently I was able to see through the depths of my own to notice anyone. Not until recently have I ever wanted to make the effort.*

"Be good, Grey." Trevor tousled his nephew's hair before he turned to gaze at me again. "Be good, Ronnie," he said with a teasing wink before he bent down to give Grey a quick peck on the forehead.

My eyes were trained on him as he left. *God, he looks incredible from behind.*

"So, Grey, what do you want to do today?" I asked, turning my gaze to meet his.

He giggled and leaned back in my arms to get a better look at my expression. With his eyes wide and filled with wonder, he captured my heart all over again. Reaching down, I traced the panes of his face while he smiled contentedly up at me.

"Want me to read you something, little man?"

Maybe I could read him some of my story ideas?

My ideas were rough, consisting of a jumbled mess of papers with various illustrations and notes, but maybe Grey would enjoy them; maybe he could help me make sense of the mess. Taking him into the bedroom, I sat down with him on my carpeted floor and pulled out my binder of ideas. To me, the binder made perfect sense, but I was sure to many, it looked like a random hodgepodge of papers scattered with ideas that were impossible to follow. I'd been working on this book for a while now, starting and stopping whenever inspiration hit or fizzled out. If it weren't for my focus on my career as an editor, I would have put far more time into my little passion project.

If I were being honest with myself, I knew the project didn't have much direction; I had no idea what I would do with it once it was finished. I knew that, regardless if I published the work or not, I would be proud of myself for completing it. This was something I loved— something that, regardless of the tragedy in my life, I never seemed to let go of. While the world could be bleak and disappointing, I found solace in this. Creating something made me feel in control; writing made me feel like I oversaw my own little world. After having my control and free will stripped from me so thoroughly, being able to create something beautiful from nothing gave me a satisfaction I couldn't begin to describe.

"I have something special to show you," I murmured, feeling a twinge self-consciousness suddenly.

His eyes widened as I opened the binder, and his little hands instantly reached for the pages upon pages of colored pictures. Looking at them, they had not made much sense. They were an array of different ideas displaying the randomness that was my mind. In various mediums, showcasing different thoughts, the pages were elaborate but hadn't conveyed the message I desired to get across. *What message* did *I want to get across?*

"Do you like the pictures, Grey?"

He giggled and peered up at me, giving me a big smile before his eyes returned to the pages. Holding him tightly in my arms with one hand, I used the other to put some of the pages in the order they were intended to go in. I didn't know how *good* the book was, but at the time, it had made a lot of sense to me; when I had created it, it had felt *right*. Just watching Grey as he took in all of the illustrations made all the sleepless nights pouring over this project well worth it. *Hell, it's not like I could sleep back then, anyway.* I had spent so many nights restless in my bed—never having felt safe despite knowing I was perfectly alone. Even now, I struggled. However, the struggle was nothing like it used to be. It seemed like Grey and Trevor were some sort of cure—a method of elevating the pain of my past. *They were just another step in my journey of moving on.*

Grey's squeals brought my mind back to the present. He slapped the first page of my "book" with his little hand and looked up at me expectantly, as if to ask, "Veronica, when are you going to read to me?" His enthusiasm caused me to sit up a little straighter as I positioned the "book" for both of us to easily see. I began to read as Grey cooed and slurred a bunch of different sounds together as if he were trying to compliment me. His tiny fingers traced the colorful pages as he took in the imagined scenes in front of him. My heart soared, enjoying the immense satisfaction of sharing my work—my vision—with someone else.

"Did you enjoy that, buddy?" I asked as my first story came to a close.

He wasn't as vocal as he usually was. Growing worried, I bent down to get a better look at his little face as his eyes remained concentrated on the book's last page. His jade eyes were filled with tears as he reached to turn the page backward, trying to reach the beginning of the book. *He likes it.* My heart felt warmed and, in this moment, I felt like I was *home.* I gave his forehead a quick kiss and soothed him by flipping back to the beginning of my humble, little story. This time as I read, Grey peered up at my face and watched as my mouth moved. I couldn't take my eyes off of him as his tiny mouth tried to form words, too. *God, I love him.* When he gazed at me, I felt like he saw *me*; and, in the depths of his guileless eyes, I found him returning my sentiment.

After a couple more of my stories and one of my story ideas, Grey was peacefully asleep in my arms. I studied him for a moment, still unable to wrap my mind around how this little boy had fallen into my life. I pressed a kiss to his temple, enjoying the smell of his lavender baby lotion before I rose with him in my arms. Not having a pack-and-play just yet, I rested Grey safely on the center of my bed before I took a seat at his side. As he lay dead to the world, I contemplated reading a book before the sketchbook that sat on my bedside table captured my attention. Without a second thought, I grabbed the sketchbook and an HB pencil before I settled in.

With my eyes on Grey and my pencil in hand, I began to sketch. As soon as my pencil began to draw the planes of his little face, I lost track of time—my entire focus was on him. I studied the way the light hit his face, causing shadows around the curves of his lips and contours of his cheeks. I worked on the subtle contours the shadows caused, remembering how difficult it was to draw children. Adults were far more interesting as subject matter; with the variations in their skin—fine lines, wrinkles, and skin discoloration—and their mature faces, every model was a completely different experience. Children were too *perfect*, I supposed. Life hadn't affected them yet. You really had to capture each one of their features correctly, or it was hard to tell the specific subject matter from just *any* child.

Before I knew it, his image was roughly sketched on the paper in front of me. As I peered down at my handiwork, an idea struck me. *Maybe I could write about him?* He had a story, and heaven knew I needed a muse. I wouldn't have to share the work with anyone; it could just be for me. *And maybe for Trevor, too.* Trevor, who didn't even know about my little hobby. *Maybe one day this could be a surprise? A gift for him.*

My attention returned to Grey as his little mouth stretched into a yawn, and his arms came up over his head in a stretch. His eyelids fluttered for a moment before they opened, and he focused his attention on me. Setting my sketchbook down on my bedside table, I watched his face become flushed and sensed a tantrum on the horizon. Quickly, I gathered him into my arms and took him to the kitchen to get his formula.

As soon as the tears began, I brought his cheek to rest against mine, hoping the contact would calm him down a little.

"Come on, Grey. I know you haven't eaten since this morning."

While his cries became softer, they continued until he had the familiar rubber nipple in his mouth. I heard my own stomach grumble as I fed him. *Well, I suppose the only surprise Trevor is getting tonight is a hot meal.* The book—if the one sketch today did eventually turn into something greater—would have to be a surprise for the distant future. Between work and watching Grey, there was no way I would be getting anything creative done.

"Want to cook some dinner with me? We can make something for your uncle?"

He was too focused on his food to answer me. While I continued to feed him his formula, I walked toward the refrigerator to catch a glimpse of my options. Thankfully, I had made a trip to Safeway the prior day, and my fridge was now full. As Grey finished up his bottle, I decided on the one meal I knew Trevor loved: cheese manicotti. The man loved anything that involved cheese, meat, or carbs. He would tolerate salad, but he wouldn't dig into it like he would a steak. After setting Grey in Harper's old highchair, which Eden had gifted me, I started to get all of my ingredients together.

"You want to watch me cook, Grey?"

He laughed and clapped his hands together, obviously eager to help. After soaking the premade noodles and mixing my various cheeses together in a large bowl, I turned to look at Grey to find him nodding off in his seat. An idea sparked at the sight of him; I scooped a little cheese onto a paper plate for Grey before I grabbed a single noodle for him to work with. As soon as he heard me coming toward him, his eyes fluttered open, and he perked up in his seat.

"Want to help me out?" I questioned as I pulled up a chair beside him and placed the paper plate in front of him.

He squealed, nearly screaming in excitement as he reached for the glob of cheese in front of him. His body wiggled back and forth in his chair as he shook with energy. I smiled. It was just too adorable to watch him nearly passed out one second and filled with energy the next. Before he could get into too much trouble, I abandoned my seat, stood up, and took hold of his little arms to guide his movements.

"Like this, Grey," I said as I helped him grab a bit of cheese to place on the noodle.

Of course, with Grey's excited, little body, it was hard to get him to do anything the proper way. He threw the cheese down and loudly giggled before he began to smash it onto the noodle. His laugh was infectious, and it didn't take long for me to begin laughing, too. My eyes watered, and I laughed so hard, my stomach began to cramp. He was slamming his hands down on the ingredients, which caused them to fly everywhere. Cheese hit him in the face, and he laughed even harder as tears streamed down his chubby cheeks.

"Is that fun, baby?"

He squealed out another laugh before the hiccups began. Pulling him out of his highchair, I wiped him off with a towel before gently patting his back as I attempted to release some of the trapped air. I felt his hiccups against my neck and continued to rub and pat his back until they dissipated.

"Let's get you cleaned up. Then, I have to finish dinner for your uncle."

A knock on the door sounded just as I finished setting the table. I took off my apron before I picked up Grey, both of us eager to see the man who had just arrived. I opened the door to find an exhausted-looking Trevor. It was obvious that a day of work under the unforgiving sun had taken it out of him. For a moment, I worried he would just take Grey and return to his apartment, but the smile that appeared on his face as soon as he smelled the dinner quickly calmed my nerves.

"You didn't have to cook again, Ronnie. I could've done something," he said, although, it was obvious he was grateful.

"I wanted to. It's nice to have someone to cook for. I'm so used to cooking for myself all of the time, and like I said before, cooking for one can become pretty sad. Well, I guess I liked having all of those leftovers," I teased as I ushered Trevor back to the kitchen. "Now, I have you to feed, and I never have to worry about wrapping anything up."

"Well, you're a damn good cook." He cursed under his breath and ran a hand through his unruly hair. "Sorry, I meant to say you're really good. A real good cook."

I blushed. There was nothing like seeing a man like Trevor flustered. Trevor looked almost childlike as he appeared remorseful for his small slip. I wasn't sure why he felt like he couldn't curse around me. *Maybe it's a female thing?* While I didn't curse much, I never cringed at the sound of other people doing so. In fact, I found it sexy when he did it. I found *everything* sexy when he did it. One word in his coarse, deep voice would cause me to melt.

"Thanks, Trev. I've been cooking for a long damn time." I winked.

Trevor relaxed and grinned at me. As soon as we were seated, he quickly grabbed a plate and shoveled a load of food on it as if he were experiencing tunnel vision. The way to a man's heart was through his stomach, I supposed. I took a seat across from him and placed Grey comfortably in my borrowed highchair. His dinner was humble compared to ours—consisting of pureed sweet potatoes and formula—but he ate with the same zealousness. While assisting Grey, I attempted to put together my own plate. While doing so, I heard a remorseful sigh from across the table.

"Shit, Ronnie, I'm sorry. I'm so damn tired I wasn't thinking. I can do that for you."

Trevor gave me a regretful smile and reached for my plate, helping me. I hadn't noticed how *spent* he looked until now. It appeared his exhaustion stemmed from more than the events of today; his exhaustion was more than a physical one—it was an emotional one, too. Despite the dark, swollen circles under his eyes, he was still intensely handsome. I couldn't imagine what all of this was like for him—working full-time while trying to keep his life from falling apart.

I would bet he didn't get much sleep anymore. If it would help things, he could stay over here with the baby … *God, no, Veronica! What are you thinking? He's not going to want to do that. Would he?* It was doubtful I would ever find out because I knew I wouldn't have the courage to ask him. Heaven knew I wasn't bold enough, and even if I *was*, I wasn't sure asking him to practically move in with me after being his friend for a few weeks was a wise move. I was sure it crossed many, *many* lines.

"Here you go," Trevor said as he passed the plate back across the table to me. "Work really took it out of me today. I'm usually not so rude."

"It's okay. You're allowed to be tired."

"I'm just not used to working under the sun, I guess. Hopefully, it won't always be fu—" He paused for a moment as he rolled his eyes at himself. "*Freaking* like this."

"I'm sure it'll get easier," I responded, my voice hopeful.

I studied him for a spell, wondering if my next statement would cause me to come across as needy. I knew he might not want me in *that* way, but I could still use another friend. Outside of my sister, I didn't have many. Due to my extremely introverted nature mixed with the social anxiety, which had developed after college, I always pushed most people away. I couldn't afford to push people away anymore. *Especially men I find attractive.*

"Any time you want to come by for dinner, just let me know. I love having someone to cook for, and it's nice not to have to eat alone." *Gosh, how sad did that sound?*

For a long time, I had enjoyed eating in solitude. When I had worked in an office setting, I loved to be able to come home and unwind with a plate of food and a glass of red wine. Now, however, I worked from home and rarely saw anyone unless I found the desire to actually plan something. So, my dinners became pretty boring. My whole day became very boring, in fact.

Trevor smiled at me, obviously noting the flush that colored my cheeks as I had posed my question.

"I like not having to eat alone, too. As much as I love Grey, he isn't the best when it comes to conversation. Really, outside of my parents, I don't have anyone to really talk to. Well, besides the guys at work. But I don't really hang out with them because I have Grey to care for. So, you're pretty much it." He winced and ran a hand through his hair, which must have been some sort of nervous habit for him. "Shit, that sounded bad, Ronnie. Even if I had loads of people to talk to, I'd still want to be with you above anyone else."

He winced again before he looked resigned and took another bite of his food. I didn't understand why he appeared so uncomfortable. I liked what he had said. It was nice to feel wanted—especially by him.

"So, it's settled, then? You'll join me for dinner more often."

"Heck, Ronnie. We can do this as often as you like. We could do it every day, if you wanted to. But, I don't want to seem like I'm taking advantage of your good nature. You don't have to buy groceries for me and cook for me and all that stuff. If anything, *I* should be buying everything."

"Why's that?" I asked confused.

"Well, I don't know … I just feel like, as a guy, I should be doing this shit for you," he said with a wave of his hand, obviously giving up on the whole "no cursing in front of Veronica" thing.

"Trev, I've been taking care of myself for a long time. I don't need a man to waltz into my life and do things for me," I said with a teasing smile.

Despite my light tone, I did hate the idea of a man doing things for me while I was willing and able to do them myself. I didn't like to rely on anyone. The only thing I had learned in life so far was this: if you needed someone to rely on, rely on yourself; you never knew when the time would come when yourself was all you had.

"Well, I want to do things for you." He paused for a moment, leaning back in his chair as he studied me. "Why don't you let me cook some nights? Or at least let me order takeout or something? I don't want to feel like I'm not contributing."

I smiled at his persistence. "That's perfect." Suddenly, I felt more optimistic than I had in a while. Now, I would have someone to talk to about my day—someone to share bits of my life with. *Perfect.*

"So, how was he today? I hope he didn't give you too much trouble. I figured he can't be too fussy because I know my mother wouldn't take care of him if he was."

"He's not fussy," I agreed. "In fact, we had a great time together."

"That's nice to hear. I know he can give my mom a hard time sometimes. But then again, everything pisses her off," he replied bitterly.

Who could possibly get pissed off by such an adorable baby? I thought. As much as I wondered about Trevor's mother, I knew it was probably inappropriate for me to ask. Whenever he mentioned her, his entire body tensed as if he were awaiting a blow. There was something that made his mother a touchy subject for him; I respected him enough to not press him. I didn't want to make him uncomfortable. He had enough going on in his life already—I didn't have to poke at subjects he obviously wanted to avoid.

"Grey is always lovely for me."

Trevor smiled at this and took a sip of his Coke. "That's just because he likes you so damn much. Honestly, I think you're the only person he ever really has eyes for."

Giggling, I responded, "What are you talking about? He stares at you like you're his entire world."

"Well, I'm not as pleasing to look at, I guess. Who would want to look at me when they could be looking at you?"

I liked looking at him. I could look at him all day.

"I don't know about that." I blushed.

"Well, Grey knows apparently."

Ten o'clock hit before we had realized how late it was. When I talked to Trevor, everything else escaped me. It was like the world paused when he was around. When he spoke, I forgot about the future, and I forgot about the past—heavens, I forgot about the present, too—as I became absorbed by him. He had become my closest friend so quickly. Everything with Trevor was easy. It was as if I had known him my entire life. Maybe that was why I felt so relaxed around him. If I were placed in this situation with any other man, I would have been filled with anxiety. With Trevor, things were different. With Trevor, I felt calm.

As he left to go back to his apartment, I was sad to see him go. Everything felt so empty without him. I almost laughed at the thought, remembering a time when I would be thrilled to return to my solitude. I had never felt lonely before. With Trevor in my life, I didn't want to look at its emptiness. Without Grey's laughter and Trevor's sarcastic comments and foul language, I felt bored here. I gave them both a quick hug goodbye, wrapping my arms around Trevor longer than I probably should have.

He felt so warm. I nearly melted against the strong muscles of his chest. It had been a long time since I felt a man's arms around me. Closing my eyes for a moment, I took in his musky scent and smiled at the wave of comfort it brought. *I want him to hold me like this forever. I want him to never let me go.* His hand moved up and down my back in a friendly gesture as his other arm was occupied with holding Grey, who was now playing with the curls of my hair. *This is bliss.*

"Goodnight, Ronnie," he murmured as he pulled away from me.

"'Night, Trev."

As he left, I knew this would be our first of many nights together.

8

If I Ever Was A Child

"Trev, why don't you just let me pick something up?"

"Why? Was it really that bad the other night?"

I bit down on my lip as I tried desperately not to laugh. Trevor had wanted to contribute to our routine dinners and had nearly set his apartment on fire in the process. I had never seen someone burn garlic bread before, but my lips had been sealed as I helped him calm the flames. Grey had had fun, at least; he had been fascinated by the flames as he had sat a safe distance away from the oven in his highchair. He hadn't been able to stop giggling at his uncle, who had been frantic. As Grey had tried to jump out of his highchair to "aid" his uncle, I had taken him in my arms and held him far away from the disaster. We had ended up getting a cheese pizza, and Trevor even attempted to eat the garlic bread after scrapping off the burnt parts, which basically were the entire piece of bread. After that ordeal, I had not been too keen on the idea of Trevor cooking *anything*.

"Trev, it wasn't *that* bad. I've just been craving Chinese food."

"Okay," he said unconvincingly. There was a silence over the phone before he continued. "I'll see you tonight, Ronnie. You know this is basically the highlight of my day? Work kicks my ass every day, and all I can think about is seeing you." There was another awkward pause before he spit out, "And Grey, of course. I just think about seeing him, too, when I'm here."

I smiled at his obvious discomfort, stifling a laugh as I heard him fumble through his words. *Maybe he did really like me more than he let on. Heavens, I can only hope.* While I loved being his friend, part of me craved something more. Besides the one hug we had shared, we haven't had any other intimate contact. I wanted to initiate it, but I didn't know where to begin. The only man I had ever shared anything with had used and abused me. Now, I didn't know which way was up when it came to love. *Romantic love… something I have always wanted but never received.* I frowned at the thought. *Maybe I could talk to Eden?*

"I understand what you mean," I finally said, hoping to ease his discomfort. "Whenever I'm editing, I always think about doing something else. It's so easy for my mind to drift. Sorry, I'm rambling. Shouldn't you be getting back to work?"

I heard him laugh.

"Yeah, I suppose so. Good luck with your work."

"You, too."

We paused for a moment, not knowing what else to say. Whenever we talked on the phone, there was always this awkward pause at the end where we both searched for the right words to say goodbye. It would have been far easier if he were more than a friend; this uncomfortable silence seemed to kill us both.

"See you tonight," I finally decided on.

"Tonight," he confirmed before we ended the call.

I leaned back against my couch cushions with a sigh. I wished I knew what I was doing when it came to Trevor. During moments like these, I hated being single. I wished I could be in a relationship, so all of this initial awkwardness would be long forgotten. While the "getting to know you" stage could be exciting, I wanted to skip over it, allowing us to finally be comfortable with each other.

It wasn't as if we weren't comfortable now, per se; we have had moments when we had been so lost in one another, we had forgotten about the uncertain state of our friendship. There was this unspoken question in the air concerning our status. Neither of us was willing to acknowledge its existence, which only made it more uncomfortable. When we were lost in these moments, and had forgotten about everything else, I saw the potential we had together. His calming presence, his rich, enthralling voice, and his dark eyes, which truly saw *me*, caused me to wonder why I didn't just snatch him up before another woman found him.

The day I summon the courage will be a shock to everyone— including myself. Maybe I should text Eden?

While Eden had once "helped" me with my love life, she hadn't involved herself recently. She had backed off of the topic a while ago, understanding how sensitive it was for me. I knew it had made her unhappy, and although she had tried desperately to hide it, I saw pity swimming in her eyes at times. She had worried for me in a way only an older sister could. Before I had the chance to overthink things and stop myself, I reached for my phone and called my sister. Eden being Eden, she answered on the second ring.

"Ronnie? Is something wrong? You never call me!"

I rolled my eyes. I had called her plenty of times. *Hadn't I?*

"You know that isn't true. I've called you before."

"You *text*," she clarified. "You treat phone calls like they're some sort of plague. So, what's up? It has to be something good if you're willing to speak to me via phone."

And this *is why I don't call you, Eden.*

"Nothing is up. I just wanted to talk to my sister."

"Bullshit."

Seriously?

"You called me for a reason. So, spit it out," she continued with her usual snippy, yet loving, voice.

I rolled my eyes again as I soaked up her teasing. Ever since we were children, she had been like this. One would think I would have been used to it by now.

"I just wanted to ask for your advice on something."

"Truly? You're coming to me for advice?" She giggled, and I sunk in my seat, feeling embarrassed already.

"*Eden*, I've asked you for advice before."

"I know, I know," she said.

I heard Harper in the background, obviously nearing the phone.

"Auntie? Is Auntie?" I heard Harper scream before her mother laughed.

"Yep, it's your Auntie Ronnie. Want to say hi to her?"

"Gimme!" I heard her respond before there was a rustling sound caused by the phone being transferred from one hand to a more excited one.

"Auntie!" she squealed, which caused me to flinch as my eardrum rang. "Miss you!"

"I miss you, too, Harper. But, I just saw you two days ago. You miss me already?"

"Yeah! Miss you. Day you come?"

"No, I don't think I can today, sweetie. I have lots of work to do."

"No fun."

"I know, I know. But maybe I can come over tomorrow, okay?"

"'Kay!" she responded, her voice perking right up.

"Can you give me back to your mom, please?"

"'Kay! Love you."

"I love you, too, sweetheart. Now let me talk to your mom, Harper."

I heard a rustling again before Eden's voice sounded over the phone.

"She's always so excited to hear from you, Ronnie. I honestly believe she likes you more than anyone else with the way she follows you around all of the time and aspires to be just like you."

"I like her a lot, too. Besides, it's nice having a little mini-me."

"Well, you've always been good with kids." She paused for a moment before she laughed and said, "Look at us. Here I am, the girl who swore she never wanted kids because she had always been terrible with them, and now I have a little girl. And you, the girl who kids love—" She stopped, obviously realizing the awkwardness that would come if she finished her train of thought. "Sorry. Anyway, why did you call?"

I was so sidetracked by her comment I almost forgot my reason. She was right—I had always believed I would have a house filled with children one day; I had always imagined when I hit twenty-five, I would be married and pregnant. But life had happened. Life had happened, and I had thrown all my old dreams away. For a long time, I had been happy if I had only managed to get through the day.

"Ronnie?"

Shaking those thoughts from my mind, I quickly responded. "Sorry. I just called because I wanted to ask you about ..." *God, am I really going to do this?* "I wanted to ask you about a friend I have."

"A new friend?" she questioned, her interest peaked.

"Yes. He's a new friend."

I could practically feel her smiling. I could imagine her face so clearly in my mind: her left eyebrow raised with interest, and her lips perked with a contented grin.

"*He's* a new friend. How new? Why haven't you mentioned him before? You haven't been holding out on me, have you?"

"I haven't been holding out on you," I responded with a frustrated sigh. "Well, not really. Trevor and I haven't known each other very long. We've only been friends for a matter of weeks." I found myself smiling as I began to talk about him; all of my frustrations were gone as soon as his image entered my mind.

"Trevor? What's he like? I can't believe you haven't mentioned him until now!"

"What's to talk about? He's only a man," I said unconvincingly.

He's so much more than that.

"He doesn't sound like he's 'only a man,' " she teased. "Ronnie, do you hear yourself right now?"

"What do you mean?"

"What do you mean, 'what do you mean'? I've never heard someone sound so breathless while mentioning someone's name."

I flushed. "I don't sound breathless."

"Whatever you say, little sister." She paused for a moment, and I could tell she was trying to pull herself together. "All teasing aside, what did you need advice on?"

With my cheeks burning, I wondered if I should continue. As embarrassing as this may have been, it felt nice to talk to someone about Trevor. However, I had my reservations. *What if things don't work out with Trevor like I had hoped? What if he doesn't return my sentiment?* I would have to face my sister; I know I would feel so incredibly embarrassed. I felt embarrassed now just thinking about it. I *thought* Trevor had feelings for me, but I couldn't be entirely sure. Sometimes, when he looked at me with those dark eyes sparkling intensely, I swore he felt something. *Something ... anything ... I'm sure his heart responded to mine.*

"Well, I don't know ..." I trailed off, filled with conflict. *Am I really about to admit my feelings for him out loud?* "I just think ... Well, I think I like him."

I imagined my sister's eyes widening before she broke into a smile, satisfied by my response. I couldn't remember the last time I had talked about boys with her. It may have been before I went off to college, when I had still been hopeful, and life had yet to make me too jaded. When I had first talked about dating with her, I had admitted I felt as if I had been venturing into the unknown. Funnily enough, I felt the same way now. With Trevor, everything felt new; I had never felt this way about anyone. With him in my life, I felt like I had fallen down the rabbit hole—faced with so many new and exciting emotions and experiences. Even touching myself felt like something brand new.

"You *think* you like him? It seems like you know. You *are* telling me, after all."

"Well, we're just friends."

"*But*," she insisted.

I could hear the smile in her voice.

"*But*, I like him. I don't know, Eden. He makes me feel ... different, I guess. Since meeting him, I just feel so different." Tears filled my eyes before I could stop them. *Why are you getting so emotional about this, Veronica?* Blinking back tears, I took a deep breath as I realized these tears were happy ones. My eyes closed for a moment, and I saw him in my mind so clearly, as if he were standing right in front of me.

"*Ronnie*," she started, allowing me to hear the tears in her voice, too. "Sweetie, that's so great! I'm so happy for you!"

"Eden, he doesn't even know I like him yet. What's there to be happy about?"

"Well, you've found someone. Isn't that something to celebrate?"

"I guess you're right."

You've found someone. I loved the way that sounded. It made me feel like I wasn't alone in this world anymore. I wished he had ventured into my life sooner. He could have saved me from so much damage—so much hurt. Nevertheless, I was happy he was here now. And, maybe if I were lucky, he would really be mine someday. I smiled, feeling giddy. Suddenly, I felt connected with the heroines in the countless romance novels I read. I felt the same joy, disbelief, and apprehension they had felt when they had found "the one."

Is Trevor my "one"? Is it too early to tell?

As I considered my romance novels again, I found the answer was *no*. While those were works of fiction, and this was something real, I knew, deep in my gut, it wasn't too soon. *Once you know, you just* know. Even before I knew, I seemed to *feel* it somehow. From my very first glimpse of Trevor—just a *glimpse*—I had known he would play a pivotal role in my life.

"He's not looking for a relationship, Eden. A relationship seems to be the last thing he needs. And I—I don't know. I *feel* ready. But, am I *really*? I don't know if I could go there again. I don't know if I could give myself to someone else—"

"You don't have to give yourself to anyone, Ronnie. That's not what love is about."

"Isn't it? Giving your heart to someone? If that's not love, what is?"

"You shouldn't lose part of yourself. When you find the right person, you won't have to give any part of yourself away—you won't have to change for them. When you love someone, everything becomes an equal balance. Sure, you'll have to make sacrifices, and every day won't be beautiful, but when it's all said and done, you'll be able to find beauty in that person. It's about supporting each other; it's about respecting each other; it's not about giving a part of yourself to them to never get back. You did that before, Ronnie. You shouldn't have to do that again."

That part I gave away ... I could never get that back. *Never.* No matter how much I wanted it—no matter how much I felt its absence—that part of my heart would always be missing. For years, it had ached, but now, for the first time, I felt growth. Despite the tiny piece of myself that was missing, creating an empty spot that would forever feel soiled to me, I felt myself healing. Soon, I might forget about the absence entirely.

Falling for someone was scary. Falling meant I had to let go of the small control I had; I had to let go of *myself.* Falling was as freeing as it was frightening. Right now, I felt like I was hanging onto a precipice, too afraid to let go. I didn't fully understand my fear—it was almost as if I were fearful of being happy. There was no denying Trevor made me happy, but would I be able to hold onto happiness forever? *What would happen to me if that happiness faded away one day?* I didn't know if I could go on living through another heartbreak.

"Ronnie, give him a chance," Eden continued as if she were reading my thoughts. When I didn't respond, she continued. "He must be a good man. I can tell by the sound of your voice when you talk about him. Why not let him in? Why not allow yourself to be happy?"

She posed a good question—the question I kept asking myself. *What was so scary about being happy? Why should joy bring such fear?*

"Eden ... I don't even know where to begin. Neither of us seem ready, and I—"

"No excuses, little sister. You know him, so I'm sure you have *some* idea where to begin."

As sad as it sounded, I didn't. Sure, I was his friend, but I had no idea how to flirt. I couldn't remember the last time I tried to win over a man's heart. Sure, I may have come across as flirty at times, but I knew if I *tried* to appear coy and flirtatious, I would only look foolish. I stifled a groan, not wanting my sister to understand how inexperienced I truly was.

"Eden ... I just don't know," I muttered as my cheeks flushed, and I itched to end the call.

"You don't know if you want to be with him?" she questioned, her voice tinted with sadness.

"No, I just don't know—" I stopped as I felt my entire body turn a pale rose. "I just don't know how to show him I'm interested."

"Are you asking me how to flirt with a man?" I heard the smile in my sister's voice.

"No! I was just asking." I paused, wishing now I hadn't started this conversation. Taking a deep breath, I paused to gain a little courage before I continued. "I'm just asking how you think I should go about it? He's not one to talk about his feelings, and neither am I."

"He's shy, then?"

"Not shy ... He's just a little self-conscious, I guess. He doesn't like himself very much, and I don't think he has the confidence to say anything to me. I don't know why. He's an amazing person. He just doesn't see it."

"Has he had issues—"

"He's had a rough past, just like me," I replied, cutting her off.

She was silent for a moment, deliberating before she responded. "Have you thought about making him jealous?"

"Why would I do that?" I asked perplexed.

"Well, if he feels threatened by another man, maybe he'll make a move. God knows you're not great about discussing your feelings, either. You two must be made for each other."

"Make him jealous …" I deliberated. "Are you sure that will work?"

"Well, I can't be sure—I've never met him—but if a man likes you, he's not going to want another man to make any moves on you. If he's thought about dating you, I'm sure the threat will cause him to spring into action."

"I don't know, Eden. I don't want to cause a rift between us."

"Well, just think about it. You don't have to do it if you think it's not the right move. I haven't met him, so I can't be sure about what's right for you both."

"I'll think about it." By just talking to my sister, I felt a weight lifted off of my shoulders. "Thanks, Edie."

"Love you, baby sis. Good luck."

Luck. One thing I would need copious amounts of.

Heavens, am I really going to do this?

I stared at his door as I contemplated my next move. I wanted to make him feel a *little* jealous, but now I wondered if that was a good plan. I didn't desire to hurt him, but what if that was the outcome? I didn't want him to believe I would even consider someone else.

Heck, he doesn't even know I'm considering him. *Deep breaths, Veronica. Deep breaths. You can do this! Step one: summon the courage to knock on his door so you're not standing here like an idiot all night. Step two: convince him you have a date. There! That's not so hard! Make him a little jealous, and he'll do all the work.*

Despite my mental pep talk, I remained immobile at his doorstep. *Veronica! You're being ridiculous! Even if he doesn't want you the way you want him, you're still friends! And friends hang out and do things together. It's not as if you're out of line.* Without allowing myself another second of contemplation, I forwent knocking on his door and merely let myself in. I stopped in my tracks as soon as I saw him. Now that I had my little "plan," I felt strange around him—almost skittish. I felt disingenuous, and I hated it. I knew I should have been going about this the right way, but instead, I was manipulating him into admitting his true feelings. *If he has feelings to admit to.* As much as I hated not being honest, a small part of me enjoyed calculating like this. If it worked, I would have everything I wanted, and if it didn't, I would still have my pride.

Putting on my brave face, I made my way toward the living room where he sat on the couch with Grey in his arms. His eyes lit up as soon as he saw the bag of food in my hands. As he gazed at it, Grey became jealous of the attention, which was no longer directed at him, so he reached up for his uncle's chin, pulling Trevor's face back toward his direction.

"You look like you're starving," I commented.

Trevor grimaced before his eyes became animated, and he shifted in his seat. He nodded and rose from the couch with Grey safely in his embrace. Giving me a small smile, he walked toward the kitchen. He was gone for a moment, and then rushed back into the living room with drinks, paper plates, and plastic utensils balanced haphazardly in his right palm. He was obviously ready to eat.

I noticed how young he looked when he was content—how carefree he seemed. I loved the moments when the rest of the world seemed to fade away, and he had the chance to enjoy life and act his age. *He's so gorgeous in his exuberance.* These moments seemed to be coming more frequently now, although, he still had his bouts of sadness—just like I did. Tonight, he was all smiles. Despite the look of uncertainty in his eyes, he seemed blissful. When he was like this, I realized how *young* he was.

At twenty-four-years old, he had already experienced so much. So many men his age still acted as if they were teenagers, but not Trevor. He had the weight of the world on his shoulders and carried it so well. So well, in fact, I wondered how he did it. Heavens knew I never handled anything with grace. I worked myself into a dark place—but not Trevor. I didn't know where he found his strength, but I was so impressed I would give anything to make that strength my own.

Observing him as he dug into his meal with a boyish grin, I wondered how he could possibly doubt himself the way he did. Did he not realize how well he was doing? Was his perception truly so warped? As I viewed him, I wondered how people viewed me. I wondered how *Trevor* viewed me. I wished for the chance to get inside of his head for a moment. *Just a moment.* I was always so curious as to what was going on in that gorgeous mind of his.

Right now, he stared off into space, abnormally quiet as we ate. He seemed to be having a moment, like my mother would say whenever I had spaced out for long periods of time. Grey grew bored in his lap and frowned at his uncle, wiggling around before giving up and reaching for a handful of rice. Quickly, I shooed his little hand away; my movement escaped Trevor's notice completely.

"Trev?"

He didn't answer; his eyes were still glossed over as he stared off into space. I nudged him, finally gaining his attention.

"What has you so lost in thought?"

He rewarded me with a soft smile, looking almost bashful as he looked down at his takeout.

"It's nothing."

He shrugged, and I knew instantly he was lying. However, I didn't plan on pushing him. I would never do that. If it were important, he would tell me. He looked down at the baby on his lap, and his shy smile transformed into a proud grin.

"Grey stood up today," he told me, changing the subject. "He pulled himself up off the floor and stood up for a few seconds before falling right back down on his ass."

The mental image of Grey's accomplishment filled my mind, and I giggled. *He's standing already?* Soon, he would be walking and talking and mirroring his uncle—his hero—everywhere he went.

"That's amazing, Trev! Maybe he'll do it for me later? That's so impressive!"

Trevor's grin widened, and he sat a little bit straighter in his seat. My heart melted as I looked at him: the picture of a proud father.

"I think he's been afraid of trying to do it since he fell," he explained as he smiled down at the little boy on his lap. "But, I'm sure he'll forget all about that and try again soon enough." He paused, choked on a laugh, and ran a shaky hand through his hair before he continued. "Hey, I wanted to ask you about something coming up next month …" He stopped, obviously feeling slightly unsure. So, I perked up in my seat, wanting to look as engaged as possible so he would feel encouraged to continue. He took a deep, shaky breath before he said, "It's my mother's birthday the thirteenth, and she's having this big party, and I was wondering if you'd like to go with me? I just don't want to go alone, you know? All my parents' friends will be hounding me all night if I'm by myself."

He grimaced, and I stifled a laugh. I more than understood where he was coming from. I understood the pressure of putting on airs for family and friends. I had always felt like I had to appear as successful and well-rounded as possible. Anything less had caused me to feel like I was an embarrassment.

"I really want you with me, Ronnie. It'll be hell without you."

I took him in for a moment, gazing at his wide-open expression, dark eyes, inked skin, and jagged scars. The fact that he feared something almost seemed comical as I studied him. He looked like the type of man who faced fear head on; so, it was interesting to consider he may have needed some help. I was more than happy to support him. Besides, any night I spent with Trevor was amazing. His presence alone had the power to make any day outstanding. I had never told him as much, but perhaps someday, I would. *You'll have to express your feelings, first, Veronica. And so far, you're too chicken to do that.*

"I'll go with you, Trev. Don't sweat it."

He grinned, and Grey giggled in his arms, obviously feeling his uncle's relaxation and enjoying the shift in mood.

"Is Grey coming with us?"

Trevor smirked at my question. "Yeah. I think my mother will want the chance to show him off to her friends."

Interesting. I would love to meet his mother. I would love to be able to understand why he tensed up every time he mentioned her.

"Well, I'm sure we're in for a fun night."

Trevor rolled his eyes and smiled at me before he took another bite of his food. I watched Grey as he struggled to grab a bite of his uncle's meal despite having a bottle of formula not too long ago. As I studied the pair, I felt my phone buzzing in my pocket; I could easily guess who was trying to reach me without even looking at the name on my phone. I slid my phone out of my pocket before I swiped to unlock the screen, displaying a message from my lovingly persistent sister.

Did it work? Details, Ronnie! I need details!

I suppressed an eye roll as I placed my phone face down on the couch. *Thanks for stirring my nerves up, sis. I wasn't nervous enough before. Now, I don't want to utter a word.* Trevor gave me a curious look as my mind worked quickly to come up with something smooth to say to him. Of course, his dark eyes made me breathless, making it almost impossible to focus. When he looked at me, my mind became consumed by him. *Which was why I'm surprised that I don't constantly embarrass myself around him.* My words could easily turn to gibberish if he kept staring at me in this manner.

"What is it?" he asked as his gaze dropped to my phone.

"It's nothing," I responded dismissively, still unsure about my next move concerning him.

However, as soon as his gaze captured mine, all of my uncertainty was tossed out the window. *Screw it!*

"It's just my sister, Eden," I finally replied. "She thinks she's a matchmaker. I love her, but sometimes she drives me crazy. She thinks since she's older, she should try to help me out. But sometimes, I wish she'd just take a hint and back off."

I knew Eden would have gotten a kick out of that if she would have been able to hear it. As I captured Trevor's gaze, I noticed the concern in his eyes. Concern and confusion and ... *jealously*? Or had that been merely wishful thinking on my part? His nostrils flared, and his chest expanded as he considered my words.

"What do you mean by matchmaker?" he asked in a rough voice.

A smile tugged on my lips as I heard nervousness lace his tone.

"Eden's trying to set me up on a blind date with one of her friends," I lied.

His nostrils flared again, and my eyes fell to his neck as his jugular vein twitched. I hid my smile and tried desperately not to look too satisfied with myself. *Look what you've become, Veronica. Look what you've become.*

"I tried telling her I didn't feel comfortable with a blind date. I wouldn't be *so* opposed if it were with an acquaintance. But if things go sour between me and one of her friends, it's going to be awkward."

I could feel Trevor's agitation as he sat next to me. He felt filled with energy as he searched for the right words. Part of me experienced remorse for making him so upset—for getting him so worked up—but another part *enjoyed* seeing him this way. I figured he wouldn't be this emotional if he didn't feel anything more than friendship toward me. If I threatened what was "his"—*am I just dreaming?*—maybe, he would open up to me just as Eden had suggested.

"What are you going to tell your sister?" he asked.

Taking a bite of an eggroll, I contemplated what to say next. I didn't want to push him *too* far; however, this was pretty fun. I had never toyed with a man before, and I found it to be strangely pleasing. Although, my enjoyment was probably due to the fact it was *Trevor* on the receiving end of my teasing.

"I'm just going to tell her to forget about it for now. I'm not really looking to date right now. I just got my career rolling, and I want to ride that wave for a while," I rambled on and on, naming all of my old excuses. "Eden's always been so codependent. She doesn't understand what it's like to actually *enjoy* being alone. She went from being a daddy's girl, to having multiple boyfriends, to finding the right guy and getting hitched at twenty-two. She's freaking out because I'm twenty-five years old and don't even have a boyfriend." *Wow, Veronica. You went*

from coy to a rambling mess. See, this is why you don't flirt with men.
"Sorry, I'm rambling," I apologized, flushing. "I just always feel like I have to defend all of my life choices to her."

I couldn't believe I was expressing all of this out loud. While her insistent behavior concerning my love life had always bothered me, I had never said anything to anyone about it. I teased her, sure, but I had never talked to her seriously about how her judgments really affected me. For a while after she got pregnant with Harper, I had felt like I couldn't relate to her anymore. She had caused me to feel like I had to pretend to be someone else—a different version of her sister.

I had known she loved me and obviously wanted the best for me, but sometimes, I had just wished she would have accepted me for who I was *then*. Thankfully, she had gotten better about how she treated me because, for a long time, I had felt inferior. Not because Eden had purposefully made me feel so low but because I had felt low about myself and seeing her so happy had been difficult.

Trevor's voice pulled me from my thoughts as he said, "It's okay. I like your rambling."

I grinned, forgetting everything else as I focused on him. "Well, that's why you're easily my best friend."

Best friend ... Well, if luck is on my side, he won't be my "best friend" for much longer. If everything goes the way I've dreamt of, he'll become so much more.

9

Time After Time

"You'll never guess what I did."

The devious nature of Eden's tone worried me. Dropping the magazine onto my lap, I looked up at her and as I saw her signature smirk, I knew the next words to come out of her mouth would irk me. Whenever she had adopted this particular look in the past, it had been due to something brewing in that beautifully scheming mind of hers. I watched while the wheels in her head turned as she leaned forward, grinning at me.

Oh, Eden. What on earth have you done, now?

"Why should I guess when you're just going to tell me?" I posed the question, arching my brow at her.

She rolled her emerald eyes and giggled. Obviously, she found whatever it was she was doing very amusing. I doubted I would feel the same.

"Well … You know Quinton's friend, Kace …"

"No."

"Yes, you do," she insisted, leaning forward in her seat even more. "Remember our Christmas party last year?"

What on earth was she talking about?

The only person I had talked to at that party was her. Whenever there was a party, I usually stuck with the people I knew well—never wanting to branch out, fearful of any awkward social interactions. I found small talk to be a bore, and small talk was all you could really engage in with strangers. Despite the love and respect that I had for my sister, I had only been able to stomach that party for an hour before I had to leave. I had been in the middle of a good mystery paperback and had wanted nothing more than to go home and change into my favorite flannel pajamas.

"Did I talk to him?" I asked; although, the prospect seemed *very* unlike me.

"Well, we introduced you two," she explained, almost seeming annoyed by my typical introversion. "Ronnie, you'll like him."

"What do you mean, 'you'll like him'? Is he coming over or something?"

"Well … you know how you wanted to make Trevor jealous?"

She didn't.

"Eden, you have to be kidding," I stated blandly.

"I didn't do anything," she responded, seeming hurt by my lack of enthusiasm. "I just—" She paused, raising her eyebrow as her expression screamed: *Really, bitch? I'm trying to help you, and you're looking at me like I'm the devil.* "I just thought going on a date with a nice man could be just what you need. If Trevor sees that, he'll definitely want to jump in and steal you away before you become someone else's girl."

"I'm *no one's* girl," I muttered beneath my breath.

"What?"

"There's no chance of that happening," I said a bit louder.

"Becoming someone else's girl?"

"No, going on a date to make Trevor jealous," I corrected. "I'm not seriously going to do that. I thought you said we would just mess with him a little. I don't want to drag another person into this."

"Kace wouldn't mind. Besides, he's seen pictures of you and thinks you're really cute. He's been hounding us to hook you two up!"

"So, you thought now was the perfect time to do that? Now, when I'm talking to someone else?"

"You're just *talking* to someone. You're not in a relationship."

"Yet." The word was quiet as it passed through my lips, but my sister had still managed to hear it.

"If you want to make him jealous, Ronnie, I'm giving you the chance."

"I don't want to make him jealous. I don't want to hurt him like that. I just wanted to tease him a little or something. I just wanted him to see what he could have with me. I'm afraid if I dated someone else—I'm just afraid I would hurt his feelings. What if this causes him to be more unsure of himself? What if this plan goes sour? Then what? It'll be even harder to get him to open up," I rambled, feeling frustration spread through my veins like a wild fire.

Eden nodded. Although, my words hadn't seemed to change her mind.

"Think about it. I'll give you Kace's number. Your date is at seven-thirty."

"I won't go," I spat out right away.

"Just think about it, Ronnie. You're allowed to be happy, you know?"

"And I will be—with Trevor."

She smiled at this, reaching across the coffee table to grab hold of my hand.

"I know."

Was I really doing this? Staring at my reflection, I barely recognized myself. My cheeks were flushed, my eyes were dancing, and my body was jittering. Running a hand through my curly mane, I tried to dismiss the need in my body. He would come soon—I knew he would. Whenever he was nearby, it was almost as if I could *feel* him. My hands dropped from my hair and made their descent, running along the lines of my curves before they rose to play with my breasts.

A smile tugged on my lips as I enjoyed this newfound peace. I watched my reflection as my hands wandered over the planes of my body again. Transfixed, I watched my slim fingers pluck my nipples until they were hard against the silk of my robe. Biting down on my lip, I suppressed a moan as my hands moved of their own accord, traveling down my body and between my legs.

A knock on the door caused my hands to halt. *Shoot!* Flushing, I pulled my robe tightly together and made sure I was fully covered as I left my bedroom to answer the door. I hadn't texted Kace, but knowing my sister, she was perfectly capable of giving him my address; although, I doubted she would cross a boundary like that. I knew I needed to text him soon to cancel our date so he wouldn't show up at the restaurant to find a vacant table.

I hoped he wouldn't take my declination personally. It was just a blind date, after all. I took a final look at myself in my hallway mirror, noting my eyes were still bright and excited, and my nipples were still straining against my robe. I covered my breasts with my hands for a moment, hoping the warmth of my palms would tame them. Another knock sounded, and I quickly pulled myself together before I moved to answer it.

I swung the door open and found an absolutely sinful-looking Trevor with a determined look in his nearly pitch-black eyes. The determination quickly faltered as he took in my apprehensive expression. Despite my efforts to appear coy, I was certain I looked bewildered. Taking a deep breath, I tried to control my façade, wanting to appear desirable without seeming stilted.

Finding the lustful look in my neighbor's eyes, I realized I didn't have to work at all—one amorous look and I knew, deep down, he was already mine. His eyes were glued to my breasts and remained there for a long pause before they snapped to meet my gaze. He looked remorseful, and I smiled, feeling sexy suddenly.

"I brought you that coffee drink you like," Trevor said, breaking the silence between us.

Look, he's being all thoughtful, and you're going to go and ruin his day, my conscience reprimanded me as I tried not to cringe. *Well, it won't ruin his day if he steps up to the plate and admits he has feelings for me.* If he had feelings for me, tonight would be special. If he didn't, then we would both be on the same page and I would know it would have to keep things strictly platonic between us.

If the one man I want thrusting between my thighs doesn't want me, I don't know what I'll do.

The thought caused an amalgam of images to play in my mind—all involving a very sweaty, very naked, Trevor.

His mouth on my lips, my breasts, my legs ... My hands running through his soft, unruly hair. His cock teasing my entrance, begging for some friction and release.

My mind floated back to reality as I met Grey's gaze, finding him posed comfortably in his uncle's arms. My cheeks burned as I realized I had been lusting after his uncle while his eyes were glued on me.

"Thanks, Trev," I replied as I wondered how I should go about this "flirting" business.

"Ronnie, what is it?"

The seriousness in his velvet voice made me tremble. I loved when he talked to me like this. His broad shoulders grew stiff, his already massive chest seemed to expand, and his tall body loomed over mine. If we'd been alone, I would have wanted him to slip off my robe and make love to me on the floor of my entranceway. However, that was not what I had planned for tonight; despite my yearning for him, I didn't know if I would be ready for *that*.

I looked away for a moment, not allowing his dark eyes to distract me from the matter at hand. Tonight, I would make him jealous, hoping it would cause him to notice any sort of romantic feelings brewing inside of him. Sometimes, men needed a little push in the right direction. While Trevor was both smart and capable, he seemed to need guidance from a woman. *A woman like me.*

"I let Eden talk me into a date, tonight," I admitted to him, trying not to squirm under his scrutinizing gaze.

His brows knitted together while his muscular body tensed as if he were receiving a physical blow. My teeth came down on my bottom lip, biting to restrain myself from telling him anything more. I stayed silent as he deliberated what to do next, obviously beside himself.

"And you want to go? I thought you were opposed to the whole 'blind date' thing?"

"I am," I admitted with a pout as I stepped aside to let him and Grey into my apartment.

This is it, Veronica. Make him jealous. Get him going. Soon, he'll be the one you're going on a date with. I felt his eyes roam my body as he followed me into my apartment, diligently moving behind me as I led him to my bedroom—the one room he had never been in.

"Eden just has a way of talking you into things," I continued as I entered the room and turned to Trevor.

His eyes were trained on my bed for a moment before they ventured around my room, appraising my desk, bookshelves, and the piles of my favorite novels stacked haphazardly on my floor. I felt his gaze drilling into me again as I walked into my closet and out of his view.

"I should've told her no," I continued as I stripped out of my robe and pulled on the first "revealing" dress I could find. "But she was just so persistent and guilted me into it."

I smoothed the tight dress over my curves before I made my way back into my connecting bedroom. Trevor's eyes lit up as he drank in the sight of me. It took all of my strength not to smile.

"Does this look okay?" I asked, forcing myself to sound unsure.

Who are you kidding? You are *unsure!*

He gave me a leisurely once-over, and I felt my skin burn under his scrutiny. His heated gaze sparked with a fire. He looked angry, which caused my body to respond even more. *He was jealous.* I could feel the emotion oozing out of his every pore as he tried to contain himself. Grey became distressed in his uncle's arms as Trevor remained stilted.

"I don't like that dress," he responded, his tone clipped.

What man doesn't like a skin-tight dress? I stared at him in utter confusion before I realized why he was being so harsh. *He was jealous. Trevor Warren was* really *jealous.* I bit down on my lip as I suppressed a joyous smile. *Don't smile, Veronica! He'll know what's up the second your lip quivers.*

Crossing my arms over my chest, accentuating my breasts for him to regard, I questioned, "What's wrong with it? It's just a navy dress."

"It's too ..." He trailed off, running a nervous hand through his hair. "It's just too *much*. Maybe you can put a sweater on over it?"

"It's not even fall yet," I admonished, giving him a dubious look. "It's not that cold out, Trev."

"Well, this is your first date, and you don't want to give the guy the wrong idea."

God, I hate when men say stuff like this. I believed no man should go on a date expecting *anything* physical. *Just because a man bought me dinner didn't mean he should expect a sexual favor from me.* Expectations such as these were the reason I avoided dates like the plague. After what had happened to me in the past, the last thing I needed was feeling pressured into sex by a man. Just the *thought* of this line of thinking caused me to fume.

"What 'wrong idea' would I be giving him, Trevor?"

His eyes widened at my sharp tone before he settled down and a smile tugged on his lips. "Well, if you don't want him to expect to come home with you, maybe you should wear something more conservative."

"Wear something more conservative"? In this day and age, I can wear whatever I want.

Fashion may have been viewed as a reflection of who we were as people, but a "reflection" was all it was. One shouldn't conjecture based on a mere glimpse of another's wardrobe. Unfortunately, I had realized a long time ago that it didn't matter what a person wore; it didn't matter whether they dressed conservatively or otherwise. If someone wanted something from another person, they would get it, regardless of a "provocation" on the other person's part.

It wasn't your fault. It wasn't your fault. It wasn't your fault. God, Ronnie. Snap out of this! You don't want to do this in front of Trevor. You don't want to have these thoughts in front of him. Not yet. You're not ready to open up yet.

When what had happened to me, *happened*, I had been wearing a sweater. A sweater that I had thrown away shortly after. Its pattern was still sketched into my brain as if it were a part of my everyday wardrobe: Antique Cream and blush with a Fair Isle design.

"Are you sure she doesn't feel this?"

"Dude, what the fuck do you think? She's fine. Stop whining so goddamn much. This was partly your idea, after all. You ... and your dickhead friend who was too 'squeamish.' "

The memory ached. I hated when they crept up on me. The voices were so vivid it caused everything to feel real all over again. *That sweater ... that damned sweater.*

"What a typical 'man' thing to say!" I exploded as I pushed the unpleasant thoughts from my mind and focused on the present. Taking a step forward, I placed my hands on my hips and continued my rant, "Men shouldn't expect anything on a date, regardless of what the woman wears. We don't owe a man sex just because he decided to buy us dinner."

"I'm not saying that," he quickly defended. He looked down at his nephew to find him peering up with wide, curious eyes as he regarded our conversation. "All I'm saying is this guy could be an asshole." He sighed as he brought his nephew up to rest on his shoulder. "And as an asshole, he could expect stuff like that. You don't know him. As you said earlier, it's a blind date."

The man had a point. I hadn't been able to handle a "normal" date, so I don't know how I could stomach a blind one.

"Well, he's probably not an asshole if he's friends with my sister," I finally decided on saying, wanting to spike his jealously as I headed into the closet to slip out of one dress and into another.

Finding a dress even more revealing than the last, I slipped it over my head and walked out to show my increasingly angered friend. The look on his face made every bit of my efforts worth it. Eden had been right—it was fun to make a man a little jealous every now and then. I wouldn't have had to resort to these measures if Trevor could have been up front about his feelings. Although, I supposed I couldn't own up to my own. I would much rather do this than lay myself out there, only to be faced with rejection. At least I could play this attempt off as a joke if I had to.

I tried on dress after dress, feeling flushed as Trevor's eyes heated up with a delicious mix of fury and desire. As his dark eyes captivated me, I had to admit I had never felt so womanly—so desirable. His gaze scanned over my every curve, appreciating all my body had to offer. While his eyes were filled with possessiveness, I felt my body coming to life. He wanted me, and to my shock, I wasn't frightened by the fact. To my surprise, my usual anxiety never made its appearance. The past had no place here with him. When he looked at me, it was like a fresh start—I was truly born again. It was as if my past had merely been a result of my overactive imagination. As Trevor scanned my body with longing, everything else faded into the background.

"What do you think about this one?" I asked as I stepped out of my closet in a very short, very tight black dress.

"Well, it's black, that's for sure," he replied sarcastically.

Grey, however, squealed in approval, which caused a smile to tug on my lips. His eyes were wide and animated, and his little hands reached out to me, begging for my attention. He could capture the attention of an entire room, so I didn't know why he tried so desperately to win mine. If only he had known how much I loved him already—how much he and his uncle had already captured my heart. A giggle escaped my lips as I watched him look away and, with great determination, attempt to stick his entire foot in his mouth. This, of course, captured Trevor's attention. He looked down at the little guy and chuckled as a wave of tension left his body.

"So, why are you asking about this, anyway?" he inquired as he stared down at his nephew. "Do I look like a man who knows anything about fashion?" Meeting my gaze again, he gestured to his worn, black T-shirt and ripped jeans, obviously not realizing how devilishly handsome he looked. "Can't Eden give you advice on this girly crap?"

"Well," I replied, keeping a level head, "I wanted a man's opinion."

A sly smile tugged on my lips as I wondered if he understood the game I was currently playing. I knew men could be obtuse at times, but I thought I had been making my intentions very clear.

What do I have to do, rip my clothes off and beg him to make love to me? Do I have to express my feelings for him through words?

I knew we were dancing around the truth, both of us too nervous to express ourselves. Sometimes, when his gaze captured mine, I was certain he felt *something*; I was certain he was as attracted to me as I was to him. Not just physically attracted, but mentally and emotionally attracted as well. I was just as intrigued by his thoughts and feelings as I was by his muscular and beautifully inked body.

He studied me, and I flushed under his intense stare, feeling myself shy away from him. His gaze softened, and he exhaled as he took a moment to drink me in again.

"Ronnie, you know you're beautiful. Anything you wear is going to look just fine."

God, words like these ... If he hadn't captured my heart and soul already, comments like these would have caused me to fall head over heels for him. As I looked upon him, I wondered why he was so hard on himself. How could he possibly believe he wasn't good? I wondered what type of man he believed he was. He was a wonderful, caring man who put everything and everyone before himself. Perhaps he hadn't always been so giving, or so good, but now he was a man I respected. *And he's so damn beautiful. Even with the sadness lurking in the depths of his irises, he's the most beautiful man I have ever seen.* This was why I needed to make him mine; this was why I couldn't wait a moment longer. I studied him a second more, my eyes trailing over the attractive lines of his body before I returned to my closet.

The tension in the air was palpable as I began to strip out of my sister's dress. The energy that surrounded us was potent, filled with our mixed desires, making it harder and harder to breathe with every second that passed. It was so strong, I nearly choked as I restrained myself. I understood I couldn't throw myself at him, knowing if I did so, I would be mortified. Standing in my closet, partially nude with a dress in my hands and my mind consumed by images of my neighbor, I knew I was considering my next step. I didn't contemplate long. As soon as the energy stiffened in the air around me, I knew he was near.

My nipples hardened against the thin fabric of my bra as my pussy began to gently pulse between my legs. A shiver ran through my body as I allowed his energy to consume me. I took a moment before I turned around to face him. Shock overwhelmed me as I found his eyes bright with a liquid fire. His gaze could have easily eaten me alive if I let it. I made a weak attempt to cover my breasts with the dress, but I had enjoyed his gaze too much to cover myself fully.

His eyes trailed over my curves, and I made no move to stop him. If it had been any other man leering at me, I would have felt afraid, skittish, and threatened. However, with Trevor's eyes on my body, I felt no such thing. With Trevor, I was a whole new woman. During the time I had been with him, my darkness had taken a short vacation, promising to be back as soon as he had to leave.

"Ronnie," he uttered in a rough voice, causing my body to tremble. "I can't let you go on this date tonight."

It took all of my restraint to keep the satisfied look off of my face.

"Why? Why does my dating life matter to you?"

"It doesn't." A nervous chuckle escaped his lips as his entire body tightened with what I could only assume was desire mixed with an inkling of discomfort due to the pressure I was placing him under. "You're my friend, and I'm just looking out for you."

My eyes rolled so hard it hurt. *Why do men do this? Why can't they just own up to their feelings? Oh, Veronica ... hypocrite, much?*

Placing all of my fears aside for a moment, I quipped, "Bullshit." I smiled as his eyes widened in disbelief before he managed to gain control of his handsome expression. "It's more than just that."

I liked challenging him.

"Why are you going on this date tonight?" he questioned.

"He seems nice," I lied with a shrug. "He comes highly recommended by Eden."

I watched his eyes blaze. I dropped the black dress onto the closet floor and reached for another selection, attempting to slip into it as he watched me. Before I got far in the process, one of his strong arms shot out and delayed me. My eyes peered up to meet his, enjoying their passion as I watched him search for the right words.

"Don't play with me," he ordered in a dark voice.

"Are you looking out for me as your best friend?" I challenged.

"No, Ronnie. I'm not."

Standing up straighter, I met his gaze head on. I wouldn't allow this man to intimidate me—*despite enjoying it.* I couldn't remember the last time I felt so alive. *Have I ever felt this alive? Have I ever experienced something so passionate in my twenty-five years?* He took a step forward, effectively trapping me against the wall of the closet.

"If you want to go on a date, I'll take you out."

I couldn't hide my smile this time. "A real date?"

"Well, we could just fake it and see how it goes," he teased me.

Playfully hitting him on the shoulder, I stepped forward, causing him to back up. "No, Trevor. I think you should try asking me out again."

"Cancel your date tonight," he ordered. "I'll take you out."

It was a demand—I liked that. I especially liked how he believed all of this was his idea. If only he knew *I* was the one who had been seducing *him.* Or perhaps, he did know that. *Maybe he was just playing along, too?*

With a playful smile, I responded, "Okay, Trev. I'll go out with you. But only because you *begged* me." I winked.

"I didn't beg you." He rolled his eyes.

"Well, I won't tell anyone about it. It will be our little secret." Pushing him out of my closet, I continued. "Now, give me a chance to get ready, will you? I don't need you breathing down my neck all of the time."

With a goofy grin on his handsome face, he stumbled out of the closet and gave me the privacy I needed. *God, I have him wrapped around my little finger. And it seems he owns my heart already.* I quickly changed into a cotton dress, which was modest, yet sexy, showing off my legs and chest without causing me to feel uncomfortable. I felt classy and effortless in it—the perfect dress for my first date with Trevor Warren. I slipped on a cardigan to complete the look before I stepped out of the closet to greet Trevor and a very excited-looking Greyson.

"You look beautiful," Trevor commented as his eyes raked leisurely over my body.

I flushed under the heat of his gaze before I beamed at him. People had told me I was beautiful plenty of times in the past, but I never felt its truth until Trevor uttered the words. Before, I had never believed it. I had imagined I was pleasing enough—attractive, perhaps—but never *beautiful.* He managed to make me feel beautiful, desirable, and worthy. He made me *feel* period.

"Do you mind if I run over to my apartment and change? I don't want to wear this to dinner," he explained as he gestured to the outfit he had worn to work.

"That's fine." I joined him on the bed and took Grey in my arms, bouncing him gently until he began to giggle against my chest. "Just hurry back. I'm starving."

Trevor winked at me before he rose from the bed and headed to his apartment across the way. As soon as I heard my front door shut, I turned to Greyson.

"So, it seems like your uncle likes me, buddy." I sounded so giddy. I hadn't felt this happy in a very, *very* long time. "Can you believe it, Grey?"

He giggled at me, his wild hair falling into his eyes before I quickly pushed it away.

"I'm being silly, aren't I?"

He giggled again.

"I just can't help myself. Your daddy makes me so happy. You know that, right? I guess he makes us both incredibly happy."

I surprised myself by referring to Trevor as Greyson's "daddy," but as I considered it, I realized I couldn't think of a better word for the pivotal role he played in his child's life. He would always be his uncle— Greyson's biological parents would never be erased; I doubted Trevor would ever want that—but for all intents and purposes, Trevor *was* his father. His amazingly, loving father who took on the rule so quickly and impressively.

Grey smiled in response and outstretched his chubby, little arms. I brought him closer to my face so my cheek was resting against his crazy head of hair. I wished I had known him when he was born. I wondered what his unruly hair looked like back then. Considering how tiny he was now, I couldn't imagine how small he must have been as a newborn; that would have been a sight to behold.

"I think we all will be happy, Grey. Together. Someday. Do you feel it, too?'

I knew he couldn't answer me, but I believed that if he could, he would have agreed. I didn't quite know what it was—I supposed it was just a feeling I had—but sometimes, I swore I could look at a person and envision a future for them. Usually, it was a future I was a part of; usually, those futures consisted of a friendship. However, with Trevor Warren, I had envisioned far more than that. I had always wanted a home filled with children, but after my rough start, I never believed it could be possible. *Never ... until now. Until him.*

"We'll be happy, Grey. I promise."

A knock at the door startled me from my contemplations. *Is that Trev? Why doesn't he just let himself in?* I smiled, realizing he was probably knocking to do this the "right" way—the traditional start to a first date. *God, he was too cute.* I giggled at the thought of ever telling him that. If I ever did, I was certain it would be the only time in his life that anyone would refer to him as "cute." I bet he believed himself to be so hard—so tough—but here he was, knocking on my door to escort me to his truck for our very first date. *Our first date ... I can't believe it!*

I opened the front door without caring how flustered I must have looked. I wanted Trevor to know what he did to me. He made my heart race and made my knees weak. He made me feel like I was the heroine in one of the romance novels I frequently read. He was my knight in shining armor, and I felt like a princess—a princess who didn't need to be saved.

"You ready for our date?"

"I guess it *is* too late to back out now," I teased. "Have you thought about where you'd like to go?"

"I thought I'd figure that out on the way. I'm sure there're plenty of places around town."

There are plenty of places, and I don't care where we end up. As long as I'm there with you. I almost said this out loud.

Almost.

10

I Got You Babe

I watched him as he drove; his gaze scrutinized the restaurant options from the driver's side window. His hands were tight on the wheel, revealing his nerves. I watched the vein on his forearm as it twitched before my gaze rose to his neck, where a vein was throbbing, too—the black and gray lotus tattoo slightly expanded with every twitch of his external jugular vein. There was something attractive about the way in which it moved. Perhaps it was due to the intensity of his aura. I wanted to reach out and run my fingertips along his throat and chest before slowly descending to his strong forearm. Of course, I resisted despite my belief he would enjoy the feel of my fingers moving across his skin.

I was so busy studying him, I barely noticed as the truck rolled to a stop. I managed to tear my eyes away from his form for a moment and found we were parked outside a small pizzeria on the edge of town. I loved this place. I wondered if Trevor somehow knew that, or if he had just happened to pick this place by chance. It *had* been the only restaurant without a plethora of cars parked out front, after all.

Whatever the reason, this spot was perfect; the perfect place for a date with my two perfect men. As soon as the thought passed through my brain, one of the "perfect men" squealed from the backseat. I peered at his content face in the rearview mirror, marveling at how happy he always looked before I returned my attention to his uncle up front. Trevor gave me an apologetic grin, and I wondered if he was worried that a place like this didn't meet my standards. *What type of girl does he think I am? Doesn't he know me better than this?*

Compared to my sister and her friends, I didn't think of myself as a "high maintenance" type. As much as I loved Eden, I was sure she would have stuck her nose up at this location. However, I wouldn't have done that even if I hadn't understood Trevor's financial circumstances. With a little baby to care for, dates should be the *last* thing Trevor had to worry about. Reaching my hand across the center console, I placed my hand on top of his, resting against the steering wheel, and gave him a reassuring smile.

"Thanks, Trev."

His eyes lit up, and he smiled in return before opening his driver's side door and sliding out of the truck. I couldn't take my eyes off of him as he walked around the front of the truck and opened my door for me. With a goofy grin on his attractive face, he proffered his hand. I took it, grinning before a chill ran through my body, energy sparking between our warm palms. As my eyes shot to meet his, gauging his reaction, I wondered if the attraction in the air was as palpable to him also.

"I know it isn't much ..." He trailed off, his voice sounding nervous.

"It's perfect, Trev."

Just like you.

His lips twitched into a smile, and for a moment, it illuminated his entire being. He wasn't nervous anymore. At least, not in this instance. I stepped out of the truck and followed him as he reached for the backseat to retrieve an extremely rambunctious Grey. While having a first date with a baby present wasn't exactly *normal*, I was happy Grey was involved. The night wouldn't have felt right if he weren't.

Grey squealed from the moment his uncle opened the door. He squirmed around in his seat, reaching out for Trevor with eager arms. His little mouth moved, trying to form words, and for a moment, I thought I saw an actual English word about to fall from his lips. However, that hint of a word turned into a string of babbles. Trevor gathered him into his embrace before he kicked the door shut with his foot and locked up the truck.

Grey babbled loudly as we walked toward the restaurant, pointing and gesturing with his little hands as if he were trying to describe the place to us. I laughed at him, feeling like I had a family of my own as we walked through the front doors. With Trevor and Greyson, my life felt *perfect*. I soaked it all in, pretending this slice of heaven was my everyday reality.

A hostess came to greet us, and her eyes locked onto Trevor instantly; they danced over his structured frame while she asked him all of the basic questions. Despite the twinge of jealousy that I felt, I knew I would have been doing the very same thing—I couldn't blame her. Trevor was so striking. It was impossible *not* to look at him even if the gaze wasn't one of attraction. With his ink, angular features, height, and build, it was unlikely for him to ever go unobserved. I knew I was lucky to be at his side despite what *he* believed. Regardless of being wounded himself, I was positive he could have had any woman he wanted, and yet, he chose me: someone equally damaged, if not more so.

The hostess grabbed a high chair for Greyson before leading us to a booth toward the back corner of the restaurant. I was grateful for her choice since I loved nothing more than feeling like I was in my own little bubble. The moment we sat down, Trevor moved to place Grey in his high chair—he stopped as he watched his nephew's eyes fill with tears. He attempted to ignore the moisture at first—which was wise because sometimes babies would give up when immediate attention was not given—but as the cries persisted, Trevor couldn't help himself and pulled the tearful baby onto his lap.

A grin tugged on my date's lips, and I wondered what he found so amusing. *Maybe the odd circumstances surrounding our "first date"?* I guessed he hadn't imagined it like this. If *he had imagined it at all.* I knew *I* had allowed my imagination to run wild time and time again. Whenever my thoughts had drifted away from my priorities, I had allowed myself to dream of a night such as this one: a night when I was Trevor's girl. In my fantasies, I hadn't pictured it *this* way. Although, currently, I didn't long for anything else.

"This is great, Trev."

He smirked at my compliment, leaning across the table to close a bit of the distance between us. "So, is this how you envisioned tonight going?"

Grey babbled a response from his perch on his uncle's lap. My cheeks flushed as I remembered the exact salacious thoughts I had about tonight. *His warm, naked body moving over mine. His lips on my neck; his tongue tracing my collarbone before dipping to nip at the skin between my breasts. His cock twitching at my entrance, teasing me until I opened my legs as wide as they went. Him thrusting between my legs until the world shattered around me, and I came harder than I ever had in the past...*

"Yes," I murmured after a heartbeat. I wondered if he saw the trace of a lie in my eyes. I wondered if he read me like a book. Finally, I looked up, giving him a coquettish smile while I felt my cheeks burn under his scrutiny.

I studied him as he pondered my answer, mulling it over in his mind.

"So, did this guy take it pretty hard when you canceled?"

Truthfully, I had already forgotten all about the other man. How could I have thought of him when I had a man like Trevor sitting in front of me? *Trevor, the man I think about every time I touch myself.* He was the first thing I thought of when I woke up in the morning and the last image in my mind as I lay down to sleep every night. Snippets from my various fantasies of mine danced through my mind as Trevor watched me from across the table. I bit down on my bottom lip to keep from smiling too broadly.

"He was hoping to reschedule for another time, but I left him hanging."

I winked and watched him nearly lose his wits all together.

"I'm sure he's heartbroken," Trevor commented, his voice sounding gruff.

"I'm sure we wouldn't have been right together."

"Why's that? Is there someone else in your life whom you see yourself with?"

Really, Trev? Who else could there possibly be, besides you? I spend every second with you. He gave me his signature cocky grin, which I had grown far too fond of in these last few months, and I quickly responded with a smile of my own. Just as I opened my mouth to give him a playful response, our waitress approached our table and stopped me. She quickly started chatting, going over the usual spiel, and as she did so, I felt Trevor's eyes on me, calculating as if he were trying to equate what I was planning on saying to him before we were interrupted.

His eyes only left my face when it came time to order. We ordered our drinks, and Trevor ordered our meals before the waitress sauntered off. Once she left, the moment between Trevor and I no longer felt organic. So, I stayed quiet. I knew Trevor was eager for a response, but I didn't know if I was as eager to supply one. It seemed my nerves had gotten the better of me, and regardless of how desperately I tried to stifle them, I couldn't seem to overcome my anxiousness long enough to adequately express how I felt.

I moved my gaze from my folded hands, where they had remained in my lap as I had tried to summon the courage to speak, to peer up at Trevor, who seemed to be in the middle of an epiphany. Now, *I* was left to wonder what he was thinking about. Suddenly, his eyes shot up to meet mine, looking at me as if he were seeing me for the very first time.

Not knowing what to do or say, I picked up where we left off, repeating my words from earlier. "This is nice, Trev. I never thought you'd ask me out."

"I guess I just needed you to tease me until I caved," he quipped.

Oh, God! Am I so easily read?

I threw my head back as a deep, belly laugh escaped my throat. My curls bounced around my face as my loud laughter became amused giggles. *He knew!* How much he knew, I wasn't certain, but it was abundantly clear he knew I had been messing with him. *How hysterical!* I had believed I had been so clever, but Trevor picked up on my game. I wondered if he knew to what extent I had planned this.

"Well, I love going on dates"—not exactly true—"but I had a feeling the night was going to be boring. Why would I want to go out with some stranger when I could go out with you?"

He smirked at my response, straightening up in his seat.

"Good point, Ronnie." *God, I love when he utters my name.* "Why would you want to go out with someone else when you have me?"

If I hadn't been smitten with him before, I would have been in this moment. With his cocky smile, kind words, and dangerous appearance, he was everything I had never known I'd wanted. Everything about him captivated me to the point I became blind to anyone else. *He's it for me.*

Our waitress returned with our drinks and Trevor reached for Grey's bottle, getting the little boy comfortable before he began to feed him. Seeing him like this always managed to take my breath away. Such a simple, intimate moment between the two of them was one of the most profoundly beautiful things I had ever seen. The intimacy almost made me feel like an intruder as I watched them. However, as Trevor peered up to look at me, I understood I was an equal part of this.

"I don't know why I would want to go out with anyone else ever," I said quietly; I was certain he couldn't hear me.

His eyes lit up for a moment, and he peered at me. If he had heard my comment, he appeared too exhausted to form a reply. As he stifled a yawn, I searched for another topic of conversation—something easy. As I thought, I considered that despite being worn out, he had still made an effort to take me out for the evening. *He must be serious about me. Why put the effort into this, if he weren't?*

"Work has been kicking my butt, lately," I commented. "I used to like content editing, but now I'm not sure if any of this is for me."

"What would you rather do?" he questioned with his eyes cast down, focusing on his nephew as he nursed him from the bottle.

"I don't know …" I trailed off, feeling almost embarrassed. "Write, I guess. I just need something different. I've been so focused on editing for such a long time; I haven't had the free time to explore much else. I dove head first into my job fresh out of college, eager to become as successful as I could, as soon as I could. And while I'm successful now, I'm not sure whether or not I'm really happy with my position."

I sighed, twirling my straw around in my Coke as I contemplated my past choices. I had been so focused on getting my mind off of things I had buried myself in work. I never regretted the decision—I didn't know if I would be here right now if it weren't for my past focus and determination—but sometimes, I wondered what my life would have been like if I had chosen a different path.

Where would I be if I had chosen a college closer to home? What if I never chased after a fantasy, leaving me with a darkness I'll never be able to escape from? Was there one decision I made that changed my entire life?

"The workload I have is a nightmare," I continued, keeping my unpleasant thoughts at bay. "Of course, it doesn't help that I've got a neighbor who I always want to hang out with."

"You're blaming me for your slacking?" Trevor questioned as another confident smile tugged at his lips.

I supposed he should be cocky. He *was* the reason for my procrastination and overactive imagination, after all.

"I'm not blaming you. I'm just saying you're quite the distraction."

"I've been told that a few times in the past."

He winked at me.

"And you're proud of that? A girl has to earn a living, Trev."

"Well, maybe one day, I could take care of you and you won't have to work."

My eyes widened at his suggestion. *Did he really just say that?* From his spot across the table, he looked just as baffled as I felt. *Has he envisioned a future for us? Together?* Despite the relatively short amount of time we'd known each other, I felt as if I had known him for years. As strange as it sounded, it felt like he had always been a part of my life, in one way or another.

Viewing the worried look in his eyes, I knew I had to tease him a bit to ease the growing tension surrounding us.

"You want to take care of me, Trev? It's the twenty-first century, so, I think I can take care of myself."

Despite my teasing tone, this statement was true. I didn't need a man to take care of me. *Not now, not ever. I could never give myself to someone completely again. I can't afford to lose another part of myself.* While being "taken care of" sounded nice in theory so did my independence. I enjoyed the luxury of not having to look outside of myself to have a single one of my needs met. *I didn't have to look outside of myself to find happiness.*

"I know you can," he insisted. "But, you deserve some time to relax every now and then. Men don't mind carrying more of the work load."

I rolled my eyes at this, and he smirked in response. While I didn't entirely agree with his ideals, I did appreciate him for thinking of a future. *A future where I had a starring role.* God knew I considered him as a starring role in my future. *In my forever.*

The waitress came with our food, but my gaze never strayed from my date and the little boy resting contently in his arms. This was my future; *they* were my future. I didn't care if this was rushed. I didn't care if the people in my life didn't approve of my decision to be with Trevor. He was what I wanted. *This* was what I wanted.

As we began to eat, we drifted into easy conversation. This was one of the things I loved about Trevor the most: he was so incredibly easy to talk to. I began a conversation, and the words would just fly out without hesitation. I didn't overthink things; I didn't put on a show for him. When we talked, I believed I could act as my true self. I didn't have to hide anything. When I was with him, things just *clicked.*

We discussed movies, literature, and the authors who'd inspired us throughout our lives. Trevor discussed, in great length, his old love for science fiction novels while describing how he had read old, beaten-up paperbacks growing up. He talked about a time where he had read many of his favorite authors, such as Kesey, Bukowski, and Palahniuk. All of which were authors I would have chosen for him to read, if he hadn't already chosen them himself.

Before he had decided to live a life on the road, leaving Colorado behind, he seemed to have been happy. However, I knew something must have changed within him. I didn't quite know what happened after he had embarked on his excursion around the country, but he didn't seem fond of any of it. I would ask him, but I didn't want to intrude. If he had wanted me to know, he would have told me. Until then, I didn't dare pressure him.

When there was a break in his ramble concerning all things literature, which had only caused my feelings for him to amplify, I replied, "Well, I've always loved Bukowski. *Ham on Rye* was a nice escape from some of the British classics I always read. When I was in college, I took every British literature course they had offered because I've been obsessed with Austen and the Brontë sisters since I was a girl. I've broken many of my books' spines even. I think I've purchased *Pride and Prejudice* at least ten different times!"

"I've never read any of that old stuff," he admitted with an almost shy smile.

As he appeared to be mentally kicking himself, I suppressed a chuckle. Just the idea of him reading one of those books for me was enough to make my happy.

"I've read older science fiction, and that's about it," he said.

"Well, I've never read any of that. So, I guess we can educate each other then?"

I winked at him, watching as he relaxed against his seat.

Just as I opened my mouth to expand on the idea, Grey became relentless in Trevor's lap. Honestly, I couldn't believe the little, energetic guy had remained so relaxed for so long. Now that he was becoming more mobile, he always wanted to be on the move—always searching for another adventure. Grey started to kick his legs, looking as if he were trying to walk away from his uncle. I giggled at him. As soon as the small noise escaped my lips, his wide, curious eyes shot up to meet mine. He reached out to me, causing my heart to melt.

"Aw, poor guy," I said, leaning over to get a better look at the fussy, little baby who had completely captured my heart. "Is it past his bedtime?"

We had been talking for so long I had lost track of time. I couldn't remember a time when I survived so long without a glance to check the time. Now that I peered around the restaurant, I found we were one of the few tables still filled with patrons. *They must be closing soon.* No wonder Grey had become so temperamental so quickly—it must be ten o'clock.

"Yeah," Trevor answered as he rocked the little boy in his arms. "I'm sorry about this."

He made eye contact with our waitress, silently indicating he wanted the bill. I glanced over at her, catching her in the act of giving my man a flirtatious grin before she headed to her POS. *My "man"? Where did that come from, Veronica? He isn't your "man." At least, not yet.*

"It's completely fine," I answered with a dismissive wave of my hand. "I love having Greyson around. He's so well tempered." My eyes dropped to the little boy's scrunched up, flushed face before I raised my gaze to capture Trevor's, smiling at him. "Well, most of the time," I amended. "Let's pay the check and get this adorable, little guy home."

"Can you hold him for a moment?" Trevor questioned as the waitress returned with our bill.

Eagerly, I reached for him, always happy to have a chance to hold him. As I rocked him gently in my arms, he calmed down, his tiny body relaxing against the curve of my chest. My right hand came up to play with his small amount of hair, trying to tame it as I watched his uncle pay the bill. I almost asked to pay half, but I knew Trevor wanted to treat me, and I didn't want to offend him by suggesting otherwise. As soon as Trevor finished laying down the appropriate amount of cash, I rose with Grey in my arms. I watched Trevor as he slid out of the booth, appearing completely relaxed for the first time since I had met him.

He led us out of the restaurant, moving toward his truck. While I attempted to keep my eyes appropriately forward, they kept wandering down to gaze at the curve of his ass; despite the numerous times I looked at it, I never felt satisfied. *God, I just wanted to bite it ... just wanted to grab onto it as he thrusted between my opened thighs.* I flushed as I continued to stare. *I guess construction jobs can really do wonders for a man's body.* As Trevor peered over his shoulder at me, my entire body went ice cold as I shuddered with embarrassment.

Oh, please, oh, please, don't tell me he caught me staring at his butt. If there's a God, he wouldn't let this happen!

Gaining my composure, I picked up my pace, walking next to him until we reached the truck. "Thanks for tonight, Trev," I commented, hoping my cheeks weren't still red with embarrassment. "That was a lot more fun than a stuffy dinner with a stranger would have been."

He opened the passenger door of the cab and rolled his eyes at me. "Well, I really appreciate that. What an amazing compliment."

I grinned at his sarcasm. I peered up at him, and with the streetlights shining down on his perfectly structured face, I thought he looked like a fallen angel—an angel who was sent especially for me. *Maybe he is.* I pushed that thought from my mind as I continued to regard him. He may not have been a fallen angel, but he had quickly become *my* angel, nonetheless. In this moment, there was nothing I wanted to do more than to kiss him. However, my nerves held me back. As the light from above reflected on his wet, full bottom lip, I contemplated how those lips would feel pressed against mine, molding against my mouth until I would scarcely be able to breathe. *Heavens, I can barely breathe now just thinking about it.*

Somehow through my amorous haze, I managed to tell him, "Tonight was amazing, Trev. I had a lot of fun—just like I always do when I'm with you."

With a heat raging in his eyes, I felt his desire to kiss me, too. However, we both remained perfectly still—neither of us gaining the courage to make the next move. Although, the next move didn't have to be made tonight. We had our whole lives ahead of us and plenty of time to kiss our day away. It didn't have to be now … despite how much I wanted it to.

He took Grey, who was nodding off under the safety of the night sky, from my arms and opened the back door of the cab for him. As he placed him safely in his car seat, I slid into my spot up front. Through the windshield, I stared off into the night, reaching up to touch my fingertips to my lips as I imagined again what I had been too afraid to do. I wanted to *physically* express how much I felt for him. In this moment, I knew I was ready to dive back into those waters. *The waters I have feared for so long.* With Trevor, I knew I had nothing to fear. With him, I could conquer anything.

At least, I hoped.

11

With Arms Outstretched

"*Why did you wait so long?*"

"*I wasn't sure about you,*" *I replied, peering over the vanilla ice cream cone in my hand to catch a glimpse of his cerulean eyes.*

"*No, you weren't sure of yourself. It's just a date, Veronica.*"

I didn't know what to say. Perhaps he was right ... perhaps I was unsure of myself. This was the first time I had really been on my own, and I barely knew which way was up. While my friends had attempted to persuade me to stay away, claiming he adopted this attitude with all of the girls, I hadn't been able to bring myself to listen to them. Despite what they said, I had never seen Preston with any other girls around campus. Maybe in his past, he had dated quite a bit, but since I had met him, I had yet to see him run around with anyone.

"*You're right. It's only a date,*" *I meekly agreed.*

"*Have you been on a date before?*" *he asked as his blue eyes sparkled.*

"*Well, I don't know if you could really call my past experiences dates. I went out with a few boys growing up, but my sister and her boyfriend always had to chaperone us. My dad never let me go out by myself.*"

"*So, this is your first 'real' date, then?*" *he challenged with a smirk.*

I felt my cheeks flush as I slowly nodded in response. This was my first real date. If only the shy, nervous girl I was a few years ago could see the man I was going out with tonight. She never would have believed this future was a possibility. While I knew I wasn't unattractive, I had never believed I could land a man like the one before me. He was just so ... perfect. So perfect, in fact, I felt like a complete slob as I sat across from him. He complimented me time and time again—he always told me how pretty and perfect I was—but I had never fully believed him. He'd claimed he could never tell a lie, so I supposed everything he said must have been true. Maybe to him, I was perfect. I loved that idea. I loved being perfect to someone. I felt wanted, womanly, and whole. I couldn't describe it. All of my life, I had felt out of step with everyone around me. With him, I finally felt as if I was where I needed to be.

"I suppose it is," I finally answered.

"Well, is it everything you hoped it would be?"

I nodded, smiling at him.

"Am I everything you hoped I would be?" he questioned as his eyes filled with mirth.

"You are."

I took another bite from my cone and blushed, reaching to wipe the ice cream from my bottom lip. He had beaten me to it, though. He reached across the small table and wiped the vanilla cream off my lip with his thumb. My eyes closed as I felt his finger move across my bottom lip, and when I had opened them again, I found him bringing his ice cream-covered thumb to his mouth for a taste.

"Sweet." He winked at me.

"Am I what you hoped I would be?" I asked in a very small voice.

"You are, Veronica." His grin widened as he continued. "You're exactly what I hoped for and more."

The memories had hit me like a tidal wave, and before I knew it, I was sitting on the carpeted floor of my living room. All it took was one simple trigger, and my mind would flood with images of him—images of my old life. While Trevor had helped me in more ways than he could ever imagine, when he wasn't here, I felt as though I was in the dark again. I couldn't grasp how I had been able to manage so long without him. The idea of dealing with all of this alone felt so foreign to me now. I was strong—I knew that. I was far stronger than I gave myself credit for. But sometimes … Sometimes, I didn't *want* to be strong.

Sometimes, I wanted someone to wrap me in their embrace and care for me the way my mother once had. Sometimes, I wanted to fold completely and allow my emotions the chance to drain from my body. It may have been good for me. However, I couldn't do that. Not now. The one person I would have wanted to open up to was Trevor, and he had far too much on his plate already. I didn't want to add to the mess of his life. Although, I felt he was more than welcome to add his mess to mine.

Perhaps you could wake up Grey ... No! I knew I couldn't use him as my life support right now. That wouldn't have been fair to him. *Would it? Maybe I could hold him, just for a little while? Just until I feel better.* He had been napping for a little over an hour, which was quite the record for him, and I was sure he would be ready to wake soon. Before I could stop myself, I rose from the floor and moved down the hallway to my makeshift nursery. It wasn't much, but it was a home away from home for him while his uncle was at work, and his grandparents were busy. Today, his uncle had a twelve-hour shift, and his grandmother was playing tennis with her friends. *How that woman could bounce back from losing a child is beyond me.* How could I judge her though? I had never met the woman, after all.

While I had never met Trevor's mother, the image of her he had painted for me was not an attractive one. The small amount he'd said about her had spoken volumes. Although, he would never say it aloud, I knew Trevor believed his mother didn't love him. The doubt swam in his dark eyes whenever he spoke about her. While it was always distant, it was there. The flash of hurt—the sliver of pain. I wondered if he realized these feelings. Maybe they were buried so deep he never had to acknowledge them. Thankfully, any conversation about his mother had ended with the mention of his brother, Dean. Trevor's eyes would always light up when he talked about his older sibling—his hero. *Just when I thought Trevor couldn't consume my heart anymore.*

When I made it to Grey's room, I found he was wide awake. On his back, he kicked his legs back and forth as he stared up at the ceiling fan in wonder. I was shocked he hadn't cried out yet. *Maybe he just woke up a few moments ago?*

As soon as he felt my presence in the room, his eyes darted to meet mine, and his arms began to wave wildly around, beckoning me to come closer. I crossed the room and reached for him, gathering him in my arms before I bounced him gently against my chest. I walked to Harper's old bean bag chair in the corner of the room and plopped down.

"Hey, buddy. You're not so sleepy anymore, are you?"

His little mouth stretched open into an "O" as he yawned—his chubby fists stretched above his head as his body became straight and still in my arms. After he was finished with his stretch, his mouth transformed into a happy smile as he balled up his body against my chest. Just holding him like this had the power to cause my mind and body to destress. I almost snorted at the thought as I remembered Harper when she was a baby. *God, babysitting that girl had been a nightmare.* I loved her with all of my heart, but she had spent her entire life testing my patience. Grey, however, was so well-tempered it caused him to barely seem real. He was always so calm and loving; he always wanted to be cuddled and held. With the way Trevor spoiled him with affection, I couldn't blame Grey for constantly seeking it. *I certainly wouldn't mind being held by Trevor all day long.*

"Your uncle will be coming soon. What should we do until then?"

He gurgled a response and grinned up at me. Without having to ask again, I reached for the pile of children's books at my side and chose the one I knew he liked the most: *Where the Wild Things Are.* His eyes lit up as I moved the book to my lap and propped him up to see the pictures. He began to giggle, wildly clapping his hands as he awaited my performance. As soon as I began to read, his laughter ceased, and he was all ears. With wide eyes and a thoughtful expression, he listened to me, watching as the fingertips of my right hand traced the words on the page in front of us. When he was captivated like this, I felt like I was the only person in the world. I felt so safe and so loved. Emotions coursed through me as I considered how long I had gone without this sort of comfort. From the moment I said, "the end" and closed the book, I was inspired.

Setting Grey belly down on the floor, I ran and grabbed my sketch pad. I came back and plopped down, quickly beginning to draw. I sketched his little face before I started to sketch the world around him— the world outside of this small room. One day, he would go out into the world and become the man he was always meant to be. Today, I would draw that. A smile tugged on my lips as inspiration overwhelmed me.

"You're going to do great things one day, aren't you, Grey?" I asked as my pencil moved across the paper of my Strathmore sketchpad.

He giggled and garbled a response before he attempted to shove his entire left foot into his mouth. Setting the pad down for a moment, I reached for him and brought him into my arms, causing him to forget all about his attempt to swallow his foot whole.

"You're going to grow up to be wonderful, buddy. I just know it."

He wiggled out of my embrace and crawled back onto the floor, playing with his stuffed animals while I continued to sketch. Time flew by quickly once I got caught up in my own head, and before I knew it, there was a knock on the front door. Grey squealed, knowing his uncle was only a few walls away.

"Ready to see your uncle, buddy?"

I scooped up my excited, little guy and bounded down the hallway toward the door. As soon as I swung the front door open, Trevor nearly slouched against the frame. He looked exhausted with his hair disheveled and covered in specks of dirt. His cheeks were slightly puffy and tanned, and his posture was weary.

"Come in before you fall over," I suggested as I stepped aside and allowed him entry.

He staggered in, wiping the exhaustion from his eyes as he made his way toward the couch in my living room. He nearly fell onto the cushion, throwing a toned arm across his eyes to shield his face from the overhead light.

"Rough day?"

"I was up all last night with Grey." He moved his arm to peer over to his happy nephew before he continued. "How was he today?"

"Perfectly behaved," I supplied with a smile. "Why? Was he trouble last night?"

"More than trouble." A tired laugh passed through his lips. "That kid never wants me to sleep."

Grey reached from him, which caused Trevor to laugh again. Despite his weariness, he wanted to hold his nephew. Closing the small space between us, I placed Grey on Trevor's belly before I took a seat beside them on the couch. Trevor's arms instantly wrapped around his nephew, holding him snuggly against his chest. As I watched the duo, I noticed both of their bodies relax, as if all the stresses of their worlds had suddenly disappeared. Trevor closed his eyes for a moment, seemingly enjoying the quiet of my apartment, before he tilted his head down to press a small kiss against his nephew's forehead.

"You two are cute together."

Trevor's eyes shot up to meet mine, and he rewarded me with a sleepy grin. "Not as cute as the two of you," he quipped. "I've never seen him take to someone so quickly. I guess it's pretty easy to be taken with you though."

He winked, and I flushed.

"Thanks for watching him today," he continued. "Tomorrow, I have the day off, so you can actually get some work done."

"It's all right. I like watching the little guy." I grinned at him before continuing. "Besides, I wouldn't want your mother to miss her game."

Trevor laughed at my comment. Rolling his eyes, he replied, "Yeah. God forbid that woman doesn't get to play tennis."

"Maybe she just needs a break." As I took in his weary eyes and defeated appearance, I quietly added, "Maybe you do, too. It's okay to just relax every now and then, Trev."

"I do relax. I relax whenever I'm with you."

"I can help you relax some more ... if you want."

His eyes heated at my suggestion. With the baby asleep and the apartment all to ourselves, the night was ours, and I wanted to reach out and take it—reach out and take him. I wanted him to make love to me until I could scarcely remember my own name. All I desired was the here and now; all I longed for was to live in the present—with him. With the one man who mastered both my mind and my heart.

"Ronnie ... are you sure? I mean, I thought we could wait. I don't want to rush you, baby. We've got the rest of our lives ahead of us and plenty of time to do this together."

"Trev, don't try to talk me out of this."

Before I knew it, I was rising from the couch and began slowly unbuttoning my blouse. Despite his words, he seemed immensely satisfied with the matter at hand. My fingers shook as they moved from button to button. I grew so frustrated I almost yanked the shirt apart to expose my flushed flesh. Trevor watched me struggle with my top as he palmed his growing erection through his jeans. After a long moment, he finally decided to help me out. His fingers moved to unbutton my blouse with expert precision. When he was finished, he moved to unbutton my jeans. My breath caught in my throat as I watched his fingers move to unzip my fly. He gave me one last challenging stare, silently questioning whether I wanted this or not. As soon as I nodded, he pulled my jeans down my freshly shaven legs.

He dropped to the floor at my feet, grinning up at me before he placed a kiss against my cotton-covered pubic bone. Part of me wished I had worn something sexier—something lace, perhaps?—while another part of me was happy to see him so satisfied with my simple choice of white cotton underwear with childish hearts. Of course, I hadn't slipped them on this morning with the plan of Trevor ever seeing them.

"You're so beautiful," he murmured.

I smiled down at him, watching as he hooked his fingers in my underwear and tugged them down the tiniest bit before he placed another wet kiss on my newly exposed skin.

"No, Trev. You're the beautiful one."

He ignored the compliment, just like he always did, and gave me a questioning stare. "Are you sure you want this? It doesn't have to be tonight. We can—"

"I want this," I interrupted. "I want you."

"Well, then ..." he roguishly muttered before he pulled my underwear all the way down and kissed my wet core.

I startled awake as I came to pieces. Flushing, I realized my subconscious had ran wild again. I wondered if I should feel guilty for my little fantasy. I considered what Trevor would think if he discovered he starred in my amorous dreams. *Don't forget about your daydreams, too. He stars in every one of them.* Rubbing the exhaustion from my face, I closed my eyes and lay in bed, trying and failing to push the thoughts of Trevor away.

Morning had passed without too much of a fuss. Without having Grey here to care for, the morning had been rather uneventful. I had gone through my old routine: breakfast, Earl Grey, reading, and editing. Oddly enough, I had found this routine no longer provided me with the solace that it once had. Now, I was constantly antsy; I wanted nothing more than to spend my time with the two special guys in my life.

A smile played on my lips as I thought of them—images of them swam in my consciousness as I sipped on my tea, unable to focus as my pen ran beneath each word of the manuscript before me in search of errors. My eyes kept leaving the page to peer at my phone, which hadn't rung once all morning. I knew he was with Grey, but I had thought he would have contacted me by now.

Clingy much, Veronica? It's ten past eight, and you're freaking out because he hasn't contacted you yet?

I took a deep breath before I frowned at my silliness. *Who knew I could become so attached?* Unable to help myself, I reached for my phone and sent a quick text. Placing the phone face down on my kitchen table, I took a sip of my tea and tried to focus on something other than him.

My fingernails *clanked* against the glass of my table as I read, and re-read, the textbook's manuscript. My eyes constantly drifted to my phone, which had laid unresponsive next to me. Trevor was busy—*I* was busy—yet, my thoughts were flooded with him. While this was a distraction, I was happy that my thoughts were positive ones. I remembered a day when my thoughts were far from pleasant.

Time passed without a single vibration from my cell. Hours had passed as quickly as minutes as I became increasingly engrossed in the work before me. Every so often, I had reached for my phone and texted him again, all while chastising myself for acting so clingy, so soon. We had been on one date, and I was acting as if we had been together for years. I didn't even know how deeply his affection ran. As I awaited a response, I wondered if his feelings for me ran as deeply as mine did for him.

This wasn't like him. He usually called—he usually said *something*, even if that something had been quick. *Is something wrong? Has something changed in the way he feels about me?* No, I told myself. I would have known if something had changed. I was certain I would have felt it. My eyes moved to the clock and widened as I realized how much of the day had already passed. *Maybe he's home right now. Maybe I can go to him!* My body rose from the couch before I considered sending him another text. *I doubt he would answer anyway.*

After I knocked and received no answer, hearing only the faint sound of crying through the door, I let myself in. Dead to the world, Trevor sat on the couch with his dark eyes glazed over, his face pensive as he was deep in thought. Lost, it took him a moment to realize I had sauntered into his apartment unannounced. When he final *did* notice me, his eyes shot up to meet mine and widened in shock before his face twisted into a look of remorse. As I regarded him, I wondered if he hadn't been ignoring me; maybe he had been zoned out like this all day.

Grey's screams attracted my attention, causing my eyes to drop to him. He was flushed in his uncle's lap with wet cheeks and a red, twisted face. *How long have they been like this?* Just as I moved to reach for Grey, Trev brought him up to rest against his shoulder.

"I've been trying to get in contact with you all day," I explained as soon as his gaze met mine.

"I didn't know," he muttered in a monotone. His face was ashen, and his dark, emerald eyes were distant. "My mind has been somewhere else, I guess."

I studied him for a moment before I shyly asked, "Can I sit down?"

His body slid across the couch, silently answering my question. His gaze remained forward, focused on the off-white wall before him, ignoring me completely. I knew his distance wasn't intentional—something had to have happened.

"Do you want to talk about it?" I asked, my voice breaking with uncertainty.

His body stiffened as he contemplated his next words. He shifted back and forth while he mulled the question over in his mind. He never once looked at me—remaining completely focused. The silence had grown heavy by the time his eyes had finally shot up to meet mine. Dark orbs scanned my features in a silent plea. A plea for what, I didn't know.

While I hadn't understood the story behind the look, I understood the feeling all too well. The pain wasn't new to me—it never would be. The pain swimming in his eyes burned so violently, it seemed impossible to repress. His eyes studied mine, scrutinizing my gaze before they traveled down to my lips; his attention danced across them, causing my body to warm and my cheeks to flush. When his tongue darted out to swipe across his full bottom lip, I stifled a groan; I nearly lost my mind at the sight. *What wouldn't I like to do to this man?*

He hesitated for a moment, and I felt my entire body stiffen. My mind screamed: *Do you really want this? Can you stand it?* While I watched him, I knew I could stand it. My body yearned for something—*anything. I want to feel the comfort of another person.* Before another thought filled my mind, he brought his lips down to meet with mine.

For a moment, the world seemed to stop. Everything fell away, and there was only him. Nothing had ever felt so soft yet so rough at the same time. His intensity consumed me, causing me to feel weightless as my body melted against his. For a moment, I barely recognized myself. With his lips pressed against mine, I wasn't able to remember the girl I once was. All I understood was the woman I was now, a woman who had met her match in every way.

His lips teased mine as he discovered me all over again. I relished in their comfort—their salty taste. As his lips moved with mine, I realized I had never been kissed like this before. Never had I experienced such passion; never had I felt so wanted. The kisses I had been used to receiving were rough, carnal, and completely mindless. The kisses I had experienced before this one had made me feel nothing more than a throbbing discomfort and a desire to break free. Everything before this had been emotionless. *But this ... this moment with Trevor ... this was different.*

"Just work with me, Veronica. Just ease up a little," he said as he groped at my breasts.

I wanted to like it, but I couldn't. I felt cold. Was this how it was supposed to be? It felt so ... impersonal.

"Do you like me?" he questioned, his voice hard.

"Of course, I do."

"Then show me."

Just as Trevor deepened the kiss, I pulled away, feeling frozen all of a sudden. I wasn't sure if I was ready for this. The images from my past were running through my mind like scenes from a movie, and I wanted to hide them in the darkest corner of my head. I wanted to protect myself like I always had. Feeling scared, I brought my eyes up to gaze at Trevor. As soon as his eyes captured mine, all of my anxiety melted away.

"What was that for?" I questioned breathlessly as my feelings overwhelmed me.

"Do I need a reason? I've been wanting to do that since I saw you."

My heart soared at his reply, and suddenly, nothing else mattered. I supposed I shouldn't have been so shocked; I saw the way he looked at me sometimes—I understood the heat behind his dark gaze. While his eyes were filled with desire, I knew there was more lurking in the depths of his gaze. There were emotions I doubted he was ready to share.

"I thought about the same thing," I replied after a moment.

His lively eyes scanned my face, possibly searching for the truth in my words. When he found it, he smiled, seeming weightless for a fleeting moment before his demeanor became grim. Whatever had happened today—whatever had prevented him from reaching out to me—had more of an impact on him than I had originally realized. My hand twitched, yearning to reach out to him to provide whatever comfort I could. *Does he like to be touched when he's upset? Would that help ease his pain or worsen it?*

Without placing a hand on him, I asked, "Are you sure you don't want to talk about it?"

With distant eyes and a forlorn expression, he sat in silence and gazed ahead. During moments like these, I worried about him. He was constantly abstracted and so very distant. I wondered where his mind was half of the time. For whatever reason, it seemed Trevor was constantly looking over his shoulder toward a past he could never touch again. While he was cerebral and kept to himself, I understood more about his past than he probably knew. After my mother died, I had always been looking over my shoulder, too; I had spent so many years waiting for her. Seeing her again had once felt like a possibility.

"Stop daydreaming, Veronica."

My older sister always pretended to be stronger than she was. Now that Mom was gone, she filled the role as if I allowed it to be vacant. I could pout all night if I wanted; I could do whatever the hell I wanted. It was my *birthday, after all. And all I wanted was for them to leave me be.* Should I apologize for not smiling? Why do I need to pretend? Who is it for? *I didn't want to smile. A smile wouldn't help me.*

Suddenly, I wondered if I was being selfish. Couldn't I put on a brave face for Eden and Dad? I supposed I could try ... for Mom.

"I'm sorry."

"Ronnie, I don't know where your mind is half the time."

After I didn't respond right away, she frowned, her shoulders dropping as she continued. "I miss her, too. But it's been four years! We have to move on."

"Move on to what?" I snapped. "What if I'm not ready for that yet?"

"We'll never be ready, Ronnie. We just have to try."

"I know." She didn't seem convinced by my answer. "I promise, I understand. I really do. But sometimes ... sometimes, I just like to remember her."

"I know you do. I do, too."

"I don't want to think that she's gone. Not yet ... not ever."

"You don't have to. She's here with us. I'm sure of it," Eden said.

"I know ... but I don't feel *her like I once did. She's fading away. I worry about her."*

"My brother, Dean, died three months ago."

His voice tore me from my musings. I wished I could find the right words, but they never came. I had guessed his brother had passed away. With the way Trevor spoke of his brother, it was hard not to realize the truth. His face had said it all before his mouth had uttered a word.

"Trev, I'm so sorry. You two were very close, weren't you?"

The muscle in his jaw twitched as he sunk into his seat. I could feel everything he tried desperately to hold back—everything he attempted to shield me from. I watched his eyes as they grew wet. What hurt the most was watching his struggle to contain his tears before they poured over his thick, bottom lashes.

"He and my sister-in-law died in a car accident." His voice cracked as he forced the words out. "They think it was a drunk driver that hit their car ..." His words trailed off into nothing as he hung his head. He almost looked ashamed. He was frozen for a long time, perfectly silent, before his body began to shake as if he were containing a scream. In this dark room, I felt like everything inside of him had quickly become illuminated. Everything he had been hiding—everything he had been shielding me from—had poured out of him. His eyes and his grim expression displayed the magnitude of emotions he'd been attempting to erase. My eyes stung watching him. I understood that he imagined himself as weak. I wish he could have seen how strong he looked in this moment. Every muscle in his body clenched as he dealt with the storm raging in his heart. *My fallen angel.* Just as that thought passed through my mind, Trevor captured my gaze. His eyes fell on the lone tear that trailed down my cheek. Carefully, he reached up and brushed it away with his fingertips.

"Don't cry for me. It's all over now, and I've been trying to move on."

His voice was suddenly strong—so were his eyes, which were weary yet filled with potency.

"I would've never known, Trev. You hide everything so well."

Outside of a few occasions, Trevor had never struck me as a man who had recently lost so much. He had always been so put together. I had never once seen him break.

"I don't know about that. I feel like I'm constantly on the verge of falling apart," he responded, seemingly reading my mind.

"You're so much stronger than you think."

"How do you know?" he questioned with a snort.

He had never been one for praise, which made me want to shower him with it—he deserved it. He deserved everything that was good in life.

No more darkness. For both of us, no more darkness.

"Because I know *you*," I said in a voice rich with conviction.

I *did* know him. I felt like he had always been with me. The feeling was chilling—it was like a part of me had always known him. It was as if we had been living parallel lives up until recently when our worlds had finally intersected.

The sense of relief radiating off of Trevor was profound. His shoulders relaxed, and the tension in his facial features dissipated. He looked years younger all of a sudden, and I wanted nothing more than to take him into my arms and hold him until there wasn't a single trace of pain.

"I saw his best friend today while I was at a diner having lunch with Grey," Trevor explained after a long, thoughtful pause. "I haven't seen Travis since Dean and Cat's wedding."

A bitter laugh escaped his throat, and I reached out, grasping his hand before giving it a light, comforting squeeze. He was lost in his thoughts again. His eyes darted back and forth as if he were looking at an image right in front of him. His brows knitted together for a moment before he took a deep breath and emitted a mirthless laugh. He looked up at me, as if he were trying to gauge my reaction, before he dropped his gaze and continued to speak.

"It was so fucking weird seeing him, Ronnie. It was as if I'd been confronted with my past, and it stung more than I ever could've imagined. When I looked at Travis, I couldn't help but see my brother, Dean. I feel like shit for feeling that way because I know he's suffering, too, but I couldn't bring myself to talk to him. It was just that he and Dean are so fucking alike. It's just a morbid reminder for me."

A morbid reminder. How familiar did that phrase sound? After Mom passed away, everything had seemed like a painful reminder of her. I hadn't been able to look anywhere without seeing her face in my mind. For a long time, I hadn't been able to make it more than a few minutes without her voice in my head or her face behind my eyes. In a way, it had been nice—seeing her everywhere had meant she was always with me. And while I had felt like I was never by myself with her in my head, I never had felt so lonesome.

Her memory had been a constant reminder that she wasn't here; her memory had never filled the hole she had left behind. Her joy, beauty, and warmth had always felt impossible to recreate. Once, Dad had expressed the emotions that filled him when he looked at me, explaining he saw my mother in me whenever I smiled—saw her spirit and her goodness. However, I had always believed those things to be unique to her and felt they could never be part of me. She was the one to stand out among the rest.

Her smiles had been soothing—her laughs had always been so infectious, and her giving heart had caused everyone to feel as if they were *home*. She had been able to say more with a single look than many could with a thousand words. Even now, I could see her so vividly, as if the last time I talked to her was only yesterday.

"Style it the way you do," I insisted, pulling at my hair.

"You don't like it?" she questioned, eyeing the updo. *"I thought this was what you wanted, Ronnie."*

"I liked the way you had it yesterday. It's my first day, and I want it to be special."

"Your first day of your last year in grade school. That is something to celebrate. You're not worried you'll look like your mother?" she teased.

"No, I want to look like you," I replied honestly.

Squeezing his hand and focusing all of my energy on him, I told the strong man beside me, "I understand. I understand more than you know, Trev. I promise it'll get better. Time may not heal your wounds, but it makes them bearable."

He'll always be with you, Trev. In your heart ... In your spirit. Just like my mother will always be with me. The people we loved would never truly leave us. The imprint they had left on our lives—even long after they were gone—would never be washed away. The people we met, the people we surrounded ourselves with, and the people we loved would always exist. Even the smallest impact could leave an imprint on us forever.

"Am I selfish for blowing him off?" Trevor asked me, his voice sounding small. "Should I reach out to him?"

"Just do what is right for you. I'm sure he'll understand that. When the time is right, you'll know."

While he didn't seem entirely sure, he seemed too tired to comment. *Time may not heal everything, but it sure does numb the pain.* Wrapping an arm around his shoulder, I watched as Trevor continued to carry the weight of the world. *Lean on me, Trev. Let someone in. Don't carry the weight on your own.*

12

Don't Think Twice, It's All Right

His weary eyes watched me as I crossed the room. After his confession, I knew I couldn't be alone tonight. However, in this moment, I could barely breathe. *Was this a good idea?* Holding my favorite picture of my mother—the *last* picture of my mother—I closed the distance between Trevor and me. In this photograph, she was smiling with such a peaceful look on her face, it brought tears to my eyes. On my mother's face was a look of acceptance. She had understood that while she didn't have forever, she had that day—that moment.

Trevor sat on the couch in my living room, giving me a curious look. His expression was guarded while he appraised me. He'd had a short while to calm down after his confession, but his energy was just as raw.

"I wanted to show you something," I murmured as I took a seat next to him on the couch. With a shaky breath, I handed him the photograph, cringing as it passed through my numb fingers. His eyes widened as he took in the image. "This is the last picture we ever took of her."

Looking down at Grey as he played with his favorite stuffed animal on my living room floor, I allowed my mind to wander. My thoughts drifted back to that day in the hospital with her. I remembered every bit of the day vividly.

I had woken up late that morning after my alarm clock had fallen onto my face. My sister had been peering down at me when I opened my eyes, laughing at my expression. I remembered that, even in my disorientated, exhausted haze, I had found the sound of her laughter beautiful. I remembered the fly, which had flown into my room the night before buzzing around, annoying Eden to no end as we had gotten ready. I remembered the way the crisp day had turned gray and the way the sky had started to weep as our family had reached the hospital. That day, my mom had woken up in time for an early lunch, and the sun had been nice enough to peek through the clouds for her. One of our nurses had pulled back the curtains for her to see the small courtyard outside her window. Mom had smiled as the vitamin D soaked into her pores, and the sun had danced over her features.

"Isn't the day beautiful, Ronnie?" she asked as she gazed outside her hospital room window.

I straightened up in my seat, leaning over the bed to get a better look at her. "It's perfect. Why don't we go outside for a bit, Mom?"

"I don't know ... Maybe if I'm feeling better after lunch, okay?"

She never wanted to tell me no.

"Okay ..." I trailed off as I ran out of ideas on how best to entertain her.

I didn't like seeing her sad. She's so bored here. It's time for her to come home. We can't function without her.

"Will you be home for my birthday?" I asked timidly.

Her eyes widened for a moment before they became slightly misty. She smiled at me and gestured for me to sit next to her.

"Come here, sweet girl."

"Mom?"

"I want to talk to you."

I rose from my chair and moved to sit beside her. She wrapped her arm around my shoulder and pulled me close.

"I want you to promise me something, Veronica."

Her voice was serious. She was always serious whenever she used my full name.

"Anything."

"Take care of Eden and Daddy for me, okay?"

"Why? You'll be out of here, soon."

Her face relaxed, and for a moment, she looked almost peaceful.

"Well, while I'm in here, will you watch out for them? Make sure they're okay?"

"Of course, Mom. Anything."

"Good." She was silent for a moment and closed her eyes to enjoy the sun's hot beams. "Why don't we sit near the window. I want to feel the sun."

"What about going to the courtyard?"

"Later. Now, I just want to sit there."

I nodded, understanding. She never did well outside her room. I frowned.

"No sad faces," she cooed as she tilted my chin up to look me in the eye. "You promised me, Veronica. Only smiles."

"Only smiles."

She had sat near the window until the sun began to set. Sometimes, when I bathed under the sun's hot rays, I thought of her. I thought of the way she had looked as the sun cast beautiful shadows across her features.

"Hey," Trevor said, his voice soothing as it pulled me from my contemplations. "Please don't feel like you've got to tell me anything, Ronnie."

"No," I replied, shaking my head as I tried to gather my strength. "I—I want to." My eyes filled with tears, and despite my might, I couldn't stop them. "You've got to know that you're not alone with this sort of pain, Trev. I've been dealing with it myself for so many years."

Before I could continue, he leaned forward and brushed his lips against mine ever so gently. Their sweetness teased me, causing me to momentarily forget about everything else. My body melted against his as I basked in the feel of him. Time suspended until he finally pulled away to breathe. He looked at me for a moment, giving me time to gather my scattered thoughts, before he dropped his gaze to the photograph in his lap. I watched him carefully as he looked at the image of my mother. As he scrutinized it, I wondered if he was noting our similar features. A smile tugged on his lips, and I felt my heart open up to him even more.

"She's gorgeous, Ronnie."

I love you, Trevor Warren. I'm in love with you.

The thought passed through my mind like a comet across the night sky, and my heart stopped for a moment as I realized the fleeting thought was true. In this moment, I loved Trevor Warren. How could I not love him? *Isn't this love? Doesn't he love me? His expression as he gazed at the photo of my mother ... the way he treats me ... the way he puts me, and everyone, before himself ... the way he hates to see me cry ... the way he wants to take away my pain ... Is that not love?* Had the idea of love really become so foreign to me I hadn't recognized it sooner?

If my mom were here now, she would chastise me for not following my heart. My eyes dropped to her picture as Trevor's words sunk in further. I quickly wiped away a tear before it fell from my thick, bottom lashes.

"Thanks. This was the last picture she let us take of her. She's wearing the wig I picked out for her. I chose my hair color so she and I could match," I told him as the memories moved through my mind like scenes from a movie.

Trevor draped his arm over my shoulder, absorbing my grief. Taking a deep breath, I cleared my mind for a moment and gathered the strength required to continue.

"She passed away when I was twelve," I muttered, barely able to recognize my own voice. "She had been suffering for a long time, and while my dad was sad, he said it was *good* because her passing meant she was no longer in pain. However, as a pre-teen, I didn't see it that way. I was angry for such a long time ... constantly looking for someone to blame. I blamed her doctors, her nurses, our *family* ... until I realized there wasn't a single person left to point the finger at. Things like that just happened. Life doesn't care if it's being unfair, Trev."

Everyone died—even stars burned out. It was natural but never easy. Even now, after so many years had passed, I still struggled. I missed her with every beat of my heart—with every breath I took. A day never passed where I didn't think of her. *What girl doesn't miss her mom?*

While the question flew through my mind, I felt young and vulnerable. Suddenly, I seemed childlike. Even as an adult—even after she was gone—I longed for her comfort, her warmth, and her unconditional love.

"How did you deal with her death?" Trevor quietly questioned, effectively pulling me away from my musings before the image of her overwhelmed me. "How'd you get better again?"

A small, wistful smile tugged at my lips. *Getting better ... does that happen for anyone?* Did we ever truly recover from a loss? Did we ever get better, or did we merely learn to accept an absence in our lives?

"You never really 'get better' again. Not fully. I'll always bear a scar—the weight of her death. I just learned to carry it. You go on because you have to. My mother wouldn't have wanted me to wallow in my sorrow and self-pity. She would've wanted me to live—to be happy and accomplish my dreams. It took me a while to realize that. And, once I did, I moved forward with my life and did everything I could to make her proud."

As I finished, I wondered what my mom would have thought of me today. If she saw me now, would she be proud of me? Would she love the woman I turned into as she had loved me as a child? As I considered it, my eyes dropped to Grey. Already, I loved him as if he were my own flesh and blood. I loved him like my mother surely loved me. *Loves me. She's somewhere out there—she's inside of my heart—and she loves me.*

Tension trickled out of my pores as my muscles relaxed. *Somewhere, she loves me.* Grey smiled at me from his spot on the floor, no longer caring about the stuffed animal pressed between his chubby, little hands. Just as I had vowed to make my mother proud, Trev had made a vow, too. Seeing Grey's bright, healthy smile, I knew that somewhere, Trevor's brother was proud of him. *Dean was probably more than proud of him.* The thought made my eyes mist.

"It's just like what you're doing," I murmured as I continued to observe Grey's gummy grin. "Grey is Dean's, isn't he?"

Grey belonged to the brother who died. The only brother Trevor probably had.

"Yes."

His answer was clipped. Despite his collected façade, his wounds were fresh.

"You're doing the right thing," I assured him. "Your brother, *Dean*, would be so proud of you."

He is *so proud of you, Trev. Don't you see that?*

The fact that this beautiful, broken man couldn't see his own worth destroyed me. It was as if he didn't understand the importance of what he did each and every day. He was giving a little boy the father he needed—the father he deserved. I didn't have to understand the lurid details of his past to know it was far from clean. He may not have been perfect, but he was perfectly imperfect, now. *He's perfect for me. He's perfect for Greyson, too.* My gaze drifted to the little boy again, who was looking at his uncle with such reverence it left me breathless. A fractured sob caused my eyes to shoot to the man beside me, who was falling apart with his face buried between his calloused hands.

Instinctively, my arms wrapped around him and pulled his muscled frame against my soft curves. He was stiff in my arms but leaned into my embrace. His body shook against mine as tears fell from his dark, wounded eyes. He was so *broken*; as his emotions ran freely, he seemed so defeated by the world. His head came down to rest on my breasts, allowing their softness to soothe him. I ran a hand through his hair as I felt his tears dampen the fabric of my cotton shirt.

I held him closer, grateful he felt comfortable enough to fall apart like this in front of me. Only when I heard Grey's cries did I pull away. After I gave Trevor one chaste kiss on the head, I went to retrieve his nephew. Pulling Grey into my arms, I tried to soothe his pain, too. Seeing his uncle fall apart agitated him. I saw how he itched to comfort him. Trevor had pulled himself together slightly by the time I returned to the couch with Greyson. Immediately, Grey screeched and flailed his arms around as he reached for his uncle.

"I'm sure all the emotion in the room is overwhelming him," I explained as I handed him the crying baby.

Trevor frowned, looking guilty as he took his nephew from my arms. I knew he felt like he had to be strong for him, but he was only human. He couldn't build walls around himself to shut everyone out; he couldn't carry the weight of those deaths alone.

Once, I had tried to be alone, too. I had tried to bottle up every emotion I had. I had never wanted anyone around me to realize how broken I was. I had never wanted anyone to tell me they understood. I hadn't cared if they understood because, at the time, I had felt like no one would fathom the pain in my heart. I had acted as if I had been the first person to ever lose someone. Now, I felt silly. I had been angry for so long because I had been too afraid to be honest. I knew Trevor wanted to be a pillar of strength for his nephew; I knew he believed, above all else, that was what Grey needed. But all Grey needed was *him*—broken or otherwise.

The love Trevor had for his nephew was palpable. It was painted on his expression as he held him close, silently willing away his pain. His love seemed boundless. I had to admit, my love for him was boundless, too. He may not have had his father—or his mother—but he had us. *Could that be enough?*

"I'm sorry I broke down like that," Trevor said after a long while. His cheeks flushed. "I don't know what the hell came over me."

"It's okay. You haven't had any time to grieve, have you? You've been thrusted into the role of a parent before you really had time to say goodbye to your brother."

His shoulders slumped as a look of relief colored his features. With a tight smile, he quietly said, "Thanks for telling me about your mom. I know that must've been hard for you."

"It's not hard anymore." I shrugged—it was the truth. After many years, I had learned to accept things—I learned how to live again. "It's personal to me, but you're part of my life, Trev. I want you to know about my past."

"When you find the one, you'll know, Veronica. I promise you. You'll want them to know every part of you. You'll want to know every part of them."

"Is that how you felt about Daddy?"

"Of course." She smiled, peering at the picture of them posed on her bedside table. *"Well, not at first. At first, I wasn't so sure. But—"* She stopped, smiling.

"But?"

"'Time waits for no one.' Someone told me that once, and it has always stuck with me. Time waits for no one, but when you find that person, time will feel like it's standing still."

"I want to tell you everything, Ronnie ..." He trailed off before he shook his head. With a clenched jaw, he continued. "I've just got to wait until I'm ready. I just don't want you to think ..."

"Don't want me to think, what?"

What could he possibly say that would turn me away? We were both damaged goods. We were both broken in so many ways—fractured into so many pieces. He wasn't the only one filled with fear; I was afraid, too. I was worried if he knew my full truth, he would turn away; I worried that if he understood the complexity of my issues, he wouldn't want me. A small voice in my head screamed I was being foolish, but my paranoia was deeply rooted, causing my vision to blur. After my past, I wasn't sure if I could trust myself.

"I don't want you to think I'm fucking weak," he finally said.

"I could never think that."

"But you don't know everything about me," he insisted in a bitter voice. "Once you do, you might not look at me the same way."

"No matter what you tell me, I know nothing would ever change the way I feel about you."

His eyes widened slightly before his back stiffened. *What's going on in that beautiful head of his?* I cared for him so much it hurt. I wanted to express that—I wanted a relationship—but I wasn't sure where to begin, or if I should begin at all. *Could I handle a relationship? Could I ever be "normal"?*

Interrupting me from my thoughts, Trevor added, "Nothing you could ever say would change my feelings for you, too."

He paused for a moment, and after a conflicted look appeared on his face for a fleeting moment, his shoulders slumped, and he dropped his gaze; his gaze fell to his nephew, who was sagging against the strong muscles of his uncle's arms. Grey smiled at me, staring up with sleepy but happy eyes before he emitted a huge yawn, stretching his chubby arms over his head. After he was finished, he giggled and shifted in Trevor's embrace, trying to get comfortable.

"I think I'm going to head back to my place and call it a night," Trev said, his tone rich with regret.

I didn't want to be alone tonight. I couldn't bear the thought of my empty apartment. I knew the quiet, while usually pleasing, would drive me mad tonight. My body needed comfort, and my mind needed to be occupied by something other than television or a good book. I needed a connection with someone. I needed Trevor. Perhaps that made me weak, but I didn't care. The thought of being alone tonight, with nothing more than my thoughts, was unbearable. I yearned to feel his body against mine, comforting me as I needed him. I wanted to feel his strong arms embracing me. I wanted to feel his hot breath against my skin. I wanted to rest my head on his broad chest to hear the sound of his heartbeat, assuring me that he's alive and well. He may not love me, but I felt loved around him.

"Can I stay with you?" I questioned, hoping my voice didn't sound too desperate. "I just don't want to be alone tonight."

His gaze darkened as he looked at me before a sad smile tugged on his lips. "Of course," he murmured. "As long as you don't mind a crying baby throughout the night."

I smiled at this, feeling a weight being taken off of my shoulders. "I don't mind, Trev."

With that, I went to the bathroom to get ready for bed. As much as I wanted to look pretty for him, I knew it was not practical to go to bed with makeup on my face. So, I washed it off, feeling like a new person afterward, and brushed my teeth. I finished up my nightly routine, running a brush through my hopeless hair before changing into a pair of pajamas, which Eden had gifted me a few years ago. I had only worn them once—I always felt silly dressing up for a night by myself—so, it was nice to wear them tonight for Trevor. As soon as I walked back into the living room, his eyes widened slightly, and judging by the look on his face, I could tell he appreciated my attire. It was nothing sexy—far from it, in fact—but I supposed I looked *cute*. He stared at me for a moment longer before he broke into a huge grin. Grey giggled, apparently agreeing with my pink pajama set, as well.

After locking up my apartment, I followed Trevor across the hall to his. While he unlocked his door and grinned at me, I breathed a sigh of relief, eager for the night ahead. This sort of adventurous behavior was certainly outside of my comfort zone. I was high from the shock as I realized what I was doing. Part of me believed I should be anxious; however, Trevor's presence alone had a way of putting me at ease.

Trevor opened the apartment door, and I noticed Grey had already begun to nod off in his uncle's arms. Trevor noticed, too, and smiled, relieved by the sight of his drowsy nephew. He ushered me inside, turning on the lights. Despite the scarcity of furniture and decorations, as well as the lack of warmth from the interior, this place felt like *home* to me. It felt comforting—just like its tenant.

"I was going to read Grey a quick story before he goes to bed."

"Do you mind if I listen?" I asked, peering over his shoulder and into the nursery.

"Of course not." His cheeks flushed.

Who knew someone so intensely masculine could blush so much!

"His favorite story is *Where the Wild Things Are*," Trevor said as he led me down the hall to Grey's room. "Usually, by the time that one's finished, he's sound asleep."

To listen to Trevor read was incredible. The deep tone of his voice soothed my mind as he told a tale I had been familiar with from childhood. While I had read this story many times, I was certain I had never sounded the way Trevor had as he read to his nephew. The care he put into every word had been captivating. His voice rose and fell when appropriate, which had caused Grey to become enthralled with the reading despite his exhaustion. Watching Trevor's dark eyes scan the pages, and the way the muscles in his jaw tensed with every word, combined with the sound of his rough voice reciting the words had captivated me, too. As the story came to its close, Grey had drifted to sleep.

"See, right on cue," Trevor said as he carefully closed the book and placed it on the floor next to his chair.

With a loving smile on his face, Trevor gazed down at his nephew, his eyes scanning as if they were trying to memorize Grey's little face—attempting to take in every feature. When he was satisfied, he rose with Grey in his embrace and carried him to the crib. Trevor kissed his nephew on the forehead, holding him close for a moment before he gently lowered him onto his back.

Quietly, we moved to leave the room, turning off the lights and cracking the door before we made our way down the hall to the living room. My entire body sagged as I walked—my mind finally in a state of ease. A smile tugged on my lips as I realized this was better than I had felt in a long while. Today, I had gotten so much off of my chest, and while I hadn't told Trevor everything about my past, I felt lighter now. Now, I felt closer to him than I ever believed possible. Never in a million years would I have imagined I could feel so close to another person.

I had so much to thank Trevor for, but tonight, I was done with the heavy. We had disclosed so much about ourselves today, so I thought it was time we just relaxed. I just wanted to *be*, with him at my side.

Pulling out my phone, I asked, "Do you want me to order a pizza or something? I'm starving."

"That's cool. I was too upset earlier to realize how hungry I was."

Pulling up an app on my phone—because why talk to a living, breathing person on the phone when I could avoid social interaction?—I began to order some food for us.

"Great story, by the way," I commented as I scrolled through the topping options on the app. "I never knew someone could sound so sexy while reading Maurice Sendak."

He snorted at my comment, and I glanced up just in time to watch him roll his eyes and shake his head.

"Thanks," he replied with a roguish grin. "Maybe I could read one of your books to you? I'm sure I'd sound sexy while reading about 'throbbing cocks' and 'heaving bosoms.' "

My eyes bulged at the accusation, and I nearly cringed as I felt blood rush to my cheeks. I was sure because of my ivory skin my blush was extremely prominent. *How does he know about what I read? Was he looking through all of my books? I only have a few bodice breakers! Were those the books he looked at?* I could have died from mortification. I knew I shouldn't be embarrassed about what I read, but the thought of Trevor knowing what I was interested in sexually made my skin flush all over.

"What books do you mean?" I managed to stutter out. "I don't have books like that."

"Whatever you say, my little liar." Trevor winked at me. "I checked out the books on your bookshelves the first night you had me over."

"Well, I only read those every now and then," I lied while I wondered if my voice sounded too disingenuous.

"For 'recreational purposes'?" Trevor asked, causing me to nearly choke as he cocked his brow at me.

If only he knew about the "material" I used for recreational purposes. Every time I touched myself, it's his face in my mind, the thought of his hands on my body.

"They happen to be great stories, thank you very much."

When he gave me an incredulous look, I couldn't help but snort.

"I've got no doubt about that."

"I guess you can read them to me," I finally said, teasing as I obliged him. "You know, to practice your oral skills."

He nearly choked on air at my comment; his dark eyes widened as he appraised me.

"I ordered a pizza," I changed the subject, knowing I wasn't bold enough to continue on our current path of conversation. "It'll be here in about twenty minutes. Want to watch a movie or something while we wait?"

Movies were safe, right? Now that we were alone in close quarters with the promise of the night ahead, I didn't know how to feel. The sensations Trevor conjured up from within astounded me. After all the time I had spent around him, I was still amazed by the way the man affected me. For so long, I had worried I would never be able to feel this way again. I feared no man could stir up an emotion within me, causing such a delicious havoc in my life. When I looked at Trevor standing before me in his inked, sinful glory, I felt everything imaginable. I wanted him to comfort me—love me—fuck me. I wanted him to pound into me until everything else turned into a colorful blur. Just thinking these thoughts caused me to feel as if I were blossoming into a new woman.

I had been meek for so long—weak for so long—and now, I felt strong and so incredibly beautiful. Trevor could make me feel invincible with a single look. When he gazed at me with eyes filled with reverence, I felt like I could do anything—conquer anything—because he believed in me.

His eyes faltered, and he looked away, running a shaky hand through his hair. I wondered what he was thinking. I wondered if he felt the sweet tension building between us, too. With a crooked grin, he nodded his head toward the couch before he crossed the room to pick out a movie. I took a seat and, unable to help myself, allowed my eyes to wander along the lines of his muscular back, which was deliciously strained against the fabric of his cotton shirt, before my eyes fell to the curve of his ass, which was perfect as he bent over a few feet in front of me.

I wonder what he would do if I reached out and ran my hand along his glutes before running my fingertips along the hard lines of his thighs. Maybe I was being perverse, but how could my mind think of anything else while Trevor was bent over a few feet away.

After a few moments, he found the movie he was looking for and opened the DVD player. I watched his muscles undulate with every movement. I was so transfixed by the sight of him, I barely noticed his film selection until the eerie title music began.

He joined me on the couch, allowing me to curl up against his hard body as we watched the Colorado mountains move across the screen, taking us deeper and deeper into the movie on a journey to the Overlook. I shuddered, cozying up to the man next to me.

"The song in the opening credits always freaked me out," I explained as Stanly Kubrick's name flashed across the screen.

"Are you okay to watch this movie? I thought you said you liked this one."

I had seen *The Shining* more times than I could count. Despite living alone, I loved being scared; I loved having to constantly look over my shoulder after a movie, too terrified to be rational. Usually, I curled up with a pillow on my lap and wouldn't utter a sound. But, with a handsome man I was more than attracted to pressed against me, I had a feeling this movie would affect me more than usual.

"I *do* like it," I quipped. "I just find it eerie, Trev."

I pressed closer to him, causing him to tighten his hold on me.

While the movie drew us in, we sat in a comfortable silence, soaking in the emotions filling the air. In the silence, I contemplated how *nice* this was—how content I felt. Our pizza arrived, and we ate while our eyes remained locked on the television, enjoying each other's company.

My mind began to drift, moving from one thought to the next with Trevor as a constant. With my gaze locked on the screen, I saw his angular face in my head, tracing its sharp lines in my mind's eye. I thought of his smile, his smoldering gaze, and his dark eyes crinkling as he broke into laughter. My mind drifted. Soon, I imagined his body— what it must look like underneath the T-shirt and jeans he always wore. I imagined his inked, muscular frame covered in sweat. I imagined his muscles as his body thrusted into mine, becoming one. My breath caught in my throat as my already overactive imagine ran wild. Just the thought of him alone made my underwear wet; I couldn't begin to imagine how I would feel if my musings became a reality.

Despite my emotional exhaustion, my body was flushed with desire. Time and time again, I tried to focus on the movie, but the fact that I had seen it many times coupled with the gorgeous man at my side made it hard to concentrate on anything more than the stirrings in my body. Every time I was around this man, my body opened up as if it had been awoken from a long slumber. In many ways, it had. My senses had been asleep for far too long; now, they were overwhelming.

Pressing my legs together, I tried desperately to ease the tension, but it was all to no avail. *Focus on the movie, Veronica. Don't push things further than your psyche is willing to go.* Although we wouldn't do anything tonight, we would eventually venture to uncharted territories. I wanted to *feel* how much he cared for me. In return, I wanted him to feel how much I cared for him. I wanted him to touch the spot between my legs, which ached for him. I wanted him to make me forget about everyone before.

With a deep sigh, I focused my attention on the movie, becoming enthralled with the plot as I pushed all other thoughts away. I kept my legs pressed together as the sensation never went away. I wondered if Trevor noticed. *Would a man even notice something like that?* I was sure I felt like a ball of tension beside him. Leaning farther against his side, I prayed one day I would have the courage to ask him to release the built-up tension coiling inside of my body.

As the movie came to its close, I breathed a sigh of relief, happy to have gotten through it without embarrassing myself. There was something about the close quarters, surrounded by darkness, which made everything so much more intimate. It was like there was only us and nothing else. In the darkness, the outside world didn't matter. In this moment, there was only him.

Wanting to break the tension in the room, which I was sure was created from my own doing, I commented on the movie, saying, "I love the movie, even though it's nothing like the book."

Wow, way to string together a coherent sentence, Veronica!

Trevor smiled at me before rising from the couch to grab another film.

"You a big Stephen King fan?" he asked with a glance over his shoulder.

"Yes," I replied, straightening my back. "I love all of his classics. I haven't gotten the opportunity to read any of his new stuff, though, since I've been swamped with work."

Trevor turned his head and gently smiled as he replaced one DVD with another. "I can't remember the last time I read something other than a kid's book."

My eyes widened at his comment. Although, I completely understood; I couldn't imagine a life without reading. In a way, books had saved my life. When I was surrounded by constant darkness, opening a book was like a hug from a forgotten friend.

"Well, you should get back into it," I replied, hoping he would find time for some self-care eventually. "You can get lost in another world."

Standing up, Trevor gave me a brilliant smile before he walked toward me, joining me on the couch. There was a tenderness in his eyes I didn't miss. I looked away as the opening credits jarred me. My eyes shot to the television to find *Basket Case* beginning. Trevor slid his right arm around my shoulders, pulling me comfortably against him. In this moment, we truly felt like a couple. We were so comfortable around each other—so open—it was as if we had known each other for many years. I didn't know if I believed in fate, but when I was with him, it felt like everything happening was predestined.

He had held me throughout the movie, and considering my state of arousal, I was hyperaware of each and every move he made. I noted the way his thumb had rubbed circles on the flesh of my arm; I noticed the heat of his skin as it had pressed against mine. I had even recognized the changes in his breathing. I hadn't been able to focus on the movie as it reached its close. Thankfully, I had seen it a few times before—I would have been mortified if we had watched something I had been unfamiliar with and he asked me my thoughts. I would have had to be vague because I wouldn't have wanted to say, "Sorry, I was too distracted with your body to pay attention to the film." *God, I would have died of mortification.*

As the credits rolled, Trevor turned his attention to me and asked, "You really want to stay the night?"

Does he not want me to? Am I being far too eager? Blood rushed to my cheeks as I tried to shove my innate shyness away, answering, "Is that all right? I wouldn't want to impose."

"Of course, it's all right," he answered quickly, standing up from the couch before proffering his hand to me.

I placed my hand in his and rose from my seat, too, following him to his bedroom down the hall. As we moved, my heart thumped wildly in my chest; so loudly I feared he may hear it. I was sure he could feel my rapid pulse as my palm was pressed so tightly against his. I couldn't help it—I had been wondering what his bedroom looked like for some time now. Just the thought of being alone with him in this room was enough to cause frantic palpitations.

Veronica, stop being ridiculous! You're not a virgin, so what do you have to be so bashful about? It's just a man's bedroom! You two aren't going to have sex, so chill the heck out!

From the moment I stepped foot in his room, I smiled. It was so minimalistic—so *Trevor*. There was a desk in the corner of the room, an older television sitting atop an equally aged dresser, and a king-sized bed with off-white sheets. While it wasn't anything extraordinary, I fell in love with it instantaneously.

"Well, this is it," Trevor said with a wave of his hand. With an abashed smile, he continued. "You can go ahead and get into bed if you want. I've just got to change into my pajamas and brush my teeth." He looked at his bed, grimaced, and said, "The sheets are clean. And feel free to turn on the TV. I know it's old, but it still works."

I spared the television set a glance and smiled, remembering having something similar when I was growing up.

"I haven't seen a CRT TV since I was a kid."

I climbed into bed, quickly making myself at home there. Snuggling beneath the sheets, I gave him a relaxed grin.

"It's really cool, though," I added.

He stared at me for a few heartbeats before he gave me a tight, uncomfortable smile. I opened my mouth to say something, wanting to put his mind at ease, but remained silent. I wondered if he was just as nervous with the prospect of us sleeping together in the same bed as I was. The question danced in my mind as I watched him turn on his heel and stalk off to the bathroom. The bathroom door shut, and the lock clicked into place. *He must not want my company. God, like I would follow him into the bathroom anyway. I bet he's naked in there. Jesus, my thoughts are too embarrassing. Thank God, I'm not much of a talker. I would embarrass myself on the daily.*

Cringing at my internal monologue, I lay in bed, considering how he would react once he joined me. As I lay there, peering up at the ceiling while my eyes traced its simplistic patterns, I realized tonight would be the first night I had ever slept with a man. In my one and only relationship, we had never spent the night together. He had always been "too busy" for that, despite my copious protests.

Even when I had been passed out—unable to care for myself— he had left me there. When I had been with him, I had been blinded by love. All I had wanted was to feel his warmth every night. Back then, I had wanted to feel loved by someone. At the time, I'd had no idea sex and power plays were all our relationship had been to him.

Trevor is so unlike him. Already, he's his polar opposite in every way.

I crammed those thoughts away—this wasn't the time or place for them. This bed signified a new beginning. Already, I knew I was a changed woman. A few months ago, I would have been crippled with anxiety under these circumstances. *A few months ago, I wouldn't have been in these circumstances at all.* However, now I was fine. I knew Trevor well enough to believe I had nothing to fear. I had a feeling he would never pressure me to do anything I wasn't comfortable with—he didn't appear to be the type.

As I waited for his return, I grabbed the remote, wanting the television to distract me from reality. The silence had always bothered me because, in silence, my mind wandered to places I intended to keep closed off. Mindlessly, I flipped through the channels on the TV. There wasn't much—at least, not for someone who had become accustomed to On Demand subscriptions and seemingly endless channels—but, I managed to find Cartoon Network. I smiled, feeling young as I lay snuggled warmly beneath the layers of sheets.

I felt him enter the room; every hair on my body seemed to stand as the electricity surrounding him filled my air. My eyes shot to him as my breath caught in my throat. He looked so *perfect*. He looked at me with bright, mischievous eyes, and time suspended. *Are we really doing this? Am I really sharing a bed with a man?* He smiled at me, and whatever anxiety was left in my body evaporated.

Suddenly, feeling bold, I patted the space beside me on the mattress and questioned, "You coming to bed? I thought you were tired?"

He gazed at me for a few moments longer before he crossed the room to join me. While a piece of myself experienced spine-tingling nerves, another, more prominent part felt as though this was the most natural thing in the world—as if we had done this a thousand times. When he slid onto the mattress, burrowing beneath the covers, there wasn't a hint of awkwardness. The tenderness in his eyes thawed my heart.

As soon as he was comfortably in bed, he reached out and gently pulled me against his side. My body stilled for a moment as a shiver ran down my spine. My back arched off the bed slightly, and suddenly, I wanted to do all of the things I had dreamt of doing with him. I wanted to become lost in his body while he became lost in mine. In the darkness of the room, we lay comfortably for a long while, neither of us uttering a word. The only sound in the darkness was the soft whisper of our breaths. Emotion sat heavy on my heart, and while I wanted to open my mouth to utter the words, I kept quiet, not fully understanding my feelings for him.

Grey's cries paused my musings. Trevor stiffened beside me, seemingly disappointed with the interruption from our quiet night together. I was disappointed, too; however, I understood what came first—I wouldn't have had it any other way. I loved Grey so much. *Just as much as I loved his uncle.*

"Do you mind if I bring his crib in here?" Trevor asked as he jumped out of bed, away from my warm embrace. "I do it most nights, so I don't have to keep going back and forth between his room and mine."

I gave him a sleepy smile and nodded before he smiled in return and left the room to retrieve his nephew. As soon as he was gone, I moved to the bathroom to freshen up, feeling paranoid now that I was in such close proximity to this man who had consumed my every thought. Venturing across the room, I heard him talking to his cute, little guy in his room at the end of the hallway.

His deep voice spoke in pleasant tones, causing Grey to coo. I smiled, touched by the interaction. I hurried to the bathroom, knowing Trevor would be back any moment, and quickly relieved myself before I washed my hands. As I lathered up with his store brand bar of soap, I eyed his toothbrush as I ran my tongue along my teeth. *He wouldn't mind, would he?* I shrugged and grabbed the toothbrush before I applied a dime-sized amount of toothpaste and began to brush. *We're close enough for this sort of thing, aren't we? I mean, we* have *kissed before.* Just the thought of his lips pressed against mine caused me to smile around the toothbrush between my opened lips as I leisurely brushed before rinsing.

Returning to the bedroom, I found Grey posed on the center of the bed, peering up at me with a wide, sleepy smile. The ends of his mouth twitched before his smile broadened, and he tried to move his little body across the bed to reach me. I looked to Trevor, who was situating Grey's crib by his bedside. Our eyes meet, and he grinned similarly to Grey.

"I used your toothbrush. I hope you don't mind."

Crossing the room, I picked up Grey and held him safely in my arms, bending down to brush a kiss against his soft head of hair.

Grey giggled at the sensation and pulled away to peer up at me. He gazed at me for a moment, his eyes searching mine, before he brought his little hand up to brush against my face.

"He likes you a lot," Trevor mused, causing my eyes to shoot up to meet his.

He was watching us with a thoughtfulness brightening his features. His eyes were peaceful—happy—as he watched his nephew smiling in my arms. For a moment, it felt like every wrong in the world had corrected itself. This was a feeling of profound relief; for so long, I had felt pathetically aimless—walking through life without a sense of direction or purpose. The periods of darkness in my life had subsequently caused me to throw myself into a career—never once had I considered anything more for myself. *After my fucked-up past, what importance was a future?*

"Well, that's good," I respond as my eyes dropped down to view the happy boy in my arms, "because I love him, too."

Grey cooed at this, causing my heart to blossom. The air surrounding us was heavy with emotions as if they were emitting through our pores. The darkness that surround my life—surrounded all of our lives—was nowhere to be found. We were each other's salvation. Holding Grey close, I made a promise to never let him go. *I never want to lose this.*

Fear nagged at the edges of my contentment. *Have I found happiness too quickly?* Things in my life rarely had been beautiful. When they had, that beauty faded into so many different things—none of those things had been happy. Any moment of happiness seemed to be followed by a moment of grief. So, now, I was terrified. *What if I managed to lose this somehow? What if these two incredible people weren't meant to be mine forever?*

I brushed away the darkness as I watched Grey drift to sleep in my embrace. His little body was relaxed in my arms, and in his sleep, he grinned. I wondered if his smile was because of me. I looked to Trevor, who was still watching us, before I walked Grey to his crib, placing him gently on his back.

"He's such a good baby," I commented tenderly.

"He's not always like that," Trevor replied with a gruff laugh, his deep voice causing my body to relax even further. "I think it's just you."

I smiled, wondering if he was merely saying that as I joined him on the bed. Laying next to him on the mattress, I found my body was like water—completely fluid and relaxed. With Trevor at my side, my body melted against the mattress; my limbs felt weightless as I drank in the sight of him. His muscular form was sprawled out on the bed, his strong legs tangled with the thin white sheets. *I want to lick every inch of him.*

His dark eyes swept over the curves of my body, giving special attention to my breasts and hips before ascending to my face.

"Hey," he began somewhat awkwardly, "how about this weekend I take you out? Just you and me? I could ask my parents if they'd watch Grey."

His face was hopeful, and his eyes were pensive as he awaited my response.

Does he really believe I'd say no to that? How could I say no to him ever? Why would I ever want to? His insecurities baffled me at times. Snuggling closer to his side, I used my body to reassure him.

"I'd like that."

I smiled as his frame relaxed significantly.

Wrapping his thick arms around me, he held me comfortably against his chest. I inhaled the smell of his cologne: earthy aromas mixed with a smell that was unique to Trev. Relaxing deeper, I nodded off as I moved with the rise and fall of his broad chest. *Who knew the feeling of someone's breath could be so beautiful?* As we lay in the darkness, I made another promise to myself: I wouldn't let this family slip through my fingers.

I deserved happiness. I deserved to be loved. I had not been used up; I wasn't the piece of garbage I had once believed myself to be. I was a good person—Trevor was a good person—and we both deserved something *more*. Until this point, life had never been easy for me. With Trevor, dealing with my demons seemed manageable.

With Trevor, all my nightmares faded away, leaving me with nothing but dreams.

13

There Is A Light That Never Goes Out

Nervous energy ran through my veins, causing even a miniscule task to become seemingly impossible. *How can I concentrate on anything when Trevor was going to be here in a few short hours?* I couldn't remember the last time I felt so excited—so bubbly. I was sure Eden wouldn't recognize me if she saw me; she would wonder where her meek sister went. With jittery limbs, a hammering heart, and a flush coloring my pale skin, I felt like a teenager.

I looked up from my makeup palate to peer at my reflection in the mirror. With glowing skin and bright eyes, I looked like a different woman. I smiled, biting down on my bottom lip to contain the happiness swelling inside of my chest. Despite myself, I giggled, and the nervous energy escaped me. Dipping my brush back into what was left of my favorite shade of shadow, I continued to get ready.

After I had left Trevor's side this morning and returned to my apartment, I had tried to sketch while I saw Grey's smiling face clear in my mind; my imagination had conjured up different adventures for him to go on as my pencil had moved across the page in front of me. However, the work had quickly become useless. I had spent most of my time with my pencil hovering over the page as I thought of my muse's uncle instead. Before I had understood what it was I was doing, I had abandoned the project and moved to sketch images of Trev.

They were a jumbled mess of frantic lines—my graphite pencil smeared across the vanilla page. Despite the streaked, hazy mess, the image still resembled him; especially around the eyes, which had been dark, soulful, and unmistakably Trevor's.

I had studied the image, feeling as if he were truly watching me for a moment, before I had tucked it away under my mattress for safekeeping. *How embarrassing would it be if Trevor knew I was sketching pictures of him like some lovesick teenager in homeroom?*

With the memory of his eyes in my mind, I finished getting ready, knowing he would be knocking on my door any second. I set the eyeshadow palate down and grabbed my favorite pale pink shade of lipstick to apply. While I had never been skilled at applying makeup— only wearing it on the few occasions I left the house to go someplace nice—I managed to pull it together for tonight; it was all thanks to Eden's guidance over the years combined with a plethora of online tutorials.

With a somewhat shaky hand, I applied the shade to my lips before blotting with a piece of tissue. I pulled it away from my lips and stared down at the imprint of lipstick on the Kleenex before peering up at my reflection. *This is as good as it's going to get, Veronica.* With my curly hair tamed, running freely down my back, and my face made up without seeming overdone, I supposed I looked beautiful. *Beautiful. I never understood why anyone called me that.* Next to my sister, I had never felt beautiful. However, Trevor had a way about him; around him, I felt gorgeous. I felt like I had *always* been gorgeous.

Standing up, I ran a hand over my light green, fit and flare dress, smoothing out the fabric before I adjusted my denim jacket. *I wonder if Trevor will like this? Am I too underdressed?* Trevor wanted to surprise me and forwent telling me anything about our plans for tonight. Despite my dislike for surprises, I didn't mind; although, now, I was worried sick my outfit would stick out like a sore thumb.

A loud knock sounded on the door and quickly pulled me away from my thoughts. I laughed at myself, embarrassed by how nervous I was already. I gave myself one last appraising look before I turned to answer the door. *I can't believe he's here! I can't believe this is really happening!* Before I yanked my front door open, I took a moment to rein in my emotions, not wanting to embarrass myself. He would laugh if he saw how animated I was. I had to play it cool. I had to at least *pretend* I wasn't bouncing with excitement.

You've got this, Veronica. Just play it cool and don't embarrass yourself in front of him too much.

I swung the front door open as quickly as tearing off a bandage, revealing him in all of his sinfully handsome glory. I nearly swooned at the sight of him. With a dress shirt rolled up to reveal his slew of tattoos on his forearms, I found it impossible to look away. I wanted nothing more than to lean forward and kiss every single piece of ink. My eyelids fluttered as I came back to reality, realizing I had been staring at him for far too long.

"Is this all right for where we're going?" I questioned, breaking the silence.

"It's perfect," he said, his eyes darkened, and his breath hitched, taking in my appearance. My eyes were glued to him, fixated on the movement of his tongue darting out to lick his bottom lip. His brows knitted together, and his concentration caused me to blush. "You ready to get going?" he asked, sliding his hands into the front pockets of his jeans while rocking back on his feet.

I wonder if he's as nervous as I am?

Answering with a quick nod, I turned on my heel and grabbed my purse. My pulse was erratic, and my skin was completely flushed. Thankfully, Trevor seemed too wrapped up in his own thoughts to notice. I wanted to present myself as calm and collected, but that was seemingly impossible around Trevor. He looked at me, and I melted. When he was near, my panties were always damp. *So embarrassing.*

My blush deepened, and I turned to find Trevor's tongue darting out to trace his bottom lip again, making it impossible to ignore the subtle pulsing between my legs. I wondered if he felt my desire—felt my need for him—as his gaze dropped to my breasts. My fingers twitched while I imagined slipping my hand into my panties, working myself over until I fell to pieces in front of him.

My fingers twitched with desire, but I stifled it, taking ahold of his hand, my body acting on its own accord. His palm was warm against mine, and with a squeeze of his hand, he pulled me out of my apartment. With my free hand, I locked up, smiling as my body tingled with energy. I felt his eyes trace the lines of my frame, and when I turned to him, he rewarded me with a heated look before leading me down the hall.

"I've been thinking about you all day," I commented before my anxiousness could prevent me.

What happened to playing it cool, Veronica?

"I did manage to get a lot done today though," I lied, not wanting him to know he constantly clouded my thoughts. "I guess I was really well rested after last night." I nearly cringed at my attempt at flirting.

I felt his body tense and his grip on my hand tighten. "Same here," he responded, his voice heavy. He was silent for a moment, and just as I was going to ask what was on his mind, he relaxed and posed the question. "Maybe we can do it again?"

I suppressed a smile, not wanting to appear too eager. My imagination ran wild as I considered what it would be like to go to bed with him by my side each and every night. *His hands on my curves ... on my breasts ... between my legs ... his warm body flush against mine. His scent mixing with my own, creating a smell that's uniquely ours.*

"We can sleep together whenever you want, Trev," I quipped with innuendo swimming in my tone.

The cool night air hit my face as soon as we opened the doors leading to the parking lot. I inhaled the crisp scent of the late summer night as Trevor's body tightened at my side, obviously reacting to my previous statement. My panties dampened further at the idea of him restraining himself. *Wanting me as desperately as I want him.*

"You shouldn't say that to me," he bit out as we reached his truck.

Turning to him, I gazed at his tense muscles; each muscle of his torso was taut through the fabric of his shirt. Even in the night, I clearly saw the tension coursing through his frame. He opened the passenger door for me and paused for a moment, letting go of my hand before allowing his fingers to curl tightly around the steel of the door's frame.

"It's going to give me certain ideas, and I'm trying my best to do things the right way."

I slid into the passenger seat, unsure of what to say. I knew he didn't desire to push me—he didn't want the physical side of our relationship to progress until I was ready for it. I couldn't describe how thankful I was for that. He didn't know my past, but I hoped one day I could tell him. One day, my story would unravel, and I would thank him for being so patient with me, never pushing me further than I wanted to go.

As Trevor slid into the driver's seat, I turned to look at him, taking in his harsh expression. Despite appearances, I knew he was always a softie—more so than he ever cared to admit. He was like a Tootsie Roll Pop: hard on the outside with a soft core. I smiled at the comparison, relaxing against my seat. I almost laughed at the idea of telling him that. I was sure he would blanch at my juxtaposition. But he *was* soft. *Soft, warm, and all mine.*

"I know you are," I finally responded, giving him a thoughtful smile. "Trev, I really appreciate it."

He smiled, too, before putting the key into the ignition and bringing the monster of a truck to life. Music filtered through the truck as the radio blared a band I'd never heard of. The lead singer's voice drowned out the booming sound of the truck's engine, captivating me. Trevor gave me a nervous, calculating look, as if he were trying to decipher whether I enjoyed his taste in music. He pulled out of the parking spot before putting the truck into drive. With another look in my direction, his hand moved to the dial to change the song.

"It's fine," I said, waving his hand away. "I'm curious what sort of music you listen to."

Although he still seemed unsure, he carefully moved his hand away, placing it back on the steering wheel. As we drove, I melted against the seat and listened to the bands on Trevor's playlist. There was something so intimate about listening to the music someone liked. It was as if you were peering into their soul.

While listening, I imagined how each song related to Trevor. Closing my eyes, I considered what each song meant to him. Every song meant something to someone, even if the meaning was shallow. There was a reason we gravitated toward certain things and distanced ourselves from others. Apparently, Trevor and I gravitated toward the same things because our taste in music was similar. Classic rock, dark cabaret, progressive rock, and metal, there wasn't a single thing Trevor liked that I had a problem with. Most of the playlist consisted of stuff I had been familiar with, except one: A progressive band I had never heard of.

"What band is this?" I asked, peering over at his structured profile.

Trevor looked at me, seemingly surprised by my interest. *What did he* think *I liked? Boy bands and pop?*

"Coheed and Cambria," he answered while his eyes remained trained on the road ahead.

When he reached a stop light, he peered over at me and gave a smile of approval.

"They're really good."

Reaching forward, I turned up the volume and shot him a grin.

He relaxed in his seat, seeming more confident around me than he ever had. I wanted him to open up to me more; I wanted him to share the parts of him he couldn't share with anyone else. And I wanted to do the same. I desired to reveal the very darkness I always tried to stifle. *Can he see the same darkness in me that I see in him? The part of us we lock away.* I pushed that thought from my mind and focused my attention on the music and the road ahead. Tonight, I would forget about all of that. Tonight, my mind would only be occupied with Trevor, and Trevor alone.

We reached the restaurant, and my eyes widened at the sight— shocked this was Trevor's choice. *Did someone give him advice? Trevor doesn't strike me as someone who frequents these types of places.* When I looked to him for confirmation, Trevor was swelling with pride at my side, seemingly content with his choice. I smiled, knowing how much thought he must have put into this evening. Although, it wouldn't have mattered where he took me; as long as I had been with him, I would have been perfectly blissful. I was sure if I told him that, he would scoff. However, it was true. *He* was the reason I was here, after all. With a sly smile on his face, he found the perfect parking spot. Seeing him so confident was paradise. I wished he were always this self-assured.

With a satisfied grin, he turned off the truck and swung open his door, stepping out before crossing the front of the truck to open my door for me. Swinging my door open, he proffered his hand, which I happily took. With a proud grin, he guided me toward the restaurant. There was something consuming about him, something that caused me to melt against his side. His piercing gaze, handsome looks, and attractive edge had me wrapped around his finger. I wanted nothing more than to ditch the restaurant and forgo the conversation to feel his body thrusting into mine.

I barely acknowledged the restaurant's impressive décor as we entered—my mind was far too occupied by the man at my side. *My lips running along the sharp lines of his jaw. My tongue tracing the outlines of his tattoos. My fingers descending his body until they reach the happy trail leading to where I want to touch him the most. His hard cock in my hands. Milking him and watching his handsome face as he falls apart ...*

I felt a smile tug on my lips as I came back to the present. I moved along, Trevor guiding me toward the table he had reserved for us in the far corner of the restaurant. He was every bit of a gentleman as he pulled out my chair for me and allowed me to take my seat first. No one had ever done this before, which caused me to flush as I sat down. He shot me a confident grin before he took a seat across from mine. His carefree temperament wavered as the hostess set the menus down before parting ways.

Dark, pensive eyes were glued to the wine list while his muscles stiffened. The jugular vein, which I had always dreamed of licking, twitched as he regarded the list with a dejected look coloring his features. *Such a taunting piece of paper.* While he seemed to try to stifle his emotions, he couldn't hide them from me. The fear on his face was evident. All caused by a sheet of paper. My heart ached for him, wishing I had a way of assuaging his affliction.

In a soft voice, I asked if he was all right. His eyes darted from the paper to meet my gaze; his face was ashen. He looked so exhausted suddenly, like the world had just crashed down around him. He gave me a weak smile, which didn't reach his eyes while his jugular vein twitched again. Reaching across the table, I took his hand in mine, gently squeezing it to remind him I was here and didn't plan on leaving.

"Trev," I said softly, "it's all right if you don't want to order a drink. I don't really drink much, and if you don't either, that's completely okay with me."

He didn't seem too convinced. He squeezed my hand, giving me another tight smile as his eyes tried to avoid the sight of anything tempting. His chest expanded with a deep breath, and he leaned back slightly in his chair before he began, "It's just—"

He immediately stopped, and his dark eyes searched mine. He peered at me as if he were searching for an answer or some sort of sign. *Does he not realize I accept him and will* always *accept him, regardless of whatever taints his past? You can't change the past, so why dwell on it?*

"It's just," he slowly continued, "I've had problems with alcohol."

As soon as the words slipped past his lips, his entire body slumped forward in defeat. My brows knitted together as I looked at him, finding his self-confidence long gone. *How can he possibly feel defeated? He hasn't given into temptation. He hasn't ordered a drink.* Perhaps he felt inferior due to his past problems—problems that could haunt him for the rest of his life. While my eyes searched his face for any clue as to what was going on inside his beautiful mind, I realized my hypothesis was most likely correct. It seemed he did feel inferior. *If only he knew how strong he really was.*

Squeezing his hand as he tried to withdraw it from mine, I murmured, "I understand. I've watched people struggle with addictions."

My mind flipped through memories of my extended family falling off of the wagon, remembering the pain and darkness the slip had caused.

"I know it's hard," I continued. "Just know that having a problem like that doesn't make you weak—nor does it make me think less of you, Trevor. You're overcoming it, and you should be proud of yourself."

He snorted as his free hand shot up to run through his unruly mane. "I don't feel proud of myself," he said quietly, almost to himself.

He looked off toward the bar, his gaze more frustrated than desirous. He squeezed my hand, and as he did, I wished there were something I could do for him. *How I wish I could take this weight off of his shoulders.* But I couldn't—this was his battle; being supportive was all I could do.

"Well, I'm proud of you."

His jaw clenched as his irritated gaze fizzled into something else. An emotion that I couldn't describe. The warmth in his eyes extinguished the darkness. *There's my Trevor again. He was lost for a moment but has quickly returned.* He may be flawed, but to me, he's perfect.

He was attempting to pick up the pieces of his fractured life; he was trying to make something beautiful out of the mess that surrounded him. I loved him even more for that. Rubbing circles on the back of his hand with my thumb, he held onto me as if I were his lifeline. Perhaps, in a way, this was true. I didn't know if it was right, but I loved that I was able to tether him to some sort of goodness. *But of course, he has Grey for that, too.* Images of Greyson clouded my head. *Trevor and Greyson: the two men I never wanted to let go of.* If I were lucky, Trevor wouldn't want to let go of me either.

If I'm lucky, this is just the beginning.

14

Never Tear Us Apart

Sun seeped through my windows, trickling through the blinds to warm my skin. I turned onto my back, staring up at the ceiling with the image of Trevor clear in my mind. My fingertips traced the curve of my bottom lip, remembering the feel of his fingers doing something similar last night. *The way he touches me ... the way he looks at me ... God, I wonder how I manage to think straight.* A smile tugged on my lips, and I quickly flipped onto my stomach, burying my face into my pillow as embarrassment overwhelmed me. I had never felt this way about anyone—*ever*. Every moment, I wanted to see him; every day, I wanted him to possess me completely. The past was forgotten. All there was, was him.

Slowly, my hands made their way down my body, toying with the edges of my underwear before they dipped inside, brushing over my trim line of hair and reaching the little nub, which always brought me pleasure. Seeing the toned lines of his body in my mind's eye, I worked myself until I reached my oblivion. As my fingers moved with determination, I allowed my imagination to run freely. My eyes closed as the vision of him overwhelmed me.

Just as I was about to speak, his fingers reached forward to gently silence me. Smiling the cocky smile I had quickly grown so fond of, he bent down to kiss my neck and ran his tongue along my collarbone as his hands made their descent along my trembling frame. His lips moved from my neckline to my exposed breasts, kissing their fullness before he paid special attention to my nipples, all while his hands made their way to where I longed for his touch the most.

"Trev," I murmured, just before a moan passed through my lips. My fingers tangled in his unruly hair, pulling and yanking as his mouth worshiped my breasts. I never wanted this pleasure to end, and I told him so. As soon as the words passed through my lips, he abandoned my breast to stare up at me, giving me another roguish grin before his mouth moved down my body, past my naval, to the apex of my thighs.

No man had ever done this to me before. Everyone I had been with in the past had been far too interested in their own orgasm to give a crap about mine. I would have been more frustrated if I had known then what I knew now. I had no idea I was missing out on something so amazing. Trevor worked me until I was weeping, and only then did he rise above me and position himself at my entrance.

"Do you want this, baby?" he asked, his eyes glued to my face as he awaited my answer.

Too overwhelmed, I could only nod. He gave me a moment to make sure I truly meant it, which made me love him even more. He smiled as he watched my expression, and after I nodded one more time, he thrusted into me, tearing my world apart.

My eyes fluttered open as an orgasm ripped through my body. As soon as the pulsating morphed into a dull throb, my face flushed, and my body sunk into the mattress. For a moment, I recalled a time when I had been repulsed by this. But my nights, once riddled with nightmares, were now peaceful; my days, once filled with sporadic episodes fueled by my anxiety, were now untroubled. Trevor had changed me. *I had changed myself.* Finding a man whom I cared for seemed to trigger something deep inside of me. *If that were even a possibility.*

Sliding out of bed, my muscles felt like Jell-O. I crossed the carpet to the bathroom with shaky legs. The smile that had been on my face since reaching my peak had yet to disappear. Gazing at myself in the mirror, I couldn't believe how much *younger* I looked—how much happier I appeared. After … *him* … I had felt used up. It was as if all my good years had passed me by in a flash, and I was only left with emptiness, acting like the darkness that swallowed me whole. With every smile, every laugh, every orgasm, I was crawling my way out of that darkness. I was traversing back to the Veronica I once was. The Veronica my family loved. *The Veronica Trevor might love.* Slowly, I began to love myself again. Slowly, I realized everything would be all right.

With a 4H pencil in hand, I tried to focus on the paper in front of me; however, my eyes kept peering at the phone resting beside me on the couch. As usual, I had been messaging Trevor throughout the day, always interested in any tidbit he wanted to tell me. Today, he was going to his first consultation with a therapist. Judging by his texts, he was nervous. Although, I had told him time and time again that he shouldn't be. Being able to open up to a stranger like that was a relief. They didn't know you, they wouldn't judge you, and they gave unbiased advice.

In the past, I had found therapy far more helpful than talking to a friend. Many friends had told me what I had wanted to hear—fearing the outcome of telling me the truth—whereas therapists had been gently honest. Sometimes, it was nice to just have someone *listen*. I had gone so many years feeling like I wasn't being heard. While Trevor had never said as much, I believed he felt similarly.

A text from him illuminated my phone. Immediately, I unlocked the device and read it.

I don't know about this. It seems so clinical.

I smiled, knowing exactly how he felt. When I had first seen a therapist, I had believed it was awkward, too. Filling out the paperwork alone had caused me to want to run for the door. Yet, Eden had been outside, which had caused me to stay put. Although she was only a few years my senior, she was far more mature than I had been. After our mother passed away, she had taken me to appointments and had made sure I had the best of everything. I admired her for that. *I still do.*

No wonder she's such a wonderful mother to Harper—she has had loads of practice with me.

You'll be fine. I know you don't scare too easily.

As soon as I put the phone down and grabbed my 4H pencil, it *pinged* again. This time, his message made me grin. At least, he was joking around, which was an excellent sign.

Nothing scares me, sweetheart.

I sent him back a quick smile emoji before I placed my phone down and focused on the matter at hand. I gazed at the picture of Grey I had printed off this morning, beginning to sketch a stylized version of his baby face. *Perhaps one day, I could give these drawings to Trevor as a gift*, I mused. With how fast Grey was growing, it would be nice to have images to look back on. His smiling face stood out on my page despite the scenery I had sketched around him. Soon, I would add color, but for now, I was only focused on getting his facial features right. I never expected a baby to become my muse, but since he had first inspired me, I had filled an entire sketchbook with images of him.

Day turned into night, and my pencil had turned into a nub as my phone began to ring. Trevor must have finished his appointment. As I released my pencil, my hand ached from being posed in one position for too long. Eager to hear Trevor's voice, I ignored the ache and reached for my phone, picking it up on the third ring.

"Hey, Trev! How did the appointment go?"

I heard Grey squealing in the background. I must have been on speaker phone. He continued to squeal, causing a smile to tug on my lips. I heard Trevor laugh at his nephew before he answered my question.

"It was fine." Grey babbled in the background, and Trevor paused for a moment to chuckle at his exuberant nephew. "Sorry, Grey's freaking out in the backseat. He's just really excited to hear your voice."

With that remark, I felt my heart melt. I was happy to hear his voice, too. I looked down at the image of him on my page, and my smile widened.

"Aw. Well, you should bring him over tonight. I'd love to make dinner for my guys."

My guys. The phrase passed through my lips before I could give it any thought. For a moment, I considered correcting myself. However, Trevor responded before I had gotten the chance.

"That'd be great." He paused for a moment, and I heard him rustling around before continuing, "Actually, I was calling to ask about tomorrow. I was thinking about taking Grey to a pumpkin patch and was wondering … Well, I was wondering if you wanted to join us?"

I smiled at the nervousness in his voice. After everything we had been through, I wondered how he could still be unsure around me. *Heck, I guess I'm equally as nervous around him. Nervous in the best of ways. Nervous for his body, heart, and soul.*

"Trev, I'd do anything with you."

I heard him release the breath he must have been holding onto. "Perfect." I heard a smile in his voice. "I'll see you tonight, then?"

"Tonight," I confirmed.

"Is an hour too soon for us to drop by?"

It's never too soon.

"No, an hour is fine, Trev. I'm looking forward to it."

"Me, too." He paused for a moment, allowing me a chance to hear the kid's song on the radio mixed with Grey's babbling. "Thanks for this, Ronnie. After today, a night with you is just what I need."

A night with you, is all I ever could need, Trev. I smiled at the thought. We said our goodbyes before I hung up, already beginning to plan for the relaxing night ahead of us.

It may have been a bit *much*, but I was certain Trevor would like it. *Who wouldn't want comfort food after a day like today?* I had made a recipe that my mom had always made for me after a particularly difficult day at school, grilled mac and cheese. Which was a mix of two of my favorite comfort foods: macaroni and cheese and grilled cheese. Of course, she had never allowed us to eat this alone. She would force us to eat a plethora of vegetables, as well.

Tonight, however, we were having the sandwiches, chips, and iced tea. I left a small portion of macaroni and cheese for Greyson, too, sure he would want something other than his typical baby food. Hopefully, Trevor would like this. If he would want it, I could do this for him every night. I liked being able to take care of him and Grey. Trevor focused all of his energy on his nephew—he needed someone to look after him.

Trevor knocked on my door early, just like I believed he would. I opened the door to find Grey restless in his uncle's arms—his curious eyes darted around my apartment before they found me. When he captured my gaze, he smiled, wiggling in Trevor's arms as he reached for me. With a giggle, I took him, holding him close as I ushered his uncle inside.

"I made something simple tonight. I hope you don't mind."

"Simple? Simple's perfect."

He followed me into the kitchen, and I turned back to look at him, finding him smiling at my little setup on the kitchen table. There was a small mountain of grilled mac and cheese sandwiches, a pitcher of iced tea, and a huge bag of Trevor's favorite potato chips. His eyes scanned the table before he looked to Grey as I placed him in his highchair. Grey's eyes were wide and animated as he took in the small pile of macaroni and cheese before him.

"Holy fu—" Trevor stopped himself, nearly blushing as he looked at me. "I mean, this looks really good, baby."

Baby. My face flushed, and as cheesy as it seemed, my heart skipped a beat as the endearment slipped through his lips. Hearing his rough, masculine voice utter the word always caused the most delicious sensation between my legs. A sensation I was far too embarrassed to tell him about.

"Thanks. It wasn't any trouble to make. It's an old family recipe."

We took our seats, and I felt weightless—my world felt sunny and unclouded. The warmth radiating between us was overwhelming. It was as if we were one happy family. *It's like we've* always *been.* If this became a routine, I knew my heart would feel full every night.

It hadn't taken long for Trevor to open up about his day—the words had flown out of him as if they had been bubbling in his breast since he had left his therapist. He had talked about his frustrations—the lack of faith he had in the therapist—before he had revealed some of his fears. I wasn't sure if it were a guy thing, but the subject of fear had always been difficult for him. I supposed one of his fears was being in a position of vulnerability. It was scary to open up completely, taking off a mask to reveal one's true self. I knew this fear intimately. *Hell, I'm too afraid to open up to him.* The fear I experienced every day was visceral.

I feared if I talked about my past—if I uttered the words out loud—it would make everything *real.* I wondered if he experienced something similar. Maybe, despite the strength he constantly displayed, he still hadn't accepted his brother's death. *How could he? Not much time has passed! He hasn't gotten the chance to breathe, let alone grieve.*

"So, you don't think you'll be able to open up to him?" I questioned as soon as he finished explaining the short consultation.

The consultation he had described seemed normal enough. His therapist, Dr. Russel, asked him basic questions and inquired after what Trevor wanted to get out of the sessions. Trevor had expressed he wanted to feel more in control of his own life, which Dr. Russel had explained would be difficult, but doable. However, Trevor hadn't seemed convinced by the psychologist's assessment; he didn't believe therapy would help him. In my heart, I knew there was more than his brother's death troubling him. Maybe one day, we could both demolish the walls we had built around us and let each other in.

Trevor took a long sip of his tea and ran a shaky hand through his hair before leaning forward to answer me. "I don't fucking know. I don't know about this sort of thing. I just don't see how merely talking about something is going to help me. What is he going to do, cure me? I don't think I'm curable. I just need to pull my head out of my ass—" He stopped, looking at me with an apology swimming in his eyes. "Sorry. I'm trying not to be so negative, Ronnie. I'm just not used to any of this."

"I know. Trev, no one's comfortable with this sort of thing at first. Opening up is hard."

"I know." He leaned back in his chair, shoulders slumping as his gaze turned to his nephew. "I just never liked talking about this shit. I don't want to open up to some complete stranger."

"Trev, sometimes that's the best thing possible. A stranger won't judge you; a stranger will listen to your problems and give you the best advice. As hard as it is, sometimes you just have to trust people and trust yourself."

I wished I could trust myself. Maybe one day, I'll blossom, becoming the most authentic version of myself. I was sure that once I did, I would feel a profound sense of relief. Perhaps I wouldn't feel so bottled up—so repressed.

"I don't trust myself," he murmured, so softly, I barely heard him.

"You will. One day, you will."

"Do you trust yourself?" he questioned, his eyes shooting up to meet mine.

"I'm starting to."

15

Everywhere

The chill in the air tickled my nose, reminding me that autumn was closing in on us. When the seasons shifted in Evergreen, the trees transformed into something out of a dream. There was nothing I loved more than sitting outside during this time with a well-loved novel in hand as I appreciated everything Colorado had to offer. As of right now, the trees had only just begun their transformation. Already, they gave me a glimpse of how magnificent they would become. With the beautiful scenery surrounding them, my two handsome guys looked almost otherworldly. If it weren't for the bite of the cold air, I would believe I was dreaming. *Trevor and Greyson ... this place ... it all seems so surreal. How have I become so lucky?* Trevor turned to smile at me just as I was about to snap a photo.

"Hey, none of that. I should be taking pictures of you," he said, coming toward me while he bounced a very engrossed Grey in his arms.

"Why's that?"

"Because you're the pretty one. I'm not exactly easy on the eyes."

I smiled at this, biting down on my bottom lip as I stifled a laugh. If only this man knew how attractive I found him. *Thank God, he doesn't, Veronica. He doesn't need to know about how often you masturbate.* He may have been *rough* looking in the eyes of many—definitely not "traditionally" handsome—but to me, he was God's gift to women. *"God's gift to women"? He's turning you into such a sap.* My smile widened before I finally appeased him by bringing my phone down to my side.

"I think you're pretty fine to look at," I flirted, surprising myself.

Every time I had flirted with Trevor, it had felt like another woman was doing the talking for me. The words had fallen from my lips before I had given them much thought. The amorous comments and coquettish smiles hadn't sounded like me.

"If anyone's the looker here, it's you." He smiled before his gaze dropped to his nephew. "Or Grey, of course."

I giggled, looking down at Grey as he peered around the pumpkin patch, his eyes wide with curiosity. To him, everything was new. Being here to watch him as he experienced this for the first time was humbling. Watching him take in the changes to the world around him caused me to feel as if I was experiencing everything for the first time, too. With little Grey around, everything was fresh and new.

"This was a good idea, Daddy," I commented, feeling Trevor stiffen, shocked as he walked slightly ahead.

My eyes were trained on Grey as I followed his uncle to the caramel apple stand stationed a few yards away from the patch itself.

"I used to love coming here as a kid. So, it's only right that I brought Grey here."

Trevor glanced down at his nephew, eyes filled with warmth, before he stepped forward to order two of the best-looking caramel apples the stand had to offer. Despite my love for the tasty treat, my eyes were glued to the man before me. There was something so sexy about him ordering for the both of us. I supposed I just enjoyed seeing him take charge; it was almost as if he were claiming me. *He could claim me right now.* My face flushed as my eyes dropped to the baby in his arms. *Thank God, he doesn't know the impure thoughts I constantly have about his uncle.* My cheeks were still tinged pink by the time Trevor turned around with two apples balanced between the fingers of his left hand.

"These look amazing," I quickly spat out, cringing at the awkward tone of my voice.

"I was obsessed with these as a kid."

He smiled, biting into one before giving his nephew a caramel-covered smile. He licked the mess away, earning a laugh from our little guy.

"The first thing my dad did when we got here was buy a caramel apple for each of us," he continued.

Despite the grin tugging at his lips, there was a distance in his eyes. Understanding, I didn't want to press him. I had never understood why some people were so insistent on bringing up undesirable or uncomfortable topics. I loathed when a person did that to me—always answering their unwanted inquires with a tight, fake smile combined with a crease of discomfort in my brow. Trevor relaxed after a few moments passed without a word from me. Even though he wasn't sharing much, I was happy he was willing to share a small glimpse of his life with his family.

Grey babbled something incoherent as he reached out for the caramel apple with his chubby, little hand—fingers outstretched as he attempted to grab a handful of caramel to shove into his mouth. Trevor managed to shove his hand away last minute before he brought Grey's fist up for a quick, apologetic kiss.

"Sorry, little guy. If I gave you a treat like this, you'd be awake for weeks." With a sheepish grin, he shifted his attention to me and said, "He barely sleeps as it is. Could you imagine feeding him sugar?"

"Definitely not."

While Grey could be tiring at times, I had come to love his exuberance. And I knew Trevor had, too.

"Sometimes, I'll doze off with him on my chest and wake up to find him wide awake, his face mere inches away from mine, staring at me like I'm the most interesting thing in the fucking world."

I snorted. It was so easy to imagine the scenario since Grey constantly looked up to his uncle. While, I doubted Trevor noticed sometimes, Grey attempted to imitate him. He would mirror faces his uncle made before he sat back and awaited attention and approval. It had to be the most adorable thing I had ever seen. Even now, Grey moved his mouth as if he were also eating before he peered up at his uncle to see if he was paying attention.

"I think he just wants to be like you," I commented before finally biting into my apple.

Trevor scoffed, nearly choking on his last bite. He shook his head, swallowed his bite of apple, and said, "If he wants to be like me, I'm in for a lot of trouble. That's the last thing I want."

"Why? You're pretty great, Trev." After a few moments without a response, I continued. "You did plan this whole day, after all."

This, he grinned at. After taking another bite of his apple, he led me into the patch, bouncing a very excited Grey in the crook of his right arm along the way. The patch had as many pumpkins as it did children, which quickly became overwhelming for our little guy. As we moved along, Grey's body worked its way into a fetal position against the crook of Trevor's arm. Throwing the remains of his apple away, Trevor brought his nephew up to rest against his chest, allowing him to burrow his head into the curve of his neck.

"Do you think all the noise is too much for him?"

"Probably," Trevor agreed, bending down to give the top of his nephew's head a quick, comforting kiss. "He's not too great with too many people at once. When there's more than a few people around, he recoils into himself. But I guess I was the same way. I was one shy fucking kid." Trevor cringed, giving me a stiff smile before he added, "I need to stop cursing around him. I don't know what I'll do if his first word is 'fuck.' "

"Yeah, that wouldn't be too good, would it?"

He chuckled at this before he turned on his heel and led us to a less populated area of the pumpkin patch. Despite being September, I was chilled to the bone. I supposed I had grown far too used to the summer. While I was never the outdoorsy type, I would open all the windows in my apartment every day so I could breathe in the fresh air while I read. I always loved the way the summer heat felt against my skin; I even enjoyed when I would sweat slightly from the high temperature—it was purifying in a way. This end of summer weather caused me to already dream of next June.

While we traversed forward, Trevor shot me glance after glance, appraising me until I felt weak in the knees. Just as I was about to question him, he moved to stand in front of me. A boyish smile lit up his features, toying with my mind for a moment, effectively disorientating me as he bent down and placed a quick kiss on the cold tip of my nose. I startled as I tried to find the words. After a moment, I gave him a shocked smile, unable to manage anything else. I staggered, but Trevor continued forward. I quickly pulled myself together and fell in step beside him.

Will it always be like this when he kisses me? When he touches me? Lord, I need to sit down before I fall down.

"Maybe we can head over there and have our picnic?" I suggested, pointing to the first unoccupied spot I saw. Truly, I didn't know how much longer I would be able to walk by his side, playing it perfectly cool—pretending like I wasn't profoundly affected by him. *Does he think I'm a jumbled mess? I feel like a jumbled mess.*

"Yeah, Grey definitely needs a break from all the excitement," he agreed, following behind me as I started to walk off toward a group of tables far removed from everything else.

Still reeling from the innocent kiss, my heart fluttered against my breastbone as I made my way across the grass to the table. I nearly fell onto the bench, feeling my cheeks heat up as I kicked myself for being so embarrassingly uncoordinated. Trevor didn't seem to notice my mishap as he took a seat across from mine and placed Grey safely in his lap. With a smile, he slid his worn backpack from his shoulders and unzipped it.

Straightening in his seat, he took out the backpack's contents while his grin widened. Trevor pulled out two giant sub sandwiches and chips, along with a small portion of hard-boiled eggs and white bread, which, I assumed was for Greyson. Grey peered at the sandwiches in wonder, smiling until he realized that meal was not for him. As soon as he saw the hard-boiled eggs and white bread, he grimaced, gazing up at his uncle with a look of disapproval. A look that was hilarious as it came from a baby. Trevor groaned, obviously sensing his nephew's impending tantrum.

"Come on, buddy. You love this stuff. You eat it at home all the time. Do me a favor and suck it up for today," Trevor pleaded, helping his nephew take a few tiny bites of his meal before he reached forward to grab his own sandwich.

Grey's eyes were glued to his uncle's movements. As he watched, his eyes filled with frustrated tears while his uncle took a huge bite of his meal. I giggled, feeling almost guilty as I ate mine. As I watched the pair, I couldn't believe Trevor had put so much thought into today. With a full-time job and an infant to care for, I couldn't believe he found the time for something like this.

My focus returned to the duo as Trevor helped Grey take another bite of his meal, grimacing as the baby grew increasingly fussy in his arms.

"Come on, buddy. I woke up early just to make all this food, and this is the thanks I get?"

Grey peered up at him, giving him a long, thoughtful look before he calmed down ever so slightly.

"Thanks, buddy," Trevor uttered, sounding tired.

"Thanks for doing this, Trev," I spoke up, wanting him to really feel my gratitude. I knew this couldn't have been easy for him. "I can't believe you woke up so early to make me lunch."

He smiled at this, looking content with himself. He should have been. He never gave himself enough credit and he had so much to be proud of.

"So," he began, peering down at the sub in his hand. "I thought tonight we could carve pumpkins and watch a scary movie?"

A smile tugged at my lips. Similar to me, Trevor seemed to enjoy beginning the fall festivities early, which reminded me very much of my mother. Before summer had even finished, Mom had been keen on putting out all of our fall decorations, much to my father's dismay. She had loved that time of year—the warm colors, crisp air, festive activities, as well as buckets upon buckets of candy. Even now, years later, I could still see her smiling face in my mind's eye—easily envisioning the look on her face as she had held me in her arms, shielding me from the "monsters" that had scared me during our favorite Halloween hayride.

"Ronnie, Ronnie, it's okay. See, they're just here to celebrate with us. They won't harm you."

"Promise?" I asked as my face remained smashed against her jean jacket, shielding me from the night around us.

"I promise. I would never let anything happen to you."

I said nothing, still afraid.

"Do you know why?" she asked.

"Why?"

"Because you're my daughter, and it's my job to protect you."

I smiled, pulling away to look around the dark forest, apprehensively waiting for the next monster to appear.

Grey's giggles brought me back to the matter at hand, and I refocused on Trevor's ideas for the evening. The effort he had put into today astounded me. I had never met a man who came close to the one sitting across from me now.

With a giggle, I replied to his suggestion. "Where did you get all these cute ideas from? You don't strike me as the type of guy who carves pumpkins in his free time."

His eyes darted away as his body stiffened. Instantly, I regretted laughing.

With his shoulders stiff, he stuffily responded, "My brother and I used to do stuff like this when we were kids."

My eyes bulged, and I instantly felt obtuse for not being more considerate. He had mentioned Dean earlier—I should have known this was something he had done with him. The fact that he was here today spoke volumes on how far he had come. I knew how difficult it had been for me to go anywhere that reminded me of my mother after she had passed. Luckily, time moved forward, and I began to find going to places where I thought of her the most, comforting. When I was in a location that reminded me of her, I felt as if she were with me, standing by my side like she always did. While it was almost eerie, the comfort it provided me with had gotten me through many hard times.

"I'm sorry, Trev," I managed to mutter as I shifted uncomfortably in my seat. "I didn't mean to hurt your feelings. It's a great idea; I was just teasing you about it."

He smiled at me, his eyes warm. My shoulders relaxed as relief overwhelmed me.

"It's fine," he said with a wave of his hand. "I just thought it'd be something you'd like to do. And, I thought Grey would get a kick out of finger painting."

Although his smile was reassuring, something in his tone suggested there was more than he was telling me. *He's thinking about his brother.* Seeing a man like Trevor—strong, muscular, and covered in ink—shattered, tore me to pieces.

"I'd love to do it, Trev. Thanks for thinking of me," I said quietly, wanting desperately to assuage his pain.

I wished I could help carry some of the weight. I wished my words provided him with some solace.

"I know things are hard without your brother. I was a mess during the holidays after my mother passed away. I was filled with so much hate and anger ..." I paused as the memories washed over me, taking my breath away.

"Don't talk to me like that—like I don't know! Stop looking at me like a child!"

"You are a child, Veronica. You know nothing!"

As soon as the words left Dad's lips, his eyes widened, and he covered his mouth.

"I'm sorry," he said, bowing his head. "It's just—"

"Save it." Stepping forward, I accused, "How could you? She hasn't even been gone a year!"

"I'm allowed to be happy, Veronica. Your mother would want—"

"Well, I don't want it! Don't my feelings matter, too? Or is it all about you?"

"Veronica," he warned as his eyes sharpened.

"Whatever. I don't want to look at you."

"I'm your father. You will—" He stopped and shifted uncomfortably on his feet.

A few heartbeats passed without a word from him. He stood, calculating, as he stared at the floor.

"Veronica," he tried again, *"why don't we start doing more things together? Like the old days. You used to love—"*

"This isn't like the old days," I interrupted. *"Those days are gone. You said so yourself. Besides, it's time to move on. Time to let go of the past."*

"Veronica," he said, pleading as I turned away.

"Besides, I don't want to do anything with you."

Taking a deep breath, I centered my focus before I continued. "I know you don't always think you're strong, but you're handling this so much better than I did."

"Don't you see that I can't stand you? The more you try to get close to me, the further I want to be. Can't you just leave me alone?" I shouted, surprising myself and my father.

"Ronnie," my sister began, stepping forward.

"Eden, how can you stand him? Are you serious? He doesn't care about us."

"Stop it, Veronica," Dad snapped.

Although he hid his emotions well, I still saw the hurt in his eyes. To him, I would always be his little girl. The girl who wanted nothing more than her daddy's attention. He didn't realize that girl was gone now.

"No, you can't be serious? She wants to move in here? I hate her! You know I hate her!"

"That's enough. She's a good woman, Veronica. She likes you and Eden so much."

"I don't care. I don't give a shit."

"Don't speak that way to me," he snapped back, growing angry.

"I'll speak to you however I—"

"Stop it, Veronica!" Eden cried, tears filling her eyes. "Stop it! This isn't you."

"Fuck both of you," I muttered as I turned to leave.

"Stay in your room. Stay in your room and think about how you're treating the people who love you. I know things are hard. Baby, I know how devastating everything is."

My head whipped around. "Really? Have you cried at all since it happened? You just bounced back," I accused.

"Have I cried?" A mirthless laugh escaped him as he shook his head. His face tightened, and his brows knitted together in frustration as he stepped forward. "My wife died. The woman I thought I was going to spend the rest of my life with is gone. The mother of my children is gone. I may not cry in front of you or your sister, but my nights are pretty lonely. I have plenty of time to be alone with my feelings then."

For the first time, I believed him. The pain in his eyes was impossible to misunderstand. I wanted to say something, anything, but I couldn't find the words. It may have been my pride that prevented me from speaking, or it may have been the fear I would fall apart if I uttered a single phrase. Mutely, I nodded and turned for my room. Perhaps I could go easier on him. He lost her, too.

"You were a child though," Trevor commented, attempting to take away *my* pain as he reached across the table to take my hand in his.

I gazed at our hands, our fingers intertwined upon the picnic table, and felt myself open up to him. He had put so much trust in me, and hopefully, one day, I would be able to tell him about every ugly, damaged piece of myself—revealing every inch of my darkness.

With my eyes on our clasped hands, I softly replied, "It's hard to deal with death—no matter what age you are."

I squeezed his hand, feeling my palm tingle against the warmth of his. For a moment, we sat in a comfortable silence until the spell that had been cast over us seemingly broke. Giving my hand a final squeeze, Trevor rewarded me with a warm smile before he let go in order to feed his nephew.

Thankfully, our conversation shifted to something far lighter: what we were looking forward to the most once October hit. It would be Grey's first Halloween, and then the seasons would shift again for Grey's first Thanksgiving and first Christmas. *All without his mom and dad. Thank God for Trevor.* I didn't want to begin to imagine where Grey would have been without his uncle. I pushed the idea aside and continued to maintain our light conversation. Trevor didn't contribute much, but I understood he had a lot on his mind—I had never met a man as introspective as he was.

"You should see Harper during the fall. My sister lets her have all this candy until she's running wild."

Trevor laughed; his attention remained captured on his restless nephew. Grey kicked in his lap, obviously bored with sitting at a table for so long. Acting like a seasoned daddy, Trevor unzipped his backpack and pulled out a blanket, seamlessly moving the picnic to the ground before Grey had the chance to throw a tantrum.

Now that we were situated on the ground, I watched in fascination as Grey crawled across the blanket toward his uncle. With determination coloring his little face, he grabbed onto the sleeve of his uncle's jacket and tried to pull himself off of the ground.

"Is he going to stand?"

Trevor grinned as his eyes glowed with pride, gazing down at his nephew. "I hope so. He stands all the time, but I'm the only one around to see him do it."

Shy little guy. With an excited smile, I watched Grey as he put all of his focus into lifting his tiny bottom off of the ground. His brows knitted together in concentration, and his little, pink tongue jutted out of his mouth as he began to yank himself up. His cheeks grew red from the labors of his work, but his hard work quickly paid off. For a few seconds, his bottom was off of the ground and his face relaxed into a smile before he dropped back to the blanket with a light *thud.* Unphased, he was quick to try again with his uncle's encouragement. With his eyes on Trevor, he found the strength to pull himself to his feet.

"Oh my, gosh! Grey!" I cried out, applauding the adorable, little guy as he stood before me. Not wanting to miss this special moment, I pulled out my cell and snapped a quick photo, earning a giggle from Grey in the process. His giggles sent him back to the ground; he fell softly on his bottom.

He was dazed for a moment before his bottom lip began to quiver—his eyes searching for his uncle. His gaze fell on Trevor, and his arms reached out, yearning for the comfort of his embrace. With a proud smile, Trevor took ahold of him and placed him on his lap. Grey giggled, staring up at his uncle as if he were his superhero.

"Aw, Trev. He loves you so much."

Crawling across the blanket, I closed the distance between us.

Looking down at his nephew in wonder, Trevor shook his head and responded. "Grey's so easy to love. Everyone who meets him can't help but love him."

His eyes grew almost cloudy as he stared off into space, deep in thought. Whatever he was contemplating caused his face to flush slightly. He seemed to shake the thought from his head before he smiled. I watched him, just as thoughtful. When he was like this, he was almost child-like. His grin was young—carefree. *What I wouldn't give to know what's on your mind right now. Are you thinking of me? Is that flush on your stubbled cheeks for me? Or, is this just wishful thinking?*

"You're right. It's easy. I'm sure you had something to do with that," I said, flirting slightly.

Trevor's brows creased with confusion before recognition colored his features, and he smirked and shook his head. "Naw, no way.

If anything, my brother and sister-in-law had something to do with it. I doubt I'm a good influence on him."

"You're more than good."

"I'm all he's got."

"Even if you weren't, you'd be everything."

Trevor smiled, but it didn't reach his eyes. I doubted he believed my words, despite their truth.

While we continued our day, venturing through the pumpkin patch, Trevor went somewhere in his mind. He was beside me, yet, he was miles away. His strong jawline was so tense the veins in his neck were prominent. His eyes, darker than usual, gazed off into the distance as if they were seeing something that wasn't there. I watched him—along with Grey, who peered up at his uncle curiously while beginning to grow fussy in his arms. When Trevor's eyes became misty, my silent question was answered.

He was thinking about his brother—I was sure of it. *Why wouldn't he be?* They had created so many memories here; his attitude now was only natural. *I wish this logic made me feel better.* Suddenly, something pulled him back to the present. His brows creased, and his eyes blinked rapidly as if he was attempting to expel a thought.

"Where'd you go?" I asked gently.

With a wistful smile, he answered, "I was just thinking about how I used to come here as a kid."

"That's the one you want, sweetie?"

"A course! This da one," I answered, pointing at my misshapen pumpkin proudly.

"Okay, whatever my little girl wants," Mommy replied as she pulled me onto her lap.

"No tickles, Mommy! No tickles!"

Her fingers attacked me, and I laughed. I shooed her hands away and laughed more. My tummy hurt, but I had fun.

"Mommy, no!" I laughed harder. "No tickles! No tickles!"

"Okay, I guess I can comply," she said and laughed, too. "How about picking this one to go home and paint, pretty girl?"

"Yep!"

"Should we go find your sister?"

"Yep!"

"Yep," she imitated, laughing. "Come on, sweet girl. Let's go find Daddy and Eden."

I nodded, wishing I had the right words to say. *What could I say to alleviate the pain of losing persons he loved so deeply? Words couldn't bring his brother back.* My eyes left Trevor as they searched for some inspiration from the scenery surrounding us. I smiled, knowing exactly what I could do to take his mind off of the past, bringing it back to the present.

"Do you want me to take a few photos of you and Grey? You know, so you can remember his first trip to the pumpkin patch?"

Trevor gave me a sheepish grin. He always hated being photographed. *How could a man like him hate being photographed? God, I would fill my phone with pictures of him if he let me.* He made a face but relented as I pulled out my phone and ushered him to a mountain of pumpkins situated near the front of the patch, surrounded by piles of hay. *Perfect place for the perfect photo.*

Grey fell into a fit of giggles as Trevor took a knee in front of the pumpkins and looked at my camera. I giggled, too, as I began to snap a few photos, captivated by the love displayed before me. As I took photo after photo in rapid succession, I wondered if Trevor had any idea how his nephew looked at him. Grey's wide, curious eyes peered up at Trevor as if he were his world. *I suppose Trev is. He's his sun, moon, and stars—his everything.*

As Trevor began to waver, trying to control the rumbustious baby, I brought my phone down and tapped to view the pictures. *They're perfect. Absolutely, positively perfect.*

"These are adorable, Trev. You should see the way he looks at you," I mused, unable to help myself.

Quickly, I closed the distance between us and knelt to show him what I had captured. Trevor's eyes widened, taking in the images silently as I swiped through the photos on my phone. Grey squealed as he viewed the images of himself, nearly cackling at the sight of each one, quite the contrast to his cerebral uncle.

In each photo, they both resembled a picture-perfect family. Through their smiles, one could easily see the love between them—the love which surrounded them. Turning to peer at Trevor, I found him regarding the pictures with misty eyes and a goofy smile. The expression was almost strange on such a darkly handsome man, which made it all the more appealing. It was as if he were a lion who was only tame around us—an animal who always bit, stopping to lick our hands. *God, he's so beautiful. So beautiful ... and so mine.*

He turned to me, and without thinking, I pressed my lips against his. The feeling of his soft lips was intoxicating; the feel of them drew me in deeper until I wondered where my mind was. My tongue darted out, teasing him, thrilling him, until he allowed me entrance, opening his mouth slightly for my tongue to slip inside. A moan escaped my lips while my nipples puckered. I wanted his mouth to trail over every inch of my body. My skin flushed as I felt my body come to life. *This is how it feels to be living. This is what I missed out on for so many years.*

Looking back on the monsters of my past, I hated them even more. They had marred my college years and had tainted my future—tainted my spirit. Until I had found myself again; until I had found a way to crawl out of the grave they had dug for me.

Another moan escaped me before I pulled away—embarrassment washing over me as I realized I nearly mauled Trevor in public.

"What was that for?" Trevor asked as his eyes burned with excitement.

"I don't know," I answered, trying to catch my breath. "You're just so cute with him."

You're so loving—it makes me want you even more, I thought, far too nervous to mutter the words.

He smiled, seemingly satisfied with my answer. Handing Grey to me, Trevor reached for his phone and said, "I want a few photos of you two."

For some reason, hearing this made me blissful. As he began to take pictures of Grey and me, I couldn't help but feel like a little family. I felt that Grey and Trevor were really mine. *Something I want now, more than anything.* A few short months ago, I had felt alone. Now, I had everything. Grey smiled up at me, content in my arms. For a moment, I couldn't look away, captivated by the blissfulness in his wide, innocent eyes. I only peered away as Trevor called out to us, continuing to snap a few shots.

As Trevor snapped the last photo, I bent down and gave Grey a quick kiss on the cheek, pausing for a moment to make sure Trevor had a chance to snap the perfect photo. When Trevor finished, I stood with Grey in my arms and eagerly closed the distance between us.

"How do they look?" I asked. "I never look good in pictures."

He playfully rolled his eyes at my comment, pulling the pictures up on his phone as he replied. "What are you talking about, Ronnie? You look just as fantastic as you do in real life."

I felt my face flush. *How could he possibly believe I was more beautiful than everyone else? Is that part of love?* My cheeks colored further at the thought.

"Come on, you know you're gorgeous," he continued, giving me a dubious look.

Not knowing what to say—what could I say to something like that? I knew a man like Trev could do better than me if he wanted to—I playfully shoved his shoulder and deflected. "Well, I definitely don't look as cute as Grey."

His eyes regarded me for a moment before a smile tugged on his lips. Apparently, I amused him. Taking a step closer, he bent down, giving me a quick peck on the cheek before he stood to his full height, which towered over my five-foot, three-inch frame.

"Come on," he said, taking my free hand and leading me toward another small apple stand located toward the back of the patch.

Grey babbled in my arms as we traversed across the field, obviously growing used to the noise coming from the plethora of children surrounding us. It was nice to see him come out of his shell a bit; he had spent the majority of our little trip with his face buried against Trevor's neck. Now, his eyes wildly scanned the sight before him, taking everything in with a gummy grin. His incoherent babbles grew louder as we reached the stand, causing Trevor to release my hand so I could grip his nephew with both hands, keeping the wild baby in check.

I listened to Grey's babbles, fascinated by his attempts at speech. I wondered if I had the opportunity to hear his little speech phonetically, if I would laugh at what he was attempting to communicate. Judging by the look on his face, he found himself very funny. He babbled as he watched his uncle pay for some treats and threw his head back to laugh at whatever he had said. I laughed, too, as I reached to adjust his hat before it consequently flew off. Trevor continued to shoot his nephew amused looks as he slid his wallet back into his back pocket and grabbed our treats and warm ciders.

"So, you grew up coming here?" I inquired as I followed him to a nearby hay bale.

He took a seat, waiting for me to do the same. I situated Grey comfortably on my lap before Trevor handed me my portion of the treat. His eyes peered off into space, gazing at nothing in particular as he took a long sip of cider, cringing as the hot drink slid down his throat.

With his eyes trained ahead and a memory seemingly taking over his mind, Trevor replied, "Yeah, I used to love coming here. Closer to Halloween, they'd have these awesome hayrides, and I'd sit in my dad's lap while Dean would sit in my mother's. We'd get so scared at the littlest things. I would bury my face in my dad's shirt and just stay like that until the ride was over. Dean loved it though. He'd always get a kick out of anything scary when he was a kid. The only thing he hated was how my mother would make him pose for all these pictures. He hated getting in front of the camera. Even when he was really popular in high school, he never liked getting his picture taken."

Immediately, he stopped talking; his eyes were puzzled as they dropped to the ground. I gazed at him, wishing I could read his mind. With his shoulders hunched forward and his body tensed, it seemed like he was erecting a wall around himself. *Or maybe he's trying to tear the walls down?* As his silence sunk in, the noises surrounding us became even more apparent.

While I sat in silence, I realized this was the first time he had talked about Dean so freely. Until now, Dean had been an abstract in my mind. All I knew about him was his current status: deceased. I knew nothing about what he had been like alive.

For a moment, Trevor had blossomed before me—seeming not as broken. The light in his eyes while he had spoken of his brother had been enthralling; in these moments, he emitted a warmth that touched everyone around him. I felt it; Grey felt it. Hell, I was certain the entire world would feel it, too, if he opened himself up to everyone. But with Trevor—and with many like him—it was one step forward, two steps back.

When Trevor would reveal a part of himself, it felt like there was a length of time following when he would recoil further. *He's rather like me in that way, I suppose.* I longed to pry him open. I wanted to see the darkness he held so well. I wanted him to tear into me, too. *One day, perhaps we can bleed together; bleed until the only thing between us is the truth. If he thinks his darkness is bad, what will he think of mine?*

Wanting him to relax again—wanting to see that carefree smile—I nudged my shoulder against his, effectively taking him out of his daze before I asked, "So, your mom never made you take any pictures?"

"No, not really."

The grateful look on his face made me smirk.

"I was usually off doing something with my dad," he expanded.

"Well, hopefully there's some photos of you. I'd love to see what little Trevor looked like," I teased.

He smiled slightly at my tone and adjusted his posture before he answered me.

"I looked like my brother, Dean. Just a little rougher around the edges, I suppose. He was clean cut and straight edge, and I was the complete opposite. But, everyone said we had the same eyes and smile. Dean looked a lot like my mom though, whereas I look nothing like her at all. My aunt used to tease me about being adopted." He laughed, shaking his head at the obvious absurdity of the thought.

"I'm sure you were very handsome."

He rolled his eyes—forever awkward when I complimented him—but the smile tugging on his lips indicated that he enjoyed my assessment.

Dropping my eyes to the babbling bundle in my arms, I added, "Just like Grey."

Now, Trevor really smiled—contentment illuminating his face.

After a day beneath the Colorado sun with an exhausting, but extremely cute, little boy, we forwent Trevor's previous plan of carving pumpkins to celebrate the upcoming holiday early and, instead, decided on a relaxing night in at my place.

"My place" sounded strange to me. Since meeting Trevor, I felt as if our two apartments were combined. We were constantly together; I was at his place some nights, and he was at mine others. Truly, it was as if we lived together, the only separation being where we slept at night. While we *had* slept in the same bed before, it hadn't become a regular occurrence. *Yet.*

When I was with Trevor, my body and mind seemed to forget about its previous spatial issues and everything else that had triggered certain anxieties. In fact, being close to him—feeling his strong, inked arms wrapped around my body—made me feel safe. In his embrace, I felt like nothing could ever harm me. I wondered if Grey felt similarly. As I considered the look on Grey's face as he laid snuggly in his uncle's arms, I knew he did.

Resting my head on Trevor's shoulder, I stared down at our little guy. He was completely uninterested in the movie playing. *Apparently, Aladdin wasn't too exciting for this baby.* Despite his obvious weariness, he tried to stay awake to spend time with us. Grey's eyelids began to flutter as he began to doze off. Just as sleep was prepared to engulf him, he forced his eyes open to peer up at me.

I heard Trevor chuckle beside me before I felt his lips pressed firmly against my hair for a quick peck.

"It's okay if you have to go to sleep, little guy. We'll all be here when you wake up."

Grey's eyes darted to his uncle, staring up at his lips as if he were trying to decipher what was being said.

"Come on, buddy. You know you want to," he continued.

Grey babbled something, his voice laced with exhaustion. His eyes darted to meet mine before they moved back to his uncle. Apparently, our silence wasn't a sufficient answer, so, he babbled again. His words were incoherent, reminding me of Eden whenever she was intoxicated: babbling and incoherent, but cute. The memory of her made me grin, and as I compared her and Grey's speech patterns side-by-side in my mind, a laugh escaped me.

"What's so funny?"

I flushed, feeling almost embarrassed for comparing his baby nephew to my drunken sister. *Not that he ever has to know, thank God.*

"Nothing," I quickly replied. "I was just thinking about my sister, Eden."

"What about her?"

I giggled again before wariness caused my body to stiffen. "It's really dumb, Trev. Not worth sharing."

What a hypocrite I was—constantly worried about honesty between us while not wanting to share the smallest thing. Trevor gave me a strange look. Although, I didn't want to see it, he appeared disappointed. *Should I tell him? Would it really matter? Perhaps he'll find it funny.*

"Okay, well, I guess you don't have to tell me then."

With a tight expression, he slid his arm down, removing it from around my shoulder before he reached for Grey, adjusting him to rest comfortably against his chest. He didn't say anything. Instead, he stared at the television as he rocked Grey gently against him.

"Trev," I stared, feeling worried all of a sudden. "It was really nothing. Just something stupid I thought of."

"If it was nothing, why can't you share it? I might find it funny, too."

Looking at his crestfallen face, I slumped against him, wishing I knew how to appropriately act around him. *Just say it, Veronica. If anything, this can be a learning experience. Test the boundaries and find where you stand.*

I took a deep breath, and while keeping a thoughtful eye on his expression, I told him. "I was just thinking that Grey reminds of my sister when she's drunk. You know because of the way he babbles."

I nearly cringed at the awkward tone in my voice.

Trevor's brows knitted together for a moment, which caused me to hold my breath, before a small smile tugged at his lips.

"You're right. I think that all the time. He's just like a little drunk: eating garbage, staggering around, babbling incoherently, and shitting himself."

Trevor chuckled at this and dipped his head down to press a kiss against his nephew's forehead, earning himself a giant, sleepy grin from Grey.

"Why didn't you ... " he trailed off before shaking his head. "Thanks, Ronnie, but I'm not that fragile. You can mention that stuff around me. I'm not going to fall to pieces."

"I'm sorry. I just—"

"Don't apologize." Reaching down with his free hand, he took my right hand in his grasp. "Thanks for caring so much. Other people in my life don't. Being with you … it's like a breath of fresh air. You're good for me, Ronnie. Don't ever think differently."

16

Time

Light reflected off the bathwater as I peered up, taking in the contorted scenery while I lay fully immersed. The hot water almost stung, but instead of shying away, I basked in the sensation, enjoying the way my skin flushed in response. I breathed in, watching as bubbles of air rose to the water's surface before popping. My bones *creaked* beneath the water as my back realigned. Closing my eyes, I tried to clear my mind, which grew increasingly impossible by the second.

Tonight was the night. Tonight, I would meet Trevor's family for the first time. Tonight, I would become even more immersed in his life. He had already captured my heart, and now, I wanted to know every part of him.

Despite my efforts, my mind began to drift. There was an insecurity regarding tonight that I couldn't stifle. *What if they don't like me? What if they take one look at me and think I'm wrong for Trev?* I didn't know what to expect, and judging by the drastic shift in Trevor's mood as of late, I already had my reservations. Lately, he seemed so distant—so withdrawn. As his mother's birthday had approached, he became increasingly quiet. Even his behavior around Grey had been different. I wondered if he was aware of the changes in himself; seeing him this way was sobering. *Is his relationship with his mother really* that *horrible?* Images of my mother filled my mind as my imagination quickly wandered. In my mind's eye, I saw her loving smile, and, in the corners of my memory, I heard her soft voice.

Suddenly, water filled my nostrils as I inhaled without thinking; I choked before I shot out of the water and spluttered. I coughed until my lungs burned and cursed for forgetting myself like that. Rubbing the suds away from my face, I slowly sank back into the water as I considered how I should deal with tonight. *Maybe I can help mend his relationship with his mother?* Having a mother—even a horrible, thoughtless one— was better than having no mother at all. *Wasn't it?*

Even if she *was* horrid, she was breathing—she was there when he needed her. Even if their relationship was strained, at least he could speak to her when he wanted. She was just a phone call away. He could hear her voice any time; see her face whenever he chose to. I didn't have that option. Never again would I be able to feel my mother's embrace or be able to confide in her—never would I be able to tell her about Trevor and Greyson. She would never know them; she would never know the happiness I had found.

I stared blankly ahead, wondering what she would have thought if she would have been able to meet the man who had become my entire universe. Thankfully, she hadn't been here to witness my darkness; she hadn't been here to witness the time my life had been shattered. In a way, she had helped me take those jagged pieces and slowly put them back together until they formed a resemblance to the girl I had once been. The memories of her warmth—of her love—had mended me. However, despite my efforts, I hadn't been truly healed until Trevor touched my heart. Slowly, I had begun to trust again. A smile touched my lips and, for the first times in days, I felt weightless. *Trev ... Oh, Trev.* With his image in my mind, I knew I could get through tonight—and whatever other challenges life threw in my way.

Accessing my appearance in the mirror, I took a deep breath as I realized after an hour of shaving, plucking, brushing, curling, and scrubbing, this was as good as I was going to get. *Not too shabby, Veronica. Not too shabby.* I smiled at my reflection, hoping Trevor would find me just as appealing. I couldn't remember the last time I had dressed up like this. In a white cocktail dress, which molded to my curves, I actually felt sexy. Gazing at my reflection, I ran my fingers along the lines of my body, paying special attention to my puckered nipples before my fingers descended farther. The alarm of my phone alerting me it was time to go paused my wandering fingers, and I blushed, realizing Trevor was waiting for me.

After I quickly threw on a purple cardigan, which complimented my dress, I rushed to leave my apartment. I grabbed my handbag and key before I locked my front door and moved to knock on Trevor's. His gasp flooded my ears as his front door swung open. That sweet sound of appreciation was quickly followed by a cacophony of sounds coming from Grey. Trevor's eyes were glued to me however, which made me shift back and forth on my feet; I gently moved my thighs together with each movement to provide the throbbing between my legs with a small amount of relief. His heated stare made me want to weep, but I knew now wasn't the time for that. *Not even close.*

His eyes moved up and down my body before they came to rest on my breasts, causing them to feel heavy against the bodice of my dress.

"What is it?" I asked, making him fully aware of the fact he had been gawking at me for what felt like an immeasurable amount of time.

"Sorry," he muttered, running his free hand through his unruly hair. "You just look incredible tonight."

I flushed, biting down on my bottom lip to suppress a girlish laugh. "You look pretty amazing yourself, Trev," I replied as my eyes took in his appearance.

In a dark blue button-down and a pair of dress pants, he looked absolutely divine. *Heavenly and sinful at the same time.* I wanted him to hold me in his arms like I was a precious jewel—as he so often did—but I also wanted him to recklessly fuck me into oblivion, making me forget about everything else. I wanted him to pound into me until everything else faded away. *One day, Veronica. One day.*

As my flush deepened, I adverted my attention to something else: Grey, who had been watching me with wide, innocent eyes. He looked just as dashing. So, I said so and stepped forward to tickle his chubby, little belly. He squealed and reached for me. Seeing the eagerness in his eyes left me breathless as my arms outstretched to gather him into my embrace. He rested his head against my chest, and I closed my eyes, enjoying the closeness as I inhaled the scent of his baby lotion and *No More Tears* shampoo. The scent reminded me of Harper and the days I had spent taking care of her when she was very little.

"You ready to go, beautiful?"

"Beautiful." I loved when he called me that.

"I thought afterward we could grab dinner somewhere. I wasn't planning on being at this thing all night," he continued.

This "thing." He wasn't excited at all, was he?

"Sounds good, Trev. Whatever you want to do," I replied as I watched him lock up his apartment before we took off down the hall.

Grey chirped in, supplying us with a response consisting of a garble of noises filled with various inflections. He gazed up at me, seemingly waiting for a response. The edges of my lips curled, causing him to garble something else. Bending down, I nuzzled his little neck with the tip of my nose before I kissed his cheek, and then his wild hair.

"I think he's got a crush on you," Trevor commented dryly with a hint of a smirk on his face.

"I guess you'd know a lot about what that's like, wouldn't you?" I teased right back—my eyes on his ass as I followed him to his truck parked at the edge of the lot. "With the way you constantly look at me," I continued as a smirk plastered on my face, "I can't imagine how hard it must be for you to contain yourself."

He stopped walking, causing me to nearly fall into him as I came to a halt, too. He looked over his shoulder, regarding me with eyes smoldering like liquid fire. Unable to help myself, as I wanted to push him to the edge without causing him to fall victim to his emotions, I winked at him and bit my lip as I suppressed a smile. His mouth dropped open. I passed by him, acting so confident I surprised myself. I heard him burst into laughter behind me; it caused me to break into a smile. As I listened to him, I decided the sound of his laughter was my favorite sound in the entire world. I would do anything to hear that sound more often. I looked down at Grey, whose eyes were shooting wildly about as he looked for the source of his uncle's booming laughter. Before I could turn around to show him, I felt Trevor approach. I gasped as his arms wrapped around my center.

I turned in his arms as my mind searched for another clever thing to say. But, before I found the chance, Trevor pressed his lips against mine. The softness of his mouth caused every witty thought to escape me. I lost myself in the kiss, and when he pulled away, I found I wasn't sated—I doubted I ever would be. His eyes scanned my face before his lips twitched into a smirk. He knew what he did to me, and he knew what I wanted. *Now, it was just a waiting game.*

My eyes glued to Trevor's knuckles, which turned white as he gripped the steering wheel. If I had my doubts about his nerves concerning tonight, now, they were long gone. With his shirt sleeves rolled up around his elbows, I could see the veins running down his muscular forearms twitch in reaction to his unforgiving grip. I reached forward and placed my hand on his thigh, squeezing lightly. My effort didn't have its desired effect. Instead of relaxing, Trevor tensed at my touch and jolted in his seat, nearly swerving into the lane on our left.

"Trev!"

"Sorry," he responded as he slowed down slightly. Throwing me a sheepish smile, he continued. "I wasn't expecting that."

"You weren't expecting me to touch you?"

He chuckled. "I guess not."

"I like touching you."

God, I sounded lame.

"Well, I like your hands on me."

He cringed as the words came out, obviously unimpressed with himself, too. He muttered a "fuck" under his breath before he shook his head.

"Are we close?"

"Too close," he quipped. "I was hoping this drive would be a bit longer, if I'm being honest. You know, so I can mentally prepare."

"That bad?" I grimaced.

"No, not *that* bad."

He was a horrible liar. Although I wanted to, I didn't press him. I turned my gaze forward, peering down the empty road ahead of us as my mind conjured images of possibilities surrounding what Trevor's childhood home might look like. I couldn't wait to see where he had grown up; I couldn't wait to see the people who had raised him to be the lovely man he was today. If they were anything like him, they had to be wonderful—wonderful, as well as incredibly giving. When the house came into view, I smiled, realizing it was exactly what I imagined: warm, wholesome, and traditional.

"I can't believe this," Trevor muttered as he weaved around cars parked haphazardly along the edges of the street leading to his childhood home. "It's like they invited everyone they've ever met."

I forced myself to suppress a laugh—there was just something about disgruntled Trevor that I loved. With his brows knitted together in obvious frustration, he continued down the dark, packed road until he found a place to park a few blocks away. He threw his truck into park with an annoyed huff and swung open his door before jumping out and popping open the passenger door to gather Grey from his car seat. I stepped out, careful in my heels as I usually stuck to flats. Tonight, however, I wanted to look my absolute best for the two most important men in my life.

The neighborhood's graveled roads felt like hell against the soles of my heels. The sharp edges of the rocks were unforgiving, and despite my efforts to ignore the pain, it was impossible for my body not to react to the sharp discomfort. Trevor looked at me, eyes searching my body for signs of distress before he frowned, looking forward to the rest of the walk ahead of us.

"Fuck, I'm sorry, baby," he commented, running a hand through his hair in an effort to tame it.

"It's fine." I shrugged. *I knew I should have opted for comfort.* "This is why I never wear heels."

He turned to me, regarding me for a pregnant moment before he replied, "Well, you look beautiful tonight, baby. But, you look beautiful in *anything* you wear."

I shook my head, smiling despite myself. I knew he was just trying to flatter me; however, I couldn't deny the girlish pleasure his compliments brought. Just hearing him call me "baby" made my heart flutter wildly in my chest. If any other man had been complimenting me, I would have assumed they were merely being nice or had some sort of ulterior motive.

However, Trevor was genuine—so genuine, in fact, I wondered if he could ever be false. Nothing about Trevor Warren was artificial. Every fiber of his being rung true, which put part of me at ease, causing me to trust his words. Knowing his compliments came from an authentic place made them all the more potent—all the more important. He always said what was in his heart.

With a flush coloring my pale cheeks, I replied, "I love it when you call me that."

"Baby? I've been wanting to call you baby for a while now; I didn't want you to freak-out on me."

I giggled at the idea. "I would never 'freak-out' on you. I like being your *anything*."

His "baby." His "girl." His "world." Anything would do as long as it meant I was his.

"Well, I'll keep that in mind."

With a confident smirk and a wink from him, I nearly melted where I stood.

Trevor stiffened beside me as we walked past the threshold of his parents' home. With a tense jaw and dark, pensive eyes, he guided me inside, never bothering to let his eyes wander. I took a quick glance around the room and discovered why he had instantly recoiled and become withdrawn. The looks he was receiving took my breath away.

This was a room filled with his parents' "friends," and they were looking at Trevor as if he were some sort of delinquent. I understood the man wasn't everyone's cup of tea—I understood the judgments one could make by looking at him. Nevertheless, their stares made me sick with anger; their judgments made me want to lash out and protect him like a lioness protecting her cubs.

Where were his parents? Shouldn't they be here to tell their friends how wonderful their son is? They needed to be defending him, explaining how well he has done under the soul-crushing circumstances. My face flushed as the anger continued to course through me. *How dare these people judge him! How dare these people not care for him like I do!*

He was beautiful—beyond beautiful—and yet, this crowd turned their faces away in disgust and prejudice. They looked at him as if they had smelled something sour. Taking a deep breath, I calmed myself down. After years of not feeling able to fight for myself, I wanted to fight for Trevor. *If I couldn't do it for me, let me do it for him.* With that thought present in my mind, I felt stronger than ever. I had dealt with so much and hadn't given myself an ounce of credit; perhaps, I'd had this strength bubbling inside of me all along. Trevor needed a strong woman in his life—someone to love him … someone to keep him honest. Grey needed me, too. He had lost so much so quickly. I could be the strong female presence he needed in his life. *The sort of presence I so constantly craved.*

"You ready to meet my parents?" Trevor asked, pulling me from my thoughts.

My eyes snapped away from the crowd to peer up at him. I found his eyes had thawed, and his expression had loosened. *Meeting his parents …* Suddenly, my strength seemed to dissipate, and I felt nervous once more. Trevor gave me a confused look, as if he was wondering what *I* had to worry about. Holding on to him as a lifeline, Trevor led me through the crowd, almost smiling as he held Grey against his chest while looking out at the attendees in front of him. Apparently, he was unbothered by their supercilious glances. *If only I could be so cool about it.*

His eyes were focused ahead on a handsome man who looked to be in his early fifties. With dark hair and a ruggedly handsome face, he resembled Trevor quite a bit. A smile tugged on my lips as I realized this man must be his father. *This is the man from before! The handsome one who helped him move.* The man's eyes brightened as his gaze locked onto his son. In this moment, I knew I liked the man. His proud, paternal smile gave me a profound sense of relief. I wanted Trevor to have parents who were just as proud of him as I was.

As soon as I noticed the beer the man was nursing, my gaze shot to my date, anxiety blooming in my chest. *How does Trevor deal with things like this? If alcohol is such a temptation, how can he walk away unscathed?* Beside me, Trevor was stone-faced and strained. His rigid form was hard to miss. His muscles were tight beneath the fabric of his shirt, bulging ever so slightly. His eyes were focused on the drink, and his energy, which I had quickly become attuned to, felt chaotic, like a wild animal attempting to break free of its cage.

I squeezed his hand in mine, hoping the small gesture eased some of his stress. His shoulders dropped slightly, but not significantly enough to ease my own anxiety. Grey, who was just as attuned to Trevor's emotions as I was, stirred in his uncle's arms as his eyes darted around the room for the source of his uncle's discomfort. My eyes moved back to Trevor just in time to find his tongue darting out to lick his bottom lip before it slid back inside, disappearing between his lips before he bit down to stifle a groan of irritation. I didn't know what he was irritated with—his father for drinking in front of him or himself for not being immune to temptation.

Trevor relaxed slightly and waved a polite "hello" to his father's colleague before his attention fell on his father. His eyes were trained on him before they wavered, dropping to the beer, appreciating the way the bottle sweated. As if he had been smacked, he snapped out of his trance, eyes widening as he peered at the man before him. Squeezing my hand, he took a shaky breath. I wondered if he was summoning the courage to introduce me. I smiled at this idea, falling for Trevor even more. *If that were even possible.*

"Dad, this is my date, Veronica Clark." His pensive face morphed into a content expression as he uttered my name. Turning to me, he introduced his father. "Ronnie, this is my dad, Arthur Warren."

Arthur grinned at me. His eyes swept over my body appraisingly before he gave his son a knowing grin. His aura was warm—similar to my father's—and I took to him immediately. Reaching out my hand, I gave him a firm shake—just like my father taught me—before letting go and turning my attention to his son.

"So," Arthur began, his voice gruff, "you're the beautiful, young lady my son can't stop talking about."

"*Dad*," Trevor bit out, displeasure mixing with shock. Letting go of my hand, he moved to run his fingers through his untamable mane as his eyes shot to gauge my expression. I flushed under his scrutiny before my attention reverted to his father.

"I'm just joking, Trevor," Arthur said in a deep, paternal voice. He smirked at his son before he continued. "It's very nice to meet you, Veronica." His eyes danced between us, and his mouth twitched, as if he yearned to say something before his son's glare inspired him to refrain. "So," he began again conversationally, "how did you two meet?"

As soon as he asked the question, it was somehow obvious he already knew the answer. However, I replied anyway as I wondered how much Trevor had told his father. *Does he talk about me frequently? Has he told his father how he feels about me? Does he confide in him?*

"Well," I answered, straightening up as I spoke to the man I had been longing to meet since witnessing Trevor's own paternal skills, "I saw him around town a few times, but I was always far too shy and nervous to ever approach him. So, when I saw he had moved in next to me, I knew I finally had my chance."

Trevor stiffened at my side, and my gaze shot to him, wondering what I had said to upset him. My gaze flickered toward his tense figure, and to my surprise, he seemed more contemplative than upset. *Had he not noticed my interest in him? Had he not realized the way my eyes followed him whenever he moved through a room?*

"You wanted to talk to me before you ever saw me move in?" he asked, in what seemed to be utter disbelief.

Was he serious?

With a small, sly smile, I answered him. "Well, you're kind of hard not to want, Trev."

His eyes sparked, and in this moment, I wanted nothing more than to lose myself in his kiss—I wanted to feel him pressed against me; I wanted him to understand the depths of my desire for him. He might not be "conventional," but he was twistedly beautiful. His originality deepened my desire for him. He was a tortured soul wrapped in a sinfully handsome package. He was a giving, unselfish man behind a gritty façade.

When Trevor didn't contribute to the conversation—finding himself far too busy peering at me incredulously—I went on to add, "We started talking when Grey was teething—I had heard his cries. So, I stopped by and helped out … and it progressed from there."

Arthur's mouth twitched into an approving grin as his gaze darted between the three of us. "Well, that's great. Trevor needs a girl like you in his life." He winked at his son.

My body flushed as Trevor snuck his arm around my waist. I tried not to look too embarrassed by my body's reaction to him in front of his father. *I swear my body will never grow used to his touch. I'll never grow bored of the feeling of his fingers caressing my flesh. I'll always yearn for this intimacy.*

I was so immersed in his energy I barely noticed as his body became rigid. Following his gaze, I noticed a beautiful woman standing across the room with a terse smile on her surgically enhanced face. *This is his mother? Was this cold, distant woman his mother?* My eyes shot to Trevor for confirmation of my theory. Judging by the look on his face, he knew this woman incredibly well. The love he had for her, swimming in his eyes, broke my heart. *Perhaps she's not as bad as you're imagining, Veronica. You haven't spoken to the woman, yet; give her a chance.*

She crossed the room, looking overtaxed despite being at her own party. *No wonder this woman doesn't have any wrinkles—she never smiles.* Feeling disappointed in myself for being so judgmental, I pushed those thoughts aside. I shouldn't judge this woman; after all, she had lost her son recently. I understood loss, and I understood that, as individuals, we all carried that weight differently. We all had different experiences as we walked down the dark, seemingly endless path of grief. I had been horrible to everyone around me after my mother passed away; perhaps, in that way, Trevor's mother was similar to me.

With this thought in my mind, I tried to ignore my gut feeling as she greeted her son with a cold, forced smile. I told myself she was grieving, but from Trevor's expression, it was far more than that. *Has she always been so cold and passionless toward him?*

His mother didn't acknowledge me, and Trevor, far too overwhelmed with emotion, didn't utter a word. Before I understood what he was doing, he handed me Grey and advanced toward his mother with arms outstretched. My heart pounded in my chest as I watched him—wanting nothing more than to see her features soften as she opened her arms to him. That didn't happen.

As I rocked Grey in my arms, I watched the scene before me with a guarded heart and misty eyes. His arms wrapped around his mother, pulling her close, and in response, she gave him *nothing*. Her arms remained at her sides, not even twitching with the desire to hold her son. Her face, so beautifully made-up, was guarded. Her eyes … her eyes were what affected me the most. The look swimming in their depths wasn't one I would soon forget. Her eyes were so *dead*—devoid of emotion completely. I wondered what she felt when he held her. *Was it truly possibly for her to feel nothing?* Could her son's touch really be so meaningless to her? I blinked away the tears in my eyes, wanting to appear strong for Trevor. In this moment, watching her with anger bubbling in my chest, I knew I hated her. She had lost so much, but she didn't appreciate what she still had.

Am I being unfair? A hypocrite? Had I been like this, too?

Trevor pulled away to gaze at her face, his eyes calculating as he took in the haunting image of his unresponsive mother. Her callousness continued to confound me. *Not even a smile. She doesn't so much as spare him a look that isn't filled with disappointment.* I didn't know what *she* had to be so disgusted about, but I knew I was disgusted with her. Trevor looked to his father, searching for what, I didn't know. When he turned his attention back to his lifeless mother, he seemed just as lost. His father seemed equally perplexed, gazing at his wife as if he were seeing her for the very first time. *Perhaps, in a way, he was.*

The tension in the room was palpable; so thick, I felt like I was choking on it. Grey, who had been impressively quiet this entire time, grew weary in my arms and started to kick—body wiggling around as he searched for a more comfortable position. I brought him to rest against my breast as my hand moved to pat his back, desperately trying to comfort him before he had a tantrum in the middle of the party. *Maybe that would be a good thing. Maybe it would help break up all of this awkward tension.*

"Ronnie," Trevor began as he let go of his mother and stepped away, "this is my mother."

This was the woman he had painted—this was Evelyn.

His voice was weak and defeated. I pushed back the tears, suppressed my emotions, and forced a smile on my face. I wondered if it looked more like a constipated grimace.

"It's nice to meet you," I lied smoothly.

She responded with a tight smile and despite myself, I went on to exchange pleasantries with her. Somewhere in my heart, I held on to the hope that perhaps she wasn't as terrible as she appeared. While I made small talk—something which I had never been a fan of doing—her eyes darted all over the room as if she were looking for an escape.

Her lack of interest deflated me. The knowledge that Trevor was watching me was the only thing that kept me going—kept me talking. While I spoke, I thought, *this was the witch who withheld so much information from her son; this was the witch who hadn't helped him along the way.* Until recently, Trevor hadn't realized Grey had many benefits waiting for him. In my own stupidity, I had always assumed he knew. He had been too shy to speak about his struggles—especially his financial ones. What man would want to open up in that way to a woman he was interested in?

While I was sure his father wasn't blameless, Trevor had told me his mother sat him down and helped him take the "next steps" after his brother and sister-in-law passed. *Some job she did.* My eyes narrowed as I wondered what sort of woman would do something so deceitful to her own flesh and blood. She noted my change in demeanor, and her gaze sharpened. With my head held high, I ignored all of her efforts to intimidate me. Later tonight, I would permit myself the luxury of allowing my emotions to escape, but for now, I would keep them nicely bottled up. As I sized her up, Trevor's words from last night came coursing back into my consciousness.

"If she didn't tell me about this shit, what else has she been hiding from me? Didn't she see me fucking struggling? Jesus, Ronnie! When Dr. Russel told me about that shit, he looked at me like I was a fucking idiot for not knowing! But how would I know about that sort of thing? I've never had to deal with this crap before."

I frowned, wishing I could do something, anything, *to make him feel better. The fact that she wouldn't tell him about all the benefits he could file for was almost unbelievable. What sort of woman would do that? Had she been so scatterbrained she had merely forgotten?*

"I wish there was something I could do." *I frowned, reaching forward to take his hand in mine.* "At least, you know now. This will be a game changer, Trev."

"Yeah, I know. But still ... how could she do that?" *he mused before falling silent.*

My eyes continued to shoot toward Trevor, who was watching his father as he finished off his beer. Arthur moved to walk toward the kitchen to grab another. Trevor turned to me with anxious eyes and asked, "Ronnie, do you mind hanging out for a bit? I need to get that stuff from my dad."

He was referring to the paperwork he needed: birth certificates, death certificates, etcetera. His eyes were intense, and the muscles in his jaw were taut as he looked at me. Bloodshot eyes searched mine, taking my breath away. I wanted to follow him; I wanted to protect him, but I knew he had to do this alone. I knew I couldn't shield him from the world—I had been shielding myself this way for so long. So, I did all I could do. I provided him with an encouraging smile before I leaned in to kiss him gently on the cheek. With Grey snuggly in my arms, I watched Trevor as he turned to follow after his father. I peered at the space he had previously occupied, sending a silent prayer for the best.

As much as I wanted to love both of his parents, they had both been so deceptive. *Why on earth had they allowed Trevor to suffer for so long when a small amount of information from them could have helped him along—could have eased his transition?* They hadn't provided Trevor with any guidance. They had allowed him to walk down this rough road alone. Trevor faced every new responsibility without fear—or at least, it appeared that way to me. While he had fought to gain control over his new life, his parents had kept him in the dark—forgotten.

Suddenly, I didn't want to be here anymore; suddenly, this party seemed like a horrible joke. While there were happy faces and smiles as far as my eyes could see, there was a coldness in the room, which was impossible to ignore. Perhaps, it stemmed from the callousness of his mother. Maybe *this* was why she ignored me: I saw straight through her bullshit. To me, her kind mask wasn't convincing.

I felt as if I had been a poor judge of character in the past—trusting when I shouldn't have; opening up when I should have protected myself—however, Evelyn's character was as clear as day to me. She may have been great to some, but as a mother, she was piss-poor.

Looking down at Grey, I muttered, "You don't realize how lucky you are to have Trev, little guy."

The words sounded almost strange on my tongue because, in his very short life, he had already lost so much—but he had gained so much, too. He had gained another father who adored him, a man who loved him far more than he loved himself. When Trevor looked at this lost, little boy, it was as if he saw the embodiment of all the goodness in the world—all the goodness he felt personally detached from.

Grey babbled a response as I sat down on a chair farthest removed from the party. While the people filling the room may have been lovely, after conversing with his mother, I was no longer in the mood to speak to another soul.

While I played with Grey on my lap, I gazed around the dimly lit room, wondering what type of people surrounded Trevor while he had grown up. Everyone here seemed so pretentious—so out of touch with reality. *Was this Trevor's life? Were his rough edges once tamed?* If he had ever been around people such as these, his strong personality must have been diluted. I couldn't picture him as docile or the least bit subdued. He was too … well, he was too *himself.* He consisted of sharp edges and a jagged heart. In this crowd, he stood out like a sore thumb; I found this beautiful. He was different than all the rest. He was unapologetically the person he had been born to be.

My legs bounced as I tried to release some of the tension brewing inside of me while I gazed at the clock, watching it as the minutes ticked by like hours. Grey grew restless in my arms, obviously sensing the nerves in my body as I thought of his uncle. *What's taking so long? What are they discussing? Is he telling his father off for not bringing all of this to his attention sooner?* Questions blazed through my mind as I remained glued to my seat.

"He'll be here soon, sweetie," I told Grey, but truly, I had been comforting myself with these words. "Why don't we give your uncle a good night tonight? After this, we can all do something nice together. Wouldn't that be great?"

He gave me a curious look, and I laughed at myself. Just staring into his wide, guileless eyes gave me such comfort. I bounced him in my lap, trying to keep us both entertained as I scanned the room again, looking for my man in the crowd. I didn't find him, but I found his mother staring at me from her perch across the room. The look on her face suggested she had just smelled something rotten. Usually, I would have felt anxious under this type of scrutiny, but tonight, I straightened my spine and met her gaze.

For a moment, she only stared at me, judging me from afar; but, as I continued to make eye contact, she looked away, pretending to have laughed at something a woman close to her had said. Even from my distance, I could see she was being false. I wondered if the people around her could tell, too.

My eyes remained on her while her gaze moved around the room. I was certain she was looking for her husband. My eyes broke away from her to search for him, too. If he were here, Trevor had to be here. I found nothing. With a sigh, my gaze returned to Evelyn. Her artificially beautiful face looked stressed—as stressed as a surgically enhanced face could look. Setting her drink down on a nearby table, she excused herself as she left the room, moving in the same direction Trevor and Arthur had taken a long while before. I wanted to follow her, but I remained in my seat, knowing Trevor needed to handle this alone.

I had no reason for alarm, but something about this situation didn't sit well with me. Every piece seemed to be falling into place, leading to something catastrophic. Something was brewing underneath this perfectly packaged exterior.

Just as my worry was about to transform into a panic, I spotted Trevor as he walked down a darkened hallway, moving to rejoin the party. The crestfallen look on his face said everything. Even from this distance, I saw the pain swimming in his dark eyes. Something had happened—something horrible. I rose to meet him.

The rest of the world faded away as he became the center of my universe. Everything around his stature was a blur as he walked toward us with his head down and his shoulders slumped. His usual stride was contorted, making him barely recognizable as he moved forward. To me, this was a different man. He was not the same Trevor Warren as he had been prior to following his father down that same hallway not even a half hour before.

I closed the distance between us, and he stopped before me, sensing me without having to look up. His eyes were locked on what was in his hand: a pile of papers holding all of the information he needed. With a white-knuckled grasp, he held a pile of papers that somewhere, had two death certificates.

When I peered up at his face, which was just as painfully contorted as the rest of him, I wondered if he hadn't truly come to terms with their deaths until now. Hearing it was one thing—seeing it was one thing—but having an impersonal piece of paper, which told you such a monstrous truth, was another. *In print, it was real.* With the evidence right in front of him, there was no denying the facts.

"Trev …" I began before I came up short.

What could I say? *Sorry for your loss? I'm sorry your parents didn't help you do right by Grey? I'm sorry they concealed this from you?* I remained silent, waiting for him to give me a sign concerning what to do next.

"Let's go, okay? I got everything. I'm ready to get going."

There wasn't an ounce of warmth in his tone. My heart dropped as I watched him pass by us without a single look. He appeared so broken—so numb. Grey reached out for his uncle, only to whimper as he received no response. I opened my mouth to say something but decided to remain silent. Instead of speaking, I followed dutifully behind, knowing the best thing I could do for him now was to give him space.

As the chill from the night hit my face, my mind conjured up different possibilities as to what had happened in the short time Trevor had been away. Every one of those possibilities made my blood boil. I knew it was irrational, but I wanted to throw myself in front of him. I wanted to experience the pain and help carry the weight with him.

Unfortunately, as I gazed at the tired man ahead, I realized this was a weight he wanted to carry all on his own.

17

You Are My Sunshine

"Do you want to talk about it?"

He was as stiff as a board beside me. Since we had arrived home, he had been almost catatonic, staring off into space as if the nothingness before him would provide him with answers. With his brother's death certificate in hand, I watched him, waiting for him to say something—*anything*—to put my mind at ease. Instead, he remained silent with a dead expression.

"Tonight … was rough," he mused to himself with eyes that were still completely void.

Not knowing what words could possibly ease his mind, I bent forward and kissed his shoulder, hoping the feel of my lips would relieve some of his pain. Grey shifted in my lap while he remained sound asleep, exhausted from his exciting night. My gaze moved back to Trevor, finding him gazing down at the little boy in my lap as if Greyson was going somewhere.

His emotive eyes moved me; his face was open, revealing his raw pain. Reaching out, I cupped his cheek with one hand, smiling at the tickle of his stubble as I reached out with my other hand to take his hand in mine. Resting our joined hands on my lap near Grey, I waited for him to respond—I waited for him to give me *anything*. I held my breath, and when he finally met my gaze, the look in his eyes left me spinning. In this moment, despite the chaos surrounding us, I knew everything would be all right. Maybe our skies would always be gray, but with him, I could still soak up the sunlight.

While his eyes bore into mine, his shoulders relaxed, and his tense expression faded into one of gratefulness. Romantic chemistry sparked between us like electricity. The energy brought us closer, and I felt tethered to him, like there was a pull between our two hearts. I leaned forward, pressing my lips against his; I reveled in their salty taste. I melted against the feel of his soft mouth. As I kissed him, I realized I never felt close enough. I wanted him to thrust into me until he poured his emotion—and everything else—into my body; I wanted to feel every single inch of him. I wanted him to drink me up like a man dying of thirst. I moaned against the pillows of his lips, opening my mouth just enough to allow his tongue entrance.

I became delirious, only pulling away when I needed air. With a shaky breath, I let go of his hand and smoothed my hair, needing to calm down before I took things further than we were ready to go tonight. My eyes darted to the movement of his hands as they rested on top of his lap in an attempt to hide his prominent erection. I stifled a gasp, unable to tear my eyes away. *It's so ... so ... Jesus H. Christ. How can Trev lack self-confidence with* that *between his legs?*

Thankfully, Grey chose this moment to awaken from his slumber, giving me an escape from my thoughts. The blush, however, did not leave my cheeks, and my pulse didn't calm. Grey yawned, stretched, and then gazed at me with a look that was so questionable it made me feel like all of my dirty thoughts were being displayed on my face. His bottom lip quivered before he began to cry. He turned toward his uncle and reached out his hands, begging for Trevor to take him. Trevor smiled slightly, although his eyes were still slightly pensive, and took his nephew, bringing Grey to rest against his shoulder.

God, he's good with him. Trevor's the picture of the perfect unconventional daddy. Trevor must have felt my stare because his eyes popped up to meet mine before he broke into a slight smile. *He looks so young like this. So carefree. God, how could anyone* hurt *him? How could his parents stab him in the back? I just want to freaking scream at them!* Anger filled my chest. I wanted to march back into that party and give his parents hell. I wanted to scream at them until they understood the irrevocable harm they had done. They chipped away at his trust—his good nature.

"He loves you so much," I mused as I tried to dissipate my anger. Greyson and Trevor were what mattered now. Everything else was just background noise.

"He said 'da' today," Trevor bragged to me.

"Aw," I cooed, knowing how that single sound must have felt. "He must've been trying to say daddy! That's wonderful!"

Trevor was not his *biological* father, but he loved Grey as if he were his own; the bond between them transcended that of uncle and nephew. It was more than that—so much more than that. It was them against the world. They were what was left of Dean and his wife; they were their legacy. Trevor should be referred to as his father—it's what he was: a protector, a provider, and a mentor. He was everything a father should be and more. *Everything his own father wasn't.*

"I *had* been saying 'dad' around him all day today before he finally said it. I just couldn't help myself. It slipped out while I was giving him a bath, and it just sounded right to me. Fuck, it *felt* right to me."

I smiled at him, unable to believe how flustered he seemed.

"Well, you *are* his dad, Trev. You provide for him, you're his mentor, and you love him more than anything. He's your world. That's what a dad is, and I think you make a sensational one."

I barely got the last word out before he crashed his lips against mine. He poured every ounce of himself into the kiss, and I returned the passion as I poured myself into him, too. Physically, I expressed every word I was too afraid to speak out loud. With my lips, I told him I desired him now and forever; I told him I wished he could have always been here.

Grey's fussiness eventually pulled us apart. The moment I broke away from Trevor, Grey reached up his small, chubby hand to tug on Trev's cheek, giving him a needy look. He seemed almost jealous of the attention I had gotten, so used to receiving every ounce of his uncle's attention. Trevor laughed before he granted Grey his wish, bending forward to give him a quick kiss on the forehead. Grey giggled at the affection before he rested his head happily on his uncle's shoulder.

"See, Trev. He knows you're his daddy," I mused, wanting to call Trevor "daddy" far more often.

He was silent for a moment before he responded. "I thought I'd insult my brother's memory in some way if I called myself that."

I considered his words, deflating at the sound of pain in his voice. "Trev, I didn't get to know your brother, but I'm sure he gave you custody of his son so you *could* be a father to him. He obviously knew you two would be perfect for each other. I'm sure if Dean could see you right now, he'd be smiling down at you. He's got to be proud of you. I know *I* am."

His dark eyes misted before they darted away, hiding his face from me. He was thinking of Dean. I couldn't read his mind, but judging by his facial expressions, it was obvious. I wished I could have known his brother. I wished I could have known the man Trevor had grown up with—the man he loved so deeply. The bond between them was long lasting. Death couldn't break it. In my heart, I knew if his brother were here now, he would have been content in this moment; his son had a father—someone whose love was limitless and unconditional.

As Trevor sat in silence for a long while, I envisioned Dean. My imagination ran wild with fictitious scenarios from their childhood, picturing two little boys who were so alike they could have been a single person. The images were clear in my mind as if they were scenes from a movie. *I wish I could have spoken to him. I wish I could have met him once before he passed away.*

With a fabricated history of them in my head, I turned my attention back to Trevor.

"What are you thinking so hard about?" I asked as I reached out to run my fingers along the muscles of his arm, wanting to provide him with whatever comfort I could.

He smiled, although his eyes were still sad. "I was thinking about getting another tattoo. One in memory of Dean."

"That's a great idea, Trev."

"I just want to have some closure. I never got any." He paused and looked at me for a moment, judging my expression before he continued. "I wasn't there when he died. They couldn't reach me before his surgery, but it's not like I would've made it back here even if they had. I would've done my best to rush back here though. If it only meant I could see Dean one last time … *alive*. Just to watch him breath before they whisked him off to surgery. I would've at least gotten to hold his hand." Tears filled his eyes as he swallowed the obvious lump in his throat. "I would've *wanted* to hold his hand and tell him it was going to be okay. He was in surgery by the time my parents got to the hospital. He didn't get to see any of his family, Ronnie." By my side, he grew hysterical. "He didn't get to see our parents before he died. He didn't get to say goodbye to his son."

Tears poured from his eyes as all of his emotions came bubbling to the surface. He could no longer hide this part of himself. Whatever happened tonight had ripped him open, tearing at all the raw wounds. I had never seen him like this; never had he allowed himself to become so exposed. Tears filled my eyes and trailed down my flushed cheeks. I was torn apart, too. As he dealt with his wounds, I dealt with mine.

"Trev …" I began, wishing I could find the right words. Reaching out, I grasped his hand, holding it so tightly it caused my knuckles to ache.

"I should've stayed in Evergreen," he mused as his tears continued to fall, transforming him into the image of a dark, fallen angel. "I would've stayed and been miserable if it meant I would've been able to say goodbye to him. *Fuck,* I couldn't even look at him in his casket at the funeral. I watched everyone else get up and pay their respects, but I couldn't leave my seat. And Cat … God, she died in that fucking car. I imagine Dean held her hand and told her to hang on … because that's just the type of guy he was. He would've encouraged her to keep going, even when he must've seen the light leaving her eyes. God, Ronnie. I don't know what the fuck I would do if that were you."

And with that, he buried his face in my shoulder and sobbed against the fabric of my cardigan. His tears ran along the exposed flesh of my shoulder, causing his warm, labored breaths to tickle. Tears continued to stream from my own eyes. Together, we fell apart, and together, we rebuilt ourselves.

"Do you know what tattoo you want, Trev?" I asked as we both relaxed in each other's embrace.

"Some sort of angel," he weakly murmured against my neck.

Slowly, he raised his head and wrapped his arms around his sleeping nephew.

"That's wonderful, Trev," I encouraged. "What a wonderful way to honor your brother."

He smiled as his bloodshot eyes searched mine. With so many built-up emotions expelled from our bodies, a feeling of peace filled the room.

I had spent the night. He'd held me all night long until I had finally drifted to sleep in his arms. In my dreams, I had seen two little boys playing. But these hadn't been the little boys I'd made up in my mind to represent Trevor and Dean. This had been Greyson and a child of my own.

With a few inspirational photographs in hand, Trevor sat in the waiting room with us at his side. Grey took in the scene around him with wide, curious eyes. He was particularly captivated by Trevor's artist's current client, who was moaning for mercy in the tattoo chair.

As I watched the woman, wondering how a person with so much ink could handle a single tattoo so badly, I contemplated getting another tattoo. With my love for art and literature, I had a long list of ink I dreamt of getting. When I was younger, I had avoided getting inked anywhere visible since I hadn't known the direction my life would take. *Hence, the small peach tattoo on my ass.* Now, however, I knew I worked in an industry that was pretty accepting of body ink and piercings. Not that I could ever see myself *covered* with them, of course. A plethora of ink just wasn't my personal style; however, one or two more tattoos seemed perfect. *I bet Trev would find them attractive, too.* I wanted something meaningful—something relevant to the woman I was today.

"Maybe I should get a tattoo," I mused as my eyes scanned the framed art on the walls.

He smiled at this, tearing his eyes away from the hysterical woman in the chair to glance at me. "Do you have any?" he asked as his eyes scanned my body.

I warmed under his gaze as I imagined what he could be thinking as he scrutinized me. "I do," I said coyly. "But I'm not telling you where. That's a secret."

"It is?" he teased me. "I'm sure I'll see it eventually."

He gave me a roguish grin, which caused my nipples to pucker and my skin to flush.

"Maybe you will," I teased back, enjoying the flirtation.

He smirked, and his cheeks flushed as he looked at me. I wondered what his reaction would be to my very small tattoo. I was young when I had gotten it and had thought the placement had been cute. Now, I honestly couldn't believe I had gotten a tattoo on my butt. *I want Trev to bite it before he kisses my pussy.* I flushed as the imagery made my core tingle.

"What tattoo would you get, if you were going to get one today?" Trevor asked, pulling me away from my overactive and inappropriate imagination.

I shrugged, too flustered to really think. "I've always wanted a literary quote inked on my skin."

Trevor smiled, pleased with my answer. "Do you know which quote you'd get?"

"Well, I always liked this one quote from *The Kite Runner*: 'For you, a thousand times over,' " I mused as I remembered the special place that book held in my heart. It was one of the first books I truly fell in love with in school. "I always thought that quote was the most beautiful thing I had ever heard."

"That is beautiful," he agreed.

The quote summed up how I felt about a great deal of people in my life. I would do anything for the people I loved. Now, Trevor and Grey had become part of that group. For both of them, I would do anything.

Trevor's artist finished up on his client and moved outside for a quick smoke break before it was Trevor's turn. I watched Trevor as he hurriedly filled out the appropriate paperwork. His brows were knitted together, and his body was tense, as if it were awaiting a significant release. Getting inked seemed cathartic to him—stimulating him and providing him with a release usually found in sex. My body flushed at the thought, and suddenly, I wanted to share this experience with him even more.

The receptionist moved toward us, indicating it was time.

"Are you all right, Trev?" I asked as we rose to meet the woman.

Trevor seemed coiled up inside of himself, as if all his emotions were waiting to be surfaced.

"Yeah, I'm fine," he responded dismissively.

His emotions seemed violent, but I didn't comment. This was an emotional day for many reasons. I couldn't begin to imagine what he was feeling.

"Just hold my hand, okay?" he said with a small smile.

I smiled in response and nodded, following him back to his artist's station as I bounced Grey in my arms. While the artist finished up his work on the stencil, Trevor took off his shirt to expose his back, which was completely free of ink. I couldn't take my eyes off of him. He was so beautiful—so perfectly imperfect. He turned around to face me as I stood right next to the mirror at this station, and I nearly gasped at the sight of his ink and piercings. His nipples were pierced, and every bit of his torso and arms were inked. He may not have been the type of man I would usually swoon over, but staring at him now, I found he was everything I ever wanted. My eyes danced around his torso before they fell to his happy trail. *I want to run my lips across the hair. I want to make him very,* very *happy.* I flushed, adverting my gaze as he lay down on the tattoo chair, situating himself on his stomach before he rested his head on his forearms.

Pulling my gaze away from Trevor, I moved to glance at the design the artist was perfecting: an intricate fallen angel, kneeling with his head bent in prayer. The wings of the design were what captivated me most; they were powerful yet fragmented and torn. The design reminded me of the man who was getting it. I smiled, knowing it would look perfect once it reached completion.

The artist finished up before showing Trevor the design. Trevor smiled and approved it before the artist transferred the design onto his skin. Trevor stood up, allowing me another glimpse of the perfection of his chest and abdominal muscles as he moved to check the design's placement in the mirror. The look on his face as he viewed it momentarily took my breath away. For the first time since his mother's party, he looked truly and incandescently happy. Tears filled his eyes as remembrance colored his features. Seeing him momentarily lost in the past made me happy. In our memories, no one is ever lost.

With misty eyes, he laid back down on the chair and smiled at the familiar *buzz* of the tattoo gun. I took a seat with Grey comfortably in my arms and observed the process. I watched the blood as it rose to the surface of his skin, appearing like little beads against the flesh of his back before the artist wiped it away, continuing the outline of the most beautiful design I had ever seen. Trevor didn't flinch in the process. Instead, he seemed to revel in the sting from the needle.

Grey was fascinated with the process, too. He didn't seem to like the idea of a man using a machine to draw on his daddy's back. His curious eyes took in the scene, trying to decipher whether or not his daddy was okay. Confused, his eyes shot to my face as he tried to gauge my reaction. He relaxed a little as he took in my calm demeanor. Eventually, he had either grown bored or had become too tired from all the excitement, nodding off to sleep in my embrace. Just as Grey was fast asleep, completely dead to the world, Trevor's artist rose from his chair to take another quick smoke break.

"How are you feeling?" I asked Trevor as his artist grabbed a pack of smokes and walked toward the back door.

He was quiet for a moment, thoughtful, before he answered. "I feel alive. So very fucking alive."

"I'm glad."

He looked so happy. I prayed he could always look this way—feel this way. I prayed this was a turning point in his life. This tattoo could be a step in his journey of acceptance.

"I know this sounds fucking dumb, but I feel like he's here right now. He would probably tease me for getting a tattoo in his honor. I can imagine him dumbly saying, 'Trev, do you really need another bit of ink.' " Trevor paused and laughed at the idea. I laughed, too. I wondered if his impression was as spot on as it seemed. "God, I miss him," he mused, resting his head back down on the tops of his forearms.

"I've never met him, but I miss him, too," I muttered.

"He would have liked you. He would probably warn me not to screw things up since you're so far out of my league."

I giggled at the idea. "I'm not out of your league, Trev. If anything, you're out of mine."

The artist returned and went back to work, finishing up the gorgeous outline. The energy in the room grew somber as Trevor became completely silent. He was basking in the moment, and I held Grey close while watching him. I felt like I was witnessing something private, but I couldn't tear my eyes away. Although Dean wasn't here, it felt like Trevor was having a private moment with his brother. I closed my eyes for a moment and allowed my mind to drift. I saw the pair of them. I saw them as children, teenagers, before finally, adults. I imagined scenarios and made up conversations. I imagined them as a mismatched pair of friends who understood one another better than anyone else. I hoped, one day, Trevor would reveal more about Dean. Until then, I would rely on the workings of my imagination.

The sound of silence snapped me back to reality. It seemed the first session was finished. My eyes moved over the outline before they misted with tears. It was perfect. So perfect, I wanted to sob. *Trevor is going to be so happy. He deserves this. He deserves all of the happiness in the world.*

Trevor slid off the leather chair and moved to check out the progress in the mirror. His hand shot up to cover his mouth, and he laughed into his palm as he stared at the reflection in shock. *He loves it.*

"Fuck, man. It's perfect. Thank you. Jesus, dude, I wish I had found you earlier."

"No problem," the artist responded as he cleaned up his station. "Two more sessions should finish it up." He paused his work to gaze up at Trevor, quietly judging his expression. "Was there a special meaning behind the piece?"

The way he posed the question suggested he knew the answer. I was sure he had done many memorial tattoos in the past. I looked to Trevor, waiting for his reaction.

"It's for my older brother," he said as he looked at the piece in the mirror again. "Dean. It's in memory of my brother, Dean."

The way he said his brother's name left me with chills. I watched him put his shirt back on with tears swimming in my eyes. It took all of my effort to keep myself composed.

After making a future appointment, we left the tattoo shop. The difference in Trevor was already like night and day. It seemed like the weight of the world had been lifted from his shoulders. He wasn't the same man he was this morning or *had* been since I had met him.

"Thanks for coming with me, Ronnie. You don't know how much it means to me."

"It was nothing," I said quietly, hoping Grey would remain asleep in my arms. "I loved being there to comfort you. I'm happy you wanted me to be a part of that experience."

"I want you to be a part of everything," he said as he came to a halt in the middle of the sidewalk.

"Trev—" I began to say before he cut me off.

"Ronnie, I feel almost silly asking you this at this point because I feel like our relationship is so meaningful already. You've quickly become my world and Grey's world, as well. I want you and I want to keep you," he gracelessly rambled.

I smiled. The anxiousness surrounding him was so endearing. *Why was he nervous? How could I possibly refuse him?*

"What are you saying?" I asked somewhat teasingly.

I wanted to hear him say the words. I wanted to hear his feelings for me aloud.

"Will you be my girlfriend?" he rushed out.

A smile lit up my face, causing my cheeks to ache. *God, I love this man. I love the way he makes me smile. I love the way he loves me.*

"Officially," he added with a smirk.

I giggled for a moment, enjoying the happy energy surrounding us. For once, I felt like I was standing in the light. I felt like the darkness had disappeared, and my life had become one long, sunny day.

"Of course, Trevor Warren. I'd love to be your girlfriend."

I leaned forward and kissed him, long and deep.

"Even though you were too stupid to ask me sooner," I teased him as soon as I broke away. "But, all is forgiven."

"I should've asked you the moment I saw you."

"You were interested in me way back then?" I questioned in disbelief.

I had suspected, but I had never been sure.

"At first, I was captivated by your beauty, but as soon as you spoke, I became captivated by the rest of you, as well."

"I was drawn to you instantly, too," I admitted, happy we were finally speaking so freely. "However, it was when I saw you interact with Greyson that I knew you were it for me."

His response was a kiss. He crashed his lips against mine, expressing everything he was still too fearful to verbalize. Time stilled as I became consumed by him. The words would come eventually. We had the future ahead of us, and I knew, one day, he would tell me everything. One day, I would tell him everything, too. But one day wasn't here yet.

So, I would bask in today.

18

Towers

"Aw, buddy. You're not ready to come out now, are you?"

Grey giggled at my expression before he continued to splash the bathwater beneath his tiny palms. He was so exuberant—it was far too early for me to feel the same way. With tired eyes, I watched him, giggling along with him every time he laughed.

After a string of syllables, he turned his attention toward me, reaching out with his little hands to capture a few of my fingers. He squeezed as hard as he could, which hadn't been hard at all, and giggled at his strength. I played along with him, feigning hurt and shock until he finally let go of my fingers and went back to splashing the bathwater. Just as I reached forward to tickle him, my phone buzzed along the sink's countertop, moving toward the opened toilet. I catapulted up and snatched my cell before it could drop from the countertop and hit the toilet water.

"Hey!" I said awkwardly as I answered the call and balanced the cell between my shoulder and ear.

"Ronnie! So much for calling me," Eden answered miffed.

"Sorry," I replied as I sat back down next to the tub and watched Greyson play. "I've been really busy."

"Yesterday, you texted me and said you would call me. What happened to—"

"Eden, what's up?" I had to cut her off, knowing she would prattle on endlessly.

"Can't I just call my sister?"

I smiled slightly at her teasing tone. "You never call to just 'talk.' Now, out with it."

"You know me too well, I guess. I just wanted to check up on you. You know, see how things were going with your hot neighbor."

I grimaced. "His name is Trevor."

She giggled at the correction. "Touchy, touchy. Sorry, *Trevor*. How's he doing? Are you two an item, yet?"

I bit down on my bottom lip as I wondered how much I wanted to reveal to my sister. If I held back information, she would be hurt—after all, she never held anything back from me—but, if I told her everything, she would be at my apartment in a heartbeat. She would harass me until I introduced her to Trevor and Grey; I wasn't sure if this was something I was ready for. Having Trevor meet Eden could very well become the equivalent to throwing him to a hungry pack of wolves. I loved her, but she was a lot for anyone to handle. Trevor was far too stoic and withdrawn for someone like her.

I mulled it over for another moment before I decided to tell her the truth, knowing she would discover it eventually. "I'm ... well," I stuttered, flushing with nerves. "We're a couple now, I guess."

"You *guess*?" she challenged.

"Well, I know. We're together, now," I said more confidently. "He asked me the other day."

"The other day? He asked you the other day, and you didn't come to me with the info immediately?"

"I was a little busy, Edie," I countered.

"Oh ..." she replied in a singsong tone. "You were *busy*? Veronica, already?"

"No, not like that." My flush deepened. "I've just been busy with work and taking care of Grey."

"Well, how lame," she teased before she began gushing, "Oh, Ronnie, that's wonderful! I can't believe it! My baby sister has fallen in love."

"Love?" I interrupted quietly.

She hadn't heard me. Instead, she continued to prattle away while my mind wandered. I loved Trevor, but hearing the word "love" regarding him, coming from my sister's mouth, was strange. I had barely come to terms with the new feeling myself, so, hearing it spoken of so freely made my heart race and my palms sweat. I hated that she could talk about love so openly while I was so closed off. *Why couldn't love feel as easy to me?*

"Did you hear me, Ronnie?"

The question yanked me away from my contemplations.

"What?" I asked dumbly.

"Lunch. Tomorrow. God, Veronica, I love you, but you really can be a space cadet."

"Thanks," I grumbled, although I knew she was right.

Since childhood, my mind had always constantly wandered. While Eden always remained in the present moment, my thoughts were all over the place; they constantly jumped from one idea to the next—one memory to another.

"So, are you down? Are you and your hot neighbor free?"

I knew Trevor's schedule by heart.

"Yes," I answered after a moment of debating whether or not I should just lie. "*Trevor* and I are free tomorrow."

"Perfect! See, was that so hard? Now, I can finally meet your boyfriend!"

"*Finally*? We haven't been together very long, so it's not like you've been waiting around."

"I know. I'm just excited."

I smiled at this. She was probably just as enthused about Trevor as I was. My happiness was all she had ever wanted. She had mourned with me, had cried with me, and had raged with me, all while she had looked for opportunities for me to find happiness again. Those opportunities had been few and far between.

Whenever I had found a sliver of happiness in the past, it had only lasted a short while. It had washed over me like ocean waves; it had passed while I had tried to stay afloat. However, I knew this time was different. Trevor was different. He wasn't just a wave. He was the entire ocean.

"I'm excited, too," I answered, smiling. "Edie ... I think it will stick this time."

"What's he like?"

I heard the smile in her voice.

"He's wonderful. He's so wonderful, so kind, and so giving. I don't think I deserve him."

"I'm sure you do. You're always too hard on yourself. Just sit back and allow yourself to be happy."

Grey began to scream for attention, finally ready to get out of the tub. I gave him a small smile and grabbed a bath towel for him.

"Sorry, Edie, I have to go. Grey's finished with his bath and is getting all fussy."

"Okay! Well, give him a kiss for me. I'll text you about tomorrow."

"Sure. You're not going to believe it when I say I'm actually excited." I chuckled.

"Excited? Who are you and what have you done with my sister?"

I giggled again. "I'm serious."

"Well, good. I'm looking forward to meeting the man in your life."

Grey squealed again before he gave me the cutest pout I had ever seen on him.

"Okay, I really have to go now. He's going to throw a fit any second."

"Love you, sis."

"Love you, too, Edie. See you tomorrow."

"Tomorrow," she promised before ending the call.

"Sorry, buddy. I can't give you all of my attention all of the time." His pout grew. "Although, I want to." I laughed, reaching for him.

I lifted him from the tub and pulled the plug, allowing the bathwater to drain. Wrapping Grey in a towel, I tried my best to dry him off as he wiggled around in my lap, babbling to me. I watched his mouth move and wondered what words he was attempting to form, if any. He babbled something, cocked his little head to the side, and peered up at me, awaiting my answer.

"You ready to get dressed and watch a movie?"

He smiled at this and clapped his hands as I rose from the ground and made my way to my makeshift nursery. Grey laughed as I toweled him dry and slid his jittery body into a onesie. Once I buttoned him up, I smiled to myself, happy to finally have him clean and relaxed.

"What movie should we watch while we wait for Daddy?" I asked as I traversed to my living room.

For so long, I had referred to Trevor as Grey's uncle; now, that sounded wrong. Although the title wasn't meaningless, it didn't seem to express Trevor's role in Grey's life. He was Greyson's father. The minute details didn't matter. So, I would call him that. He *deserved* to be called that—he had earned it.

After I settled Grey comfortably on the carpeted floor in front of the couch, I knelt in front of my modest television and scanned my DVD selection. My eyes wandered from DVD to DVD before they settled on one of my favorites: *Anastasia*. Growing up, I had known every song. With my mom near, I had murmured along with "Once Upon a December," until I had fallen asleep in her lap. Today, I could share a similar experience with Grey. As I popped the disk into the player, my eyes began to mist.

Suddenly, I could see the major draw to having children. In a way, I could live vicariously through Greyson. I could experience everything through Greyson's eyes as if it were brand new. Nostalgia washed over me in waves as I remembered what it felt like to grow up. With Grey, I felt young again—I felt like I did before life had marred me.

My phone came to life on the couch beside us as the third movie began. Relaxed, I reached for it. This was the first "lazy day" I'd had in a long time. I smiled as I saw Trevor's name light up my screen. Whenever he messaged me, I felt special. Which surely was silly, considering I was his girlfriend, but he had a way of making me feel like I was the most important person in the world. I was grateful for that.

I'll be home soon, babe. How's Grey?

Being referred to as "babe" always managed to make my heart flutter.

He's been perfect. He's only had one tantrum today, and it was short. But we both want you home!

I'll be back soon. Don't have too much fun without me.

Never.

I had almost written, "I love you." Thankfully, I had some sense and kept my text short. When I told him my feelings, which I someday would, I needed for the words to be expressed in person. I wanted to see his eyes as he heard the truth. The words carried so much weight—meant more than they could ever express—so, I wanted to be present for their impact. I wanted to see firsthand the change they made.

As we waited for Trevor to bust through my front door, I thought of the words "I love you." I thought of the fact that I had never said those words to anyone outside of my family. Even when I had believed myself to be in love with *him*—the man from my past who didn't deserve a name in my mind—I had never told him. He had held enough power over me already; if he truly believed he'd had my heart, I would have never broken free of him. The way I had felt about *him* was entirely different than the way I felt about Trevor. My feelings for that other man didn't hold a candle to my feelings concerning the man in my life now. Trevor made me feel loved. When I thought of his face in my mind, I experienced a profound sense of relief.

Even in my dark times, which still crept up on me every now and then, the image of Trevor had the power to put my heart and mind at ease. Although he wasn't always by my side, when I needed him, I could picture him, and the image felt like a warm embrace; phantom arms wrapped around me as if he were holding me against his chest. It was like somewhere in the world he knew I needed comfort. Trevor felt like home. I had never known I was wandering until he rooted me. Honestly, I hadn't even known I loved him—*really* loved him—until recently.

I had fallen for Trevor before I had even been aware love had found me. I had realized my feelings for him a few nights ago when I had been all alone. The darkness had crept up on me, surprising me as I had curled up with a book on my recliner. That night, the book had been unable to captivate me, and my mind had wandered, brushing against the edges of dangerous topics, which I had kept buried away in my subconscious. One moment, I had been okay, and the next I had tears filling my eyes.

Suddenly, I had been drowning. The darkness had been pulling me deeper into the abyss as I'd tried desperately to swim back to surface. Depression was tricky that way: one moment, you believed you were all right, and the next, you couldn't breathe. Trevor had kept the darkness from sinking its claws into me. Trevor and little Greyson. I had thought of him—I had thought of how much he meant to me. The more I had thought, the more I began to realize my feelings. I realized I never wanted to leave them behind.

"What would Trevor think of you if he saw you like this?" I whispered to my reflection.

I looked so ... broken. I looked broken, and I hated it. I hated the power I had allowed someone to have over me. I hated that they had the privilege of going on with their lives, probably forgetting all about me, while I had to suffer.

It was debilitating. Until I met Trev. He made things better. He made me feel like me again. He gave me hope.

"He would feel so sad for me," I told my reflection.

He would want to do something to assuage my pain. I imagined his face in my mind—I imagined his smile. I imagined the way he talked to me like no one else really had, with a voice filled with so much love and warmth.

Love ...

Someone else talked to me similarly.

Someone who was long gone.

I smiled as I thought of her. My mom would have loved Trevor. If she knew the way he made me feel, she would push me toward marriage in a heartbeat. My smile grew. I had been so confused with my feelings toward Trevor. After all the shit that had happened in my past, I hadn't been sure if I could trust my heart. Now, I knew I had to listen to it.

I loved Trevor.

I loved him.

He was my other half.

As cheesy as that phrase had always sounded to me, there was no better way to describe his role in my life. When I saw his face in my mind, all my pain washed away. He was the best medicine. He was the best friend. As a boyfriend, he made me feel like I was the only woman in the world. He made me feel beautiful, and more importantly, he made me feel like I was worth something. I wondered if I made him feel something similar because, to me, he was worth everything.

"I love Trevor," I said aloud, feeling the darkness washing against my heart trickle away.

"I love you, Trevor," I practiced.

I loved him. Now, nothing would ever be the same. He was my future—the past no longer mattered. I wouldn't let it. The shadows couldn't affect me anymore.

I had far too much to live for.

Grey's little hands grabbing at my blouse caused my mind to center. I peered down at him before I realized our third movie had reached its end. Feeling lazy, I grabbed the television remote and switched to daytime cartoons. Grey perked up on my lap instantly, obviously recognizing *SpongeBob SquarePants* from his days with Trevor. Just as we got settled in and Grey began to laugh at every image presented on the television, Trevor shuffled in, kicking my front door shut behind him.

"How did lunch go with your dad?" I asked as I tried to read his blank expression.

He looked handsome—he *always* looked handsome—but today, he also looked tired. Not just physically, but mentally, too. He looked like a man who had been through the ringer. He gave me a small, crooked smile before he took a seat on the couch next to Grey and me. He threw his arm over my shoulder and exhaled, sinking into the couch cushions as if he wanted to disappear.

"It was fine. He seemed really out of it," he replied as he stared at the TV.

"Did he patch things up with your mom?" I asked, unable to help my curiosity. This was why he had lunch with his dad today, after all. They had had a fight after the party. Trevor had seemed bleak about it. Apparently, they had seemed fractured beyond repair.

"No," he said slowly as he continued to gaze at the dorky cartoon sponge on the television. "They're getting a divorce."

Typically, I would have felt horrible hearing news like this. However, Evelyn had rubbed me the wrong way. Everything about her seemed artificial and narcissistic. I didn't know what to think of his father anymore. I felt for Trevor but believed the situation was possibly for the best.

"Oh, sweetheart," I empathized as I nuzzled up against him. "I'm so sorry. I know that must be difficult."

He shrugged, seeming almost bored with the topic. "I don't know. I guess I never really had a good relationship with her. I just hope my dad isn't suffering."

Of course, I hoped that, too.

"Did he seem to be in pretty bad shape when you saw him?"

"No, he just looked tired—so fucking tired." He grimaced, turning his head away.

Reaching forward, I grabbed his chin and gently turned him to face me. I licked my lips and then pressed them firmly against his. He groaned against my mouth and opened ever so slightly to allow my tongue entrance. His tongue flirted with mine, and he kissed me until he was breathless. Only then did he pull away a fraction. I smiled at him, feeling flustered, and he rewarded me with a small peck on the lips.

"Grey's missed you all day," I commented, changing the subject.

As if on cue, Grey became needy and reached for Trevor, pouting until his daddy picked him up and held him against his chest.

"Stop being so fussy, little man. Dad's home. Chill out."

As I watched the pair, I thought of the conversation I'd had with Eden this morning. Somehow, I would have to convince Trevor to meet my sister. Thankfully, he barely knew anything about her; otherwise, convincing him would have been no easy feat.

"What is it, baby?" I heard Trevor ask, causing my eyes to shoot up to meet his.

Toying with my hair, I shrugged, feeling myself sink against the couch cushions. "It's nothing."

"Ronnie," he admonished, sounding very father-like suddenly.

"Okay," I gave in. "It's just ... my sister really wants to meet you. Since I told her I had a boyfriend, she's been wanting to have you and Grey over for lunch."

"Wow, she works fast." He chuckled.

That's Edie for you.

"We don't have to go if you don't want to," I continued, not wanting him to feel pressured. "I know it's really soon, Trev."

"No." He waved his hand dismissively. "It's fine. I want to meet your sister. Didn't you say she has a daughter? Maybe she and Grey can become friends and have playdates."

I smiled at the hopeful note in his voice.

"Okay, well, I told her you have the day off tomorrow. So, maybe we can go then?"

He gave me a dubious look. I watched as the corners of his mouth twitched.

"Is it that obvious I'll say yes to anything you ask?"

"Well," I blushed, giving him a coquettish smile, "it's not *super* obvious or anything. It's just, you've never let me down before."

"I never want to let you down. *Ever.*"

I'm counting on it.

19

Here Comes Your Man

I wondered if it was strange to be fearful of my own sister. Although I knew Trevor had nothing to worry about, anxiety bloomed in my chest. My fingers shook as I worked on buttoning my flannel. After trying to work one button into the small slit in the fabric for a few moments and failing, a nervous laugh escaped my lips, and I dropped my hands. *It's going to be fine, Veronica. What are you so worried about?* Eden would love Trevor. She would love any man I had feelings for. My eyes rose to gaze at my reflection in the mirror in front of me. The blotchy girl staring back at me inspired another nervous laugh to escape.

My nerves were blatant. Redness appeared on my neck and chest in spots; the blotchy blush covering my pale skin caused me to become even more agitated. *I can't see Eden looking like this. I'd never hear the end of it!* She would take one look at me and tease: "Look at this lovesick girl." She would have been right—I *was* lovesick. So lovesick Trevor had taken up every space in my mind. *While still leaving room for Grey, of course.* I was certain I wouldn't need to express my feelings for him to my sister; she would be able to take one look at me and know all the things I feared voicing.

Before my brain could register my body's movements, I placed one foot in front of the other, moving toward the front door while I ignored the anxiety irritating my chest. Today would be a good day, and if it wasn't, it would pass—just like everything else.

Whatever happens, happens.

I took a deep breath and grabbed my purse before I gave my appearance one final check in my hallway mirror. Slowly, I steadied my hands and finished buttoning my flannel, breathing in and out as my anxiety melted away. *Today will be an important day. Make it count.* With a smile, I left my apartment.

As I knocked on Trevor's door, I heard Grey's squeals coming from inside. My smile grew as it always did when they were near. Seeing them had a way of making everything better. The door swung open to reveal a freshly shaven Trevor in a button-down shirt which pleasantly displayed every muscle in his torso. He was gorgeous. It wasn't just his outward appearance that caused me to believe that—his kind heart had a way of shining through; it illuminated him from the inside out. His lips twitched into a smile. In this moment, I realized just how much I loved him. I loved him so much it hurt to look at him. I wanted to launch myself into his arms and never let go.

Of course, I couldn't do that now—Grey was here, staring at me with guileless eyes and a bright grin. My eyes darted from him to meet his father's gaze. Trevor was appraising me, taking in my fall outfit, which had been completed with a light scarf and matching beanie. I'd believed I looked cute when I had put it on, but now, I felt self-conscious.

I always wanted to look beautiful for Trev—at least, at first. Then, when we would get to talking, I would forget all about my tiny, yet nagging, insecurities and focus my mind on him. Right now, I hadn't a single insecurity. *What woman can with a man staring at her like this?*

His lustful stare fizzled into a look contaminated with nerves. I stepped forward, attempting to reach out for him to ease his stress; instead of accepting my comfort, he handed me Grey and stepped aside to give me space to enter his apartment. I entered and helped Greyson into his light jacket while keeping an eye on Trevor. He shook off my gaze as he pretended to be cool and collected.

Whenever he was especially nervous, he would become silent. He would only utter a word if he had to. Otherwise, he was lost in his own thoughts.

Grey babbled to me as we headed out. I kept shooting glances in Trevor's direction, wondering what he could be pondering so intensely. He was my future, therefore, he had nothing to worry about. *Of course, he doesn't know this, Veronica. You're too nervous to ever open up to him!* the voice inside of me screamed.

"Trevor," I said, instantly grabbing his attention. "You don't have to worry about today. My sister and her husband will love you. I promise."

He rewarded my comment with his signature crooked grin—although, today it looked more like a grimace. Not long after I finished speaking, Trevor was lost in his own world again. As we found our seats in his truck, he was a ball of nervous energy at my side.

"Trev, will you chill out?" I asked as I gently nudged his shoulder with mine. "Eden and Quinton will love you. I promise. And Harper will be an instant friend to Grey. Just you wait and see."

He sighed, not appearing too convinced. "If you say so, Ronnie. It's just that I've never made a good first impression on anyone."

"You made a good first impression on me," I quipped.

He grinned at this and reached across the center console to grab hold of my hand. "What did you think when you first saw me?"

A sly smile tugged on my lips as I gave him a once-over and replied, "I thought you were extremely hot, and I just wanted to …" *Let you fuck my brains out. I wanted you to let me lick every one of your tattoos.* "Never mind."

"What?"

I mulled it over for a moment before I decided to be honest. "I wanted to run my tongue along the outlines of all of your tattoos." My eyes scanned his exposed skin as I imagined what his unexposed skin looked like. "What did you think when you first saw me?" I asked, changing the subject.

"I thought you were incredibly beautiful and way out of my league," he was quick to respond.

Grey babbled loudly in the back seat as if he were trying to give his two cents. Trevor smiled at his exuberant son before he reached forward to turn the radio dial to a popular kid's station. I took a deep breath, enjoying the positive energy in the car for a moment before I texted Eden, informing her that we were finally on our way.

While we drove, I gave Trevor directions and watched his facial expressions fluctuate between peacefulness and anxiousness. He was lost in thought as we moved onto the highway. I wondered what he was thinking. Today was a big day, and he had been contemplative since we'd left our apartment complex.

"It's this exit," I said, gesturing to the off-ramp.

He gulped as he signaled and moved over to the farthest right lane. "So, is your sister … nice?" he mumbled.

I snorted.

"Of course. I wouldn't introduce you to her if I thought she was mean."

He smiled and flushed slightly before answering. "I know, I know. I'm just being ridiculous. I just want shit to go well, you know?"

"It will." I reached forward and brushed my fingers over his white knuckles, feeling his hands relax slightly around the steering wheel. "Now, take a right here, and it's the first neighborhood on the left."

After that, Trevor didn't say a word. He was quiet at my side, so coiled up I believed he might snap. We reached my sister's home, and I smiled at the familiar sight of her brick house with her dream wraparound white picket fence. Her living situation was the portrait of the American dream; her life was very dreamlike, too. Trevor rolled to a stop next to Quinton's car and parked, trying to calm his nerves. He wasn't succeeding; he still looked just as riddled with anxiety as he had when we left our apartment building.

"Trev …" I began before his forced smile cut me off.

He exited the truck and moved to the cab to retrieve Grey. I took a deep breath, saying a silent prayer for smooth sailing before I opened the passenger door and exited the truck, too. Eden must have been standing at the front door waiting for us because as soon as we were gathered in her driveway, she bolted out of the house while displaying an exited look on her beautifully made-up face.

"Ronnie! *Finally*! I've been waiting for you to show up all morning!"

"I told you lunchtime," I replied as I stepped forward to hug my tiny sister.

She wrapped her arms around me, squeezing me hard, before she took a step back and appraised my two guys. "They're even cuter than you described," she whispered with a wink.

I rolled my eyes at her. Eden's stage whispers were always so dramatic. I turned my attention to Trevor, who looked skittish as he stood perfectly still.

"This must be Greyson," Eden cooed as she moved toward the little guy. She took hold of his hand and gave it a small, polite shake. I watched as she shot Trevor a pretty smile and continued. "Ronnie talks about him all the time. She talks about him almost as much as she talks about *you*." She winked at him.

I rolled my eyes a second time and stepped forward to join my sister. "Trevor, this is my sister, Eden," I said, introducing them finally. "Eden, this is my boyfriend, Trevor."

"You don't know how happy I am to finally meet you," she shamelessly gushed. "I've been trying to convince my sister to bring you over for lunch since she started talking about you."

Trevor's gaze shot to me and he smiled. His eyes danced with mirth. The expression on his face seemed to jokingly say, *God, your sister is a bit* much, *isn't she?* I almost laughed out loud before I gained control of myself. Eden was wonderful, but I knew her gregarious, outgoing nature had the possibility of coming across as overbearing.

When neither Trevor nor I said anything, Eden continued. "He's so adorable, Trevor. You must be so proud of him."

Trevor's posture straightened. Suddenly, he seemed to warm up to her.

"I'm proud of him," he confirmed as a smile tugged on his lips. "Grey's amazing and just *so* smart. He'll grow to be a lot smarter than I'll ever be."

While Trevor was shy, he flourished when he was able to talk about his favorite subject: Greyson. Whenever Greyson became the topic of conversation, Trevor could go from a man of few words to someone who was just as chatty and outgoing as my sister.

Eden looked at him for a moment before turning her gaze to me. She seemed to be judging the energy between us, and after a heavy moment, she smiled.

"I'm just so thrilled to see my sister happy. You have no idea how many jackassess she's dated."

"Eden," I sharply warned as I threw her a look of disapproval.

"Sorry, sorry," she apologized, smiling as her eyes teasingly beseeched my forgiveness. "It's just good to see you with someone nice."

My muscles relaxed, and I leaned back on my heels as I grinned at her. While I was no longer tense, I still *hated* when she brought up a single whiff of my past. It wasn't a discussion I wanted to have yet, and I feared the mere mention of it could spur questions.

I heard the sound of the front door open and close and turned my head to find Quinton coming our way with an excited but shy-looking Harper in his embrace. As he walked, he sized Trevor up. *God, what is he thinking?* I knew Trevor looked brutish, but after my previous discussions with Quinton, I knew he would be able to see past Trevor's intense exterior. From my words alone, he already knew Trevor was a good man.

"Hey, Ronnie," he said as he came to stand with us. His blue eyes shifted to Trevor and he smirked, obviously wanting my boyfriend to feel the heat a little bit. "You must be Trevor," he continued. "I'm Quinton, Ronnie's brother-in-law." He sized my boyfriend up before he gave me an impish grin.

He likes him. They like each other. I can already tell.

A blush stained my cheeks as happiness coursed through my veins. In this moment, everything felt so perfect—like I was right where I needed to be. *Here, with Trevor and Greyson and my family. Maybe one day, they could all be my family ... Until then, they are all merely mine— all having a piece of my heart.*

"This is our little girl, Harper." Quinton introduced her as he took another step closer. Staring down at the little girl, he pressed, "Say hi, sweetie."

She looked up from beneath her lashes and leaned against her father's chest.

"Hi," she softly said.

She gave Greyson a curious glance before a smile tugged at her lips.

"I three," she said, holding up her fingers for Greyson to see. Her gaze turned to me before she questioned, "Who that?" She pointed at Greyson, who was staring back at her with inquisitive eyes.

"This is my son, Greyson," Trevor explained as he took a step forward.

"He cute." Harper giggled, approving of him before she placed her thumb in her mouth.

While I watched the encounter, I hoped Greyson could become a friend to Harper. While he had Trevor and me, he needed someone young to relate to. He needed a friend to play with. *Maybe one day ...* I stopped myself. The last thing I needed to be meditating on was the possibility of babies with Trevor. *Although, it does sound wonderful.* More *than wonderful. Maybe we could start practicing tonight?* I pushed the thought from my mind as I returned my focus to my family, intent on enjoying the day.

Time with my family had flown by in an instant. It had been so wonderful I had felt like I was living in a dream. A dream where I had everything I had ever imagined wanting. There had been instances when I had been silent and absorbed the energy surrounding me. Although, these moments weren't outlandish or extravagant—like something that would usually stick in my memory—I knew I would remember them forever. Sometimes, when I experienced a moment—a feeling—I knew it would be an instance that would stick with me. Whether it was watching a movie with Trevor or having lunch with my family, I would feel the moment's importance. It was almost as if my mind would say, *Enjoy this. Enjoy this while you can. Not all moments are like this.*

Over lunch, Trevor had spoken with ease. He had easily fit right in. Quinton had spoken to Trevor like he had known him for years. They had discussed work and their likes and dislikes. While it had been small talk, it hadn't felt that way. It had felt like two friends speaking after a long separation. I was happy for them—Trevor needed more friends in his life. Part of me wondered if he had secluded himself because he felt undeserving.

I worry about him.

"Can I play with baby, Dada?"

Harper's question refocused my thoughts. After an hour and a half of sitting at the dining room table, she was now eager to move around. Quinton gave Trevor an inquisitive look, and Trevor nodded at him, indicating it was all right. After sitting in his father's lap for so long, I was sure Greyson was eager to move around, too. Quinton moved away from the table and helped Harper down from her seat before retreating to the kitchen. Harper ran to the living room as she hollered for Greyson over her shoulder. Trevor smiled and rose from his seat with Grey safely tucked in his arms. He walked after Harper, obviously eager for his son to have some playtime with another kid.

"Well, Ronnie, he really is something," Eden said as soon as we were alone.

When she waggled her eyebrows at me, I had lost it, falling into a fit of giggles.

"Seriously, though," she continued, laughing, too. "Where do you find them? He's so … *handsome.* I would have never guessed he was your type though."

"I never knew he was," I murmured before Quinton called out from the kitchen.

"Want a beer, Trevor?" he hollered, causing me to freeze in my seat.

I had warned them. I hadn't delved far into Trevor's past—I barely knew his past myself—but instead, politely explained Trevor didn't drink. The implications had been obvious. So obvious I thought I had been completely clear with them. Eden threw me an apologetic look before she rose to join her husband in the kitchen.

"No, thanks. I'm good," I heard Trevor respond.

As I sat at the dining room table, I imagined what his face must look like. I was sure he looked stricken—the way he always looked when alcohol made its play.

While I sat, I hoped Trevor wouldn't be too upset if he discovered I had opened up to my family. While I had said very little, I had said it without consulting Trevor first. While his best interest had been in my mind, perhaps it hadn't been my place.

I heard Grey babbling from the living room, and I relaxed. *Everything must be okay, then.* I watched Eden dart from the kitchen to join them in the living room. Quinton lagged behind, shooting me an apologetic smile, too, on his way. I rose from my seat and moved to the living room as I heard Grey babbling "da" again and again.

"Was his first word dad?" I heard my sister ask.

"Well, 'da,' " he corrected her.

"That's just the cutest thing I've ever heard," my sister gushed as I joined them in the room. "Harper's first word was 'no.' "

Trevor smiled at her before his gaze dropped to his son. "Well, I doubt he knows what he's saying."

I loved this about him—he was so humble. He never wanted to admit to being content; this made me particularly sad. It was as if he felt underserving of happiness, making all of his smiles worth even more to me.

"I'm sure he does know, Trevor," I said as I joined them on the floor. *Of course, he knows. He loves you, after all.* "Trevor is an incredible daddy."

Trevor's energy had seemed to shift as soon as the sentence had passed through my lips. I hoped he understood how proud I was of him. How proud *everyone* was of him. For a moment, as he smiled while staring off into the space ahead, I believed he knew he was good. Just for a moment, he seemed to feel worthy.

You are *worthy, Trev. If I could, I would give you the world. If I could, I would spend the rest of my life trying to make you smile like this.*

20

Disarm

September came and went as the air grew colder. I had fallen into a routine of taking care of Greyson and his ruggedly handsome daddy. Never had I felt more at peace than I had as the autumn chill descended on Evergreen.

Looking back on my life last year at this time, I wondered how I had managed. Now, the thought of being alone, with nothing more than the ghosts of my past to keep me company, made me feel melancholy. I had allowed myself to be less happy than I could have been for a very, *very* long time. *I couldn't help it, though. It wasn't my fault. None of it was my fault. I knew this now.*

I looked up from my sketchbook, peering over at Greyson as he played in the grass. He was getting bigger and more independent by the day. I wished he could always be like this: so little and loving. One day, he would grow up to be the man he was meant to be and would move on with his life. *I hope I'm there to see this.* I had become so attached to him already. The thought of letting him go now was unbearable. *That won't happen. Trevor loves you. This could be your life forever.*

From my spot on the grass, I leaned back against the oak tree behind me and closed my eyes, allowing the crisp, early-autumn wind to tickle my face. Grey's babbles made me smile—he was enjoying the weather, too. I opened my eyes again and looked at him, finding his cheeks slightly flushed from the wind. Reaching out, I plucked him off of the ground and cradled him in my arms, nuzzling his face before I pulled away to look at him. His smile was serene.

"Life starts all over again when it gets crisp in the fall." I remembered the Fitzgerald quote with a wistful smile. He had been right;

fall felt like a new beginning. Grey giggled against my neck and began to play with my hair. *I hope every day will soon be like this.* I held him close, enjoying the moment. These moments were becoming more and more common as each day passed.

"What do you think, Grey? Isn't this wonderful?"

He gave me a gummy grin, beaming at me. He babbled a few words in response, causing me to wish I could hear his sentence phonetically.

"It's wonderful. I haven't had a fall like this ... in a very long time," I admitted, snuggling him closer. "This is your first fall, isn't it?"

He giggled at my question and leaned back to get a better look at my face.

"You're experiencing your first everything. I've got to say, Grey, I envy you." I paused for a moment, calculating, before I grinned and continued. "Well, I suppose I'm experiencing some new things, too. For instance, I've never been in love before. I've never had a family of my own."

Of course, Trevor and Greyson weren't truly my family, but they *felt* like they were. We felt like one unit; our lives were intertwined.

"I love you, Greyson," I murmured those three words out loud.

I loved Greyson unconditionally—like his mother would, if she were alive. *She still actively loves him. I'm sure somewhere in the universe ... somehow ... she's there, watching him grow.* Suddenly, I wondered what Grey's mother would think of me. I wondered if she would approve of the woman I was; I wondered if she would be happy that I was here to take care of her son. While she wasn't here to answer me, I believed she would be satisfied. I believed she would love me just as I would love her, too. I loved her now. I loved her, and I loved Dean, too. *I wish they were here.*

As much as I loved having Greyson to care for, I wished he still had his biological parents. One day, he would learn the truth about them. One day, his heart would break just like mine had when I had lost my mother. One day ... but not today. He needed to enjoy these blissfully ignorant and perfectly happy moments. *Perfectly happy moments will* come again, but once his eyes were opened, he will change. Trevor can't shield him from the world forever.

"I love you, Greyson," I said again as tears pricked my eyes.

Perhaps one day, I would be able to say those words to Trevor. He deserved to know the truth.

Closing my eyes, I relaxed against the tree's trunk and imaged *her*, Greyson's mother, Cat. In my mind, she was beautiful. I pictured the love that must have swam in her eyes while she looked at her son. I envisioned the hope she had once had for him. I imagined all the possibilities she must have seen while looking at him. I imagined she had pictured him as a teenager and as an adult. I believed she had pictured an entire life for him where he made her proud every step of the way. She must have felt every emotion I felt now.

In my imagination, she smiled at me, her beautiful face beaming. As I daydreamed, I felt Greyson's fingers playing with the ends of my hair. I smiled and slipped further into my musings.

"He's so big already. I would have never imagined ..." the image of her muttered as her eyes were glued to Greyson.

"He surprises me every day," I responded. *"He's always doing something new and different. He's so smart ... so smart it astonishes me. He'll grow to be better than anything I could ever be."*

Her gaze turned to me. "He loves you, you know?"

"I know," I whispered.

"Take care of him. Love him for me, Veronica."

I gasped, surprised as she said my name. "I will," I answered her, as I watched her image turn away.

"Hold him tight for me," she said over her shoulder as her image began to fade in my head. *"Tell him you love him every day. Do that for me."*

"I will," I answered again before her image disappeared in my thoughts.

My eyelids fluttered open as my body sagged against the tree. Tree bark tickled the skin of my neck as I considered my brief delusion. I felt like I had just spoken with a ghost. *Or an angel ...* My gaze dropped to Grey. His eyes watched me expectantly; a smile never left his face. I held him tightly—for her.

Trevor appeared haggard as he entered his apartment later in the evening. He ran a shaky hand through his hair and attempted to smile for me, obviously not wanting to seem so grim.

"Baby, we don't have to go out tonight," I said as I stood from my spot on the couch and traversed across the carpet, pulling him into a hug. "Grey and I would be just as happy eating in."

He pulled back to smile at me. This time, his smile reached his eyes.

"That sounds good, babe. I'll just have to take you out some other time."

Then, he bent forward and pressed his lips against mine. The softness of his lips juxtaposed with the roughness of his kiss always had the power to take my breath away. His tongue darted out and traced the fullness of my bottom lip before he pulled away to look at me. I blushed under his gaze as his eyes wandered over the panes of my body. In a pair of yoga pants and a sweatshirt and without a trace of makeup, I didn't *feel* sexy; however, as he stared at my breasts, hips, and thighs, I began to feel a tingle between my legs, feeling gorgeous. He bent forward and gave me another quick kiss, teasing me. He pulled away, leaving me breathless.

"We just need to run to the store first," I told him, still reeling from our shared passion. "Do you guys want to stay here? Or, we can all run to the store together?"

In this moment, I felt like we were truly a family.

"We can all go," he answered with a grin. "Just let me change real quick."

My eyes trailed after him as he moved toward the bedroom. I looked down at Grey, who was perched on the floor with one of his beloved stuffed animals, and found he looked at the empty space his father had just occupied with inquisitive eyes.

My gaze shifted back to Trevor, who had left the bedroom door ajar. If I peered tenaciously enough, I could make out his firm body moving around in the dim light of his bedroom. Biting down on my bottom lip, I watched as he slipped his shirt off, pulling it over his head to reveal a broad chest, defined abdominals, and ink covering every inch of exposed skin. Although I couldn't see *perfectly* clear, I swore I saw a few piercings, too. I flushed as I watched his strong, muscular arms reach to unbutton his jeans and nearly passed out as he unzipped his fly. As if he knew I was watching, he turned away from me before dropping his jeans to the floor, revealing nothing else underneath.

Holy fucking shit! For the love of all that is holy. That's his freaking ass! Okay, calm down, Veronica. You've seen an ass before; one man's ass isn't different from another's. Oh, who the hell am I kidding? Trevor's ass is completely different than any other man's. Trevor's ass is perfect. Absolutely divine. I want to kiss it, and bite on it, and spank it. I want to grab it as he drives into me, taking me to places I never knew existed.

Grey's cries brought me back to the present, and I noticed they caused Trevor to speed up the process of changing. Now, I was really flushing. I wondered if Trevor knew the small peep show he was allowing me. *Or* wasn't *allowing me.* Trevor came bolting out of the bedroom, giving his son an apologetic glance as he reached to pick him up off of the floor. As soon as he turned to meet my gaze, I turned red, remembering what I had witnessed a few moments before. *Perfect ass; perfect abdominals; perfect ... everything.* I bit down on my bottom lip to stifle a moan as my eyes roamed leisurely over his body.

"You ready to go?" he asked so casually I wondered if he hadn't stripped in front of me on purpose.

Wishful thinking.

With a bashful smile, I nodded. Although, I wished I could see his unclothed body again. He stared at me for a moment before he smirked, obviously noting my blush. That smirk made me want him even more. There was something about the quiet confidence he had at times that made me want to drop to my knees in front of him. As we headed out, I imagined it, wondering what my lips would feel like wrapped around his cock.

The drive to the supermarket had been short. Grey had spent the duration of the time babbling loudly in his car seat. I had held Trevor's hand over the center console, basking in the sensation caused by his thumb rubbing circles against my palm—I had enjoyed the warmth of his skin against mine. I had never imagined handholding could be so intimate, but with Trevor, it was. The feeling of him had kept my mind occupied until we had reached the supermarket. Quickly, I had become distracted by the exciting prospect of grocery shopping.

"Okay, we'll be in and out really quickly. I promise," I assured Trevor as I slipped out of his truck.

Despite his tired eyes, Trevor gave me a knowing smile, which said, "Baby, I know you're going to take your sweet time." In the time he had known me, he had grown accustomed to my supermarket shopping habits. I always did a good lap around the store, looking through every department before I even *reached* the food. Trevor was different—always in and out. If he could be anywhere, he would want to be in his apartment with his little guy. He hated spending time on things that didn't matter. This was another thing I loved about him—he was a homebody, like me.

As we entered the store, I pulled out the list of groceries I had snatched off of my refrigerator. Trevor gazed at me as he bounced an exuberant Grey in his arms.

"Let's do a quick lap before we head to the groceries, okay?"

Trevor stared at me for a second before a laugh escaped his lips.

"Real quick, huh? Somehow, I don't believe you."

"Trev, I promise. I won't be long," I said as I pulled a cart for myself and guided him to the women's clothing section.

Thirty minutes later, Trevor was restless. I felt guilty, but every time I asked if he was all right, he reassured me, claiming he *liked* watching me shop for clothes. Due to my distaste for the mall, supermarkets were the only places I regularly purchased clothing. If Trevor was bored, at least Grey seemed to be entertained while I shopped. His hands moved from fabric to fabric, running his little fingers curiously over the different tops and discovering how each of the materials felt. As his fingers came across a plush, oversized sweater he giggled, being tickled by the material. Trevor smiled at this before he turned his attention to me.

"Do you mind if I take him to the toy department?" Trevor asked, appearing bored despite wanting to be with me.

Looking up from the pile of clothing in my hands, I answered him. "That's fine. I've got to try on this stuff anyway. Just call me if you get lost." I winked.

My eyes followed him as he walked away, drifting down the aisle toward the toy section in the far right corner of the store. I noticed my eyes weren't the only ones consumed by the sight of him. Other women seemed just as smitten. I gave a glare to one of the women in particular before returning to my shopping. I supposed I had to grow used to going out with a man like Trevor. He commanded attention wherever he went. His aura, ink, and attractive stature were all impossible to miss. Although he never said so much to me, I was sure he got hit on constantly. Perhaps he was so accustomed to the attention he no longer considered a little flirtation as something notable.

Chattering pulled my mind away from my shopping, and I looked up from the clothes in my cart to find a group of women gossiping nearby. Usually, I wouldn't eavesdrop on a conversation—I was usually far too wrapped up in my own thoughts to do that—however, the subject matter of this conversation made it impossible for me to ignore.

"I couldn't imagine having someone like that."

"Yeah, I could definitely use a young guy to help me around the house … entertain me whenever Jack's away."

"Hell, he could entertain me while my husband was in the same room. With him around, who has time for anyone else?"

One of the women snickered before her eyes shot over to meet my gaze. She gave me an artificially apologetic smile before she returned her attention to her friends. The group of them seemed so *fake*—so insufferable. Perhaps this was just my jealousy speaking because, usually, I wasn't harsh to other women. Usually, I tried to be understanding— almost to a fault—but these women irked me in a way I couldn't ignore.

Trevor wasn't just a piece of meat. *Of course, I frequently daydreamed about his body, too. But it was different when I did it, dammit! I was his girlfriend. I could think about his cock if I wanted to! These women, however* ... I flushed at the jealous feelings burning a hole in the pit of my stomach. Trevor was so much more than just his appearance.

"Can you believe out of all the women in the world, he—"

"Jesus, Karen. She can probably hear you."

The woman, Karen, rolled her eyes at her friend's comment, seemingly put out. "Oh, calm down. I wasn't going to say anything, Beth."

The group shot me another look before they rolled their carts away. Surprising myself, I started laughing. Once I started, it felt impossible to stop. Something about the way they spoke was hilarious. It was astounding that, at their age, they still didn't understand love. Maybe they had never experienced it themselves before, but love wasn't about shallow things. Love wasn't about finding the best-looking partner or most wealthy partner or even the "perfect" partner. I believed love wasn't about finding anything; I believed love found you.

Maybe one could look at their partner and wonder if they could do better, but would they want to? Would they want to do "better," or would they merely want the person they had, realizing they were perfect for them? There's a reason Trevor and I had found each other. I wasn't sure if we were well suited for each other in every way, but I was sure we were meant to be together. We were perfectly imperfect. Our jagged edges smoothed and fit together like pieces of a puzzle. *Pieces of a puzzle we could never form with anyone else.* Due to this, I knew I shouldn't feel self-conscious. I shouldn't worry if another woman was smarter than me, thinner than me, prettier than me, or richer than me because they weren't *me*. There would always be someone better, but I would always be the one and only Veronica Elizabeth Clark. I would always be uniquely myself.

I shopped for a while longer, placing a few more items in my cart before I decided to seek Trevor out. Hopefully, they found something interesting, and they weren't merely meandering about while waiting on me. After the long day Trevor had, I felt guilty for taking so long to browse the clothing section—something I could have done anytime I came alone.

I moved through aisles of toys and action figures before I came across them. Trevor had a book in one hand and Grey situated comfortably in the crook of his other arm. In front of them was a woman. While she was older than us, I could tell just by viewing her profile that she had been heartbreakingly beautiful her entire life. She looked familiar, but for the life of me, I couldn't place her. She even *felt* familiar. I was certain if I had seen her face at some point, I would be able to recognize her now. She didn't strike me as someone to be forgotten.

With long chestnut brown hair and lovely features, she was striking. Her body was slight but had subtle curves where any woman would want them most. She looked to be in her late forties and, judging by the way she was dressed, appeared to come from money. This woman looked like she had walked off the set of a classic movie, reminding me of Veronica Lake or Katherine Hepburn.

Realizing I had been gaping at her, standing awkwardly at the end of the small aisle, I moved forward to introduce myself.

"Hey, I'm Ronnie Clark," I said awkwardly as I watched her turn from serene to skittish. I wondered if I made her uncomfortable. *Was she after Trevor?*

I shook my head at the thought. While she seemed interested in him, she didn't seem interested in him in *that* way—the way many women were. Her fascination seemed strangely different. She looked at Trevor as if she were seeing a ghost. Her green eyes, while beautiful, looked haunted. She looked far older all of a sudden as she apologized and moved back over to the cart she abandoned before leaving the aisle. I stared after her, perplexed as I watched her retreat.

"Who was that woman?" I questioned as I turned my attention back to Trevor.

He looked just as haunted—just as unsettled as the woman had. His entire body was rigid as if he had just received a physical blow. *What did I miss? What had happened?* I wanted to ask, but Trevor seemed just as confused as I was. He stared at the spot she had just occupied as if he were waiting for her to reappear. He was lost in his own thoughts again as he searched for an answer.

Baffled, he finally answered. "I've no idea."

His voice was gruff and uncomfortable. Judging by the look on his face, she felt familiar to him, too.

21

Turning Page

"Tonight's the night," I whispered as the sun trickled through the shades of my bedroom windows.

As the morning sun danced across my face, I felt like a different woman. Tonight, would change everything—I could feel it already. While my body relaxed against the mattress, soaking up the vitamin D, my body came to life. My muscles tickled with the start of a new day, and my body became lethargic as my mind filled with images of him. With the image of Trevor in my mind's eye, I felt my core begin to pulse gently against the fabric of my panties.

I didn't know if tonight was destined to be the night Trevor and I finally had sex. While I wasn't sure if I was ready … I wanted it. I wanted him to touch me; I wanted to feel his lips on my body, kissing, sucking, and biting, until I writhed beneath him; I yearned for the feeling of his cock moving inside of me, creating the most delicious friction. I wanted to come on him. I desired sharing my pleasure with another person. I was tired of finding a release by myself.

For a long time, I was all I had ever wanted—I had been too fearful to ask for anything more. Now, however, I wanted to find myself all over again as he pleasured me. In his arms, I knew I would be reborn. As he thrusted into my body, showing me more pleasure than I could have ever imagined, I knew I would forget all about the past—all about the men who haunted me.

Even now, I heard their laughter in my mind, playing on a loop like a broken record.

I pushed those memories aside before they plagued my mind. A faint whimper of a memory could transform into a loud *bang* in seconds. Centering my mind, my right hand began its descent down my body. My fingers paused at the elastic band of my cotton underwear; they ran along the band before my index finger shot out and lifted my underwear just enough to slip my hand inside. My fingers ran along my pubic bone before I met my wet lips.

I bit down on my bottom lip as my fingers began to play with my folds—first, slowly before I increased my speed, creating a wonderful friction, which caused my clit to tingle. Next, my fingers wandered there. I rubbed circles around my clit as I pictured the possibility of Trevor's hands on me later this evening. My eyes rolled back in my head as my skin grew hot, turning red as I created friction with my fingers. I was flushed all over.

My pussy was wet, begging for attention, which I was more than happy to give. I slipped one finger inside, enjoying the silken feel as I slowly moved the finger in and out. I reached down with my free hand and began to play with my clit while my right hand added another finger. I pictured his mouth on my breasts, sucking on my nipples while his hand played with my pussy. I imagined him biting, licking, and sucking until I fell to pieces, orgasming around his fingers. The thought of his strong body dominating mine made my core begin to flutter. I worked my fingers faster, wanting my entire body to shudder as my orgasm ripped through me.

Trevor filled my mind again. I remembered the sight of his nude body from the other day when he gave me a little "show" while he changed. I remembered the way his muscles rippled against his inked skin. I remembered the way his ass looked—perfectly taut. I remembered wanting to lick each and every inch of his body until he came in my mouth. With that thought as clear as day in my head, I rode out the last waves of my orgasm.

I opened my eyes, gasping for air as I came down from my high. Licking my lips, I tried to remember the taste of him. *I suppose tonight I'll get another taste. Hopefully,* more *than just a taste. I want all of him.* Tonight, if I were lucky, I would experience *everything* with him. And tomorrow, I would feel like a changed woman. A woman who was no longer afraid. A woman who had finally found herself in the darkness.

My heart pounded as I heard his knock at my door. Running my hands over my sleek black dress, I moved to answer it. I was certain my chest was flushed and blotchy—I was too skittish to look at my reflection to check. I couldn't help the feelings that raged inside of me. My nipples already strained against the fabric of my dress while my body reacted to his arrival. *This is it*, my mind said as I grabbed the doorknob and swung the front door of my apartment open.

I believed *I* looked good, but Trevor looked incredible. In a black button-down with sleeves rolled up to exhibit his muscular forearms, black slacks that fit him perfectly, and black shoes, Trevor looked devilishly handsome. His dark eyes and even darker appearance triggered something in me. Suddenly, I felt bashful in his presence.

"Do I look all right?" I asked, emitting a nervous giggle.

With an incredulous look, he responded, "You look sexy, baby. Very sexy."

I flushed. It was strange facing him after having him star in such vivid fantasies earlier. However, I forced myself to meet his gaze. I was done being bashful and coy all of the time. *I masturbated to the thought of him, now I just have to own up to it.*

Just as I finished this thought, Trevor grabbed my hand and gently pulled me out through the doorway. My body molded against his as I gazed up at him, happy to feel his hands on my figure and his flesh against mine. He looked at me for a moment, pressing his hips against mine before his gaze dropped to my lips.

I felt my breath catch in my throat as I watched his tongue dart out to lick his full bottom lip before he bent down to close the distance between our mouths. His lips were warm against mine, causing my body to melt against his. As I basked in the feelings sparked by his passionate kiss, I felt myself grow wet, wanting him now more than I ever had. I became breathless as he moved his body against mine, giving all that he had to the kiss. I gasped against his mouth, needing air before I became too overwhelmed. With a soft, cocky chuckle, he pulled away.

"Later," he promised me.

After grabbing my purse and locking up my apartment, Trevor ushered me down the hallway with his hand on the small of my back, his thumb dangerously close to my bottom. I smiled, feeling cherished in his company.

As we drove, Trevor rolled the windows down, letting the autumn air flow through the truck. I soaked the air up, smiling at the way it tickled my skin and eased the tension between Trevor and me. I leaned back against the passenger seat and watched the cars zoom by us while I tried to ignore the potent sexual tension that swam through the air.

The astriction between us became palpable as he weaved in and out of traffic toward our destination. As the cold air stung my lungs, I realized this was the happiest, most relaxed moment I had ever had because, tonight, I felt like we were driving toward our future. Tonight, I felt like my life would change.

We pulled in front of Guard and Grace, a steakhouse in Denver, and I took a moment to peer out of my window, shocked. I couldn't believe Trevor thought of this place. This was a spot I had always wanted to go to but never could afford. While Trevor pulled up to the front of the restaurant to drop me off, I couldn't stop smiling. Trevor was beaming, too. With a proud look in his eye, he leaned across the center console and planted a kiss on my lips. What should have been chaste lasted longer than we both expected. If it weren't for the blare of a horn, we probably would have remained in the front seat of his truck, making out all night.

"You go ahead," he said with a devilish grin. "Go wait inside, and I'll go park."

Feeling as if I were living a dream, I leaned forward and kissed him once more before sliding out of the truck. I was on cloud nine. The horn from the car behind us blared again, causing me to cringe. *What's with this dick?*

Feeling bold, I turned on my heel and gazed at the car for a moment before I curtseyed and flipped him the bird. I giggled to myself, feeling so young suddenly as I continued into the restaurant. As soon as I passed through the restaurant's front doors, I forgot all about the irate driver. This place was divine, with a modern interior and a beautiful décor. *I've never been to any place like this before. If this is a dream, I hope I never wake up.*

In a daze, I moved to the hostess stand and waited for my equally impressive date. As soon as Trevor entered the restaurant, looking dark as sin, all eyes quickly flew to him. Each expression varied. Some seemed shocked by his appearance, some were curious, and some gazes—mainly coming from older women—were appreciative. I didn't blame the women; I couldn't take my eyes off of him either.

"This is incredible, Trev," I whispered, feeling childlike as I beamed up at him.

Trevor joined me near the hostess stand and wrapped an arm around my waist as we waited for the couple before us to finish speaking with the woman behind the podium. As soon as it was our turn, the woman became flustered, looking Trevor up and down before she sputtered out a question, inquiring after a reservation for the evening.

With a cocky grin Trevor seemed to naturally produce, he responded with his name. The deep baritone of his voice caused the woman to flush, and if I weren't so smitten, I would have wanted to rip her hair out for looking at my man the way she was. However, I was far too secure in my relationship with Trevor for that sort of behavior. *Wasn't I?*

"Right this way, Mr. Warren," the young woman said as she grabbed two menus and a wine menu, all while giving my date a speculative look.

While she was beautiful, Trevor's gaze remained on me. He guided me through the restaurant with a gratified look on his face. Now that the night I had dreamt of was finally happening, I barely knew what to do—I didn't know how to act. I would enjoy tonight as if I were enjoying a dream. *But this wasn't a dream. Thanks to Eden, this night is finally happening.*

As we were ushered to our table, I took in the crowd. The dining room was gorgeous, filled with what appeared to be the wealthiest populace of the city. I drifted toward my seat, ignoring the unwanted stares Trevor and I were receiving. I promised myself I wouldn't allow anything to ruin our evening. Once I realized I had the strength within me to control my outlook, every day became lovely in its own way. *Especially my days with Trevor.*

Our table was located in the farthest corner of the restaurant. I smiled, feeling secluded from everyone else. While Trevor was the center of my attention, I could still see the leers I received in my periphery. It seemed Trevor noticed them, too. After pulling out my chair and allowing me to be seated first, he moved to the opposite side of the table and situated himself so he placed a barrier between me and everyone else. I smiled, thankful for him as always.

"So, what do you think of this place?" he asked as soon as we were alone.

I peered down at the menu, slightly concerned about the prices. *I know Trevor works long hours, but after all of those bills ...* I wasn't disillusioned when it came to his financial situation—times were tough. However, I decided not to comment. I could easily picture the face he would have made in response to my prying. He would have blanched, embarrassed by my assumption. Then, I would have felt absolutely horrible.

I bit down on my lip for a moment before my eyes rose to meet his, and I answered, "It's great! It's just so ... *fancy*." I giggled and peered back down at the menu.

He studied me for a moment and then laughed to himself. "Well, I thought my beautiful girlfriend deserved to go someplace nice."

Beautiful girlfriend. Beautiful girlfriend. Beautiful girlfriend. God, he could say those words to me all night, and I would be perfectly content.

"Besides," he continued jovially, "I put some cash aside just so I could take you out. I just wanted to treat you like a princess, I guess. I wanted to make tonight special for you."

This was the softer side he rarely revealed. I knew being open like this made him feel weak. I supposed this was what made falling in love so frightening. You really felt like you were falling; you opened yourself up to a person and relinquished control of your heart. The later was the part I feared the most. For so many years, control had been all I had. Control had been my constant friend. After someone robbed me of my free will—not one time, but many—control had been all I had to cling to. Now, I felt myself letting go. I felt myself allowing the walls I had built to breakdown.

"It is," I finally said as I met his gaze. *Allow yourself to fall. Give yourself the chance to break free.* "It was going to be special no matter what you had planned. I'm having a wonderful time already, Trev."

Every time his name fell from my lips, I felt warm. He looked at me for a long while, seemingly mystified. There was something in the air around us. Something that made me want to hand over my heart—as wounded as it may have been—to Trevor. While a comfortable silence surrounded us momentarily, I wondered if he felt similarly.

"I don't think you realize how special you are to me. Seriously, Ronnie. I've never been good about putting my emotions into words, but you mean everything to me."

His words were rushed and obviously unrehearsed. Like him, his words were raw, passionate, and authentic. He didn't have to say he loved me—not yet. He didn't have to sing me his praise and write sonnets in my name. He didn't have to work to impress me. To me, words didn't matter; actions were more meaningful than anything. So, while he hasn't uttered the words, I knew he loved me. Just as I loved him. I knew because of the way he looked at me, the way he talked to me, the way he encouraged me, and the way he inspired me to be the best version of myself. So, those three words didn't matter just yet. Perhaps one day, they would. For now, however, I was perfectly content with being everything.

"Trev," I began as a small smile tugged on my lips, "I *do* realize that. I feel the same way about you. You're all I think about. All I—"

Our waiter arrived at our table before I could finish my sentence. A fraction of me was thankful because I had been rambling, and *nothing* good ever came from my ramblings. Truthfully, I believed if we hadn't been interrupted, I would have professed my love for him. *God, how embarrassing would that be?* The waiter's voice pulled me away from my train of thought before I became too mortified with what I had so narrowly escaped.

He was talking about the drink specials for the evening. My eyes shot to Trevor, feeling somewhat defeated for him. I hated to put him in the path of temptation. I could only imagine how hard all of this was for him. Every day took so much strength. It was always easier to give up than it was to shape up and fight back. Concern trickled through me as I took in the sight of him. With a rigid posture, tense muscles, and pensive eyes, he looked like he wanted to bolt.

The waiter asked for a drink order to which Trevor responded by spitting out an answer, explaining that we would stick with our waters. I couldn't ignore the slightly peeved look we then received from our waiter. I realized he had decided in the few seconds he had spoken to us that we were cheap. In my freshman year of college, I had waited tables to earn some extra spending money. So, I understood the anxiety that came with surviving off of tips. It had caused me to think things like: *They seem cheap. Will they stiff me? Maybe I shouldn't be* too *nice.* My eyes turned to Trevor to find he was equally peeved.

Much to my surprise, he grabbed the drink menu and scanned the list until his eyes fell upon the miniscule, non-alcoholic section.

With a small smirk, he stopped the waiter and said, "We'll have two espressos as well. Thank you."

He seemed spiteful as the waiter retreated.

"What was that all about?" I asked as our waiter reached his POS station.

"Nothing." He shrugged nonchalantly.

Despite his casual tone, I knew there was something brewing.

"I just didn't like the way he was looking at me," he continued, staring after the waiter.

"He's an asshole," I agreed, knowing the exact look Trevor was referring to.

He had looked at Trevor as if he weren't good enough to eat here. I searched for the words to make him feel better but came up short. So, I decided to play with him a bit.

"He's probably just jealous," I said smugly.

He snorted at my assessment. "Jealous of what?" he asked incredulously.

"He's probably just jealous of how hot you are." I paused, trying not to smile too widely at the shocked expression that colored his features. "Actually, I'm just a little annoyed with his timing. What I wanted to tell you was how important you are to me, too. You and Greyson are my world, Trev."

Without a single moment of hesitation, he replied, "You're my world, too. If it weren't for you and Grey, I don't know what type of man I would turn out to be. When I'm with you, I feel *better*. I feel like you allow me to be a better version of myself. You see the man in me that I never imagined I could be."

"You're a good man," I replied a heartbeat later in a tone overflowing with conviction. "You're too hard on yourself. You're such a wonderful father and such an amazing boyfriend. You don't give yourself enough credit."

As soon as the words had left my mouth, Trevor straightened in his seat. He wasn't perfect—no one ever could be—but he was *mine*. He was mine, and I would be keeping him forever. *He may not be the hero in his own story, but he was the hero in Greyson's and mine.*

The waiter returned with our drinks. After he had placed them on the table, Trevor reached forward and grabbed ahold of his espresso. He then took a sip with a thoughtful, calculating expression. He pretended he was some sort of espresso connoisseur, making me want to snicker. He masked a look of disgust before he threw the waiter a cocky smile.

My eyes drifted from his face back to the menu. I felt guilty as I looked it over—everything was so expensive. I never liked spending too much money on myself. I always found it frivolous. I had to stifle my nature as I focused on the man before me. He wanted to spoil me, and I wasn't going to argue with that. So, I kept my worried thoughts to myself as I scanned for the cheapest thing on the menu, hoping my choice wouldn't offend him.

"Ronnie, just get whatever you want. It's on me tonight, so, you don't have to worry," Trevor insisted as if he had read my thoughts.

His eyes implored mine, silently beseeching me to humor him for the evening. In this moment, I understood that, for him, part of this evening was about proving himself capable of taking me out on a date. Despite being beautiful, his self-esteem was floundering. *I just want to make him happy.*

My eyes scanned the menu once more before landing on the seafood selection. I found something moderately priced, the Scottish salmon, and ordered, hoping my choice would please Trev. His eyes danced across my face for a moment before he smiled at me. His smile faded into a vacant expression as his mind seemed to drift to something other than food. As I regarded him, I wondered what he was thinking of. Then, I blushed as I watched his distant gaze fall to my breasts. *Was he thinking of me the way I so frequently thought about him?*

I realized I wasn't the only one watching him; the waiter was standing, facing him, with an expectant look as his pen hovered over his pad of paper, waiting for Trevor's response. I coughed, hoping to pull Trevor away from his fantasies. He snapped quickly out of it and gave me a guilty smile before ordering, looking almost childlike.

With his eyes on the menu, he said, "We'll take the Maryland crab cakes as a starter, and I'll have an eight-ounce New York strip for my entrée with a loaded baked potato for my side."

The waiter smiled at this, obviously pleased with the dollar amount of our bill so far, before retreating, leaving us alone.

Instantly, we fell into an effortless conversation as we sipped our espressos. Despite being an introvert by nature, conversations with Trevor were always uncomplicated. We could bounce from one topic to the next seamlessly. It was as if we were the same person or perhaps two people who had known each other their entire lives. *Our souls have known each other for a very long time. God, that's so cheesy, Veronica. You've been reading far too many books!*

Pushing the countless romance novels I had read aside, I pondered the fact that I had never met someone I wanted to bare my soul to. Of course, there wouldn't be any soul baring tonight. Our conversation, instead, surrounded our work and hobbies.

"You're writing a children's book? How did I not know this?" Trevor asked as he nearly choked on his drink.

I flushed. I never liked talking about my creative ventures. I had always believed I would jinx them somehow if I spoke about them to anyone. I constantly worried about the many "what ifs" that came with chasing a dream. *What if I'm not good? What if I embarrass myself? What if I set out to do something and don't reach my goal? What if I talk about something, only to have it fall through in the end? What if I'm a failure? What if I'm a success? What if all of this will lead to nothing?*

"I don't like talking about it," I explained as I finished off my espresso and set it down on the table.

"You don't like talking about it? Why? It's pretty fucking impressive."

"Well, I guess I don't want to jinx it?" I said, posing it like a question. "I'm worried that if I talk about it too much my ideas will never go anywhere."

"I get that," he agreed, smiling at me. "But I'm sure they will go *somewhere*. One day, they will."

"Thanks, Trev."

"What's the book about? You can at least tell me that much, can't you?"

My flush grew. I didn't want to tell him the subject matter. I wanted it to be a surprise. I wanted to watch Trevor's eyes light up as I revealed Grey's face on every page. I wanted him to be proud of me for telling a fictional adaptation of his little boy's story. So, I had no intentions of spoiling it.

"You'll see it once it's finished one day. I don't want to ruin it."

He shrugged and nodded. "Okay, I won't pressure you. Just know I'm really proud of you. You never cease to amaze me, Ronnie. Seriously, you're unlike any girl I've ever met. I thought I'd been lucky in the past, but I had no idea what luck was until I met you."

"I feel the same way," I agreed as I leaned forward in my seat. "The guys before you ... Well, they never cared what I had to say, I guess. We definitely didn't talk about any of this stuff."

"What did you talk about?"

Even now, I hear the sound of his laughter in the back of my head. I hate his fucking laughter.

"Nothing," I answered, wanting to change the subject. "So, before you left Colorado, what were you like?"

Now, Trevor seemed to want to talk about something else.

"Honestly, my last few years of high school were shit. *I* was shit. I spent the majority of my time drinking, partying, and trying not to flunk out. Before that, I had been as straight edge as could be, but once I started hanging out with a different crowd, I got deep into some shit. When I was younger, though, I was the biggest nerd. Dean used to tease me relentlessly for staying inside to read comics or play video games when I could be outside playing ball with him. I never knew shit about sports and never wanted to. I was always too wrapped up in something else."

"I think I would have liked you ... back when you were a self-proclaimed nerd."

While my tone was teasing, my words were true. I had never been the partying type—I was far too bookish and introverted for that—but if I'd met Trevor before that life had touched him, I believed I would have liked him very much.

Our appetizers arrived while we were deep in conversation; I had barely noticed the waiter as he came and went. Our gazes remained locked while we began to dig in. His eyes made my body warm. He looked at me as if he would look away for a second, I would disappear. As we ate, we talked about our favorite books, movies, and television shows. Slowly, we learned more and more about each other. We finished our appetizer quickly, laughing at how hungry we had unknowingly been, and continued to talk while we waited for our entrees.

"I'm into anything, Trev, really. You name it, I'll watch it. I'll see anything once," I said as we moved the topic toward our favorite movies.

"Anything? What are your favorites then? Any standouts?"

"Well, that's just as hard as asking me to pick my favorite book. I have copious amounts of both. I mean, haven't you seen my collection?" I laughed as I considered his question. I had always been horrible when it came to picking my favorite *anything*. "For scary movies, I love *The Shining* and *American Werewolf in London*. For romances, I love *Where the Heart Is* and *Rebecca*. Oh, and *While You Were Sleeping*. I can't forget about that! Wait, and *You've Got Mail*! Have you seen that one?"

He shook his head, appearing amused. "Haven't heard of it."

"It has Tom Hanks. It's brilliant," I informed him. "I also love *Millennium Actress*, *Crimson Peak*, *Evil Dead 2* ... I don't know. My tastes are all over the place."

Trevor's grin grew. He reached for my hand, took it in his, and brought my hand to his mouth for a quick kiss. His warm lips felt like heaven against my skin. He held my hand there for a moment, letting it hover near his lips before he brought our joined hands to rest on the table.

"Those are perfect choices. See, you're my type of girl." Squeezing my hand, he said, "I'm glad you're into horror, too. Dean and I would watch tons of that shit growing up. We would have movie nights in our living room, and Mom would get so mad at our selections. But now, I can see how two kids watching *Cannibal Holocaust* isn't the best thing in the world." He snickered.

"I would watch tons of different stuff growing up, too. I've watched that, plus every single Stephen King film adaption. I loved *The Hills Have Eyes*, *The Nightmare on Elm Street*, *Last House on the Left* ..." I trailed off, almost laughing at Trevor's shocked expression. *I feel so natural around him!* "Don't look so shocked, Trev. I told you before my dad really *would* watch those movies with me growing up. How'd you think I heard about most of them?"

Trevor smiled, relaxing against his seat. "So, what's your dad like?"

"Well, you'll be meeting him soon enough so I suppose you'd want to know," I said, teasing him.

As I had uttered the last sentence, Trevor had been taking a drink of water. As soon as I had said "meet" and "soon," he had nearly choked.

"How soon is 'soon'?"

I giggled and leaned back against my seat, mirroring him. "Not *that* soon, so, don't look so terrified. My dad's a good man, I promise. He's busy with work right now, but he'll come up to see me eventually. When he does, he'll want to meet my boyfriend."

He shifted uncomfortably in his seat. "What does your dad do for a living?"

With a proud smile, I answered, "He's a fire chief in Austin, Texas."

Suddenly, Trevor appeared worried. If he only knew my father, he would realize he had nothing to fret about. Although he had a tough exterior, my dad was a giant softie. I supposed he was much like Trevor in that way, so I believed they would get along perfectly.

"He sounds really cool," Trevor responded, his voice strained.

"He is," I agreed. "And he'll love you, Trev."

Before I could prattle on about my father, our waiter returned to our table with our entrees in hand. As soon as our food was placed in front of us and we were left alone, we dug right in, previous conversation forgotten. After taking my first bite, I realized why the food was so expensive—it was divine. Everything about this night was divine—the food, the ambience ... Trevor. Trevor, the man who seemed more like a dream than an actual person.

With his face in view, I barely noticed the scenery around us. I barely noticed the darkening skies or the quietness. With him near, everything else was hazy. Faintly, I heard the rain as it pattered against the windows we sat next to. The rain ... and then the thunder, as darkness descended. It was just past six o'clock in the evening, yet, as I peered outside, I found it looked as if it were midnight. I shuddered at the roar of thunder, hoping the rain wouldn't ruin our perfect evening.

Trevor reached across the table and took my hand. "Are you afraid of storms, baby?" he asked.

With a flush, I shook my head. Trevor's eyes judged my expression for a moment and then he flagged down our waiter. I wanted to stay, but as I stared out the windows, I feared if we didn't head home soon, we wouldn't reach our apartment complex tonight.

The weather was already fierce, and it would probably only grow worse as time ticked on. We quickly finished our food, and our waiter brought us our check. Trevor paid and left a generous tip. As soon as he finished signing his name on the merchant's receipt, my eyes darted back to the window, staring out at the violent skies.

"Ronnie, everything will be okay," Trevor said as he rubbed comforting circles against my palm with his thumb. I turned my gaze to him and he smiled at me. "Besides, you've got me to comfort you." He gave me a roguish grin.

He stood up and walked around to help me out of my chair. *Always the gentleman.* While I didn't need his help, I smiled at the gesture and placed my hand in his, allowing him to lead me to the door.

It was pouring by the time we reached the outside. The wind looked as violent as the rain as we paused to gaze out at the street. Trevor's eyes were wide with disbelief before his gaze turned toward me, giving me an apologetic grin.

"Just wait here, and I'll pull the truck around and pick you up!" he yelled over the sound of the downpour as he zipped his leather jacket all the way up to his neck to protect his body from the bite of the autumn chill.

I knew he was being chivalrous, but I didn't feel like appeasing him. Not tonight. Tonight, I wanted to have fun. I wanted to feel alive in every possible way. So, I rolled my eyes at his suggestion and smiled at him.

"I'll be fine, Trev. Let's make a run for the truck together. It's not like you parked far away. I can see your truck from here."

He gave me a dubious look before he shrugged his shoulders, not wanting to argue with me. I giggled, excited to run out into the rain. I hadn't done so since I was a child, and as I peered out into the night, I found the idea seemed so freeing. I wanted to be my old self again. This just felt like another step.

Trevor took my hand and squeezed it as we both looked out at the downpour. It was beautiful as it pounded down against the pavement in an unrelenting manner. I smiled. I smiled so hard my cheeks hurt as a memory flooded my mind.

"Sweetheart, I don't want you to catch a cold," Mom said as I pulled her toward the sliding doors leading to our backyard.

"Come on, Mommy! Just for a second! It's so fun," I insisted with a pout.

She looked at me and then looked at the rain before a smile lit up her features. "Okay, but we're only dancing for a little bit, understand?"

"A little bit," I repeated with a nod of my head.

She laughed and pulled open the sliding glass doors before we both darted out into the backyard. The rain tickled my cheeks as I giggled, staring up at the sky. We ran to the middle of the yard and paused. Mom smiled at me for a moment before she reached out to take my hands in hers. Humming a nameless tune, we began to dance under the rain. First, I had tried to dance seriously, but she made me laugh too much for that. After a few minutes, we were wiggling around for the entire neighborhood to see. I couldn't stop laughing.

"Mommy! Mommy! Twirl me again! Again!"

She laughed before she picked me up off the ground and spun me in the air. We spun around again and again. She never let go. When she was breathless, she paused and held me close as the rain continued to beat down on us.

"I love you, Mommy," I said into her hair before I threw my head back to let the rain hit my face.

"I love you, too, my little Ronnie." She paused for a moment and kissed my temple. "Stay like this forever. Promise me."

"I promise. Forever."

"On the count of three, we'll make a run for it together!" Trevor yelled to me.

I threw my head back and giggled, feeling childlike.

"One! Two! Three!" we shouted before we took off into the night.

As I ran in the rain, like I had done many times as a small child, I couldn't control my laughter. I couldn't control the laughter or the tears that pricked my eyes and eventually slid down my face. I thought of *her*, I thought of my past, and I thought of where I was today. I thought of how far I had come. *She would be proud of me in this moment. She always wanted me to stay the same.* And then I had an epiphany. I *had* stayed the same. Through all the shit, through all the darkness, I was still the same Veronica Elizabeth Clark. I was still the girl my mother loved. I was still the girl my family loved. I was still the girl *I* loved. As I ran in the rain, I realized I had never changed. I had been lost, but I had *never* forgotten myself.

Through the downpour, I turned to look at Trevor, only to find he was staring back at me. His eyes were warm with lust and passion. I wanted him. If we took things further tonight, I would never regret it. I was finally ready to move forward. I wanted to continue to discover myself all over again.

I could barely contain my lust as we reached his truck. He opened the passenger door and helped me slip inside. He tried to play the role of a polite gentleman, but his gaze wandered over my body. I tried to imagine what I must have looked like now that my already tight dress was wet and molded to the curves of my body like a second skin.

I felt my nipples pucker against the fabric as my body yearned for him. His hands roamed my figure, coming to rest on my hips before he gave them a light squeeze. I moaned at the contact. The noise was quickly silenced as Trevor smashed his lips against mine, soaking up my passion. The rain poured down on us, soaking the upholstery of his truck, but he didn't seem to care—he was too wrapped up in me. I was thankful for that because all I ever wanted was this moment.

Lightning struck the ground and caused me to nearly jump from my seat, effectively breaking the kiss. I sulked for a moment as Trevor let go and closed my passenger door before jogging around the front of the truck to slip into the driver's seat. As he closed the door, my gaze shot down to my outfit, and a laugh escaped my lips. I was completely drenched head to toe and found I had never looked better. I straightened up to look in the rearview mirror and found my makeup was smeared across my face.

I giggled as I abandoned the sight of my reflection to look at Trevor. The wolfish look in his eyes nearly took my breath away. His eyes were so lust-filled I found myself melting against the damp upholstery of my seat. His gaze was on my breasts as they heaved against the fabric of my dress. I tried to regulate my breathing, but it was useless. I couldn't recall the last time I felt so amorous—so incredibly *horny*. Trevor's tongue darted out to lick his lips, and I nearly lost it. My panties became just as wet as my clothes.

I wanted to reach out and touch him. I wanted to run my hands along the planes of his body. I wanted to lick every inch of his skin, paying extra-special attention to his ink. I wanted to feel my mouth wrapped around his cock. I wanted to climb across the center console and hike up my dress before I unzipped his fly and impaled myself onto his length. Looking down, I found his cock was hard, straining against the fabric of his dress pants. It looked so thick and generous. My hands inched to touch it. I wanted to see if I could wrap my entire hand around his thickness or if it would be too much of a struggle. Slowly, I tore my gaze away from his cock. The energy in the air seemed to crackle around us and our eyes met.

Silently, we asked ourselves if we were really doing this before we answered the question with a kiss. Our lips desperately met again while I brushed my breasts against the hardness of his chest. His soft lips tasted amazing, and his tongue felt better than any of my wild fantasies had suggested. He had kissed me before, of course, but this was so different. As the rain fell around us, shielding us from the outside world, I fell deeper in love than I ever imagined possible. His lips conveyed the three words he was still too afraid to say aloud, and soon, the rest of his body would express those words, too.

22

Lost My Pieces

With a darkened sky and a heavy sheet of rain surrounding us, it felt like we were completely alone—shielded from everything else. I felt like we were lost in the middle of nowhere; the world around us faded away, and the sounds inside became jumbled with those of the rain hitting Trevor's Ford F-250. Time suspended as Trevor's lips worked against mine. I felt breathless, mindless, and lethargic against his muscled frame. I wanted all of him, and I wanted him to take all of me.

My breasts heaved against the fabric of my dress, and my body was slippery from the rain. I was crushed against him, gasping for air as his tongue played with mine. Trevor moaned into my mouth, sending shockwaves through my system before he jerked away from me to catch his breath. His dark, emerald eyes were wild with lust, and his expression was tense as if he was using every ounce of his strength to restrain himself.

His breathing was erratic as he searched for the semblance of control I doubted he had. Even in the darkness, I could see how much he desired me. After a quiet moment, his eyes rose to meet mine, finding a passion that matched his own. A moan escaped his lips as he reached across the center console to grab ahold of me. His lips pressed against mine again, and I felt my inhibitions slip away. His tongue darted out and he tasted me, licking my bottom lip as he moaned against my mouth. My body flushed as I tried to move closer to him, wanting to feel every inch of his body against every inch of mine. He felt the same way and pulled my body over the center console to rest on top of his.

The horn sounded and scared us both, and I giggled as I realized my bottom had slammed against the steering wheel, causing the harsh sound, before Trevor pulled me down on his clothed crotch. With a devilish smile, Trevor slid back his driver's seat and pulled me to rest comfortably against him. His lips moved over my neck, kissing and sucking until I could barely think. My body was flushed, warm against the wet fabric of my dress and jacket, and my pussy begged for friction.

Slowly, I felt my body begin to move against his. My pussy worked back and forth against his thick erection, and I enjoyed the way he gasped at the sensation. I didn't feel like myself; perhaps it was because my mind couldn't form a single coherent thought—my head was too clouded with lust. It had been so long since my body had found its release with another person. It had been so long since I had been comfortable enough to so much as *try* it. Now, my fear was long gone. Here, my past had no weight. Here, I felt like the woman I had been. Horrid memories poured out of my veins, evaporating into the air as Trevor's lips pulled me toward the future.

After one more long, heated kiss, Trevor pulled away, causing me to pout. Even if he had just broken away to breathe, I missed the contact. His eyes dropped to my open legs and his erection, which was pulsing against the zipper of his dress pants, begged to be released.

"We can't do this here," he said, which caused me to pout again. "Don't give me that look! It'd be public indecency or some shit like that."

I laughed at how angry he looked. I knew he was just trying to be a gentleman; he didn't want to fuck me like some cheap prom date in the back of his truck. *I love him even more for that.* Despite his concerns, I still wanted to tease him a bit. I wiggled my way off of his lap, making sure to pay special attention to his throbbing cock before I slid back into my seat.

I smiled at the sound of his moan and smiled even more at the sound of his frustrated groan, which had escaped from his lips as soon as our bodies had no longer been touching. Grinning, I looked out through the windshield. The night was blurred by the sheet of rain splashing against the glass. I couldn't believe how confident I was tonight. It was almost as if my past had never happened. In this moment, I was only the woman I was *currently* and not the girl I had been. That made me happy—blissfully content.

Trevor pushed his seat forward and started up his truck. My body shuddered as the vehicle roared to life. He flipped on his windshield wipers to their fastest setting and turned on his headlights. Combined, they did little to illuminate the road ahead, which made me nervous. As I turned to look at him, I found he appeared dead set on reaching Eden's house tonight. Grey was waiting for us there, after all. I was eager, too. I was hoping to see Grey again after I had a little alone time with his daddy, but now, that idea seemed too dangerous.

The roads in downtown Denver were beginning to flood from the deluge of rain, but once Trevor pulled onto I-70 to reach Evergreen, the roads seemed more promising. I felt hopeful. *Perhaps I can have my night alone with Trevor after all. Eden expressed that she wasn't expecting us until at least after midnight.*

My hopes were shot as I found the road conditions worsened as we grew closer to our exit. We turned off the highway onto 40 East and after a few minutes, we reached a standstill of backed-up traffic. Trevor and I gazed at the situation in disbelief. Finally, I was ready to open up to him completely—physically and emotionally—and now *this*. The situation would have been comical if it weren't for my frustration.

"Do you know another way to Evergreen?" I questioned as I peered ahead at the emergency vehicles blocking the road.

He chuckled, shaking his head in response. I wished I could be of help, but I had always been horrible with directions despite having lived here my entire life. I only went to a handful of places around town. I was a hermit, after all. I watched as a few cars ahead turned, causing us to slowly inch forward. Trevor looked slightly nervous as he kept moving toward the police officers redirecting traffic. As soon as he was close enough to speak to them, he rolled down his window and masked his expression. He and the cop chatted for a moment as Trevor asked about road closures and different routes. With a grim expression, the cop explained many of the roads had been flooded and were now closed off. I laughed in disbelief, unable to wrap my mind around our misfortune.

Tonight of all nights!

While looking at Trevor's worried expression, I suddenly felt horrible for thinking of sex. He was worried about Grey. If we couldn't make it to Eden's, this may be the first night Trevor had to spend without him. With a pensive look, Trevor thanked the officer and turned his car around, heading back to Denver. He looked so worried—so lost. He wanted to be with Greyson; he knew how worried the little boy would be if he weren't there.

Reaching across the center console, I rested my hand on his thigh and squeezed slightly, hoping the small gesture would provide him with some small comfort.

"As much as Grey wants you there, he needs his daddy safe. You're all he has left, and we can't take risks because of that."

God, if Grey lost us in an accident, too ... it would be so horrifying ... It would be so sickly ironic and devastatingly cruel. As much as I wanted to see Greyson, as much as I wanted to assure him Trevor and I were all right, I knew we couldn't take the chance. We couldn't go back tonight.

The rain began to fall more heavily, causing the road in front of us to become barely visible. Trevor leaned forward in his seat as he attempted to see through the sheet of rain to the car in front of us. All I could see was the blurred visions of brake lights and colors as they inched forward down the interstate, and all I could hear were the sounds of horns and water hitting glass, iron, and steel.

Through the heavy rain, I couldn't make out a single sign on the interstate. The driving conditions mixed with the lust I still felt tingling in my body caused me to be on edge. I felt like I was standing at a precipice about to tip over into foreign waters. With a shaky hand, I reached for my phone, wanting to shoot my sister a quick message of warning.

I managed to type a message, informing her of our situation, before I pulled up hotel listings on my phone, searching for vacancies near our current location. Trevor pulled off the interstate at the next exit, hoping there was some sort of lodging. Having no luck with the options on my phone, I placed it on my lap and stared out my passenger window in an effort to see our options.

We had come across a motel, but Trevor hadn't seemed in love with the idea of spending the night there because he had continued forward, searching for something better. After a few more minutes of searching, we had approached a hotel, which looked to be way out of our budgets. Trevor seemed to mull it over for a moment before he smiled slightly and pulled into the parking lot.

He parked close, but we both knew it wouldn't have made difference—we were getting soaked regardless. I wanted to feel the rain against my skin; I wanted to bask in every aspect of tonight. With a giggle, I swung my passenger door open and eagerly ran out into the night, kicking the door shut behind me.

The rain felt amazing as it brought my body to life. I was aware of each and every inch of my flesh as energy flew through my every nerve ending. Lifting my head toward the sky, I smiled as the water tickled my face. I heard Trevor get out of the truck and felt him move toward me. I turned my head to gaze at him and found him immobilized a few feet away, staring at me. I felt my nipples pucker under his amorous gaze. I turned my body to face his and smiled at him, hoping he felt the happiness as it flew through me. His eyes widened as he looked at me, and his jaw dropped slightly. I giggled at his expression before I turned and made a run for the hotel. I laughed even louder as Trevor chased after me, feeling childlike and carefree.

My laughter stopped as I entered the hotel's lobby and several patrons gave me wide-eyed, confused glances. I was certain I looked crazed with my wet clothes, smeared makeup, and carefree laugh. However, I didn't care; I had never felt more beautiful in my life. As soon as I caught my breath, I took in the sight of the hotel lobby. With high ceilings, marble floors, and expensive furnishings, it seemed like a one-night stay here would cost a full month's rent.

Slowly, I made my way toward the front desk and waited for Trevor to appear. He walked in a short while later, and his eyes widened, too, at the sight of the hotel's interior. He patted his wallet in his pocket as he moved toward me. The hotel clerk looked between both of us as if she were trying to discern our relationship.

"One room, please," Trevor said as he pulled out his wallet.

The blonde continued to stare at us both as if she were attempting to compute something. I would have felt offended if it weren't for my newfound confidence.

After an uncomfortable moment, she asked, "Do you require a room with two queen beds?"

Trevor gave her a dubious look before he shook his head and answered, "No, my *girlfriend* and I would like one room with one bed."

I giggled at his abruptness. Trevor was funny when he was frustrated with someone. His patience with this woman seemed to be running thin.

"Sorry, sir," the blonde stuttered before she began to type away on her computer.

Trevor rolled his eyes and reached out to take my hand. As the woman looked for a vacancy, Trevor turned his attention to me, peering at the smeared makeup on my face before his eyes dropped to my drenched attire. He stared at my breasts for a moment, which strained against the fabric of my dress before he smiled at me.

The look in his eyes made me feel like a goddess, and before I could express any of the thoughts weighing heavily on my mind, Trevor leaned forward and kissed me. At first, his kiss was light and teasing, but it soon turned into something *more*.

I opened my mouth, moaning against him, giving him the opportunity to slip his tongue inside. His tongue gently teased mine as my body moved flush against his. The sound of someone clearing their throat interrupted our kiss. We pulled away to find the hotel clerk staring at us with a constipated look on her perfectly made-up face.

"We have two suites available," she informed us with an annoyed expression.

Trevor smirked as he pulled me more tightly against his side.

"As long as it has a nice king-sized bed, we'll take it."

The woman peered at us as if she were using all her strength to refrain from saying anything sarcastic. *I'm amazed she's able to remain professional with us taxing her like this.* Trevor smiled as he handed her his credit card, wanting to soften the blow a bit.

From the moment she saw his crooked grin, her flirtatious aura was back, and she smiled at him in response. Trevor's eyes widened slightly before his face morphed into a confused expression. *He should know by now he can't look at women like that—they get too flustered. It's like he doesn't realize the power he has over others.* Trevor looked at her and then looked at me before his face flushed slightly. *God, I wonder what he's thinking. He couldn't possibly be thinking about ... No, there's no way.* Now, I was flushing, too.

"Enjoy your stay, sir. Let me know if there's anything you need," the hotel clerk said as she handed him the envelope containing two keycards.

It was impossible to misunderstand the innuendo in her tone. Trevor gave her a small, uncomfortable smile as he gripped the envelope and guided me away. I looked up at his tense expression as we walked toward the elevators. Suddenly, this all felt so real. Excitement bubbled in my chest while nerves played around in my mind. The last time I had sex ... I pushed the thought aside quickly, knowing it would only bring pain.

You want this, Veronica. You've wanted this with him for so long. Just let yourself open up! This will be a freeing experience if you just let yourself feel.

I just needed a little more time to clear my head. I knew as soon as I entered that hotel room, I would want him, and before that, I just wanted to think.

"Why don't we get some dry clothes, hygiene essentials, and snacks?" I suggested awkwardly as we walked by a gift shop, and I pulled him inside.

While he appeared confused, he didn't say anything. As soon as we were inside, I let go of his hand and roamed around the store on my own. My eyes took in the various knick-knacks, touristy shirts and sweatshirts, candy and snacks, refrigerated food and drinks, magazines, books, and various over-the-counter medications. I looked at everything other than Trevor, too nervous to meet his gaze. I paused at a selection of sweatshirts displaying "Colorado" across the chest as I felt Trevor pause behind me. I shivered at the sensation of his breath tickling my neck.

"We can just take all of our clothes off and hang them on the shower rod to dry, then, there wouldn't be a problem," he quietly suggested in my ear.

I felt my body still as desire moved through my veins. My pussy tingled at his suggestion, and suddenly, I wanted nothing more than to go to our room.

"We don't have to go all the way," he assured me in a stiff, uncomfortable voice. "I can just taste you if you want. Or we could do nothing."

He didn't want to make me feel pressured. He wanted me to know that my feelings mattered to him more than anything else. *I love you, Trevor Warren.* I turned around so quickly I nearly knocked him to the floor. I grabbed him, yanking on his shirt to pull his face down to my level before I crashed my lips against his. My body was on fire as I kissed him with every ounce of passion I held. I didn't care who could see us—I deserved this. I deserved *him.* I had overcome so much to get to this point, and now it was my chance to enjoy everything I had gained.

I pulled away to peer up at his face, wanting to see if his expression matched my own. It had, and my body grew even more desperate.

"Let's go to our room," I suggested as I still gripped his soaked shirt. "I can't wait any longer."

He kissed me again before he lifted me up off the ground. The tips of my shoes trailed along the marble floors as he pulled me toward the exit. I realized there was an older man working near the cash register staring at us behind the thick frames of his glasses.

I gave him a bashful smile before Trevor shocked me by picking me up completely and tossing me over his shoulder. I laughed as he walked briskly toward the elevators and bounced back and forth on his feet as he waited for one to arrive. The elevator dinged and opened to a vacant car. Trevor spanked my bottom as we entered before he set me down on my feet and smiled at me. The doors to the elevator closed, and Trevor approached me with a wicked grin on his face. Cornering me, he pressed his body against mine as his lips found my own.

I was delirious as he kissed me. His hands skimmed my body and ran over the lines of my curves before he found my breasts. They felt heavy in his hands, and I gasped as his fingers wrapped around my puckered nipples, tweaking them as he enjoyed my small, hushed moans. I deepened our kiss, biting down on his lip. My eyes opened in surprise as I tasted the iron of his blood. He didn't seem to mind my violence; his hands became more aggressive as they played with my breasts. I bit down on his lip again, playing with him, and he moaned before pulling away.

"Fuck, baby," he expressed with a rough moan.

His tongue darted out of his mouth as he licked away his blood. I smiled at him, feeling turned on by the sight. I didn't wait for him to fully recover and crashed my lips against his again. I felt his cock throbbing against my belly. I didn't know how much more teasing I could take. The elevator doors opened with a *ding*.

We rushed out, almost falling into the hallway. Drunk with desire, we continued to kiss as we moved toward the end of the hall, stumbling as we searched for our room. We found the room, and my heart sped. I reached forward and grabbed his shirt, trying to unbutton it as he slid the keycard to unlock our door. The green light flashed on the lock, and we entered. The room was beautiful, but I could barely pay attention. Now that we were alone with sex on our horizon, I felt nervous once again.

You can do this, Veronica! Believe in yourself! You love him more than anything, and he loves you, too.

Upon seeing my expression, Trevor said, "Baby, we don't have to do anything you don't want. That's not what tonight is about. I'd love to just lay in bed with you and hold you all night, if that's what you want." Despite his words, Trevor looked disappointed as he reached down to adjust his erection in his pants.

Biting down on my lip, I smiled at him. A blush colored my features as I realized just how much I wanted him. I wanted him more than I wanted anything—*ever*. I shook my head, moved toward him, and said, "I want you, Trevor. All of you."

He gave me a grin in return and stepped forward so there was barely an inch separating us. He reached out and held my right hand in his; his palm was warm and comforting. His aura filled the entire room. I peered up at his eyes, and the emotion swimming in them took my breath away. He looked at me with so much love it left me breathless. His gaze was so warm and sincere. Tonight, he would make love to me—*truly* make love to me.

No one's ever made love to me before—not even close.

We would express physically all the things we were too frightened to say aloud. Every kiss felt like a new experience; every touch felt so intimate. I wanted him to fill me up and never let go. I needed him now. I knew I couldn't wait any longer.

I gave him a warm kiss before I pulled away and began to undress myself. I felt almost bashful as I disrobed. I wanted him to like what he saw. Unable to meet his gaze, I slipped out of my dress. My body flushed as I watched his hand move toward his erection. Now, it was massive and straining against his pants. It looked painful, and I wanted to relieve it of its confines and take it into my hand. As he stared at me, I realized I had stopped moving. My dress was gathered around my waist as I watched him reach down to unzip his fly. His cock sprang free, nearly hitting his stomach as it throbbed in the air. It was beautiful. *Well, as beautiful as a throbbing erection could be.* It was long, at least nine inches, and thick. A vein, which led to the head of his cock, pulsated and made me lick my lips. *I want to lick that vein before I kiss his tip. I want to watch his face as he watches me.*

Trevor took his cock in his hand and wiped the pre-cum away from the tip. My mouth felt dry all of a sudden, and my body felt slightly worried. *How on earth am I going to take that thing inside of me? It's too thick. Maybe I'm just making excuses, but Jesus!*

"You still want to do this?" he asked, obviously noting the hesitancy in my gaze.

Staring at his cock, I gulped, and with a shaky smile, I answered, "Of course." Then, I dropped my dress, allowing it to pool at my feet.

His jaw dropped, and his cock twitched. I blushed as he scrutinized me. I was curvier than the average figure, but Trevor didn't seem to mind. His eyes moved over my breasts, my small waist, my curvy hips, my strong thighs, all the way to my feet, which were still in my flats. I kicked them off and smiled at him, now only standing in my lace push-up bra and panties. As he looked at my lingerie-clad body, he stroked himself, nearly pushing me over the edge. He walked toward me and closed the distance between us. Seemingly unable to help himself, he rubbed the tip of his erection against my slightly curved belly, causing me to moan with desire. I closed my eyes for a moment, and when I opened them again, I was even more confident and determined.

I want this. I want to find ecstasy with another person. I want to be free of my pain.

As my eyes scanned over his body, I said, "Let's get you out of this shirt."

Eager as I yanked off his shirt, I nearly drew blood as I pulled his buttons open. I felt so uninhibited and free. I had never felt more in love. Never had I believed this level of intimacy was impossible. The depth of my emotions surprised me.

We were far from shallow waters, and I was ready for him to pull me in deeper.

I gasped as I saw his newly exposed skin. Tattoos covered every inch of his chest. His nipples were pierced, and I wanted to know what those steel bars would feel like in my mouth. *Later*, I promised myself as I reached to pull his pants off. My panties became drenched as I pulled his pants down and took in the sight of his strong, inked legs.

Now that I was really looking at him, I found the tip of his cock was pierced, too. I almost salivated at the sight. He was so different from any man I had ever known. I would weep for him. I would become delirious with desire for him. I was sure my body would always yearn for his. My pussy pulsed as I wondered what his pierced cock would feel like rocking inside of me. Reaching out, I took his cock in my hand. I smiled at its warmth and flushed at the size of it. With one hand, I began to pump his length, and with the other, I reached out and grabbed the back of his head, pulling his hair as I yanked his head down so I could kiss him. My lips moved against his; his tongue devoured my mouth.

Pulling away to breathe, I murmured, "You're so fucking sexy, Trev."

His eyes widened at my words before they darkened. He looked like he could break me if he wanted to, but I knew he was too tender for that. We made our way toward the bed while we touched and bit every inch of exposed skin we managed to reach. As he touched me, I knew this would be something beautiful—a shared experience we would never forget. He made me feel special and loved. I was ready to give myself to him completely.

As soon as we fell onto the mattress, he was on top of me. He kissed my body and began his descent down to the apex of my thighs. He kissed the inside of each wet thigh before his tongue trailed along the lines of my lace panties. He gave me a roguish grin before he pulled the fabric away with one, fluid tug. He stared at my pussy with wide, lust-filled eyes. Trevor licked his lips at the sight of my landing strip leading to my wet, flushed core. I held my breath as he leaned forward and licked my glistening folds before running a finger between them. I shuddered at his touch as my back arched off the bed.

"You're so fucking wet, baby," he moaned as he ran a finger up and down my slit, playing with my clit before he dipped one finger into my tight pussy.

As I quivered, he added another finger, causing my legs to spasm around him. My core clenched around his fingers as he worked me into oblivion. Feeling my orgasm fast approaching, I did what I frequently did when I was alone and pulled down the cups of my bra to play with my nipples. The action felt even more erotic with Trevor's eyes watching my movements.

"I've been waiting for you for so long," I murmured as I continued to play with my nipples.

The statement was true in more ways than one. I had waited for the physical part of our relationship for so long, constantly playing with myself as I thought about him, but I had been waiting for *him* for a long time, too. Unknowingly, I had been waiting for a man like him to come into my life. Trevor gave me everything I needed and more. He loved me with respect and patience I doubted I would have been able to find in another man.

Trevor stared at me for a moment, his eyes glistening with shock, before his head dipped down to lick my pussy in one long stroke. Seeing his head between my thighs nearly sent me over the edge. I shuddered against his mouth as he kissed me in the most intimate of places. I was close—so close I could taste it. No man had ever made me come before. The last man—the man I didn't even want to think about—had never come close. I controlled every orgasm I had ever had, but tonight, that was about to change.

"Let go, beautiful," Trevor encouraged before he began to suck on my clit.

I felt myself tighten around his fingers before my pussy began to wildly pulse. I cried out, grabbing his hair to hold him in place as I rode out my orgasm. *I feel free! Finally, I feel free! My body has been caged for so long. I've only known my own touch for so long, but finally, that's changed. Finally, I can trust someone. Someone who loves me; someone who cares for me more than he does himself. And I care for him, too. I love him, too.*

As I came drifting down from my orgasm, he kissed his way up my body until his lips met mine. I tasted myself as he kissed me, and I moaned at the sensation of his cock resting between my opened legs. While he kissed me, I grew restless. I wanted him more than I could describe. Feeling my need, he pulled away to look at me.

"Do you want this, beautiful? It doesn't have to be tonight," he assured me in a tense voice.

It was abundantly clear he was using all of his strength to restrain himself. I smiled and reached behind my torso to unclasp my bra, exposing my breasts to him completely. His mouth was on them in an instant, licking my nipples before he sucked them into his mouth. I ran my hands through his unruly hair and kissed the top of his head to encourage him to continue sucking. A few moments passed, and my core throbbed for him. I couldn't wait a moment more. I needed him.

"Please, Trev. I can't wait any longer," I begged.

He moved up my body and kissed me softly on the lips before he left the bed and ran toward his pants. He slipped his wallet out of his back pocket and grabbed a condom before he moved back to me.

As he walked, he said, "I want you to know I wasn't banking on this being the end result of our date. I just like to be prepared."

I didn't care if I had been a forgone conclusion or not. My mind was too filled with desire to think of anything else. My breathing was heavy, and my body was lethargic as he joined me on the bed again. With a sexy look in his dark eyes, he ripped the condom wrapper opened and pulled out the rubber, staring at my heaving breasts as he slid it into place. With a smile, he settled between my legs.

"You're clean, right?" I asked, knowing it was the important thing to do despite the question sounding awkward. "You've been tested and everything?"

He nodded and replied, "I was tested when I returned to Colorado. I'm clean. You?"

A shy smile tugged on my lips as I stared down at his sheathed cock. "I'm clean," I confirmed.

Trevor gave me an almost terrified look. His eyes asked, *"We're really going to do this, aren't we?"* I gave him a reassuring smile, although I was nervous, too. I had never made love before. In the past, I *thought* I had, but now, I realized I had never come close. I had to be in love to make love. I had never been in love with anyone other than Trevor Warren.

He kissed my forehead once before lowering himself onto his elbows. He positioned his cock at my entrance and paused for a moment. I could feel his tip flirting with my pussy. He pressed against my entrance but didn't move farther. He was giving me time to change my mind if I wanted; there was no chance of that happening. I opened my legs even wider before I smiled at him, hoping I didn't look as nervous as I felt.

He looked at me with eyes filled with love, and slowly, he pressed into me. I gasped as his cock pushed past my entrance. He moaned and stared down at his erection. I peered down, too, and found only his blushing tip was inside of me. With my eyes, I captured his gaze and encouraged him. In one, hard thrust, he was inside me, filling me up to the point where it was almost painful. I cried out, my back arching off the bed as my body grew accustomed to his thick cock. I moaned, and my legs tightened around his waist.

His size was uncomfortable, yet pleasurable at the same time. I peered down at our joined bodies and found there was still an inch of his cock waiting for entrance.

"Do you think you can handle more?" he asked, and I could tell he was trying desperately not to sound too hopeful.

Biting down on my lip, I nodded and braced my body to receive the rest of him. He pulled out for a moment before thrusting back into my tight core, causing me to gasp. I cried out as I finally felt all of him. He was impressive and so perfect. We felt like puzzle pieces made especially for one another. I wanted to worship his body for the rest of my life. My eyes fluttered opened as I appreciated the feeling of him sheathed inside of me. *He's perfect. In every way, he's perfect.*

"We did it," I teased before he silenced me with a kiss.

He took it slow, obviously wanting our first time to last as long as it possibly could. With his lips and body, he worshiped me, kissing me and playing with me everywhere as he thrusted deeply inside of me. I believed every kiss was his way of saying, "I love you," and I imagined every single touch was his way of saying, "I want to belong to you forever." He didn't say the romantic words out loud, but he didn't need to. I understood him better than he understood himself.

I returned the sentiment through my own kisses and touches. With my body, I expressed how much I loved him. With my mouth, I expressed how much I wanted him with me forever. The emotions in the air overwhelmed me as I felt myself begin to fall to pieces around him. *This is what sex should feel like. This is how a man should treat me,* I thought to myself as he moved inside of me. Finally, I thought, *this is love. This is what unconditional love feels like.* Our love mixed with our desire perfectly. Suddenly, I wondered how I had lived in this world without him for so long.

I was going to come any moment. Reaching down, I grabbed ahold of his ass and encouraged him to buck more wildly against me. I wanted him to fuck me. I wanted him to pull me over the edge so we could experience that sweet oblivion together. He moaned as my hands massaged his muscles and thrusted into me more violently. He reached down, and with determination, he began to play with my throbbing clit. I was so close to the edge I couldn't see straight.

"Come for me, my beautiful girl," he whispered in my ear as he continued to play with me. "I want to feel you come on my cock."

I moaned and stiffened beneath him as I found my release. My core clamped around his cock, pulsating around him and pulling him more deeply inside of me. He began to fuck me, *really* fuck me, and held nothing back. I grinned at his enthusiasm, never feeling more freed. I spanked his ass and cried out as he sent me over the edge again, spiraling toward another orgasm. Then, I felt him come, too.

"I love you so fucking much, Veronica Clark!" he screamed out as he came.

My eyes widened, and I wondered if he realized what he had just said. Before I could ask him, he fell on top of me, completely spent. Our sweat mixed together, and our scents combined as the weight of his body pressed against mine. He kissed me once more on the lips before he rolled off of me and pulled my lush body against his. I was breathing hard, and my mind was reeling. *I just had sex. I just had sex! I can't believe it. I just made love to the man I love more than I ever thought possible.* I stared out the hotel windows into the dark night as my mind continued to reel in disbelief.

I went from a broken, anxiety-ridden woman to a woman who finally had her power back. I could finally express myself. I could finally live how I wanted to. I could finally love with my entire heart. All because I had found love, and more importantly, I had found myself. I knew who I was again. I knew the power I had inside of me. I had finally conquered my demons.

In this moment, I promised myself I would never lose myself again. I couldn't afford to. I promised myself, and I promised my new family. I smiled as I felt a weight being lifted off of my shoulders. *I found myself. Veronica Elizabeth Clark. Finally, I'm free of my past. Finally, I have a future to look forward to.*

Eyeing Trevor, I said, "The night is still young, and I want you again," as I slid onto his lap.

I wanted to say, *"I love you, Trevor Warren. I love you more than I can describe, so, let me spend my lifetime showing you."*

And one day, I would. Tonight, however, my body would become lost in his.

The End of Part I

About the Author:

Lizzie Lee is a twenty-four-year-old bibliophile who lives in Carmel, Indiana. When she's not writing, she enjoys attempting Pinterest projects, online shopping, studying Japanese, and watching horror movies. *Jagged Hearts* is her second novel.

Visit her website:

www.lizzieleeauthor.com

A Special Thanks to ...

The process of writing this was amazing ... but it wouldn't have been nearly as amazing without these people. I love you all! Thanks for your continued support. You don't know how much I appreciate all of you.

Sally Hopkinson, Paige Britton, Sherry Franklin, Ciara Shayee, Bethany Siedl, Rosario Serna, Ruthie Vasquez, Stephanie Graham, Erica Howe, Debra Ross, Monica Patterson, Amanda Wallace, Krystal Kinder, Anastasia Wolfe-Walker, Melissa O'Neal Laskarzewski, Keera Corbett, Teresa Roberts, Kyra Kerber, Jade Stanley, Allie Welch, Araceli Macias, Jennifer Santa Ana, Deb Neese VanAntwerp, Marianne van den lerssel, Suzanne Baxter, Becca Rogers, Amy Beer, Cindy Robson, Karen Peters, Zowie Adamson, Deidre Victoria Ballard, De Parry, Kerstin Window, Christy Wicklund, Patti Blomstrom, Leah Rogers, Mairead Gallagher, Rayne Chan, Christine Graf Taggart, Sarah Medlin, Charli Coloquhoun, Bronwyn J Goulding, Audelia Muniz Resendes, Emalee Wahl, Kelsey McClain, Miranda Sanderson, Julie Appleby, Kelly Creagh, Rosario Serna, Casi Rice, Jennifer Reynolds, Lindsay Lupher, Consuelo Hernandez, ZN Willett, Tanya McLeod, Judy Allen, Mysty Kame, Jada D'Lee, and Beth Anderson.

Made in the USA
Columbia, SC
01 February 2019